Pra...

"The relationship between Cal and Stella is unique, complex and deeply sensual. Their forbidden romance keeps the tension ratcheted high."
—*RT Book Reviews* on *Otherworld Protector*

"A beautifully written spell-binder, with dashes of the occult and a climactic ending. Set between wars, this exceptional book also has a supernatural touch. It is captivating and very steamy."
—*Goodreads* reviewer on *Valley of Nightmares*

"This story is a roller coaster of adventure with twists and turns that kept me frantically turning the pages.... I can't wait for book two in the series."
—*Goodreads* reviewer on *Otherworld Protector*

Praise for Sharon Ashwood

"Ms. Ashwood's characters leap from the pages."
—*Romance Junkies*

"Sharon Ashwood is all that is good and right in the paranormal romance genre."
—*Bitten by Books*

"Ms. Ashwood knows how to write paranormal novels, leaving the reader with one heck of an impression of her talent."
—*Coffee Time Romance & More*

ONE NIGHT
WITH THE VALKYRIE
&
ENCHANTER
REDEEMED

JANE GODMAN
SHARON ASHWOOD

If you purchased this book without a cover you should be aware that this book is stolen property. It was reported as "unsold and destroyed" to the publisher, and neither the author nor the publisher has received any payment for this "stripped book."

Recycling programs
for this product may
not exist in your area.

ISBN-13: 978-1-335-24997-5

One Night with the Valkyrie & Enchanter Redeemed

Copyright © 2018 by Harlequin Books S.A.

The publisher acknowledges the copyright holders of the individual works as follows:

One Night with the Valkyrie
Copyright © 2017 by Amanda Anders

Enchanter Redeemed
Copyright © 2018 by Naomi Lester

All rights reserved. Except for use in any review, the reproduction or utilization of this work in whole or in part in any form by any electronic, mechanical or other means, now known or hereafter invented, including xerography, photocopying and recording, or in any information storage or retrieval system, is forbidden without the written permission of the publisher, Harlequin Enterprises Limited, 22 Adelaide St. West, 40th Floor, Toronto, Ontario M5H 4E3, Canada.

This is a work of fiction. Names, characters, places and incidents are either the product of the author's imagination or are used fictitiously, and any resemblance to actual persons, living or dead, business establishments, events or locales is entirely coincidental.

This edition published by arrangement with Harlequin Books S.A.

For questions and comments about the quality of this book, please contact us at CustomerService@Harlequin.com.

® and ™ are trademarks of Harlequin Enterprises Limited or its corporate affiliates. Trademarks indicated with ® are registered in the United States Patent and Trademark Office, the Canadian Intellectual Property Office and in other countries.

Printed in U.S.A.

H HARLEQUIN®
™ www.Harlequin.com

ONE NIGHT WITH THE VALKYRIE

JANE GODMAN

I love paranormal romance. It's a genre in which everything is supercharged (including the romance). Additional powers, other worlds, magic and danger...all of those things provide both readers and writers with a mini-vacation from reality.

This story is dedicated to my fellow paranormal romance lovers, who encourage me to keep building fantasy worlds and creating larger-than-life characters. Thank you for your support!

Chapter 1

Adam Lyon had dodged mtany bullets in his life. Until now, they had always been of the conversational variety. For the first time ever, the fire and fury being unleashed around him was not in a boardroom…and it was not of his own making.

He thought of his time in Syria in numbers. Two weeks. Seven towns. Ten uncomfortable hotel beds. Fifteen thousand dollars. One question his guide had asked over and over.

"Where is the American called Lyon?"

Despite its seriousness, the question had become a source of amusement between Adam and his guide, Yussef. Something to lighten the darkness of their mood. As they toured the Damascus bars with Danny's picture in one hand and a wad of American money in the other, Adam had joked that at least Yussef had made it clear they were seeking a Western mercenary, not a man-eating beast from the United States.

The answers—or half answers and hints—he got in one of those bars had brought him north to this desolate, shelled-out town called Warda. They were the reason he was now crouched in the corner of a half-ruined, empty office building with all hell raging outside. His arrival had coincided with an intense new outbreak of fighting.

Yussef had brought him to this building, the deserted workplace of one of his friends. The terrified guide had advised Adam to hide here while he attempted to negotiate a way out of town. He explained that Warda was the center of an ongoing battle for supremacy between ultrahardline government fighters and radicalized rebels.

And you walked into the middle of this place before you checked that out. Nice going, Lyon.

That had been an hour ago, and Yussef had not yet returned. Adam might have known the guy for only two weeks, but Yussef didn't seem the type of person to run out on his responsibilities. Apart from anything else, Adam hadn't paid him for his services, and he knew Yussef had a young family to feed. No, he had a horrible feeling about the reason why Yussef had not come back. His only hope had been killed, injured or captured. Which left Adam on his own. Not a new situation, but not one he had ever faced with bombs and bullets going off all around him.

As an American in Syria, Adam had known all along he was kidnap fodder for both sides in the ongoing conflict. He hadn't entered into this trip lightly, and hadn't gotten into this country easily. It had been a question of weighing his own safety against the need to find his brother. In those circumstances, Danny would always come first. A year ago, Danny had volunteered with a medical charity and come to Syria. Now, as the ground beneath his feet shook in time with the explosions just outside the building, and his ears rang in protest, he realized that kidnapping wasn't his most immediate problem.

I am in so much trouble here. Now there are two missing Lyon brothers, and no one back home knows where either of us is.

The thought galvanized him and he got to his feet, pleased to find his legs were steady. There was no point sitting here waiting for death. May as well head on out and meet it face-to-face.

As he staggered toward what remained of the front door of the building, the shooting outside intensified. Something else happened at the same time. Everything got suddenly darker and a whole lot weirder.

Automatically assuming the change was caused by dust from the explosions, Adam rubbed his eyes to clear them. It didn't help. If anything, his vision darkened even further.

This is it, he decided. *I've been hit. They say you don't always feel pain.*

He was about to grope around his body for a bullet wound when the door flew inward and a black cloud filled the foyer.

"What the...?" *Chemical weapons. I am so screwed.*

The amorphous mass of darkness that had poured into the space began to shift. Within the quivering cloud, Adam could make out three winged figures. Although their features were indistinct, they were female and they were on horseback.

Hallucination. But what a way to go.

One of the figures moved slightly ahead of the others, materializing more fully. Her voice echoed in the small space. "I seek the American Lion."

Adam decided he may as well go along with his own delusion. That whole lion joke between him and Yussef had clearly taken a grip on his imagination. "That makes two of us. If you find him first, tell him his brother said 'hi.'"

Fascinated, he watched as the forms manifested themselves completely. His senses seemed to be heightened to the point where he could observe every detail of the illusion in front of him.

The horses' coats shone like satin as they plunged and reared with restless energy. Adam was only mildly surprised when each animal unfurled giant wings at the same time as it snorted steam and pawed the ground. This was all going on inside his head, after all, so why should anything that happened come as a shock to him?

The woman who had spoken dismounted and took a step closer to him. Adam took a moment to congratulate himself on the quality of this fantasy. Two weeks of enforced celibacy had clearly done wonders for his imagination. It also seemed he might have a previously unexplored warrior-princess fetish.

This tall, slender vision possessed silken skin, impossibly blue eyes and flowing, gold hair. She and her companions were dressed in identical silver helmets adorned on either side with decorative wings, and a tight scarlet corset over which was fastened a fish-scale breastplate. Each of them wore a cloak made of feathers so pure and white they could only have come from the breast of a swan. They carried shields and spears, and had short swords in sheaths strapped at their waists.

In other circumstances, Adam might have spent more time enjoying this visual feast. Since Armageddon seemed to be unfolding in the street outside, he didn't have another minute to waste. It couldn't be wrong to barge past a figment of your own imagination, could it? As he took a step forward, the woman placed an unexpectedly solid-feeling hand on his chest, halting him.

"I am Maja, Valkyrie shield maiden." She spoke clearly enough to be heard over the sound of automatic gunfire. The echoing note had gone and her voice sounded almost normal, although her accent was hard to place. "I must take the bravest of the fallen back to the great hall of Valhalla."

As Adam gazed into Maja's incredible eyes, trying to decide how his mind had endowed a make-believe creation with so much detail, one entire wall of the building collapsed.

Although his body was intact—there were no bullet wounds, after all—this shock-induced delusion hit him hard. Dark spots danced at the edges of his vision as dizziness overtook him and the dust scented floor rose up to meet him as he sprawled at Maja's feet.

The man facing her with an expression of bewilderment clouding his handsome features was not a warrior. He was clad in pants made from a faded, heavy-duty blue cloth and a lightweight, khaki jacket, under which he wore one of those garments she had heard described on other earthly visits as a T-shirt. On his feet were scarred and dusty boots. *Not combat clothing*, Maja decided. He carried no weapons. More importantly, he was alive.

Maja wasn't interested in living people. Her task was simple. Odin the Allfather wanted the souls of the bravest warriors who died in battle. They would join his army-in-waiting. The role of the Valkyries was to swoop into the scene of conflict and escort those souls to Valhalla, the great Hall of the Slain, within which Odin's elite fighting force lived.

This land called Syria had recently become a scene of such great strife that even the Valkyries had turned their attention in this direction. Although their chosen warriors were usually Norsemen, Odin wanted the finest for his army. If that meant widening their search, then his shield maidens must follow the Allfather's will. Brynhild, the Valkyrie leader, who was also Maja's older sister, had been at the end of her wits as she planned this mission. There was desperate fighting going on in two places at the same time and Odin's demands were becoming more difficult to fulfill.

"The American Lion." Brynhild had shaken her head as she pored over her charts. Finding the bravest warriors wasn't an exact science. Brynhild could predict where each fighter would be; she had an idea of the danger they would face, but she couldn't be certain who would die. Odin remained insistent. Only the best would do for his army.

"One name crops up over and over in the stars. The Allfather is determined to have the warrior known as the American Lion. The Norns tell me he will be here in the town of Warda—" Brynhild had pointed to a dot on her map "—and there will be intense fighting there today." She had moved her finger to another location, also in Syria, but many miles away. A frown descended on her face. "Yet there will be ten other warriors, all of whom Odin wants, in this other town at the same time. Each of them is less likely to survive than the American Lion. Do I risk the chance at ten warriors on the gamble that the American Lion will die today?"

"Why don't I go to Warda, while you take the other town?" Maja had said.

It would be a chance to prove herself. To step out from beneath the shadow of her older sisters. The skepticism in Brynhild's eyes as Maja had made the suggestion told her everything she needed to know.

I am still seen as the baby of the family.

It was always the same. Maja was the youngest of the true Valkyries. The twelve true daughters of Odin made up the group of female fighters whose job was to claim the finest souls for their father.

There was a hierarchy among the ranks of the Valkyrie. For many centuries Odin's daughters had been the only ones considered worthy to bear the title of shield maidens. As the population of the mortal realm grew and humans became more adept at finding ways to kill each other, Odin had widened the numbers of Valkyrie to include faeries, dryads and nymphs. Known as his stepdaughters, these new recruits were of lesser rank than Odin's own flesh and blood.

Yet I am treated like a new recruit! Like a stepdaughter, rather than a true daughter.

Maja knew she was seen as a problem to be solved. She was that unheard of a rarity...a disobedient Valkyrie. Most of her rebellion took the form of minor insurgencies, such as wearing her helmet at the wrong angle or arriving for training a few minutes late. Now and then, however, she had been known to use the worst word of all. She had asked why. There were regular how-do-we-solve-a-problem-like-Maja conversations between Odin and Brynhild. They didn't know what to do with their bad Valkyrie.

Maja had no idea why she was different. One of the difficulties about being the daughter of gods was that her parents were not exactly approachable. Growing up, she did her best to conform, tried to fight the desire to question why the Valkyrie way was the best way and accepted her punishment when she inevitably failed.

She was never given the same level of responsibility as her sisters, even though she had demonstrated her capabilities over and over. It made her more determined than ever to show them what she could do.

After some intense debate, she had worn Brynhild down. Even as she mounted her great winged steed, Magtfuld, Maja got the feeling her sister was indulging her, allowing her to have her own way, but not expecting anything of her. It infuriated her that Brynhild might think she wasn't up to this simple task. She had arrived in Warda fired up and ready to take this American Lion back so she could lay his body in triumph at the feet of the Allfather.

It was intensely annoying to arrive at the location Brynhild had given her to be confronted by the wrong man. A living, breathing man. A man who, now that she looked more closely at him, dared to have a hint of amusement in his dark brown eyes alongside the perplexed expression he wore. It was as if he couldn't quite believe this was happening.

Those eyes made Maja pause. Maybe it was because she had never interacted with a living human being until now. Maybe it was because they were so incredibly beautiful. Whatever it was, she wished she had more time to spend looking into them.

When he fell, she experienced an unexpected dilemma. Her hand had actually twitched with the impulse to reach out and help him up. Luckily, he had hauled himself to his knees before she had forgotten herself and touched him.

"This has been fun." He had to shout to be heard above the chaos around them. "But I think it's time I was going."

As he spoke, a group of men wearing dark clothing and carrying machine guns burst in through the damaged wall. They carried a white flag that bore a painted image of a hooded, grinning skeleton carrying a scythe. Putting his words into practice, the man darted out the open front door and into the main street of the small town. His action left Maja with a scant second in which to react. Since the American Lion was not where he was supposed to be, she should probably leave Warda right now. That would be the Valkyrie way. But the man had mentioned his brother. Did that mean he had further information? Was his brother the American Lion?

"Go to Brynhild." She issued the order to her companions, ignoring their disapproving looks. She was the shield maiden in charge on this mission. They would not dare voice their reservations out loud. "Tell her I have been delayed, and that I will rejoin her at Valhalla later."

Obediently, the two Valkyrie departed. The fighters who had entered the house paused in astonishment to watch the winged horses rise into the air. Within seconds, the Valkyrie and their steeds had become a swirling cloud. Less than a minute later, they had disappeared. Maja's own horse would remain hidden in the shadows until she needed him.

Maja cast another glance around the damaged foyer. How could Brynhild have been so mistaken about this location? With a shrug and a swirl of her swan feather cloak, she ignored every prompting of her Valkyrie training and followed the man who had spoken of his brother out into the street. As long as she didn't interact with him, or—the Norns preserve us—interfere in his future, what could possibly go wrong?

Adam glanced left and right as he exited the office building. Although he'd believed he'd blacked out back there, he now knew he hadn't. In the same way, he knew his body hadn't suffered any physical damage. He had been fully conscious when he'd imagined the Valkyrie, clearly suffering the effects of shock.

This was a living nightmare, and his subconscious was clearly responding with a subliminal message. *Don't worry. We'll send a beautiful Valkyrie to the rescue.* Just as he had been coping with that little treat for his senses, the arrival of a group of armed men bearing the dreaded Reaper flag—probably the most feared symbol in the world—had brought him sharply back to reality.

The terrorist organization known as the Reapers had risen to prominence in recent years, spreading its brand of hatred and fear across the globe. The Reaper himself, the shadowy leader of the group, was the most wanted man in the world.

Captured by the Reapers, the most feared killers on the planet? I don't think so.

Now, Adam's heart pounded against his rib cage and

the hairs at the back of his neck stiffened until they felt like pins being driven into his flesh. The car in which he and Yussef had arrived was ablaze in the middle of the street. The roar and crash of grenades and the staccato sounds of gunfire were deafening. As he tried desperately to find a way out of this living hell, a small figure caught his attention and he paused, his eyes narrowing as he followed its progress through the dust and smoke.

The boy—Adam decided it *was* a boy—was bent almost double as he ducked inside a drainage ditch at the edge of the road, clutching something tightly to his chest. As he drew level with Adam, with only the span of the street separating them, another grenade went off, throwing the fleeing child off his feet.

Adam moved swiftly, closing the distance between them, sliding into the ditch and crouching beside the boy to inspect him for injuries. The child seemed stunned rather than maimed, and he gazed up at Adam with wide, uncomprehending eyes. As he checked him over, Adam saw that what the boy was carrying was a small dog. Despite the mayhem going on around them and the strangeness of the situation, the bedraggled canine licked Adam's hand and wagged its tail.

Cradling the boy against his chest, Adam shielded him and the dog from the gunfire with his own body. From his size, he judged the child to be about eight years old.

"Where are you going?" He mimed a gesture to go along with the words.

"I speak English." There was a trace of pride in the words. The boy pointed in the direction of the road out of town. "I go to the mission."

Another grenade hit close by and Adam decided

waiting around in a ditch wasn't the best idea for either of them. Scooping up both the boy and his dog, he stayed low as he broke into a run. He had gone only a few hundred yards when the bullet hit him. Even though there was surprisingly little pain, he recognized what had happened instantly. It felt like someone had punched him hard in the back of his left shoulder.

I've really been shot this time. There should be more pain.

Blood, hot and sticky, began to pour down his back. The pain did hit then. Like a demon digging its claws gleefully into his muscles and sawing on his flesh with razor-edged teeth. As his vision blurred, Adam staggered and veered wildly across the road. Determinedly, he kept going. Getting the boy to safety was all that mattered.

"Let me help you." The voice was cool, feminine and vaguely familiar. It sounded like the speaker was used to giving orders. As an arm slipped around his waist, he gazed into the clear blue eyes of the woman who had burst in on him as he sheltered in the ruined office building.

Her name came into his head through the mist of unconsciousness that was trying to claim him. *Maja.* Since leaving the house, she had disposed of the horse, helmet, cloak and weapons. Even without those items she was still the same unmistakable warrior princess.

Great. Just when I think I'm being rescued, it turns out to be a figment of my pain-filled imagination.

"Lean on me." For an apparition, she was surprisingly strong, and Adam was grateful for her support. With her arm around his waist, he could drag his feet along with her in something that resembled a walk. Somehow, he was still able to carry the child and the dog.

"This way." From within Adam's protective hold, the boy gestured to a large, run-down building, half-hidden behind a drystone wall lined with dusty olive trees. "The lady will help us."

The next few minutes passed in a blur. As Adam staggered into a tiled courtyard, Maja vanished. At the same time, a tall, gray-haired woman came out of the building and issued a few commands in English. Three men in local dress emerged and followed her instructions. One of them took the boy from his arms, then Adam was carried inside and strong hands lifted him onto a portable examining table.

Exquisite pain followed as the woman probed the wound in his shoulder. After that, he dipped in and out of consciousness. He was aware of her clipped English tones telling him how lucky he was. He tried to laugh, to make a joke about the sort of luck that had brought him to Warda on this day. He wasn't sure his voice had worked, but it didn't matter because sweet, blessed darkness swept over him once more.

When he regained consciousness, he was in a small room. He took a moment to assimilate his surroundings. He was lying on a narrow bed with a broken ceiling fan above his head and a window with cracked shutters painted a faded shade of green. Oh…and his shoulder hurt like a demon.

"Where am I?" Since he was alone, he had no expectation of a response when he tried out his voice. Sure enough, it sounded like he had gargled with broken glass.

"Tarek called it 'the mission.'"

Startled, Adam began to turn his head in the direction of the voice. The movement caused darts of sheer agony to shoot through his shoulder. He guessed the woman who had removed the bullet had done so without the benefit of anesthetic. He continued the movement of his head, slowly this time, and carefully.

Maja was seated on a chair near the window, her blue eyes fixed on his face. Her expression was one of mild curiosity. As if he was an interesting specimen she was studying and about which she was making mental notes.

"Who is Tarek, and who the hell are you?"

"Tarek is the child you rescued. And I have already told you I am Maja, Valkyrie shield maiden."

"Of course you are." Adam closed his eyes, too weary to pursue this strange alternate reality his mind appeared determined to force him into.

"Are you going to die?" The question had the effect of opening his eyes again. Fast.

"What sort of question is that?"

She got to her feet and he took a moment to appreciate the way the red corset fitted her curves. Who needed painkillers with that sort of distraction around? "What you did with the boy was brave. If you die, I can take your soul back to Valhalla and my journey will not have been wasted."

"Sorry to disappoint you, but I'm planning on sticking around." That was his ambition. Whether the government forces and the rebel opposition who were unleashing mayhem on the local area allowed him to fulfill it? That was another matter. Although sound was muted by distance, he could still hear the battle raging.

She bit her lip. "I was afraid you might say that."

With those words, the ultraefficient, ice maiden facade slipped slightly and he saw another side to her. Briefly, he caught a glimpse of a frightened expression flitting across her perfect features. The swift change intrigued him, and he made an attempt at getting himself into a sitting position. It wasn't successful.

"Can you lend a hand?" She might be something his mind had conjured up, but he seemed to be able to put her to use to get his body working. Sure enough, Maja slid an arm around his waist and, with some effort on both their parts, Adam managed to maneuver himself upright. "And some water would be good."

She reached for the glass at the side of his bed and held it to his mouth. "None of this is helping."

Adam took a long gulp of the lukewarm liquid. His shoulder was more painful than anything he could ever have imagined, but his head was clear. He still needed to know where Danny was, and Maja was a distraction he could do without. But she was looking at him with such wretchedness in her eyes that he found it impossible to ignore. "Helping what?"

"My defense." She placed the glass back on the table next to the bed. "By interacting with you, I have broken the Valkyrie Code." Her lower lip wobbled slightly. "By saving you instead of letting you die and securing your soul for Odin's army, I may have signed my own death warrant."

Chapter 2

Maja knew she was putting off the inevitable. Sooner or later, she would have to return to Asgard, the home of the gods. Once there she would have to confess all to Brynhild. Not only had she failed to find the American Lion, she had interacted with a mortal. Worse than that, she had committed one of the worst possible sins known to a Valkyrie. She had saved a man from death. A man who had likely been about to die in the performance of an act of great bravery.

This man had been a prime candidate for Valhalla. While he didn't seem to be a warrior, the courage he had demonstrated when he rescued Tarek had been remarkable. Maja was sure many of the so-called heroes of Valhalla would have abandoned the boy to his fate. Her heart had lifted with an emotion she didn't recognize as she watched him cradle the child in his arms and break into a run.

She didn't know what had prompted her to go to this stranger's aid when he was shot. Maybe it was the wild streak in her nature that Brynhild had always deplored. Maybe it was those intriguing dark eyes of his. Whatever it was, she had acted without thinking. Thoughtlessness was not a trait that was encouraged in the Valkyrie.

The consequence of that action was that she was sitting in this box-like room, with its cracked plaster and concrete floor. The only pleasant thing to look at within its four walls was the man himself. Maja had never seen a man as handsome as this one. From his dark, wavy hair to his chiseled features and muscular body, everything about him was perfection. But it was those eyes that drew her attention over and over. Darker than the storm clouds that surrounded Asgard, they could appear soulful one second, then lighten with humor the next. Maja felt herself being drawn into their depths. Which was an unforeseen circumstance. She had been told humans couldn't weave spells, yet he seemed to be working a strange and powerful magic on her.

"I don't understand." The man's voice forced her to focus on what he was saying instead of the melting darkness of his gaze. "How could you be punished for helping me?"

"Because I am a Valkyrie." Why was he finding this so difficult to understand? Surely everyone knew what a Valkyrie was? "My mission is to take the souls of the dead back to Valhalla. By saving you, I have deprived Odin of a warrior for his army."

"Maja." Those incredible eyes fastened on her face.

What now? She had spoken to him, saved his life. According to the Valkyrie Code, the only thing she could do now to make things worse would be to have sex with him. If he asked her to do that... Maja felt a blush burn her cheeks. Was he going to ask her that? Surely not. She didn't know much about these things, but she'd have expected some sort of preliminaries. And just because she had broken part of the Valkyrie Code, that didn't mean she was likely to further, and forget her vow of purity. Not even for a man whose gaze did strange things to her insides.

"Yes?" She hoped the slight squeak in her voice hadn't betrayed the unchaste trend of her thoughts.

"Why do you seem so real? Am I going mad?"

Before Maja could answer, the door opened and the woman who had operated on the man's shoulder to remove the bullet entered. Maja promptly faded into invisibility. She was aware of the man looking around him in surprise at her disappearance, but he said nothing. Apparently, mortals were smarter than she'd been led to believe. Maja wanted to hug him to express her gratitude. Maybe even kiss those perfectly carved lips. The problem with that idea was that she would have to tell Brynhild about it on her return to Valhalla. Honesty was high on the list of Valkyrie values. Lying, or hiding the truth, never occurred to Maja. Somehow, she didn't imagine her sister would approve if she discovered kissing a human had been added to the growing list of crimes.

Maja had only ever heard of one case of a Valkyrie breaking the Code. On her first mission, Silja had become separated from the group and had asked a mortal man for directions. On her return to Valhalla, Odin had ordered her execution, but Brynhild had intervened. Silja was now locked away in a tower in Valhalla, forced to spend the rest of her life in isolation. Maja wasn't sure her own future held anything as lenient.

"Ah, you're awake." The surgeon had a hearty, clipped manner of talking. "You passed out while I was removing the bullet. Since we don't have access to anesthetic here, it's often a relief when that happens."

"Is this a hospital?" the man asked.

"No, although I am a doctor." The woman held out her hand. "Edith Blair."

Maja watched as he took the hand and shook it. "I'm Adam Lyon. Thank you. You saved my life."

"Tarek tells me of your own heroism. He said he would have died in a ditch if it wasn't for you. He has been talking of superheroes ever since."

Even though she was invisible, Maja held her breath. Would Adam—she wrinkled her nose at the strangeness of the name—give her away?

"Maybe Tarek has been reading too many comic books?" he said.

The frown on Edith's face eased slightly. "Maybe. It's very hard to provide a rounded education for these children. Even harder for Tarek, who has learning difficulties."

Briefly, a flash of pain crossed Adam's features. Edith appeared not to notice it, and it was gone as fast as it appeared. Maja wondered why those words had provoked such a strong reaction in him. Learning difficulties? What did that mean?

Edith shook her head. "I warned Tarek not to go out today, but that dratted dog of his escaped and he insisted on going out to find it." She pursed her lips as she studied Adam. "I would normally suggest rest, but these are not normal circumstances. I'm surprised no one warned you about the dangers of this region for an American, Mr. Lyon."

"They did." Adam's face was expressionless. "I'm looking for someone and it's likely he's in this area." With his good hand, he reached into the back pocket of his jeans and withdrew a photograph, which he held out to Edith. "This is my brother, Danny Lyon. Have you seen him?"

She studied the picture carefully before shaking her head. "I'm sorry." Her manner became brisk as she rose to her feet. "I'll have someone drive you to the border with Lebanon in the morning. The worst of the fighting seems to be over, so you should be safe tonight. You've had a lucky escape, Mr. Lyon."

Maja made sure Edith was gone before she reappeared.

"Invisibility is one of your more unsettling habits." Adam's expression was unreadable as he observed her.

"You said that was your brother." Maja pointed to the photograph. "Is he the American Lion?" Adam had said his own surname was Lyon. It was close enough. Perhaps all was not lost. It seemed safe to assume there was a connection.

Adam regarded her through narrowed eyes. "Maja, even if you are a figment of my imagination, I am not going to help you steal my brother's soul."

"I am not a figment of your imagination, and I do not steal souls," she protested angrily. Leaning over the bed, she prodded him in the chest with one finger. "I escort the fallen to their next destination."

Adam appeared to find her anger amusing, a fact that stoked her fury even further. Grasping her wrist, he pulled her closer. "I don't care what you do. Let's leave my brother out of whatever the hell is going on in my screwed-up head."

Squirming to break free of his hold, she was conscious of his superior strength. Despite his injury and the pain he must be in, he held her easily.

His nearness was having the strangest effect on her. Although she was still struggling to escape, she was no longer sure getting away from him was what she wanted. A strange sensation was sweeping through her, a combination of lassitude and excitement. The warmth of his touch seemed to seep into her bones. As Adam drew her toward him, she faced a decision: keep fighting, or give in to the promptings of her body. His lips were inches from hers, the smile that flitted across them too tempting to resist. Slowly, enjoying the flare of surprise in his eyes, she lowered her head and kissed him.

Adam decided that, at some point, he must have floated out of his own body and into a trance. His theory wasn't finely tuned, but he had conjured up Maja back in the office building. Maybe out of shock or terror? A desire to escape the situation? Then, when the bullet was being extracted from his shoulder, it seemed he had developed the fantasy even further. He didn't care how it had happened. There was no point trying to make sense of it. As dreams went, this was the sort he needed right now. Even a truckful of painkillers couldn't have numbed the ache in his shoulder the way Maja's kisses did. Her lips met his with shy, sweet promise. He'd forgotten what this sort of kiss was like. First-time kisses. Nervous kisses. Not-quite-perfect kisses.

"I've never done this before." She raised her head,

a blush staining the creamy perfection of her cheeks. "Am I doing it right?"

In response, he pulled her back down and took over. Adam had kissed many women in his life. As his lips met Maja's he realized with a pang of sadness that this had become a meaningless activity to him. It served a purpose only as a lead-in to sex. But kissing Maja took him on a whole new adventure. Possibly it was the circumstances, the danger, almost dying, the fact that she couldn't possibly be real...but this was the most erotic experience of his life. When he slipped his tongue inside her mouth, he sensed a moment's hesitation before she tentatively returned his caress. A soft groan escaped him as he tangled his good hand in the silken mass of her hair. Liquid fire throbbed through his veins, sending a hit of heat straight to his groin. He had never wanted anyone the way he wanted this woman, this woman who was a fictional character from his fevered imagination.

Maybe if I keep kissing her none of that will matter.

The weight of her body pressing down on his was perfection. He never wanted to return to reality. He inhaled her scent. She smelled like spring meadows. As out of place in a Syrian war zone as...well, as a kiss with a Valkyrie. And she tasted like honey. He wanted to lick every part of her to find out if the rest of her body tasted as sweet. As he slid a hand over her shoulders and dipped lower into the back of her corset, tracking her spine, he marveled at the satin feeling of her flesh.

Sometime later, he was never sure how it happened—to be honest, he didn't really care—she nestled into the crook of his good arm on the bed next to him, her tempting Valkyrie curves pressed up against him as the kisses continued. He marveled at the way his brain was feverishly finding release from the nightmare he had endured.

Since arriving in Syria he had witnessed the horror of shattered lives. This was a land of blood, pain and tears. And now he had come close to death himself. Was his resourceful mind creating this image of feminine loveliness to compensate for the hell of this place? Okay, if he was going to make her absolutely perfect, he might not have gone for the whole warrior-on-horseback theme. That was a kick in his psyche he hadn't seen coming. But as fantasies went, Maja was more than adequate. If she was here to compensate for the horror of the day just gone, she was doing a damn good job.

He had reached a point where the pain in his shoulder was nothing compared to the throbbing of his erection. The heat of Maja's body was driving him crazy with desire. How could a dream feel so deliciously warm?

"Maja, I need…" As he spoke, he fumbled to undo his jeans with his right hand.

Her eyes widened as she leaned on her elbow. "I have never seen a naked man before." Her voice was a husky murmur as she watched him free his rock-hard cock from the confines of his briefs. "Can I touch you?"

Not only was his horse-riding apparition a gorgeous, blue-eyed blonde, she was also a virgin. That was another unexplored side to his fantasies he hadn't anticipated. Reaching out a hand, she stroked it downward in a long, slow movement, tracing the long, thick length of his shaft. Any pang of conscience Adam may have had, any thoughts of discussing the implications of losing her virginity with her even though she was a figment of his imagination…all of those mixed-up thoughts flew out of his head.

He hissed in a breath as her other hand moved inside his clothing to cup the heavy sac between his thighs. Pure sensation ricocheted through him.

"So strong," she whispered, color staining her cheeks as she drew in a ragged breath. "So much power right here in my hand."

Adam used his good hand to tug her corset and the chemise beneath it roughly down. Her breasts were creamy and firm, tipped with delicate pink nipples. As his lips moved down her neck, she arched her back, squirming against him. Her hands continued to caress him, driving him into a frenzy. Moving lower, his lips covered her nipple, sucking her as she gasped. Pleasure threatened to overwhelm him. His cock hardened and throbbed with an urgency he had never before experienced.

What was it that made her so different—apart from the fact that she wasn't real? It was in her response to him. The way she quivered at his touch, her expression when she looked at him and the tiny sounds of appreciation she made. Adam wasn't a vain man, but he knew he was considered handsome. Cynically, he sometimes wondered if it was him or his bank balance his partners found most attractive. Those doubts didn't arise with Maja. It was clear she couldn't get enough of him and that, in turn, increased his own desire to furnace levels. His hand moved lower, finding the heat at the apex of her thighs. This corset hadn't been designed for a one-armed man to remove with ease. His creativity had deserted him when it came to the costume department. Luckily, Maja herself came to his aid, wriggling out of the offending article until she was lying naked in his arms. And as his fingers skimmed the soft curls between her thighs, the fantasy was back on track.

Maja wound her arms tightly around his neck, pressing her face against his uninjured shoulder as her legs parted to allow access to his probing fingers. She gave a soft moan as his thumb brushed her clit, and the sound was so incredibly erotic that Adam almost came there and then. He slid one finger inside her and she rocked against him, welcoming the intrusion. Adding another finger, he kept up the pressure with his thumb, circling the tiny, hard bud until he felt her shudder as her internal muscles clenched tightly around his fingers.

"Oh!" She tilted her head back, staring at him with a question in her eyes. "What just happened to me?"

He gave a soft laugh. "It's called an orgasm. Didn't they teach you that at Valkyrie school?"

The blush deepened further. "We are not taught anything about our bodies, and definitely not about sex. Since it will never happen to us, we have no need to know."

Although the words struck him as strange, Adam couldn't wait any longer. His injury meant there was no way he could do this conventionally, or gracefully. Using his good arm to lift Maja across his body so she could straddle him, Adam claimed her lips in a kiss and pulled her down onto his steel-hard cock. Even in the grip of a fantasy a brief, bizarre thought about protection flashed through his mind. He dismissed it. This was his imagination; the responsibilities of reality were not going to derail it.

No matter how much pain or danger he was in, his body was demanding more from this woman than he had ever believed it was possible to crave. Maja gave a little cry as he entered her.

"Is this okay?" A condom might be a detail too far,

ensuring his partner's well-being wasn't. He was still the same person, even in a dream.

"It feels so good. Pleasure and pain at the same time. We were taught this is wrong…" Her voice was hesitant at first, then, biting her lip, she ground her pelvis against his. "But nothing ever felt so right."

Running his good hand over the luscious curves of her ass, he released a groan of male exultation. Nothing had ever approached the surging, blistering heat of desire that flamed through him. Would he ever be able to cope with reality again after such an incredible dream?

Stop overthinking. Your body is compensating for the trauma it's been through. Just enjoy it.

His lips found the hard, pointed tip of a nipple again and drew it into his mouth. Maja's soft, feminine cries filled the air as her hands moved to his head, holding him tightly to her. As he sucked her sweet flesh—tasted her, *branded* her—he felt his desire spiral out of control.

Above him, Maja writhed with pleasure, moving in time to his rhythm. Encased in the satin confines of her tight muscles, Adam thrust his pelvis up, and she met his movements with perfect timing. They were both poised on a knife edge, ready to tip over. Adam felt his body tighten and wished he could make the feeling last forever. To keep these wild, searing sensations crashing through him, knowing he would never be able to recapture such perfection.

"God, Maja. I'm not going to last long." The words were a hoarse groan.

Each movement was like a white-hot surge of ecstasy building, tightening his sac and moving like lightning up his spine. Maja gasped, her muscles clenching and unclenching around him as she panted her way through another orgasm. Pure rapture hit him, firing its way along his nerve endings in a series of ever wilder explosions. *Never like this*. This was the storybook orgasm to complete his perfect fantasy.

Maja lay very still on top of him, and when he had recovered his breath, Adam smoothed a hand down the length of her hair. "I'm sorry. That was over way too soon." Was he seriously apologizing to the star of his erotic dream?

She lifted her head, a hint of mischief in her smile. "I might not know much about these things, but I don't know why you are saying sorry. That was very nice."

He laughed. "Maja, if I wasn't injured, and if this wasn't some sort of crazy delusion, I'd show you that we can do a hell of a lot better than nice."

The smile disappeared and a frown appeared in its place. "This can't happen again."

Since this was going on inside his head, surely he should be the one to make those decisions? Adam was too tired to ask the question out loud. Instead, he drew Maja back into the crook of his uninjured arm and closed his eyes. She felt good there. Warm and comforting. Almost immediately, he felt sleep begin to tug the edges of his consciousness. He needed to rest, but he wondered if slumber would drive away this wonderful, wakeful dream. It was a disappointing thought. He doubted if he would ever again conjure up an image as powerful and realistic as Maja.

Chapter 3

Warda was eerily quiet as Maja made her way back to the place where she had left her horse, Magtfuld. Most of the buildings were reduced to mere shells after the bombings, although some still smoldered in the pre-dawn light. Several cars were blazing, and she guessed they would soon join the graveyard of abandoned vehicles that littered the side of the road.

Even in this scene of utter devastation, there were signs of life returning to normal. An old man drove a herd of goats down the center of the street, seemingly not noticing the strangely clad woman who passed the other way. A family huddled in what was left of a bullet-riddled house, pulling blankets around themselves as they watched Maja, who hadn't used her power of invisibility, with listless eyes.

I should do something. Try to help them. Even as

thoughts of anonymous rescues that would remain hidden from Odin and Brynhild entered her mind, she dismissed them. *You have already done enough to secure your death sentence.*

How had this happened? How had she gone from being the ice-cool shield maiden carrying out her mission as Odin's representative here in the mortal realm, to a quivering mass of raw emotion? Adam Lyon. That was how.

The thought of him almost stopped her in her tracks. Instead of continuing in her determined stride, she wanted to find somewhere to hide away, to curl up tight and examine the whirlwind of feelings that were buffeting her body. The memory of his touch was almost too much to bear. Too intense. Too perfect. Just the thought of him made her internal muscles clench with remembered longing.

No one told me how much I would enjoy breaking the Valkyrie Code!

She had been taught only that sex was forbidden, not that it was pleasurable. Maja choked back a laugh. *Pleasurable? Try magical. No one told me how much I would want to do it again...and again.* But even in her dazed state, she knew this was not a reaction to the physical act itself. This was about Adam. He had changed her life. Changed *her.* But now she had to face the consequences.

Indulging in daydreams about her handsome mortal lover wasn't an option. After the storm of their lovemaking, she had allowed herself the brief indulgence of lying in Adam's arms and watching him as he slept. But she had done so knowing that she must leave him. It was time to go back to Valhalla and confess both her failure and her crimes. Her failure was bad enough. If the true American Lion had been in Warda during the latest outbreak of fighting, Maja had found no trace of him. But her crimes? They must surely be the worst ever committed by a Valkyrie. The only words they were permitted to exchange with their target must be relevant to the mission. The penalty for a Valkyrie who was found to have spoken unnecessarily with a warrior was imprisonment.

But Maja had done so much more. Not only had she spoken to Adam, she had saved his life. And then, as if driven by some inner madness, she had violated the Code in the worst way imaginable. *I lay with him in his bed. I took him into my body. All the things I have been warned against... Yet I cannot find it in me to feel shame. Even though I will admit my transgressions, I will do it with my head held high.*

There was no place in Asgard for a Valkyrie who had lost her virginity. On her return, Maja should expect her execution date to be set immediately.

With her usual disregard for convention, she had once asked Brynhild about the reasoning behind the rule about Valkyrie purity.

"Wouldn't it make more sense if, instead of recruiting stepdaughters, it was the descendants of the true Valkyries who enlarged our force? Our daughters and granddaughters could learn the shield maiden way from an early age."

Once Brynhild had recovered from the shock that Maja had dared to speak of such a topic, she had taken her sister's hand. Her expression had been the half-resigned, half-bemused one she reserved only for Maja. "You must never speak of this matter again. It is unseemly and unwise. The decree about virginity dates back to the very first Valkyrie ride. There was an incident that took place after the fighters were brought to the great hall—" Brynhild had shuddered as though the memory was still distasteful to her. "The warriors felt that the duties of the Valkyries included meeting their carnal needs. Sadly, some of our older sisters did not refuse their demands, and the result resembled an orgy. It was so shocking that Odin was forced to introduce the death penalty to ensure there would be no repeat. The distance between the men of Valhalla and the Valkyries must be maintained." She shook her head. "We will not dwell on the past, but these things are decided for good reasons."

The Valkyries lived a separate existence from the gods, but Maja had caught glimpses now and then of pregnant women. In addition to the scandal Brynhild had alluded to, she supposed sex, childbirth and babies would interfere with the smooth running of Valhalla.

Now she had joined the ranks of those who brought that look of horror to Brynhild's face.

I have no defense. If I met Adam once more, I would do it all over again.

It was something she could never explain to Brynhild, Odin or to anyone else, partly because she couldn't understand it herself. The magic of that all-too-brief time she had spent in Adam's arms lingered in the thrill that trembled through her body. It really had felt like magic. As if an incredible, heart-stopping spell had been cast upon her. She would die as a punishment and as an example to other Valkyries who might be tempted to stray from the path of purity, but the brief life that was left to her had been changed forever by the touch of a mortal.

The office building in which she had first met Adam had not fared well. Only one wall remained in place and that was leaning precariously outward. Twisted iron girders pointed skyward like gnarled, accusing fingers and the entrance doors hung on damaged hinges. Maja, probably the only individual in Syria who could not be harmed by any of the warring factions, stepped into the deserted foyer and felt a chill finger of dread track its way down her spine.

Magtfuld was gone.

When Adam woke some hours later, it was to the discovery that he had been right. Maja had disappeared and the room was in semidarkness. The light told him it was early morning. He lay still, wondering what, apart from her absence, had changed. Then he realized the bombing and gunfire that had continued intermittently throughout the previous day seemed to have finally stopped.

His shoulder throbbed unbearably; his whole body was tense and weary, yet at the same time he was experiencing a curious sense of peace. Aware that his zipper was undone, he attempted to fasten himself up one-handed. Feeling the evidence of his release on his body, he grimaced. What sort of fantasy had that been? While the imaginary sex had been better than anything he had ever experienced in reality, it had been over too soon. Shouldn't a man be the superhuman, lasts-for-hours star of his own dreams?

Just as well it was *a dream, since I didn't give a thought to protection.*

He spent a few minutes wishing he could summon her again. It was a foolish hope. Dreams like that came along once in a lifetime, and he supposed Maja had answered a deep-seated need inside him during a combination of terror and trauma. For someone who had always been rigorously in command of every aspect of his life, it was a strange sensation. *I lost control.* A smile touched his lips. *And I liked it.*

It was just as well that the corporate world would never discover that the bad boy of the boardroom had a weakness. Finding the time to leave the helm of his vast media conglomerate of newspapers, magazines, TV and internet news publishers, and publishing houses had been difficult enough. If it had been for anyone other than Danny it wouldn't have happened. Getting shot was an added complication. Hopefully, his injury wouldn't put him out of action for too long once he got home. Adam had built a global brand on the strength of his personal charisma. He couldn't spare even a minute to let that slide.

Struggling to his feet, he made his way to the curtained-off commode. With normality restored, he returned to the bed and propped himself against pillows that were as hard as bags of cement. It was impossible to get comfortable, so he settled for the best he could do... which was somewhere between discomfort and agony.

He would be leaving Syria today. For the sake of his battered body and his damaged psyche—anyone who needed the sort of illusion he had created for himself in the form of Maja had a few unresolved issues—it was time to go. He thought of the beautiful countryside he had seen on his travels, with its rolling hills full of olive and lemon trees. Everyone he encountered had been warmhearted and helpful. This was a heartbreaking land and he would leave it with regret. For the first time ever, he felt the need to do something with his life other than make money. Although he had no idea what it would mean in practice, being here had unleashed a need within him that he intended to explore on his return home. The worst thing about leaving Syria was that he would be going without having accomplished what he had come here for. He still hadn't found any information about Danny.

Danny had battled with learning difficulties all his life. It infuriated Adam that some people couldn't figure out that didn't mean Danny was dumb. He was a whole lot smarter than Adam in so many ways; it just took him longer to learn things. Their father had died when Danny was a baby and their mother had remarried almost immediately. Although their lifestyle was privileged, their stepfather was not a warm man, and despite their age difference, the two brothers had grown closer than ever. When their mother died, Adam had been twenty-one. He hadn't needed her deathbed reminder to care for Danny. His eleven-year-old brother had moved in with him. Adam had found a school that specialized in helping students with Danny's needs. Even though the diagnosis of severe dyslexia had come late, the teachers had supported him well and Danny had thrived. He had graduated high school and, refusing Adam's offers of help, had found himself a job in a charitable foundation working with refugees.

Adam had done his best to talk him out of coming to Syria, but Danny had a stubborn streak a mile wide. Adam smiled. It was a Lyon trait. His own was several miles wider. His mind conjured up an image of his brother in the days before he'd left. So sure of what he was doing, so dedicated, so determined.

"That's where we differ, Danny. You have strong prin-ciples, and are prepared to stand up for them." Adam re-membered his own words just before Danny left.

Danny had returned his gaze steadily. "Don't sell yourself short. You're the person who raised me."

Adam had given a self-deprecating laugh. "I have no illusions about myself."

Once Danny got to Syria, the brothers had main-tained a regular communication. Calling, messaging, emailing whenever they could. Then Danny's attitude had started to change. He had always been upset about what was happening in Syria. Suddenly, instead of wanting to help in a humanitarian way, he began to talk about taking real action. That was when Adam started to get concerned about him. When the communication stopped, his concern turned to fear.

He found out from the organizers of the charity that Danny had gotten friendly with a group of men he'd met in one of the local villages. It was only after Danny left the nonprofit that the organizers discovered his new friends were mercenaries.

Adam withdrew the photograph of Danny from his pocket and looked at the familiar face. At the clear, laugh-ing eyes so like his own, but lacking Adam's cynicism and ruthlessness. His fist clenched hard on his thigh.

I must find him. I have to take him home.

The opening of the door interrupted his thoughts and a small, tousled head inserted itself into the room.

Tarek smiled when he saw Adam was awake. "I can put the light on?"

Adam nodded. "Please do."

Tarek's presence was a welcome interruption. The dog he had carried with him on the previous day also seemed to consider himself included in the invitation. After bounding into the room with a shrill bark, the little creature leaped onto the bed and made several enthusiastic attempts to lick Adam's face.

"He likes you." Tarek took the chair at the side of the bed. "He knows you saved us when the Reapers were chasing us."

The dog might have been a terrier, but his unkempt appearance meant his parentage was indeterminate. He was young and friendly, and once his initial exuberance had died down, he curled up on Adam's legs with a contented sigh. Having him there felt curiously comforting.

"What's his name?"

"Leo." Tarek must have been aware of the sudden intensity of Adam's gaze, because he clearly felt the need for further clarification. "I named him after the man who gave him to me."

Leo. It was a long time since he'd heard his brother's childhood nickname. *Leo the Lyon.* It had been their private joke. Adam felt sharp, unaccustomed tears stinging the back of his eyelids.

"Is this the man who gave you your dog?" He held out Danny's picture.

"Yes." Tarek laughed delightedly as he looked at the picture. "How did you know it was him?"

Although he smiled, his hand reached out for Leo, tangling itself in the wiry fur as though the dog was his comforter.

"Tell me some more about this man, Tarek."

"You sound just like Maja. She wanted to know all about the warriors I have met."

Adam sat up so abruptly it felt like a red-hot wire

had been inserted into his shoulder. He also dislodged Leo, who whined a protest. "Maja?"

"The lady with the long gold hair. The one who was dressed like a superhero." Eyeing him with concern, Tarek clearly felt further explanation was necessary. "She brought us here after you were shot."

Adam slumped back on his pillows. The action dislodged something from his hair. A single feather, so pure and white it could only have come from the breast of a swan, drifted down and landed on the worn sheet next to his hand. His fingertips closed over it.

I am not a figment of your imagination. He heard her voice saying the words. Stunned, he remained still for a few minutes, letting Tarek's chatter wash over him.

There were too many questions vying for dominance in Adam's mind. When had Tarek seen Danny, the man who had given him his dog? What did Tarek mean when he said the Reapers had been chasing him? Surely he had just been in the wrong place at the wrong time when Adam rescued him?

Somehow, all the other questions were pushed aside and Adam asked the one that mattered most right now. "Did you see where Maja went?"

Tarek started to answer, but his words were drowned out by the sound of gunfire coming from just outside the building.

Being stranded in the mortal realm without her steed shouldn't feel like a reprieve, but it did. Maja had no doubt that recalling Magtfuld was Brynhild's way of punishing her. Cutting her off from any means of returning to Valhalla would ordinarily feel isolating and frightening. Right now, it felt like she had been handed a lifeline.

This was temporary, Maja told herself, as she did a final check to make sure she really couldn't call Magtfuld from the shadows. Her guess was that Brynhild's plan was to leave her in the mortal realm just long enough to make her suffer. Then her sister was likely to send a rescue party. The message? *Don't step out of line again.* By dismissing her companions, Maja hadn't conformed to the behavior expected of a shield maiden. Brynhild didn't do anger. She did retaliation. Cold, calculated and carefully planned.

This way, Maja might have time to at least salvage part of her reputation. Maybe, just maybe, she could still track down the American Lion. She had an outside chance of succeeding, but she may as well make the attempt. And the key to the whereabouts of the brave warrior she sought was back at the mission. The only brief glimpse she had gotten into his whereabouts had come when Adam had responded when she had mentioned him. His words had suggested that the American Lion was his brother. Although he had refused to discuss the matter, he had not denied it. And Maja had subsequently become somewhat distracted from the topic.

A blush tinged her cheeks. Was she being honest with herself? Was she really seeking the American Lion, or was she looking for an excuse to go back to Adam? She decided the two things were so closely entwined that it would be impossible to separate them. *Tell yourself that. It sounds so much better than the truth...that you cannot stay away from him.*

Unearthing her cloak, helmet and weapons from the space beneath the stairs where she had hidden them, she decided the only way she would know for sure about any connection between Adam and the American Lion would be to ask him outright.

A heavenly dawn light was breaking through the wispy cloud as Maja retraced her steps. She had never had a chance to appreciate the beauty of the mortal realm on previous missions. Although humans had a terrible capacity to cause harm to each other, this world of theirs had the power to move her with its magnificence. The contrast between the destruction that had taken place within the town, and the rolling countryside around it, unveiled now by the emerging light, could not have been starker.

As Maja followed the road out of the village, she picked up the sound of conflict. They were, after all, the sort of noises with which she was most familiar. Angry, raised voices, growled instructions, cries of pain, shocked protests, and gunfire. But it was her job to know when there was hostility in the air, and her finely tuned Valkyrie senses had told that the fighting in Warda was over. Yet this disturbance was coming from the direction of the mission.

Breaking into a run as she used her invisibility as a shield, she dashed into the courtyard in time to see a group of five men dragging the three male mission workers and Edith Blair out of the old house. They forced the frightened group to their knees, holding guns to the back of their heads. One of the attackers paced up and down in front of them.

He barked a question at them in Arabic. The Valkyries had a unique understanding of all mortal languages, but the man repeated the words in English as he paused in front of Edith. "Where is the boy?"

Maja had to admire the woman's courage as, despite the gun pressed into the base of her skull, she maintained eye contact and spoke coolly. "I know a number of boys. You'll have to be specific."

His lips drew back in a snarl. "Don't play games. We are looking for the boy called Tarek."

As he spoke, a movement just beyond the edge of the building caught Maja's eye. Her senses were keener than those of most mortals and she doubted the leader of the group who were seeking Tarek would have seen it. The house was surrounded by a drystone wall. Roughly shoulder height, it dipped in places and had some glaring gaps in its uneven surface.

It was through one of these gaps that Maja caught sight of a man's arm. It was the briefest glimpse, but it made her heart bound. The arm was strong, corded with muscle, and a white bandage stood out starkly against the tanned flesh of the shoulder. The man's hand was wrapped protectively around something. Maja could just make out a mop of dark, curly hair.

She breathed a sigh of relief. Adam would protect Tarek. Now it was up to her to keep Edith and her mission workers safe. Any thoughts of the Valkyrie Code were long gone as she strode into the midst of the action.

The Valkyries were not just pretty faces who collected souls for Odin and waited on his soldiers. They were highly trained warriors. Martial arts, street fighting, hand-to-hand combat... Maja was as equally comfortable with her fists and feet as she was with a sword or a gun.

Using her invisibility to give her the element of surprise, she drop-kicked the leader of the attackers in the head. He hit the ground like a fallen statue. As Maja materialized, sword swinging, before his openmouthed followers, she was conscious of a buzz of pure elation. Being the bad Valkyrie was starting to feel very good.

Chapter 4

When the shooting started, the only thing on Adam's mind had been to get Tarek to safety. Since he had only a sketchy idea of the layout of the house, and he guessed the gunmen were on their way inside, he decided the best option was to get outside and try and find a hiding place.

Ignoring the searing pain in his shoulder, he had shielded Tarek with his body as he pulled open the door and glanced left and right. His room opened onto a narrow corridor that, despite the noise, was still empty. Adam judged it was a situation that was unlikely to last long.

"Which way will get us out of here?"

Tarek, still clutching Leo tightly to his chest, didn't hesitate. "Left."

A few feet brought them to a utility area with an in-

dustrial-size sink and a washing machine that was in
midcycle and seemed to be doing its best to start a small
earthquake. Through an open door, Adam could see a
small courtyard lined with garbage cans. Beyond that
was the familiar undulating countryside.

Keeping hold of Tarek's upper arm with his good
hand, he skittered into the morning sunlight at speed,
assessing his options the whole time. Making for the
hills was no good. They would be too exposed out there
in the open. He had no idea what these people wanted.
The fact that they were prepared to burst into a charitable mission firing guns didn't make Adam feel inclined
to stick around and converse with them. As far as he
was concerned, their motives could remain shrouded
in mystery.

As they passed the garbage cans, they drew level
with the wall that bordered the property. At the same
time, the shouting from within the house intensified.

"What are they saying?" Adam asked.

"They are looking for me." Tarek's voice wobbled
on a new note of fear.

There wasn't time to ask for clarification about that
statement. Instead, the words strengthened Adam's resolve to get the boy out of harm's way. The other side
of the wall seemed like a good place to be right now.
There were no guarantees the bad guys wouldn't think
to look there, but at least they wouldn't be so vulnerable,
and they could keep moving while hidden from view.

There was no way Adam's injury would allow him
to climb the shoulder-high wall, but its poor state of repair meant there were places where it had deteriorated
and become almost a pile of rubble. After scrambling
through one of these, he and Tarek clung to the rough

rocks on the opposite side of the mission building, making their way along the length of the wall until they were in line with the main entrance.

Hearing Edith's voice, Adam paused, viewing the scene at the front of the mission through a gap in the stones. What he saw made his blood turn to ice. The kindhearted English doctor and her three assistants were kneeling on the ground with their hands behind their backs, while men with guns stood behind them.

Adam slumped slightly, feeling the rough-hewn rocks pressing into his back. What the hell was he supposed to do? Save the boy or try to help Edith? He almost laughed aloud. *And what exactly are you—a one-armed man—going to do against five gunmen?*

In the end, it came down to one simple fact. He couldn't cower behind a wall while people who had helped him took a bullet to the head. Even if the only thing he could do was walk out there and provide a momentary distraction for the gunmen—*and let's face it, that's likely to be all I can do*—then he would do it.

"Keep going along this wall," he told Tarek, ignoring the boy's look of horror. "Get as far from this place as fast as you can. Don't look back."

Giving Tarek a push to spur him on, Adam moved back in the direction they had just come, finding a broken-down place in the wall. Taking a breath, he clambered over the gap before his resolve faltered. Clenching his jaw to hide his fear, he stepped into the courtyard.

He fully expected the force of five weapons to be turned on him as he walked toward the group of people in front of the mission doors. Instead, no one even glanced his way. That was because their attention was focused entirely on the strange behavior of the leader of the group of militants. Without warning, he stopped screaming at Edith. His head spun so sharply to the right that Adam, still several feet away, heard a crack. It was as if his neck had just broken from an invisible kick to the head. Then the man dropped to the ground.

His followers were still regarding him in surprise, when the reason for this phenomenon was explained...to Adam, at least. Maja appeared from nowhere, holding her Valkyrie sword in both hands. As she swung the weapon above her head, her eyes met Adam's. The expression in those blue depths reassured and warmed him. She was flesh and blood and she knew what she was doing. He took a moment to feel glad she was on his side.

"Get his gun." She gestured for Adam to go toward the unconscious form of the leader as she approached the other militants. They were briefly stunned into immobility by what had happened, but Adam wasn't hopeful that was going to last.

Sure enough, as Maja drew closer, the man who held his gun at Edith's head raised it and pointed it at the Valkyrie instead. His hand shook wildly as he barked an order at her. Adam could understand the reason for the awestruck expression on his face. With her proud stance and golden hair streaming out behind her, Maja resembled an avenging angel as she bore down on him.

Adam's injury made him feel close to useless, but he was going to do everything he could to help Maja fight these thugs. It looked like he wouldn't get the chance, for the man fired at the precise moment that Adam managed to stoop and snag the leader's discarded gun. As the bullet hit Maja in the abdomen and she doubled over, Adam couldn't believe the force of the emotion that swept through him.

Out of the corner of his eye, he saw Maja go down, and he wanted to roar like a wounded animal in response. He would never have imagined himself capable of anything so primal and raw. Thought took second place to feeling. Acting on nothing but instinct, he raised his arm and fired an answering shot.

Adam's bullet hit the rebel in the throat; the man's body hitting the red dust shook the mission workers into action. Two of the militants had been taken out, which meant their chances were improving. Seizing the initiative, they turned on their attackers. Although gunshots rang out, Adam didn't see anyone get hit. But that might have been because his attention was on Maja.

After being struck by the bullet, she had dropped to one knee. Now, she was up again and powering forward at a run that would put an Olympic sprinter to shame. Adam shook his head to clear it. He had seen that bullet hit her square in the center of her body. She should be dead or dying, sprawled in the Syrian dust.

She's real, but she's not human.

Right now, he couldn't see a problem with that. As Maja thundered into the fight, sword discarded, Adam was very thankful to have an invincible warrior princess on his side. He watched in admiration as, in one stylish movement, she brought a foot up under the chin of one of the rebels while swinging her elbow full force into the windpipe of another. They would be debilitating blows in any circumstances. He had a feeling, from the way those men crumpled like discarded toys, that from Maja, they were more. She must have a strength over and beyond anything mortal. Those men were never getting up again. The fifth rebel clearly shared his conviction and attempted to run.

"We can't let him get away." Edith sounded almost regretful. "If he goes back to his masters and tells them what happened here, the mission is finished."

Adam helped her to her feet. Edith turned her face away as one of the mission workers fired the final shot at the fifth attacker.

"We need to dispose of these bodies. Fast." Adam's face was grim. Had he ever envisaged a situation in which he would utter those words?

As he surveyed the scene, Maja moved toward the drystone wall. As she neared the gap, Tarek burst through the opening and hurled himself into her arms, twining his small body around her like a monkey climbing a tree. An unusually subdued Leo came to sit at her feet.

"Don't leave me, Maja." The boy's desperate plea reached Adam's ears.

Maja's voice was soft and reassuring as she cradled Tarek to her. "You are safe now. We won't let them hurt you."

Her eyes met Adam's over Tarek's head and there was a silent appeal in those blue depths. When she said "we," she meant the two of them. With an emotion close to shock, he realized he would be the boy's rescuer. He would do whatever it took to keep him safe, and do it happily. For the first time since Danny's disappearance, Adam had someone to care for. He might not like the circumstances, but he didn't dislike the feeling.

Edith was organizing the removal of the bodies. Her men would load them onto the mission truck and drive them out into the desert. Sadly, a pile of anonymous corpses lying in the red sand was not uncommon. Their clothing, with its telltale Reaper insignia, would be burned. No one wanted the Reapers seeking revenge for the deaths of their comrades.

While that activity was taking place outside, Maja carried a terrified Tarek into the building.

"I know you told me to run." He turned his head to look at Adam, who had followed them inside. "But my legs would not work."

"It's okay." Maja could see the lines of pain etched into Adam's face and wondered how he was still standing. "My legs were feeling the same way."

They went into the kitchen and sat at the table that occupied the center of the room. There was a jug of water and Maja poured glasses for Tarek and Adam. They both gulped the lukewarm liquid gratefully.

"Why were those men looking for you, Tarek?" There was a gentle note in Adam's voice that surprised Maja.

Tarek's hand tightened convulsively in Maja's and he turned wide eyes to hers as if seeking reassurance. "You are not in any trouble," she explained. "We can only help you if we know the truth."

Her words seemed to help him reach a decision and he nodded. "It is because I know who he is." He drew a deep breath as though the words were being dragged up from somewhere deep inside him. "The one they call 'the Reaper.'"

Maja was watching Adam's face and she could tell Tarek's admission had a powerful effect on him. His eyes darkened and a frown line pulled his brows together. She sensed he was trying not to express disbelief, and she was glad when he won his internal battle. She might not know much about these things, but if they

were going to support Tarek, they had to show him that
they believed him unconditionally.

"I don't understand." Maja looked from Tarek to
Adam. "Who is this man?"

"The Reaper is a vicious murderer and one of the
most feared terrorist masterminds in the world," Adam
said. "His network extends across the globe, but his
headquarters are thought to be in this part of the world.
I'm saying 'thought to be' because no one really knows
anything about him. His true identity is carefully concealed. Armed forces have been hunting him for the
last two years with no luck."

While his words revealed a disgust for the man who
could unleash that sort of terror on the world, they
didn't explain the sadness she had seen when he first
heard Tarek's words. Sensitivity wasn't Maja's strong
point, and patience was not considered a virtue in the
Valkyrie, but she decided to wait in case Adam had
more to say. After about a minute, during which he appeared lost in thought, he spoke again.

"A bomb was planted in the office of my Boston
newspaper headquarters after we published an article
condemning the activities of his terrorist group. Luckily, a security guard saw a suspicious package and raised
the alarm before it went off, so no one was killed. The
building was destroyed."

He smiled, and her heart gave a strange little leap.
It was most perplexing, because there was no one she
could go to for advice about that. She suspected there
was nothing actually wrong with her heart, and that its
erratic behavior was an Adam-related occurrence. Until
now, she had never envied mortals. Their lives seemed
short and drab. Now, she wondered if she might have

been wrong. If she had been a mortal woman, she probably would have been able to ask someone about the unnerving effect Adam had on her. She could always ask *him*, of course. Maybe just not right now...

"And the heroic security guard is still alive, so he wasn't picked up by one of your squad mates and transported to Valhalla."

The words heralded a change in approach. They were a definite signal that he no longer viewed her as a figment of his imagination. Which meant he knew what had happened between them had been real. Real and devastating. The thought tipped her world slightly off balance. She had an uncomfortable feeling Adam knew exactly what she was thinking. How had it suddenly gotten so hard to breathe?

Tarek. He was the focus here. The only thing that mattered right now. Yes, she had a whole heap of other problems to deal with, but the child's safety had to come first. She didn't know any other children, but some new instinct, more powerful than anything she had learned in Valkyrie training, told her that. She turned back to the boy. "How do you know this man?"

"I don't know him. I have never met him, but I heard my father talking about him on the phone." Tarek clung to her hand. "I was supposed to be in bed, but I sneaked onto the landing and listened. I was frightened because my father was shouting and he sounded scared. He kept saying 'you have to listen to me.'" He swallowed hard. "I don't think they listened to him."

"Do you know who he was talking to?" Adam asked.

"My father called him 'sir.' Only once, he said his name. Then, he called him 'Shepherd.' I remember everything he said because it scared me so much. He

said the Reaper wasn't one man, it was a con-sor-tium."
Tarek spoke the word carefully in the manner of one
who had rehearsed it many times. Out of the corner of
her eye, Maja saw Adam sit up a little straighter. "But
he said one man was the brains behind it all. My father
said he had two years' worth of evidence on this guy. It
was enough to bring him down. The next day—the day
after my father made that phone call—they bombed the
university where he worked and my father was killed.
That was two weeks ago."

Maja wrapped her arms around the trembling boy,
holding him close. "Why would they come for you,
Tarek? How did those men know you had this information?"

"I don't know." Tears filled his dark eyes. "You are
the first people I have told."

"It's possible they were just taking no chances. Getting rid of any family members just to be sure," Adam
said. "But you definitely heard your father say the name
of the man behind this corporation?" As Adam asked
the question, Maja sensed he was reining in a feeling
of urgency.

"It was an easy name to remember. It sounds like
a name from a fairy tale," Tarek said. "It was Knight
Valentine."

Adam's reaction surprised Maja. Hissing out a
breath, he got to his feet. Although it was clear he was
still weak and in pain, he paced from one end of the
small room to the other for several minutes, clearly lost
in thought. That name meant something to him, and
whatever the meaning was, she sensed it wasn't good.

Maja, meanwhile, spoke softly to Tarek. Reassuring him that he had done the right thing in telling them

everything, she promised they would make sure the Reaper would not be able to find him. Could she carry through that promise? She knew nothing of this world, and she was now an outcast from her own. In an act of rebellion so complete, she had ensured she could never return to Valhalla. That was just the start of her personal problems. Odin was famed for his vindictiveness. He was unlikely to let a rogue Valkyrie live in peace. Scratch that. He was unlikely to let a rogue Valkyrie *live*. And live where? All she knew was her warrior lifestyle, and she wasn't human, so even if she might be able to hide from Odin, there was no place for her here in the mortal realm.

"I will get you out of here." When Adam came back to his seat, his firm voice, together with Maja's encouragement, seemed to boost Tarek's confidence.

Even so, the boy raised troubled eyes to Maja's face. "Will you stay with me?"

She lifted her own eyes to Adam's, seeking confirmation. He nodded. "I'll stay with you. We both will."

Reassured, Tarek went off to find Edith, to organize food for Leo.

"How will we keep our promise?" Maja asked. "How will we get him out of here?"

Adam grinned. "I haven't figured out the finer details. I'll admit that getting a child, a Valkyrie—" the grin turned into a grimace "—and a dog out of a war-torn country is going to stretch my ingenuity. But I'll think of something."

Sitting at the kitchen table in the mission, they planned the operation long into the night. Edith had handed over the keys to her car without blinking. Much the way she had accepted the presence of a corset-clad, sword-wielding Norsewoman in the heart of Syria. Adam suspected that the Englishwoman's life contained many interesting stories. Maja was just one more.

"You can't fly out of Syria without a visa, and we don't have time to obtain one for Tarek," Edith said. She spread a map of the region on the table. Tracing various locations with her finger, she pointed out a route. "One by one, the surrounding countries have closed down their borders. You won't be able to take Tarek across at any official points without the correct documentation, but if you have money, there are places where it can be done."

"I have money." Adam's jacket might be torn and bloodied, but the concealed inner pocket still contained thousands of US dollars and his cell phone. He had a feeling that his best asset in the next few days was sitting at his right-hand side, studying the map in silence. A Valkyrie warrior who could use her invisibility to his advantage was going to be more useful than any amount of money when it came to getting Tarek out of this troubled land.

"The best way out of here will be to drive across the border into Lebanon." Edith tapped the map. "I have a contact near the old port of Batroun. He will take you by boat to Cyprus. From there, you can arrange to travel to the United States."

Those words were the sweetest Adam had ever heard. Even so, it seemed he had a long way to go before he could say he was safely home.

"Does Tarek have a passport?" That was Adam's biggest concern. Maja could take care of herself. Her invisibility would prove to be a handy trick when it came to border control.

Edith nodded. "It was among the possessions that were brought here from his home. It's in my study, along with his other proof of identity."

"So, our biggest problem will be Leo." Adam was thinking ahead. How the hell was he going to get the dog into the United States?

"I'm not going without him." Tarek's expression became stubborn as he wrapped his arms around his pet.

Edith pursed her lips, disappeared briefly and returned with a Leo-sized gym bag.

"He won't like it." Tarek eyed the bag gloomily.

"He'll have to put up with it if he wants to come with us." Adam kept his voice firm. He was in charge, and everyone else—including Leo—had better get used to the idea.

Leo sniffed the gym bag thoughtfully, clearly decided it wasn't too bad, and with a weary sigh, clambered inside it and curled up. Tarek laughed and clapped his hands. "He thinks it's his new bed."

The dog remained asleep as they set off. Three hours later, as dawn broke, Adam figured they must be approaching the point at the border where Edith had thought they would be able to bribe their way across. Following the route she had suggested, their journey had been uneventful, though the roads were poor. Adam had been driving one-handed over the potholes. His whole body was rattled, his shoulder was throbbing and he felt drained of energy.

Maja turned in her seat and studied Tarek as he slumbered in the rear, one arm draped protectively over the gym bag. Even clad in Edith's cast-off clothing, Adam's Valkyrie companion was proving to be a severe test of his ability to remain focused on the journey. Baggy linen pants, battered sneakers and a blouse that might once have been white but was now a faded gray color, made up an uninspiring outfit and covered her figure. Her hair hung in a braid almost to her waist and a baseball cap topped her head. How was it that she still managed to look like the hottest thing he had ever seen? Every time he looked her way, his mind went into overdrive as he pictured the lush curves beneath those drab clothes. At the same time, his body remembered how she had felt in his arms and demanded a replay.

Focus. He was in charge of this bizarre rescue mission. Driving over the border into Lebanon would be difficult enough. Coping with a hard-on at the same time? That really was not going to help matters.

"This is a seat belt." He indicated his own. "It's designed to keep you safe."

He flicked a glance in her direction and encountered her steady blue-eyed stare. "I don't need it."

"I was forgetting. It must be useful to be invincible." He turned his gaze back to the road. "Is there anything that can hurt you?"

"Only Odin's will." Something about the quality of her voice made him look back at her.

The depths of those incredible eyes were suddenly twin pools of fear and sadness. The change was so abrupt, it shook him. During the drive thus far, he had managed to avoid conversation. Tarek had been awake for most of the time, and they had talked of inconsequential things. Big topics such as what would happen once they reached safety, how Adam was going to deal with the information about the identity of the Reaper, and what had happened between him and Maja…well, they could wait for another time. A time when they were safe. But when Maja looked at him as she did now, his defenses were stripped away. He wanted to know everything about her, including why she was hurting.

Just as he was about to ask her to tell him more, they crested a hill and the sight he had been waiting for came into view. A concrete wall, roughly twelve feet high and topped by barbed wire, stretched as far as the eye could see in both directions. The road passed through the wall, but the opening was guarded by a group of men in a variety of military uniforms. They sat around a few trestle tables, eating and playing cards. Adam didn't know whether to be relieved or disappointed at the interruption to the moment of intimacy.

"We're here." He nodded, and Maja shifted in her seat as she followed the direction of his gaze. "This is the border."

Chapter 5

Adam slowed the car as they approached the border. Edith had explained that this was not a recognized checkpoint. The gap in the border wall was not meant to be there, but corrupt officials were turning a blind eye to its existence. The men who were guarding the border were smugglers. They would allow Adam and Tarek to cross for a price. She had stressed that they were ruthless bandits who would not hesitate to kill them if they thought it would be more advantageous. In addition to her car, Edith had given Adam one of the guns they had taken from the Reapers. It rested in the well between the front seats, out of sight, but within reach if he needed it. A constant reminder of the danger they were in.

Adam surveyed the scene. He was used to skirmishes, but prior to his arrival in Syria, they had been of the bloodless variety. He knew his business opponents would describe him as a killer...within the corporate environment. Ruthless and without scruples, Adam had a reputation for doing whatever it took to achieve his goals. He stayed within the law, but it was well known that if there was a way to bend the rules, Adam Lyon would find it.

But this? Facing a group of five armed outlaws, miles from anywhere, with only his wits, a gun and a pocketful of hundred dollar bills? This was outside his experience. Add in the fact that he had taken on responsibility for an eight-year-old child—*and a dog, don't forget the damn dog*—and the whole situation strayed into the realms of the ridiculous.

He turned his head to say as much to Maja, but she had vanished. Although the passenger-side window was fully wound down, Adam hoped she was still with him, poised for a fight. Since they hadn't discussed tactics, he couldn't be sure. That was the problem with invisible companions. They were hell when it came to communication.

The men halted their game of cards as the car approached. One man rose to his feet and, with his machine gun held in an ostentatious pose across his chest, raised a hand for Adam to stop. With a pounding heart, he hit the brakes and wound down his window.

"Do you speak English?" Adam asked. His heart rate spiked further as the man looked in the rear window at Tarek's sleeping figure.

"A little." He came back and leaned on the roof of the car. "You want to cross the border?"

Relieved that he didn't have to embark on a lengthy explanation, Adam nodded. "How much?"

A speculative look crossed the other man's face as he eyed Adam, then the car. "Wait here."

Abruptly, he turned away and strode back to his companions. Adam watched as they talked among themselves for a few minutes. There was much gesturing and pointing in Adam's direction. He wished he could hear what they were saying. Were they discussing how high to set the price? Or deciding whether to kill him and Tarek, take the car and their belongings and dump their bodies in the desert?

Just when the tension was becoming unbearable, Adam's attention was drawn to another man. He had moved slightly to one side of the group and, while the others were talking, he seemed to be distracted. Every now and then, he would raise a hand as though swatting a fly. His movements gradually became more pronounced, until he appeared to be shadow-boxing an invisible opponent.

Adam felt a tiny flicker of hope flare inside him at the thought. *An invisible opponent.* He had been worrying that all he had was his wits and a pistol, when in reality there was a far more powerful weapon on his side all along.

The man reeled back, raising his hands and clawing at his throat. His face darkened and his eyes bulged. As he dropped to his knees, his companions finally became aware that something was wrong, and rushed to his aid. It was too late—the man's head was wrenched around to the right with a sickening twist and he was flung facedown in the dirt. The others halted in their tracks, their expressions stunned.

Immediately, another of the men staggered as his head jerked sharply back, and he cried out in shock.

He covered his face with both hands, but blood gushed from between his fingers. Adam's best guess was that someone—that same invisible someone—had kicked him in the face, breaking his nose and probably loosening several teeth.

Panic broke out among the group as a third member dropped like a stone. Clutching his groin, he curled up in the fetal position, a high wail issuing from his lips. Adam allowed himself a brief moment of masculine sympathy. Maja was clearly fighting hard in every direction. He was just thankful she was on his side. That superhuman strength in the form of a kick in the balls wasn't something he ever wanted to experience.

The remaining two reached for their guns, turning toward Adam as they made the connection between him and the mayhem being unleashed. Adam reached for his own in the same instant that Maja became visible. Stooping to pick up a weapon discarded by one of the fallen men, she shot another bandit in the back as he approached the car.

Four down. At the same time, Adam fired a shot through the car's open window, hitting the fifth man squarely in the chest.

It was the second time he had killed a man in two days. He had known when he came to Syria that he was entering a country where his own life would be in danger. Had he envisaged a situation in which he would be forced to kill? Perhaps it had been at the back of his mind. It didn't make him feel any better. Didn't take away the feelings of nausea and guilt. Telling himself that this man and the terrorist back at the mission would have murdered him without a second thought didn't alter his feelings. Something inside him had changed when he pulled the trigger. That didn't mean he wouldn't do it again.

"Get in." He gestured to Maja as he viewed the scene. They were leaving dead and wounded bandits in their wake. He doubted the authorities would be too concerned, but he didn't want to hang around to find out. He grinned at her as she slid into the seat next to him. "We have a border to cross."

"Thank you."

Adam's eyes were warm on her face as he spoke, and Maja took a moment to enjoy the sensation. After crossing the border into Lebanon, they had traveled for a few more hours until they reached the old coastal city of Batroun. The peaceful blue-and-gold harbor was such a contrast to the strife they had left behind in Warda that it was a shock to her system. Tranquility was outside her experience. When she came to the mortal realm, she entered scenes of bloody battle. This was a new phenomenon.

As she sat on the harbor wall, the warm sea breeze tugged strands of hair loose from her braid and caressed her face. Below them, Tarek threw sticks for Leo to chase along the sand. It was easy to imagine, for a moment, that they were here to enjoy the beach scene.

This mortal capacity to keep going was something that amazed Maja. This land had been ripped apart by war, yet its people continued to find happiness in their daily pursuits. And in each other. The thought brought her back to Adam. Everything brought her back to Adam.

She forced herself to concentrate on what he was saying instead of how he made her feel. Because how

he made her feel was dangerous. Exciting, arousing…
but forbidden. Was that part of the attraction? If this
attraction had been allowed, would it be as powerful?
Was this all part of her rebellious streak?

"Why are you thanking me?"

"For saving my life. At the last count, it was three
times." He grinned, and it was as if he had just poured
boiling water over her. Instantly, her whole body was
burning with longing. With an effort, Maja restrained
herself from clambering into his lap. "Are you sure
you're a Valkyrie and not my guardian angel?"

"No. A guardian angel is assigned to protect and
guide an individual. We have no training in that role."

She was about to embark on a more detailed explanation of the differences when Adam caught hold of
her hand. Laughing, he raised it to his lips. The action
silenced her. Very effectively. It also made her blush
all over.

"I was joking." He lowered her hand, but kept it in
his, placing it on his leg and holding it there. "Teasing you."

"Oh." Maja was still recovering from the brush of his
lips on her hand. Now she had to cope with the sensation of his hard thigh muscles beneath her palm. How
many different ways was he going to torture her? "I
don't know much about these things."

"Don't tell me… Odin doesn't encourage the
Valkyries to have fun?" Adam raised a brow.

"We don't have time for enjoyment."

That made him laugh even more. Maja watched him
with mild bewilderment. She didn't know what she'd said
to provoke his mirth, but she liked it. Originating deep
in his chest, the sound of his laughter washed over her,

warm and pleasant. His shoulders shook and she could see the muscles of his abdomen tightening beneath his T-shirt. It was an extension of his smile, a joyful sound that made her want to join in, even though she wasn't sure why.

When he had recovered enough to be able to speak, there was still a suspicion of breathlessness in his voice. "Maja, the last few days haven't given me much to celebrate, but you have been one of the high notes."

She wrinkled her nose. "Is that good?"

"Yes, it's good." Briefly, he squeezed her hand before releasing it. "Now stop making me laugh. It hurts my shoulder."

They had come to the beach in search of the contact Edith had suggested to them, Ali El-Amin.

Having eaten bread, olives and minced lamb at one of the restaurants on the main harbor road, they were waiting now for the last of the fishing boats to return. Ali's wife had described his boat to Tarek. Blue and white, she had said, with a picture of a butterfly on the side.

"There!" Tarek ran up to them, pointing excitedly in the direction of the water. "There is the boat with the butterfly."

Adam raised a hand, shielding his eyes from the still bright sunlight. Maja followed the direction of his gaze. Sure enough, Ali's boat was being dragged ashore. The man who was hauling it was young and stocky. He looked tired and dispirited as he secured his vessel and spoke briefly to some of the other fishermen. His attitude suggested disappointment with the day's catch.

Adam got to his feet and Maja rose with him. "Let's go and see if we can buy ourselves an illegal boat trip to Cyprus."

* * *

Ali's expression was suspicious as he listened to Tarek's interpretation of Adam's request. When he spoke, his response was brief and dismissive. Hunching a shoulder, he turned back to his fishing nets.

"He said he is not a smuggler." Tarek's small body drooped with disappointment.

"Ask him how much. Say he can name his price," Adam said.

Tarek spoke again. Although Ali continued with his task, Adam got the feeling he was listening to the boy's words. *Or am I deceiving myself? Having come this far, am I refusing to believe we can't make the final step?*

The problem was it felt too final. He had come here to find Danny and he was going home without him. Coming to Syria had been a long shot. It was a country with a unique set of problems. Communicating, traveling, finding information about his brother...they had all proven every bit as difficult as he had anticipated. Faced with a choice between doing nothing and making an attempt to find Danny, Adam had felt obliged to try. The realist in him told him this was always the likeliest outcome, that he would leave—if he got away at all—without any information. That stubborn streak he had? It was telling him the search wasn't over.

Adam was exhausted, running on adrenaline and determination. The strength of will that got him through the toughest deals was about all that was keeping him upright. He knew what his rivals said of him. Arrogant. Obstinate. Inflexible. Those were among the more generous labels he had heard applied to himself. As long as he got his way, Adam didn't care what they called him.

Now, his shoulder was in agony and the strong, reliable body that he pushed so hard in his day-to-day life was sending him insistent messages that it needed rest. This trip wasn't like the usual demands he made on himself. This wasn't like a fourteen-hour-day at work, followed by a sleepless night. Shock, blood loss, disappointment, and exhaustion had all taken their toll. If he didn't get to safety soon, he would collapse.

But there was something other than his own willpower keeping him going. He cast a sidelong glance at Maja. The evening sunlight lent a golden tint to her skin and the breeze blew tendrils of hair that had escaped from her braid about her face. She raised a hand to brush them away, and even that simple gesture caught him full force. She was stunning and he could watch her forever. Every movement and expression held him spellbound.

Maja's presence was energizing him. Not only because she had come to his rescue so many times during this adventure. He wasn't sure he'd have survived without her, but there was more to it than the way she had rescued him from physical harm. Her allure was keeping his waning strength going. It wasn't macho posturing around an attractive woman. Adam had never succumbed to that sort of display of virility. And without being vain, he knew he didn't need it now. The attraction between them was mutual. He had the memory of the most explosive sex of his life as proof. But he also felt it in the highly charged atmosphere. Maja was too inexperienced to hide her feelings. Even so, he wasn't sure subterfuge was an option for either of them. The magnetism was overpowering. Despite the danger they faced, Maja was uppermost in his mind. Pushing out all other thoughts, she was spurring him on.

"He said you can't afford his price." Tarek's voice intruded into his thoughts.

Reluctantly, Adam withdrew his gaze from Maja. Reaching into the concealed pocket in his jacket, he withdrew the wad of hundred dollar bills. "Tell him this is a deposit."

Adam was prepared to do whatever it took to get them to Cyprus, where his credit card would be good again and his cell phone would work. Somehow, having been to Syria, he felt closer to Danny. He understood Danny's motives. Adam wasn't giving up on his younger brother. He never would. *I should have stopped him.* Even though Adam had tried to talk Danny out of coming to this part of the world, he couldn't shake the feelings of guilt. The sense that he could have done more, then and now. Tried harder to talk Danny out of it. Been more persuasive. Traveled to more of those sorry, ruined towns. Spoken to more sad-eyed people.

Ali's attitude changed dramatically at the sight of the cash. Along with a new enthusiasm came an ability to speak English. Casting a quick glance around, he beckoned Adam closer. "Not here. Meet me at the Masa Bar. Ten minutes." He gestured to one of the beach bars before turning back to his nets.

The Masa Bar was already filling up, but Adam found a table overlooking the beach. Ordering beer for himself and Ali, and soda for Tarek and Maja, he sank back in the comfortable chair.

"I may never get up again," he sighed. Leo, obviously approving of this plan, curled up on his feet.

It soon became clear why Ali had chosen to meet here. The thumping beat of the music and the constant chatter of the noisy customers meant that, although their conversation had to be conducted in a shout, no one could overhear what they were saying. When Ali joined them, he drained half his beer appreciatively before he spoke.

"I can take you to Cyprus, but it is not easy."

Adam patted his jacket pocket. "I'll pay."

Ali shook his head. "Go to Turkey instead. Much easier."

"No." Adam wasn't budging on this.

Ali sighed and gestured for a waiter to bring him another beer. "You are a US citizen, yes? Why not call your embassy? They will get you out of here."

"The boy is Syrian." It explained everything. Syrian refugees were an international problem. Desperate to escape their own land, they had exhausted all the escape routes into neighboring countries.

"Ah." Ali turned to Maja. "And you?"

She seemed confused, so Adam came to her rescue. "It's complicated."

Ali accepted the explanation without comment, appearing lost in thought as he drained his second beer. "Okay. The weather will be good tonight. We leave at midnight."

In the hours between meeting Ali at the Masa Bar and joining him on the boat, they attempted to get some sleep in the car. Tarek dozed, but Maja stayed awake and worried about Adam. He looked increasingly weary. His face was pale and the fine lines about his eyes appeared more pronounced. Although he closed his eyes and leaned back in the driver's seat, she got the feeling he didn't sleep. When the time came, they abandoned Edith's car in a side street and joined Ali at the harbor.

Maja was surprised when Ali led them to a dinghy instead of to the fishing boat they had seen earlier.

"Faster," he explained as she climbed carefully into the small craft. "I am using my brother's speedboat. We can reach Cyprus in under two hours this way."

Maja didn't like water. It was a fact she had decided not to mention to Adam. He had enough worries to contend with without introducing her phobias into the situation. Besides, they were getting to Cyprus by boat; they weren't swimming.

The sea was mirror-still as the motor-powered dinghy skimmed across the water and Batroun disappeared in the moonlight. Within minutes, the dinghy bumped the side of the speedboat. Ali secured it to the stern of the larger vessel.

Even though there was no light except that thrown out by the full moon, Ali sprang nimbly from the dinghy onto the rear of the speedboat. Holding out a hand, he helped each of them in turn onto the deck. Handing out life jackets, he explained that they should remain seated during the journey. He also gave Tarek a length of rope and instructed him to keep Leo leashed the whole time.

"I am not turning back if your dog goes overboard."

Within minutes the boat had chugged to life and they were gliding over the dark waters. Tarek soon became engrossed in the technicalities of what Ali was doing, and their conversation switched to Arabic. Ali seemed content to answer the questions the boy fired at him, and Maja turned to look at Adam, who was leaning back in one of the cushioned seats that lined the deck.

"You have pushed yourself hard," she said.

"What choice is there?" Adam nodded in Tarek's direction. "What happens to him if I crumble?"

Although she understood what he was saying, she was confused by the depth of his commitment to Tarek, a child he had only just met. Maja shared the same determination to ensure the boy was safe and well, but she had an advantage over Adam. She was invincible, while he was hurting, driving himself to his physical limits.

He hadn't talked much about his brother, but it was clear he had wanted to find him. Maja understood responsibility. But there was more than duty in Adam's eyes when he looked at the man in the photograph. There was an emotion so powerful it tugged at her heart. But there were other feelings as well, ones she couldn't name. They were similar to the ones that made her want to wrap her arms around Tarek and protect him from harm.

"Was there an alternative to this?" she murmured.

Although they were in darkness, he turned toward her and she could see his face in the moonlight. He raised a questioning brow.

"Was there another way to help Tarek without putting yourself at risk?"

He lifted his good shoulder in a one-sided shrug. "You saw those guys who came to the mission. They weren't playing nice. If they'd found Tarek, they would have killed him, because they suspect he knows the name of their leader. He can tell the world who the Reaper is." Adam gave a mirthless laugh. "What they don't realize is the world won't listen to him."

"What does that mean?"

He shifted position slightly, resting his good arm on the seat cushions behind her. "I read an article some months ago that speculated about the very thing that Tarek said. It suggested that the Reaper wasn't driven by religious or political motivation. I wonder now if the anonymous author of that piece could have been Tarek's father. Whoever wrote it believed the Reaper was a large consortium or group of businesses."

"Some of the warriors in the great hall at Valhalla died fighting this thing you mortals call terrorism. They thought they were battling against an ideology. I don't understand how they could have died because of something that was run by a business."

"Exactly. The article I read was widely discredited for that reason. No one was able to believe such a thing could happen. Even though, throughout history, appalling atrocities have been committed for monetary gain, it was impossible to believe that acts as awful as the Reaper's brand of terrorism could be done for profit."

The boat had changed course and Adam's face was shadowed from the moonlight, but she could tell his expression was troubled.

"But Tarek said his father had proof of this man's identity?"

"And he was prepared to go public with his name." Adam lowered his voice as he cast a glance toward where Tarek was still chatting eagerly with Ali. "He died the day after he spoke it out loud."

"You knew that name." Maja studied his profile as he turned to look out over the moonlit water. "When Tarek told it to us, you knew who he meant."

Adam was silent for so long she wondered if he wasn't going to answer her. "Knight Valentine is one of the best-known names in the business world. He is a billionaire property developer. No one in their right mind would believe him capable of something like this."

"So you think Tarek's father was wrong?"

Maja felt there was something more to this. Intuition wasn't necessary to the Valkyries. They needed to be strong. Get in, get the job done, get out. That was what made them effective. More wasn't required. But where Adam was concerned, Maja was developing an extra sense. Now and then, she could tune in to his feelings. She didn't understand why that was, and she wasn't sure she liked it. It was outside her sphere of experience to get so close to another person. But it was there. She was stuck with it. Right now, she sensed his turmoil and something more. She thought it might be anger.

"No, I don't think he was wrong." He turned back to face her. "I know Knight Valentine well—too well for my liking—and I know there is nothing he wouldn't do for money or power."

"How do you know him so well?"

"Knight Valentine is my stepfather."

Chapter 6

"Larnaca."

Adam followed the direction of Ali's pointing finger and saw a line of lights on the horizon. It was the sweetest sight he had ever seen. Ali's next words jolted him out of his happiness.

"Patrol boat. British."

Some distance away, but between them and the welcoming lights of Larnaca, a searchlight was scanning the dark water.

"What can we do?" If Ali said they would have to turn back, Adam might just pull out his gun and use it on him. That was how close to the outer limits of his endurance he was right now.

"There is only one thing we can do." Ali swung the wheel to the right. "I know these waters well. We get in close to the shore and keep out of sight. Play a game like the cat and the mouse." He shook his head. "It could take many hours."

Frustration was a slow-burning fuse inside Adam's head. It bristled outward, brushing over his skin until his whole body was screaming with tension. Relaxation? Neutrality? Going with the flow? Not Adam. He created the flow. He controlled his environment.

Upon leaving college, Adam had taken over a small niche magazine, working day and night to turn it into a thriving business. From there, he had developed his media conglomerate, using the internet to expand until the Lyon logo became instantly recognizable. Now, at age thirty-three, he headed up an empire that comprised over a hundred companies. The name Lyon was an everyday part of the music, media, lifestyle and entertainment industries across the globe. He had always been in charge.

Coming away to Syria had been easy in one sense, because he'd hired the best people and trusted them to take over in his absence. It was difficult in another sense because he had never been out of touch with the deputies of his various companies for such a prolonged period.

He didn't know how to do this. To hand over control to someone else. To wait it out. To be helpless.

"My sister is the Valkyrie leader." Maja's voice intruded on his thoughts and his initial reaction was to shut her out. His nerves were too taut for him to listen to stories about her family tree. But her voice was soothing. A bit like the lulling motion of the boat as Ali weaved in and out along the rocky coastline. "Her name is Brynhild. It is her job to find the bravest warriors and to take them to Valhalla to be part of Odin's great army. But finding those fighters isn't an easy task. She has to rely on the Norns, the Norse goddesses of fate. And sometimes they are not kind."

Despite his gloom, Adam's lips quirked into a smile. "Is this your way of telling me to suck it up?"

"I don't want you to suck anything, Adam." That way she had of taking everything literally should be annoying, but it was part of her. He even found it endearing. "I know how tired you are. This is just a setback. We will be in Larnaca soon."

And suddenly it didn't seem so bad. Frustration wasn't a demon gnawing on his nerve endings. He wasn't happy, but he could live with his impatience. And all it took was a few words from a Valkyrie. Maybe he should employ Maja as some sort of stress relief guru. *Who knows? Maybe one day she might be able to talk me into a decent night's sleep. Even into taking a vacation...*

He forced his muscles to loosen as he eased into a more comfortable position. Inactivity didn't come easily to him. Inactivity under cover of darkness while on the run from a British patrol ship? That was the worst kind of torture for someone used to being in control. As Ali danced the boat in and out of the rocky coves, Adam turned his head and studied Maja's profile. She appeared outwardly serene, yet she had to be worried about what the future held. *By helping you, I may have signed my own death warrant.* That was what she had said to him back at the mission.

"Why did you come back?" He hadn't even been sure what he was going to say until the words left his lips.

She turned her head to look at him, and even though he couldn't see her eyes in the darkness, he felt the weight of her gaze on his face. "I had no choice." For a few moments, it seemed that might be all she was prepared to divulge. Then she sighed. "I returned to the building where I first saw you to find my horse, Magtfuld. He was gone. I had no way of returning to Valhalla."

Adam wasn't sure what to do with that information. Had he wanted to believe she had returned to the mission for him? But what would that mean in reality? For him? For them? For the future? They had been thrown together by the need to rescue Tarek, but anything longer term would be—he searched for a suitable word—*bizarre*. Because although she had stepped out of his fantasies and into his reality, Maja wasn't mortal.

And I don't do relationships with human women, never mind the nonhuman variety.

Until his father died, Adam's life had been normal. His parents' marriage had been a happy one, and he had known what a normal, loving relationship looked like. His perception changed the day his mother married Knight Valentine. He didn't need anyone else to tell him what he already knew. His view was skewed by what he had seen in his mother's second marriage.

Adam was still that thirteen-year-old boy who had built himself and Danny an imaginary fort in which they could hide away, sneaking only occasional glimpses at the outside world. Now, he flirted, dated, engaged in some steamy and enjoyable sexual encounters, but whenever things got a little too real, when anyone got too close, he pulled up the drawbridge and withdrew.

It had been different for Danny. Too young to be seriously affected by the train wreck of what was happening around them, and protected by Adam, he hadn't established the same defense mechanisms. Adam envied him his light-hearted approach to life. *Normal. It's called normal.*

Maja hadn't come back to the mission because of Adam. She had come back because she had no choice. And now he felt…cheated. Disappointed, because he wanted it to be about him. And that was screwed up, and perverse and everything he didn't want to be…but suddenly was.

"So you are stranded?"

"It looks that way." Maja's voice could sometimes lack emotion. Now she sounded lost.

"Forever?"

"I don't know. I don't understand what this means." She raised a hand to her throat and the simple gesture caught at something inside Adam's chest. She affected him in ways no other woman ever had. This power she had over him had nothing to do with whether she was human or not. "I think it is my sister Brynhild's way of punishing me for defying her." Her smile was rueful. "Valkyries are not supposed to be defiant. But it is worse than that. I have broken the Valkyrie Code. The outcome will not be good."

"You said you feared the death sentence because you helped me," Adam said. "Is it really that bad?"

"I have only known of one other Valkyrie who broke the code recently. Her name was Silja and she was imprisoned for life."

"What did she do?" Adam wasn't sure he wanted to hear the answer.

"She spoke to a mortal man. It is believed she was lost and asked him for directions."

Ah. He could see why Maja might have cause to be

alarmed. With that realization came a new feeling. The weight of his responsibility here settled on his shoulders. It was uncomfortable and he didn't like it. What had he wanted? Hot sex—hot, *unprotected* sex; his mind insisted on reminding him of that not so insignificant detail—with a warrior princess and then walk away? *I didn't want anything from this. I didn't know she was real.* After everything that had happened since that night, the thought seemed petulant and he put it aside. She had felt real enough when he was pouring himself into her. She had been real enough when he was calling out her name as he succumbed to the wildest orgasm of his life.

Whether he liked it or not, they were in this together. Not just because of Tarek. Maja was stranded here because she had helped Adam. He didn't know what he might do to help her in return. He didn't even know if there was anything he *could* do. But telling himself he wasn't involved didn't work. He had no idea what his involvement looked like, and right now his tired brain was incapable of trying to work it out. All he knew was that as well as a Syrian orphan and his dog to care for, he also had an abandoned Valkyrie. He wasn't sure his luxury New York penthouse was going to be the ideal home for this unique group of visitors.

Ali had been right. It was several hours before the patrol boat left the waters around Larnaca. Although they were in danger, those hours were mind-numbingly boring. Even Tarek fell silent and was reduced to sighing wearily now and then. Maja found the time passed in a strange manner. It would seem to slow to a standstill and then speed to a gallop. It alternated this way as

Ali skillfully maneuvered the speedboat in and out of the rocky coves along the shoreline, using them to keep out of sight of the patrol boat's powerful searchlight.

Eventually, he was happy that the boat was gone. "We can go ashore now." He pointed his vessel in the direction of the lights of Larnaca. "Not into the town center. We will take the dinghy to a nearby beach and walk the rest of the way."

By the time they finally felt the sand crunching beneath their feet, they were a bedraggled and weary group. It seemed to Maja that they were embarking on another journey. Although they had left behind them the strife of Syria, this was not their final destination.

Ali explained that Larnaca was popular with tourists. "Even at this time of the morning, the town will be busy."

"Good." As they entered the town, Maja could see the grayish tinge to Adam's face in the light cast by the overhead streetlamps.

"Before we check into a hotel, I need to find an ATM and a pharmacy," he announced.

Maja raised her brows in a question. She had no idea what he was talking about.

"An ATM is a machine that dispenses cash. I have to give Ali the rest of his money. A pharmacy sells medical items. I want to change the dressing on this wound." He grimaced. "And I need painkillers."

Ali led them to the main street, pointing out the places Adam sought. While Adam inserted a card into a machine in the wall and withdrew the money he needed, Maja looked around with interest. This town was different from both Warda and Batroun. Although it was now early morning, there was an atmosphere that was tangible. There were still a few people on the streets and they seemed to be determinedly enjoying themselves.

Ali, following the direction of her gaze, seemed to feel some explanation was needed. "Tourists. People come here on vacation."

It was difficult to process that information. In such a short space of time, and not far away, they had left behind them so much pain and suffering. Yet here, people were partying as if this was all there was. Maybe the human capacity to do that, to make the best of here and now, was a good thing. Maybe she should try it before she left the mortal realm.

Adam handed over the rest of Ali's money. "I wish you good luck," he told him. "And thank you."

Ali shook hands with each of them in turn. He ruffled Tarek's hair. "Keep practicing your Arabic. It is your heritage."

As they watched him walk away, Tarek slid his hand into Maja's. "How could I forget my Arabic? I know it better than English."

"Perhaps it is easy to forget one language if all you hear is another."

"I won't forget." His little face was serious and his voice was determined.

They found a twenty-four-hour pharmacy and Maja waited outside with Tarek and Leo while Adam purchased the items he needed.

When he emerged, he looked even more exhausted. "Now we find a hotel."

"How will we know which one to choose?" Maja asked. The seafront was lined with imposing, brightly lit buildings. All of them had the word *hotel* in their name.

"Easy. We find the one that looks the most expensive." He nodded to Tarek. "Time for Leo to go into hiding."

The little dog seemed happy to clamber into the gym bag and curl up inside. Maja zipped it up and carried it as they walked along, inspecting the hotels until they found one with which Adam was happy.

"This one." He paused at the entrance of the largest and most elegant.

Set slightly back from the promenade in its own gardens, the Cyprus Sands Hotel didn't look like the sort of place that would welcome three tired, dirty travelers with no luggage except a suspicious-looking gym bag. As Adam strode purposefully inside and up to the reception desk, Maja kept that thought to herself. Holding Tarek's hand, she followed him.

"I need a suite."

How had she not noticed that air of authority about Adam until now? Even though he was almost dropping to his knees with exhaustion—his clothes dusty, his jacket torn and bloodied—he exuded the calm confidence of a man used to getting what he wanted.

"We only have our premier suite available, sir. It's our most expensive." The desk clerk was polite, but slightly wary.

"I'll take it." Adam handed over his passport and credit card with a mixture of boredom and impatience. His manner brought about a remarkable change in approach from the clerk, who was suddenly very eager to please.

Within minutes they were in the elevator, another new experience for Maja, and Tarek was eyeing Adam with respect. "Do people always look at you like that?"

"Like what?" Adam regarded him with a trace of amusement.

"I don't know." Tarek's English was usually good, but now he struggled to find the words. "Like you are the king."

Adam laughed as the elevator reached their floor. "I hope so, because right now I want king-size room service."

That suggestion found favor with Tarek, and after he had bounded around the suite, exclaiming at the size and luxury of the rooms, the view from the balcony, and the mini-bar, he returned to study the room service menu.

"Burger and fries for breakfast?" Adam wrinkled his nose. "Tarek, your stomach must be made of iron. Is it okay for you to eat these things?"

"It says here the meat is halal." Tarek pointed to the menu.

"How about you?" Adam held the menu out to Maja.

"I don't know what half these meals are." She seemed to be spending all her time confessing her ignorance of all things mortal. "What are you having?"

"Toast, eggs and a gallon of coffee. Shall I order the same for you?" She nodded and he picked up the phone. Having place their order, he sank back in chair. "After I've eaten, I'm going to sleep…for about a week. I suggest the two of you do the same. Then we can take care of the practicalities, like getting some clean clothes and getting out of here."

Tarek had fallen asleep as soon as he and Leo had shared his burger and fries. The little dog was now curled up protectively beneath the boy's bed. Maja closed the door on them with a smile.

"Maybe I should have made him bathe first, but he was exhausted."

"We all are. I think sleep comes first today." Adam rose from his chair. Every movement felt like an effort as he picked up the bag of items he had purchased at the pharmacy. "Can you help me with this dressing? I can't reach it on my own."

"Of course." She followed him into the bathroom.

Before he did anything else, Adam swallowed two extra-strength painkillers with a glass of water. When he tried to slide his jacket off, he found to his dismay that he couldn't get his left arm working properly. Without saying anything, Maja came to his aid. After easing the jacket carefully off his right shoulder and arm first, she repeated the action on the left. Although the stiff material rasped against his injury, Adam bore it. Anything was better than trying to pull the garment off by himself.

His T-shirt was more troublesome. Maja had to hook her hands into the hem and pull it up inch by inch. Adam was able to raise his right arm above his head to assist her, but his left arm was useless. She managed to get the garment over his head and gently drew it down his injured shoulder. It hurt like hell, and he had no idea how he was ever going to get it back on again, but it was done.

The dressings Edith had put in place were neat and efficient. Blood had seeped through, staining the white bandages dark red, and Adam wondered what that meant about the state of his wound.

"Can you remove these dressings?"

Maja bit her lip. "I am not used to living people."

"That's not exactly reassuring, but I need your help anyway."

A smile trembled on her lips. "You don't understand. I'm scared of hurting you."

"Maja, it's probably going to hurt like hell whichever one of us does this. But you have the advantage over me. I can only use one hand."

She nodded determinedly. "I'll do my best."

Adam sat on the edge of the bathtub and Maja came to stand over him. Her fingers were hesitant at first as she got to work removing the adhesive bandages that Edith had used to hold the sterile dressings in place. Gradually, as he sat very still and didn't make a sound, she gained confidence. Once the dressing was stripped away, Adam rose and went to look in the mirror. The wound at the front of his shoulder was large and ragged, although Edith's stitching had carefully pulled the edges together. It was this injury, where the bullet had exited and ripped through his muscles, that was causing him the most pain. There was some dried blood around the stitches, but he couldn't see any signs of infection. Turning to get a look at his back, he saw a smaller, neater wound where the bullet had entered. Again, it didn't appear to be infected, and he said another silent thank-you to Edith for her medical skills.

Withdrawing a pack of antiseptic wipes and a pair of disposable gloves from the bag, he handed them to Maja. "You need to use these to clean the wound thoroughly."

He returned to his seat on the edge of the tub. Maja bent her head to her task. At the first tentative touch of the antiseptic wipe, Adam hissed in a breath and she looked up at him.

"I'm sorry."

"Not your fault. And it has to be done." Clenching his jaw so hard he thought it might shatter, he nodded for her to continue.

She worked efficiently then, seeming to sense that hesitation would only prolong his agony. Meticulously, she cleaned around and between each stitch until every trace of dried blood was gone. When she had finished cleaning the wound at the front, Adam shifted position and she repeated the process with the injury to the back of his shoulder.

"You are good at this."

"I'm a Valkyrie. I know how to follow instructions." Her breath tickled his neck, momentarily distracting him from the pain.

Finally, she was finished, and all that was left for her to do was cover his injuries with clean dressings. The back one was quick and easy. The wound at the front of his shoulder took longer. Maja had to use the scissors in the hotel sewing kit to cut two sterile dressings to fit lengthwise over the stitches, then secure them in place with adhesive bandages.

When she had finished, she studied her handiwork with her head tipped to one side. "It's not very neat, but I don't think it will come off."

Her hand was resting on his abdomen and her face was inches from his. It was incredible how quickly exhaustion could disappear in the right circumstances. And these circumstances felt very right. As he looked up at her, Maja's lips parted as if she was about to say something else. Then, as if she sensed the change in his mood, a faint blush stained her cheeks.

Adam leaned forward, ignoring the protest from his

shoulder, and caught hold of her braid, drawing her closer. His lips brushed hers and that feeling thrummed through him again. The same one he had felt back at the mission. Kissing a Valkyrie was like an out-of-body experience. Sweet, heady and darkly delicious. Maja's mouth opened eagerly beneath his and he held her head while he kissed her gently. Slow and easy. It wasn't because she was a Valkyrie. She could be a royal princess, an A-list celebrity, a wicked witch or a faerie queen. How she made him feel had nothing to do with the label she wore and everything to do with who she was on the inside. It was because she was Maja.

This wasn't going anywhere. Not because the heat between them was gone. It was there in the background, waiting to ignite anytime they wanted it. But right now, they needed this and nothing more.

Cradling her face between his hands, Adam ran his thumb over her lower lip. "Let's get some sleep."

And, wrapping his good arm around Maja as they lay in the huge bed, Adam was surprised to find slumber enveloping him almost immediately.

Chapter 7

When Maja woke from a deep sleep, she experienced a curious feeling of panic. Until now, she had never been roused from slumber in a strange place. Throughout her life, it had always been the same. When she opened her eyes, she was always in her room at the palace in Asgard.

Now, she was in a room she didn't recognize. She fought off the mists of repose as she briefly struggled to piece together the events that had brought her here. There was one very obvious clue. Her back was pressed up against a warm, hard body and a possessive arm was tight around her waist. She studied that arm for a moment or two. Strong and sinewy. Corded with muscle and lightly covered with dark, masculine hair. The hand was big and capable, with neatly trimmed nails. A memory

of what that hand could do to her body came flooding
back and she squirmed slightly.

The movement made Adam murmur in his sleep and
she subsided back into immobility. The last few days
had been a whirlwind in which every second had been
taken up with Tarek's safety. She had no brothers and
she didn't know any children, but her protective feelings
toward Tarek were strong and unswerving. She guessed
these must be the maternal instincts she wasn't meant
to possess. Since she would never have a child of her
own, she decided she liked caring for Tarek. In doing
so, she had barely had a moment to consider her own
situation, but it was time to reflect on it now.

She was a runaway Valkyrie. It was no good telling
herself that this was all Brynhild's fault for leaving her
stranded. The right thing to do—the *only* thing to do—
would have been to wait patiently until Brynhild sent
Magtfuld or came herself to take her back to Valhalla.

*But I would have been returning to face a death
sentence.*

It didn't matter. Obedience was the Valkyrie watchword. Questioning the will of Odin, or Brynhild as his
representative, should not have entered Maja's head.

*But it did. So what does that make me? A damaged
Valkyrie. Not the first in the history of time to dare to
think differently, but the first to do it so spectacularly.*

It seemed she had a faulty gene. She was a shield
maiden who didn't follow the rules. Having broken them
once, she had continued further down the route of disobedience, flouting the Valkyrie Code wildly at every
opportunity.

And I'm not sorry. Wherever this adventure led her,
and it was likely to lead her straight to Odin's court of

law, she would not have missed it. This time in the mortal realm had made her see her own life in a new light. She touched a finger to her lips, recalling that brief, tender kiss in the bathroom. Adam had made her feel alive in a way she had not imagined possible. She had never been Odin's puppet, mindlessly following instructions. She had a will of her own. She had emotions, strong ones. And she had choices. Having broken free of her bonds, she found that, despite the fear and uncertainty, she liked this new and unexpected freedom.

Going on the run in the mortal realm was the ultimate act of defiance. Even if Odin might be inclined to show her mercy for her previous misdeeds—with difficulty, she stifled a laugh at the thought—this would be the crowning sin. But Maja didn't fool herself that she would be able to hide forever. If Brynhild could use the Norns to track down the bravest warriors, surely she could use the same method to find her errant younger sister? Or did her tracking system work only for mortals? It was a question Maja had never needed to ask. Until now...

There was a knock on the door and Tarek called her name. Maja eased carefully away from Adam and slipped quietly into the next room.

"I need to take Leo for a walk."

Maja looked at the clock on the wall. Mortal time wasn't an easy concept for her, but she calculated that they had been asleep for several hours and it was now afternoon. Although this felt like a safe place, she didn't want to let Tarek go out alone.

"I'll come with you. We are not supposed to have Leo with us, remember? We need to take him downstairs in the gym bag."

Tarek rolled his eyes, but complied. Leo, who seemed to have accepted the bag as his fate, hopped in and settled down.

"Should we leave a note for Adam?" Tarek asked.

Maja nodded and snatched up a piece of paper from a pad in the sitting room, scribbling a few words on it before leaving it on the table. They made their way down in the elevator and exited the hotel into brilliant sunlight. Once outside, Maja, for the first time in her life, became aware of what she was wearing. All around them people had the maximum amount of flesh on display. As they walked through the hotel gardens, past a vast swimming pool and onto the promenade that ran the length of the beach, Maja was conscious of women with beautiful, bikini-clad bodies. In contrast, she wore Edith's travel-dusted, all-concealing baggy blouse and pants. A few strange glances were cast in their direction. She supposed a grungy woman and boy who withdrew a scruffy dog from the bag they were carrying before tying a piece of rope around his neck and walking him along the promenade did look out of place.

While her appearance should probably be the last thing on her mind in the circumstances, she was acutely aware of the contrast. She was also conscious that she didn't want Adam to start making the same comparisons she was. If he saw all this golden flesh and glossy hair, she was fairly sure that the warm light she had seen in his eyes last night would quickly disappear. The problem was, she had no idea what she could do about it.

She was still pondering the problem by the time they had walked the length of the promenade and returned to the hotel. When they got back to their suite, Adam had showered and was in the sitting room talking on his cell phone. He was wrapped in a towel and the sight of his bare chest and abdomen did something primal to Maja's midsection. It was as if her heart and her stomach were fighting to change places.

He looked up as they walked in and the smile in his eyes only intensified the feeling. *I could have stayed in Valhalla, continued in my safe life and not risked Odin's wrath. But if I had, I would never have known this feeling.* There was no contest. She would make the same choice every time.

She pointed Tarek in the direction of the bathroom. "Your turn."

A few minutes later, she heard the sound of the shower.

Adam ended his call and indicated his shoulder. "Your dressing survived." He flexed his arm warily. "And it feels easier. Probably a combination of sleep and painkillers."

She was achingly aware of his nearness. Of the fresh, clean smell of his body and the delicious sight of his muscular torso. After her walk on the promenade, she was also conscious of the shortcomings in her own appearance. "What happens next?"

"I've been making arrangements to get us out of here. If I was alone, I'd simply book a seat on the next flight to England. From there I'd get a transatlantic flight to New York."

Maja stared blankly at him. Every conversation they had seemed to reach a point at which she confessed to not understanding what he was saying, but this one had gotten there superfast.

He grinned, appreciating her confusion. "A lot of British tourists visit Cyprus, so there are several flights every day to England. It is a useful place for Americans to fly to because there are international flights across the Atlantic Ocean to my hometown, New York. Does that make more sense?"

"A little. But you can't do that this time because you are not alone?"

"No. Tarek really needs a document called a visa to get into America." Adam frowned. "But it would take a long time to arrange that. So I'm hoping to pull some strings."

Maja's brow wrinkled in an effort to concentrate. "What sort of strings are these?"

Adam laughed. "I keep forgetting I'm talking to a Valkyrie. It's an expression. It means I'm going to try and manipulate the system. I was just on the phone to my attorney. He is the person who deals with legal matters for me. And I was making arrangements to get us a private plane. It will be expensive, but it's the only way I can see this working."

"Expensive? That means it costs a lot of money, is that right?" Adam nodded his confirmation. "And money is very important in your world?" He nodded again. "And you have a lot of money?"

"I do."

"Then you must be a very happy man, Adam."

The laughter faded, and in its place she saw a flash of something darker. It might have been pain.

"I should be, shouldn't I?"

No matter how hard he tried, Adam was unable to arrange a private plane for the same day. They would have to stay in Larnaca for another twenty-four hours. In one sense, he was relieved. He hadn't completely recovered from that grueling journey, but he was starting to feel more human again.

After they had all showered and eaten, his next task had been to take his companions shopping. Trying to persuade Tarek that he needed only a basic wardrobe was hard enough, but Maja's sudden, inexplicable desire to own a bikini came like a bolt from the blue.

"We are only here for a day. How much swimming and sunbathing are you planning to do?" At the same time as he was saying words, Adam was wondering why he was trying to talk her out of it. The image of Maja in a bikini was, after all, a very appealing one.

"We could all go swimming." Tarek joined in the conversation. "You, too, Adam."

"I was thinking more of sunbathing than swimming," Maja said.

They left the store, having purchased new swimwear for all of them. Adam had the strangest feeling he had just lost control of part of his life. If that was the case, he wondered why he should be in such high spirits as they returned to the hotel. It was a mood that infected them all, even Leo, who dashed around the suite excitedly as they unpacked their new purchases, which included a collar and lead.

At Tarek's request, they ordered pizza and watched a film. It wasn't long before Tarek's eyelids were drooping, and Maja tucked him up in his bed before heading for the bathroom with bottle of bath oil she had purchased earlier.

Adam snagged a beer from the mini-bar and went out onto the balcony. The night air was warm and he savored the crisp, cold taste and the salt tang of the sea breeze. It was some time later when Maja emerged from the bathroom. Wrapped in a white bathrobe, with her hair fluffed up from the dryer, she looked impossibly desirable...which reminded him of something he needed to say to her.

"Do you want a drink?" He tilted his beer bottle toward her.

She wrinkled her nose at the smell. "Is there anything else?"

"There's wine in the fridge. Or there's a coffeemaker."

"I'll get some water in a minute." She came to stand next to him, leaning over the balcony rail. "I have only ever come into your world when there is conflict." She gestured to the beach scene below them. Although it was quiet, there were people wandering back from restaurants and bars. "I've never seen this side of it. It's very beautiful."

"It can be." He took a slug of his beer. "Maja, I need to talk to you about what happened between us back at the mission."

She kept her eyes on the beach, but he sensed the tension in her. Although the light over the balcony door was dim, he could see the blush staining her cheeks. "Oh."

It wasn't exactly encouraging, but this needed to be done. "We didn't use any protection."

Maja hung her head. "I don't know what that means." Her voice was barely audible.

Adam took pity on her then. She was clearly eaten up with embarrassment, and he wasn't helping the situation by treating her as if she was experienced at this sort of thing.

"Maja—" he set his beer down on the table and caught hold of her upper arms, turning her to face him "—look at me." Obediently, she lifted her head. "I just want to know if this is something we should worry about. I don't suppose you use any birth control?"

It was a long shot. She had told him that she hadn't been taught anything about her body because sex was something that would never happen to her. It seemed unlikely, in those circumstances, that she would have any need of contraception.

Her confused expression told him she still didn't understand. Of all the ways Adam had anticipated this conversation going, a basic explanation of human anatomy had not been one of them. "Maja, when we had sex, I ejaculated inside you. That means there is a chance that you could be pregnant. Unless your body is different from that of a mortal woman?"

She shook her head. "My body is mortal. I just have extra powers." Her lip wobbled. "And there is nothing we can do about this?"

"Hey." He drew her closer, running a hand down the shining mass of her hair in a soothing gesture. She smelled delicious. Fresh from the bathtub, clean, with her own sweet undertones. "Let's not worry until there is something to worry about."

"You don't understand. I have already broken the Valkyrie Code in so many ways. I may as well have ripped it up and thrown the pieces into Odin's face. He is likely to hunt me down and have me killed for my crimes. But a child? Living proof of my shame? That is something he would never permit."

There were so many things wrong with that statement Adam hardly knew where to begin. He settled on the basics. "Shame? Sex isn't shameful."

"Maybe not in your world, but to a Valkyrie it is the worst thing imaginable."

"Is that how it felt to you? Like the worst thing imaginable?" Adam ducked his head to get a better look at her face. He wondered where he was going with this. Was it about his ego? Had he become so insecure he needed reassurance about his performance? But he knew it wasn't that. That night had been magical. He needed to know Maja had felt it, too. He needed to hear her say the words.

"You know it didn't." Her voice was a husky whisper.

"Tell me how it felt." *Shit.* He didn't know how it had happened, but the atmosphere had gone from serious to searing in seconds. What had happened to his promise that, from now on, he would keep his distance? To hell with promises. What did promises matter when, right now, he couldn't concentrate on his own breathing because he wanted her so much?

She tilted her head back to look at him. "Like the most wonderful thing in the world."

And he was lost. Utterly. His hands loosened the tie of her robe and slid inside as his lips plundered the soft flesh of her neck. Maja quivered in his arms as he held her, chest to chest. It was hard to tell where her trembling ended and his began. Impossible to tell whose heartbeat he felt pounding through him. She was like a fever in his blood, storming through him and wiping out the last remnants of his control. Ignoring the pain in his shoulder as he scooped her up into his arms, he carried her through to the bedroom and placed her on the bed.

Maja's eyes were the color of violets as he lay next to her. "I don't understand. We still don't have this protection you spoke of."

"No, we don't." He slid the robe from her shoulders, kissing his way down her body. "But there are other things we can do."

* * *

It didn't matter how many times she told herself this was wrong, that she had enough trouble, that getting in deeper was not the way to go. Where Adam was concerned, she was long past the point of no return, fighting what she felt was trying to hold back the inevitable. She was drawn to him like a moth to a flame. Her feelings were just as heated, and they had already proved just as destructive.

Adam's lips reached her breasts and he paused, raising his head to stare at her. Through half-closed eyes, Maja drank in his expression and shivered. He looked worshipful, intent…almost savage. He looked like he was about to devour her. Her chest rose and fell in time with her hurried breathing, and her dark pink nipples were already rock hard. Lowering his head, Adam swiped his tongue over one delicate bud and her head fell back as her hips jerked upward sharply.

Hungrily, he covered her nipple with his mouth as he worked her robe out from under her and threw it on the floor. Maja arched upward, her hands locking in his hair as he sucked on her sensitized flesh. Heat tore through her and she gave herself up to the sensation.

Licking and kissing his way lower, he moved down her body, sending electric currents of arousal pulsing through her. His hands spread her thighs wide and he moved his head between them. Maja jerked in shock as his tongue flicked her clit.

His hands drew her closer as his mouth closed over her slick entrance. Maja cried out, her fingers clenching in the sheets as he sucked and licked her. His tongue pushed inside her with slow, even strokes, and she bucked wildly against him until he had to hold her down with his hands on her hips.

Her body was wild with arousal now, tightening, higher and harder, until she was stretched out of control. She shuddered, gasped, pleaded, but that delicious mouth continued to torment her. His tongue commenced a relentless, magical rhythm. Licking, circling and caressing, before driving deep inside. Then his lips returned to her throbbing clit, sucking hard as he pushed two fingers into her. She arched up to him, her muscles quivering as he drove into her, and her control broke. Waves of pleasure broke over her and she gasped his name as she was pulled under. Adam continued to lap at her as she shuddered wildly.

Finally, he shifted position and came to lie beside her, pressing a kiss to her lips. Maja could taste herself on him and the feeling made her squirm with pleasure. She slid her hand down his body to the front of his pants, to where his erection was rock hard and straining at the cloth. Fumbling slightly, she undid his zipper to free his cock and stroke his length. His breath was an indrawn hiss.

"I want to please you now." Lightly, she drew her finger around his tip, and Adam shuddered.

"That feels so good." His voice was hoarse.

"I want to make it feel even better." She wrapped her hand around his erection, then, leaning over him, took the head of his cock between her lips. Pausing, she looked up. "Is this okay?"

His reply was a tortured groan as he tangled his fingers in her hair and guided her, pushing her mouth back down to his erection. Experimentally, Maja ran her tongue along the length of his shaft, flicking it lightly on the underside. Adam's whole body jerked, and she took that to be a sign of approval. He held her in place with a hand at the back of her neck while she moved her mouth up and down. Although her movements were hesitant at first, the sounds of his ragged breathing increased her confidence and she grew bolder, taking him deeper. The suction of her mouth on his hardness added to her arousal, and her moans vibrated against his shaft. She decided she liked this new sensation of being in control.

Adam thrust his hips upward rhythmically in time with her sucking. Gaining in boldness, Maja moved her hand inside his pants to cup the tight sac between his legs. The action tipped him over the edge and his hot release filled her mouth. His fingers tightened in her hair as he called out her name.

Adam drew her up and into his arms, holding her close against his uninjured side. Lying in his arms felt right and Maja curled into his body, listening to his breathing as he dozed. It was tempting to imagine this could last. That she could find a place here in the mortal realm. She slid an experimental hand over her flat stomach. What if there was a child? A tremor of fear ran through her. Odin's grandchild? Proof of an impure Valkyrie? She couldn't imagine the storm of wrath such a situation would provoke. As she stirred restlessly, Adam flung out his good arm to draw her closer.

For now, she would focus on him and on Tarek. Their safety was what mattered. This Reaper was threatening them, and she would help Adam any way she could. After that, she would return to the subject of her own problems. *I will take care of myself...and anyone else who comes along.*

With that thought, she closed her eyes and enjoyed the warmth of Adam's body against hers.

Chapter 8

Adam had called it pulling strings. Whatever those strings were made of, Maja decided they must have a powerful effect. Two days after leaving Cyprus, they were finally approaching his hometown.

Tarek was beside himself with excitement as he gazed wide-eyed out the airplane window. "New York City." His voice was breathless with wonder.

"He has only just recovered from the luxury of this airplane," Maja said. "Now you are taking him to a place that he thinks of as a wonderland."

Adam had just finished another lengthy phone call. "My attorney is meeting us when we land to go through the immigration formalities."

Their story was straightforward. Edith had given Adam Tarek's documents and a letter confirming that he had no living relatives. Since Adam was one of the wealthiest men in the country, his attorney couldn't see any reason why there should be any problem with his proposed adoption of a Syrian orphan, and therefore Tarek's immediate entry into the country. It would be an emergency family-based immigration.

"And you will do this for him?" Maja turned away from Tarek's enjoyment of the view to look at Adam. "You will make him your son?"

He seemed surprised at the question. "I have already begun the process."

She moved closer to him, placing a hand on his shoulder. "I have known many men who call themselves brave."

Every mortal man she had ever known had earned that title. That was why they had been at Valhalla.

"But what you are doing, Adam Lyon, is the finest thing I have ever known." Swiftly, she pressed her lips to his cheek.

A strange sensation came over her. Something sharp stung the back of her eyelids and her throat felt tight and raw. Her lip trembled and, as she blinked in surprise, water spilled from her eyes and trickled down her cheeks. She had never felt so vulnerable. When Adam looked at her in concern and she tried to explain what was happening, the only sound she could make was a muffled whimper.

"Maja, are you crying?"

"I don't know. I've never cried before." When he caught hold of her and tried to draw her into his arms, she found to her horror that the symptoms became worse. Tears poured down her face like water from a dam, and she made a noise like an injured child.

"Crying is a demonstration of sorrow or pain. I have

seen warriors in the hall at Valhalla who shed tears
when a comrade dies in battle or the pain of an injury
is too great to bear." That was her only experience of
tears. "I can't be crying now. I feel good about what
you're doing for Tarek."

The plane had every luxury and convenience, and
Adam reached for a tissue from the dispenser on the
table and handed it to her. Placing his right arm around
her shoulders, he drew her against his side. "Crying can
be a response to any strong emotion, whether positive
or negative. It's a way of releasing your feelings."

"But I don't have feelings." The words made her cry
even more. She pressed her forehead against Adam's
chest. Somehow, having him there to lean against while
she was buffeted by sobs made the storm of sensation
easier to bear.

Adam gripped her chin between his thumb and forefinger, tilting her face up to his. "Who told you that?"

"The Valkyries are not allowed emotions." It was
what she had been told throughout her life. Moods, sen-
timent, passion…they were for mortals. Such mundane
things were beneath the daughters and stepdaughters
of Odin. Purity, duty and loyalty: They were the only
things that mattered to the shield maidens.

"Bullshit." Adam didn't mince his words. "You said
yourself you have the body of a mortal woman." He
drew her out of earshot of Tarek. "And when I hold you
in my arms, Maja, I know you have the same emotions
as a human. Whoever fed you that line was trying to
destroy the real you, turning you into a robot instead
of a woman."

"But we were taught that feelings are destructive."

"They can be. Anger, hatred, greed, grief. They can

all bring about terrible damage. But feelings can be wonderful too. Love, happiness, empathy, excitement. Feelings are dark and light." His face seemed to tell its own story about that. "You can't have the good ones without the bad. And existing in some neutral place where you don't have either? That world would be a very dull place."

What he was saying struck a chord within her. Her world *was* a dull place. A place of drudgery and servitude. But it was all she knew…and now she no longer had even that. She had lost her place in the only life she had ever known.

Was Adam right about her? That she was able to feel, but had been conditioned to believe otherwise? It was a scary thought. After all these years, she wasn't sure she was ready to deal with this sudden revelation. Being shaken out of her certainty was not something she wanted to confront on top of everything else that was happening. And crying was definitely not an experience she wanted to repeat.

Fortunately, the tears seemed to have stopped. After using more tissues to remove the traces of wetness from her cheeks, she blew her nose—another unpleasant side effect—and gave a determined nod. She wasn't sure whether her intention was to show Adam or herself that she had recovered from her unseemly display.

Further conversation on the subject was suspended when the pilot announced that they were beginning their descent, and requested that they take their seats.

"What do you need me to do next?" Maja asked as she buckled her seat belt.

"Well, your presence would take some explaining." Adam smiled. "Getting Tarek into the country is going to take some legal haggling. But you? Not only do you have no documents, you have no identity. Not as far as the mortal realm is concerned."

I have no identity. It was true. So why should it matter? *Would* it matter if anyone other than Adam had said it?

"So I need to be invisible?"

"Yes. And you have a very important job to do." Adam jerked his chin in the direction of the plane's luxurious bedroom. "Make sure the damn dog stays quiet."

"This is your home?" Later that day, Maja's voice contained a note of awe similar to that of Tarek's as they stood together at the full-length windows and studied the view of Central Park.

The question shouldn't have required any thought. He had occupied the penthouse apartment in this prestigious building for two years. But it didn't feel like home. He clearly remembered the last time anywhere had felt like home. He had been thirteen, Danny had been three and their father had still been alive.

"This is where I live."

"Alone?" She turned full circle, surveying the luxurious space.

"Yes, alone. Well, most of the time." Aware of how that sounded, he decided the statement needed clarification. "My brother used to stay with me regularly."

Why had he done that? He had never before felt the need to discuss his private life with a woman. Why change those boundaries now? Maja may have come into his life in a bizarre way, but that didn't confer rights upon her. He had no idea where this unusual relationship was going, but it wasn't forever. How could it be?

She lived in another world, and she would go back there. Adam didn't do any sort of relationship, and even if he had, that was taking long distance to extremes.

"And I'm not alone right now," he added. Maja still looked slightly stunned at she turned back to face him. "You, Tarek and Leo are here."

"But this…" She swept her arm around the room. "It's—" he could see her struggling to find the right word "—frightening."

"Frightening?"

Adam watched her as she moved closer to the window. She was wearing the jeans, sweatshirt and sneakers they had purchased in Larnaca, and her hair was tied back in a loose ponytail. It was hardly the most alluring outfit, but he was captivated all over again by her. Every time he looked at her, he burned with desire. And something more. Something that scared and intrigued him at the same time.

When Maja turned back to face him, her eyes were troubled. "This life of yours is not going to be easy to learn. I want to help Tarek, but I have no idea how to do that. This is as strange to me as it is to him."

"He wants you here. That's what matters." *I want you here.* The thought startled him.

She nodded. "And I will keep my promise. I will be here to help him settle in his new home." Her brow furrowed. "As long as you don't mind?"

Mind? He wanted her here. If he told her that, he would make himself vulnerable. And this fascination she held for him would pass. He was sure of that.

"Maja, this is what we agreed. Now stop worrying and come and see the rest of the apartment."

"There's more?" Her face was serious, but her eyes were teasing. Maja had just made her first joke.

Tarek had overcome his initial shock and was now running in and out of the four spare bedrooms, trying to decide which he wanted. Leo, entering into the spirit of the chase, was barking wildly as he skittered at his heels.

"You can stop that." Adam spoke sternly to the dog. Leo obediently subsided into silence, flattening his ears and wagging his tail. "We have downstairs neighbors."

As Tarek and Leo disappeared into one of the rooms, Adam turned to Maja. "I'm not fooling myself that the adjustment is going to be as easy as it looks right now. He appears to be resilient, but he's been through so much."

"I think finding friends his own age will help," Maja said. "And he was very determined not to forget his Syrian heritage."

"You're right." Adam had almost forgotten Tarek's words when they had parted from Ali in Larnaca. "I'll see if there are Arabic classes he can attend."

As he showed Maja around, he stretched his injured shoulder, grimacing at the continuing tightness of the muscles. He had a feeling it was going to take some intensive physiotherapy—and probably a lot more pain—before he had a normal range of movement in that arm.

The second floor of the apartment contained Adam's bedroom, bathroom and closet. Maja surveyed the huge bed in the center of the bedroom without comment. Only a slight blush revealed that she could have been speculating about their sleeping arrangements.

"What is your daily routine?"

Her question took his thoughts away from the pleasurable image of her in his bed. Although he wasn't happy at the interruption, Adam forced himself to think about a return to normality. He could hardly say his life was back on track, but he was here. He would have to face his responsibilities again, along with some new challenges.

And Danny was still missing. Normality would never be quite the same without him. Until he knew where his brother was, there would always be that nagging worry at the back of his mind, that need to keep sending out inquiries, to keep trying to find him.

"Work." When Maja raised an inquiring brow, he elaborated. "That's my daily routine. Dawn till late. I work."

"Do you do any other things?"

"Sometimes. But not often." He couldn't tell her the only other thing he did with any regularity. *Does that make me a workaholic sex addict?* It sounded scarily accurate.

"And now you have returned? Now you have Tarek to care for?"

"That changes things." He sat on the bed, patting the space next to him. Maja joined him. "I didn't expect to return from Syria with an adopted son." He saw her look of concern and shook his head. "Don't get me wrong. I'm not sorry we did this. But I went there to find my brother and I still intend to do that. And there is something else I have to do."

Her eyes were troubled. "You are talking about the Reaper."

"I can't keep the information I have about the Reaper to myself, Maja. People have died—are dying—because of this evil consortium. And if Tarek is right—" he drew a breath, fighting the emotions and the memories "—if Knight Valentine if behind this, then I don't just have a duty to do something, I *want* to do it."

He couldn't begin to explain what those words meant. Their father had still been alive when Knight first featured in Adam's life. A handsome, smiling figure, he was a friend to both his parents. Once Robert Lyon had died, Knight was almost permanently at his widow's side. To the outside world, he was the support grieving Belinda Lyon needed. Always attentive, always careful not to do anything that would upset her sons. *He upset me just by breathing.*

From the first moment he saw him, Adam had disliked his stepfather. He couldn't explain why, then. Later, of course, he knew. And despite Knight's smiles and reassurance, Adam knew the feeling was mutual. Now his mother was dead, and the two men rarely saw each other. The occasional party, an unavoidable meeting now and then. If he saw that cold smile once every six months it was too often for Adam.

"But you could get hurt." Maja reached for his hand, lifting it to her cheek. The more time they spent together, the more he was noticing these small gestures of affection from her. It was fine with him. "What will I… What will Tarek do then?"

"I'm a survivor."

A grim smile twisted his lips. How many times had he said that to Danny? *"I'm a survivor."*

And Danny would reply the same way every time: *"I'm a thriver. We have more fun."*

"You are going to see him." Maja had a knack for stating his next move.

"I have to." Not by choice. Adam would never willingly look into Knight Valentine's eyes. Blank and dark, they were the eyes of a shark. Although they seemed to look right through him, Adam knew the truth. Those eyes viewed the whole world as prey. "Oh, don't worry. I won't tell him about Tarek. But I want to see if I can shake him up."

Adam almost laughed at his own foolishness. Nothing rattled Knight Valentine. He was the one who did the shaking. Known for his dirty dealing and dodgy connections, he had managed to claw his way to the top by kicking everyone else out of his way. He had billions. Now it looked like he wanted to rule the world.

Maja nodded decisively. "In that case, you are not going alone."

Adam regarded her in surprise. "I thought you were in enough trouble. What would Odin say?"

"Odin can add this to the list of my crimes." She smiled, and he decided he liked this new, mischievous side that was emerging. "If he can find me."

Nothing was going to stop Tarek from seeing the sights on his first evening in the most famous city in the world. Adam was surprised to find himself enjoying the experience of his hometown through the eyes of an eight-year-old…and a shield maiden from Valhalla.

Instead of his usual annoyance at the crowds, noise and dirt of Times Square, he relaxed and joined in with their enjoyment. Felt the thrill of the buildings looming overhead. Smelled the mingling aromas from the wares of the street vendors at the busy intersections. Listened to the sound of music in the distance. Watched cabs racing by or screeching to a halt when hailed by a customer. Looked up at the theater marquees and won-

dered which show would bring the brightest sparkle
to Maja's eyes. Took her hand as she held Tarek's and
they zigzagged between the seething crowds. Waited
with the crowds for the crossing light to change. Joined
in the dash to the other sidewalk as horns honked and
tourists chattered.

His doctor had called at the apartment and Adam's
left arm was now in a sling. Stronger painkillers had
taken away that residual scream in his muscles every
time he moved. Follow-up medical appointments had
been organized. The fear that he would be left with permanent damage was receding.

I'm having fun.

When had he had been able to say that? Had he *ever*
said it? Maybe now and then when Danny was small
and he'd taken him out for the day. Just the two of them.
It had been their way of escaping from the rigid formality that prevailed in their stepfather's home. Later,
when Danny had lived with Adam, they'd had more opportunities to enjoy each other's company, but Adam
had been building up the business. They had become
missed opportunities.

So this was what happiness felt like. Who'd have
known all it took was pizza, soda, a child's laughter and
the thought of going home with a sexy Valkyrie on his
arm? Even the prospect of a visit to Valentine Tower
the following day couldn't quite take the edge off his
pleasure. He was happy to sit back and watch Maja as
she chatted to Tarek about the sights they had seen. The
light in her blue eyes loosened something in his chest
he didn't even know had been tight. The slender length
of her thigh pressed against his in the restaurant booth
felt like it was meant to be there. And when she shifted

in her seat to talk to him, her smile tilted him off balance ever so slightly. Just the way he liked it.

Although Tarek said he was looking forward to starting school in a few days, there was a worried look in his eyes. Adam had seen that expression before. In Danny's eyes. His brother had hidden his fears from the world beneath a cheerful exterior. Only Adam knew how hard he fought to overcome his problems. There was no denying the twin issues ahead for Tarek. Not only would he be studying in his second language, he also had learning difficulties. They didn't have his records from his teachers in Syria, so they would need a diagnosis from his new school. It would feel like he had two mountains to climb every day.

"The teachers at the school I have in mind understand each student's needs and adapt their methods to focus on special education." Adam did his best to reassure him. "It's the school my brother transferred to when he was eleven, and it made a huge difference to him. Believe me, no one is going to force you to do something that is too much for you."

Tarek seemed reassured by what he was saying. They finished their meal with ice cream and planned a shopping expedition for the following day to buy more clothes.

"We bought new clothes in Larnaca," Maja pointed out. "Why do we need more?"

Adam laughed. "You must be the only woman in the world to think two pairs of jeans and two sweatshirts is enough."

She looked bemused. "It's your money."

He was about to tell her how much he was going to enjoy spending it on her when he got the strangest feeling that they were being watched. It wasn't anything he could pinpoint. Just a slight crawling sensation up his spine, making the hairs on the back of his neck prickle. When he looked around, he couldn't identify the source of his unease. The restaurant was busy, crowded mostly with families. They blended in, looking like two parents with their child. No one seemed remotely interested in their table.

Syria has gotten to you. And the thought of tomorrow's meeting is unnerving you. Get over it.

It didn't matter what he told himself, the feeling persisted. As he asked for the check and they got ready to leave, he had to resist the impulse to keep looking over his shoulder. When they got outside onto the busy sidewalk, the sensation grew stronger. It felt like invisible eyes were boring into his skull. What *was* this?

Annoyed at the way his mood had plummeted for no good reason, he hailed a cab. As he was holding the door open to allow Maja and Tarek to get in, Adam took a final look around. People. Lights. Movement. And there. Over to his left. One man, standing totally still, allowing the crowds to flow around him like a river. That guy was the source of his unease. Without knowing why, Adam knew.

He was tall and muscular, clad all in black, with a shaved head. Adam was fairly sure he hadn't seen him before, but while there was nothing threatening in his stance, the sense of menace he emanated was tangible, eating up the distance between them.

As he joined his companions in the cab, Adam slewed his body around to keep his gaze fixed on the sidewalk. The man watching him didn't move, didn't flinch. As the car pulled away, he maintained eye contact, letting Adam feel that silent gaze.

Even after Adam could no longer see him.

Chapter 9

Tarek had selected the best room. With full-length windows dominating two walls, it was far too grown-up for a child his age, with every possible luxury to distract him. Maja gently pried the TV remote control from him as she explained the need to get into a routine.

"When you start school, you will have to be rested each morning so you are ready to learn."

"When I'm at school, will you be here to look after Leo?" He looked very small as he snuggled down in the huge bed. "He'll be lonely on his own."

She knew it was his way of checking that she wasn't going away. While she didn't want to make promises she couldn't keep, she also didn't want to cause him any anxiety. When the time came for her to leave, they would deal with the best way to tell him. For now, she was here.

As much as it hurt her to think about leaving, she knew it would have to happen. It frightened her to think how much this already felt comfortable. How much she enjoyed being here with Adam and Tarek. How hard it was to think of their lives going on without her.

Against all the odds, she was enjoying being a mom to Tarek, slipping into the role naturally without even knowing how it was done. Her own mother, the goddess Freyja, was hardly a warm and caring role model. Yet somehow, Maja was finding her way and Tarek seemed to appreciate her efforts.

"Leo will be fine." She bent and kissed his cheek. "Go to sleep."

When she went back into the sitting room, Adam was standing by one of the windows. The room was lit only by the lights of the city below them and the moon. Maja felt unaccountably nervous as she approached him, as though she was meeting him for the first time. As though, without the drama and fury of Syria and their escape, without Tarek to focus on, they had nothing. They didn't know each other...

Before she could speak, Adam caught hold of her wrist with his right hand, pulling her to him. He bent his head until his lips were inches from hers. Her nervousness evaporated, and was replaced by a delicious anticipation.

"I thought you'd decided to spend the night in there."

"Tarek wanted to talk." Her heart had begun a disturbing, uneven rhythm.

"What about what I want?" He brushed his lips across hers. Soft and warm and teasing.

"What do you want, Adam?" The words came out with a gasp.

"You, Maja. All of you."

He backed her up against one of the pillars, pinning her in place with his body. There was nothing soft and teasing about the way he kissed her this time. His tongue was velvet fire invading her mouth; his hips ground hard against her, illustrating exactly what he wanted. If the pillar hadn't been there, Maja would have melted in a hopeless puddle of desire at his feet.

"I guess this means we don't have to discuss our sleeping arrangements?"

He rested his forehead on hers. "I don't plan on letting you get much sleep."

Taking her hand, he led her up the stairs to his bedroom. He flicked a switch and the room was immersed in low-level lighting.

"I'm going to need some help with the clothes. Let's start with yours."

His gaze warmed her as she removed her clothing, and Maja resisted the desire to hide herself from his gaze. The half-light showed her the appreciation in his eyes as they roamed over her body. That look was as powerful as a touch. By the time she stood naked before him, she was shivering with need.

"Maja. You are incredible." There was a new note in his voice. Hoarse and demanding, it conjured up images that made her want to get on her knees and beg. "Now my clothes."

He was so virile and commanding. So masculine. It was this that appealed to her, made her feel so alive with longing. The knowledge that she could touch and stroke this big, beautiful male body made her shiver with pleasure.

He had already removed his shoes and socks. Standing on tiptoe, she undid the sling, which was fastened at the back of his neck, and placed it to one side. With fingers that weren't quite steady, Maja undid the buttons on his shirt and pushed it down his right shoulder.

Her fingers skimmed the hard muscle of his abdomen as she reached for his belt buckle, and he sucked in a breath. She liked the idea that her touch provoked such an extreme reaction from him. He affected her so profoundly, it felt good to have proof that the feelings were mutual. There were other clues. Each time he kissed her, she could feel his heartbeat. Now, as she unbuckled his belt and reached lower, she could feel his erection straining against his zipper.

When his pants fell to the floor, Adam kicked them aside. Maja's eyes widened as he moved toward her, walking her backward until her knees hit the bed. For an instant, as she sank into a sitting position, her eyes were level with his cock and she experienced a powerful desire. She wanted to taste him. Before she could do anything about it, Adam was beside her, drawing her down next to him. His lips found hers and she was lost in him.

She tingled with desire... Every part of her actually burned. He was seducing her with his touch and she loved every wicked caress. She wanted all the things she had been brought up to believe were wrong. Welcomed them along with the intimate pleasure of his fingertips on her flesh.

"This protection you talked about...?"

"Taken care of."

Moving his hand between her legs, he found the exact spot that craved his touch, and Maja's whole body combusted. She writhed against him, returning his kisses frantically as he rubbed her sensitized nub exactly the way she needed. Helplessly, she spread her legs wider and rocked her pelvis against his hand, straining to get nearer to him. To close every gap, so there was nothing between them, not even air. Every stroke of his fingers, every tiny movement, the friction against her slippery flesh, was exquisite torture. His lips against her mouth, the rich texture of his tongue, the longed-for, forbidden taste of him. *This is what my body was made for. I was made for Adam.*

His mouth moved lower, finding her nipple, tugging on the hardened tip. Maja cried out. It was too much. Not enough. She needed more. But more would drive away the last remnants of her sanity. Her body started to tremble and she threw her head back.

"Please…"

"Please what?" Adam's eyes were hooded, a wicked gleam in their depths as he watched her face. "Tell me what you want, Maja."

"More." She licked her lips, her head thrashing from side to side. "I want you…"

"And you'll get me. Every part of me. But not yet." His teeth shone white as he smiled. "I told you we were going to do better than nice this time."

Ignoring her little cry of frustration, he moved lower, burying his face between her legs. Maja squirmed as he licked her from her entrance to her clit, sucking hard before going back to penetrate her with his tongue. Her back arched off the bed. Need powered through her like a firestorm scorching her flesh. Her whole body thrummed, her breathing came in ragged bursts and her heart pounded in time with the rhythm of Adam's demands.

She took her weight on her elbows, wanting to see him, watching his dark head as he devoured her. Adam locked his eyes on hers, his intense stare searing soul-deep into her.

Although Adam's eyes on her body could draw out desires she never knew existed, the look in them now triggered a different exchange. Maja was transfixed by the emotion in their dark depths. They told her he was hers, to do with as she wished. In that instant and beyond. It was a connection that transcended the physical bond between them, taking her feelings to new heights.

Her legs began to shake, and her eyes shuttered closed. She was hanging on to a precipice, and as Adam sucked harder, she let go. Falling into an abyss that was both terrifying and exhilarating, she tensed in response to the mindless sensations ripping through her body.

"Relax. Just let it happen." How did he know she found trust hard? Even with him, it was hard to let go of the prohibitions that had been so much a part of her life.

But this was Adam. She did trust him. She let go so completely, she thought she might pass out. Just at the point where the darkness took over, pure hot light rippled through her, tipping her over the edge of infinite pleasure. Moaning and gasping, she tumbled headlong into it as a thousand stars exploded inside her head.

Adam held her close as she trembled wildly, kissing her and stroking her hair. She heard him reaching for something before he muttered a curse.

"I'm going to need your help."

She opened her eyes, allowing the room to stop spinning. Adam was holding a small foil packet.

"This is a condom. It's the protection we need. Can you help me by opening this?"

She took the packet from him and tore it open. "Tell me what else to do."

Adam took the small rubber object from her and placed it over the head of his cock. "You need to roll it all the way down."

Maja moved her hands to replace his. "Like this?" Slowly, she guided the condom down his shaft, watching his face the whole time.

His eyelids fluttered. "Exactly like that."

When she had finished, he caught her to him with his good arm. "Getting a condom on has never been so enjoyable."

His tongue tangled with hers, and he shifted his weight onto his right elbow as he moved over her. Spreading her legs apart, he pressed against her opening. Maja lifted her hips, urging him on.

"Yes, Adam. Now, please." Getting the condom on had fired her desire up to peak levels again and she couldn't wait any longer.

Slowly, he eased the tip of his cock into her. And it was perfect. Nothing could compare to this moment. To the swirl of sensations provoked by Adam pushing into her inch by inch, allowing her to adjust to his size.

"You feel so good around me." The words were a husky murmur against her lips when he was all the way inside her. "So hot and tight."

Maja wanted to grip his shoulders, to hold him tighter. She clasped her arms around his back, holding him as close to her as she could, wanting every inch of his skin on hers, feeling his muscles flex as he moved.

His right hand reached around her to cup her buttock, angling her hips to take every last inch of him, and she gasped at the fullness of him stretching her, of his body opening her to him. When he began to thrust, it was slow and consuming, accompanied by heady kisses. And heat, nothing but scorching heat. It radiated from them, so powerful that Maja felt she was absorbing him through her skin. He was imprinting himself into her. She could feel his passion everywhere. In the touch of his lips, the glide of his tongue, in the fingers that gripped her ass cheek, in every ridge and vein of his cock, in every beat of his heart.

She took him. Met his movements with a matching fever of her own, her body revealing the emotions she had believed she couldn't feel. There was no hiding place. No pretense. She gave him everything. *All of you.* That was what he had said he wanted. And Maja didn't hold back.

From a life of near sensory deprivation, she was flung into a world of color and light, taste and scent, touch and texture. And Adam was at its center, the intimacy between them the source of this swooping emotional high. So many feelings were crowding in on her at once, it was overwhelming. She didn't know their names, but she guessed there was joy alongside the passion. And a sense of wonder that something so incredible could happen to her body. That Adam could make her feel this way and she could give him pleasure in return. And it was perfect...

"Please." She was coming apart, her hands clawing at his lower back, her hips lifting in time with his thrusts. Arching. Panting. Moaning. "More."

In response, he began to thrust harder and faster. Maja's back arched off the bed in a frenzy of pleasure as she matched his rhythm, grinding her pelvis against his. Deeper. Rougher. Frenzied and frantic, she could feel Adam losing control in the same instant that she began to climax.

"Maja." Her name was a hoarse groan on his lips as, shaking, he kissed her passionately.

That kiss heightened the sensations in Maja's body. She was conscious of her muscles tightening and releasing around his cock. Her whole body was stretched taut, while her mind was empty of everything except *this*. There was a building of pressure, of her nerve endings vibrating wildly, the feeling moving out from her core to her lower belly and her thighs. Spreading fast, like wildfire, setting her whole body alight, holding it in a grip of rapture so tight and fierce that even breathing was painful.

Nothing could compare to this feeling. Maja almost laughed when she thought back to the person she had been before she had her first orgasm. Back then, she'd have listed life's most amazing physical experiences as a hot bath after braving the snows of Asgard, an intense workout or slipping between fresh, clean sheets. This? It was pure pleasure fizzing through her bloodstream, totally connecting with every part of herself.

Even when the initial storm had subsided, she was left trembling in its wake, forcing herself to remember to breathe. Her head was still spinning, her body tense, her limbs heavy. She became aware of her curled toes, her fingers digging deep into Adam's flesh, her heart hammering in an attempt to restore its normal beat.

Her internal muscles were still shuddering, giving fluttering echoes of the powerful surges of moments earlier. Like the aftershocks that followed a violent earthquake. She could feel Adam's cock jerking in time with the movements, and she squirmed with pleasure.

Adam kissed her again, softer this time. Easing out of her, he moved to one side.

"Tell me that was better than nice."

"It was wonderful." If she searched forever, she wouldn't find the words to describe how perfect it had been.

He went to the bathroom and she guessed he was disposing of the condom. When he returned, he drew her to him, holding her tightly against his chest. Maja pressed even closer, loving the feel of his skin on hers. Slowly, he kissed her lips, then down to her neck, before returning to her mouth again.

"Get some sleep. We have an important meeting tomorrow."

Maja slowly lifted her head to look into his face. Rolling onto his side, Adam threw his leg over her thigh to pin her to the bed, as though keeping her where he wanted her. It felt right. Maja's chest fluttered with something that was more than desire. The connection between them went so much deeper than that. It felt like he was in her heart and mind as well as her body. She couldn't wish him away and she didn't want to. Whatever happened in the coming days and weeks, she would be content with this. She had made a promise to Tarek, but it went deeper. She would be here when Adam needed her.

Adam watched Maja as she slept. He had switched off the light, but the drapes were open, allowing the moonlight to highlight her face. In a way, things had been easier when he thought she was a fantasy. Now he could touch her, talk to her, hold her in his arms and have mind-blowing sex with her. But she would never be part of his life. Some crazy quirk of fate had brought her to him at just the right moment. He had jokingly asked her if she might be his guardian angel instead of a Valkyrie, and in typical Maja style, she had started to lecture him about how the cosmos didn't work that way.

Maja might as well have been a protecting spirit. She had appeared in his life when he was at the point of death, and had watched over him ever since, hauling him out of one dangerous situation after another. And her genuine care for Tarek shone through everything else, demonstrating that she wasn't the unfeeling warrior she liked to portray herself as. She also happened to be the most perfect woman he had ever met. Setting aside her looks, she was smart, compassionate and— even though she appeared not to know it—she had a killer sense of humor.

Just my luck. I find there might actually be a woman of my dreams. The catch is, she comes from another world.

They had so many other things going on that maybe they should have resisted this incredible attraction between them. Adam almost laughed out loud. He may as well try to resist the impulse to keep breathing. It would be easy to say Maja was an addiction. She was more. She was a need. While she was here with him, he had to have her. He had experienced intense cravings in his business life: the need to complete a takeover, to see an acquisition through, to beat a competitor. Those things faded into insignificance beside his hunger for Maja.

But the issues facing them were enormous and growing. They might have escaped the immediate dangers of Syria, but that didn't mean they were safe. They kept a huge secret. If Tarek was right about what he had overheard, then the task ahead of them was enormous. Knight Valentine was one of the most well-known men on the planet. Though he was not universally liked, he was well-respected. He was a business leader, charitable donor, friend to presidents and princes, a man whose clever, sharp-featured face had dominated the world's media for three decades.

If Adam took his story to the press, the first question—after the reporter he approached got up off the floor and stopped laughing at the absurdity of the story—would be "why?" Why would Knight Valentine, the man who had everything, risk it all to become the brains behind the Reapers?

Only Adam, and possibly Danny, could answer that question. Only someone who had lived with Knight, and seen that the man had no soul, could truly understand what he was capable of.

Going to the press with the Reaper story wasn't their only option, of course. Adam didn't expect great things from his meeting in the morning. Knight wasn't going to crumble, confess all, express remorse and give himself up. The best Adam could hope for was to look Knight in the eye and see his suspicions confirmed, or try and get evidence that he was the Reaper. The trick would be to do that without giving Knight any clue as to what he was doing. Adam had no problem about placing himself in the firing line of his stepfather's rage, but he had Tarek to think of now. And Maja, of course... but somehow he sensed his feisty Valkyrie might enjoy using her skills against the man who had chosen to use terrorism as a means of making money.

How did that work? It was such a cynical concept, Adam found it hard to grasp the thinking behind it.

Last night, while Maja had been settling Tarek into his new room, he had found that article on his laptop, the one he suspected could have been written by Tarek's father, and reread it. The author of the article explained his or her beliefs in simple terms. The Reaper's targets were not random. There had been a map illustrating the point. Although the human toll was high—loss of life and injury were devastating features of a Reaper attack—the strikes took place inside high-profile office buildings, shopping malls, hotels and restaurants. Each time, the targeted organization suffered crippling after-effects. Knight's businesses had never been attacked, but the writer didn't mention that, and it wasn't conclusive proof of his guilt. The article argued that rival organizations would benefit hugely from such a situation. Adam recalled the outcry that had followed the publication of the article. It had been denounced as the worst kind of alarmist journalism. What kind of monster would set out to profit from global terror?

Adam conjured up an image of his stepfather's face and knew exactly what kind. He knew exactly how evil his stepfather could be.

His thoughts moved on to another aspect of the problems facing them. When he'd told them about his father's conversation, Tarek had mention another name. He'd said his father was speaking to a man called Shepherd. That was an interesting snippet of information that Adam needed to explore. If Shepherd was the high profile person Adam suspected he might be, they would have to tread carefully, particularly as Tarek's father had been killed the day after that call.

But the Reaper was not their only problem. The man watching them last night had not been a figment of Adam's imagination. He had no idea who the figure was, but he had been very real and very menacing. Could they have been followed from Syria? Could the Reaper already know Tarek was here in New York? Or did their mystery watcher have something to do with Maja? Had Odin sent him to let her know he was coming for his rebel Valkyrie? There was always the possibility that he could have been paparazzi. Adam was well-known. A picture of him with a mystery woman and kid would be worth something. Although Adam hadn't seen any sign of a camera, it was a possibility. The least worrying one. Because the guy had looked like trouble. More trouble.

For Adam personally, there was also the issue that he'd returned from Syria without finding Danny. The feelings of guilt and despair that had driven him to go to such desperate measures to find his brother hadn't gone away. If anything, having been to Syria and seen the suffering there for himself, they had intensified. The problem was his inquiries had reached a dead end. He had no idea where to go next. The only person he could think of to ask for help was Edith Blair. Although she hadn't recognized Danny's picture, she might be able to ask some questions among her network in Syria. Adam was intending to send some money to the mission, so he needed to speak to her, anyway.

Also on the list of problems facing them was the question that had been gnawing at the back of his mind since he had realized Maja wasn't a figment of his imagination. They had spoken of it only once, but there was still the lingering unprotected-sex issue hanging over them. What if she *was* pregnant? It was all very well to keep telling himself she would be gone soon. But what if that meant she would be leaving and taking their child with her? It wasn't like she would be moving to another town, another state or even another country. Maja belonged to another *world*. One that didn't allow visitation rights.

It was all very well to tell himself he would worry about this if and when it happened. His mind persisted in returning to the issue. And he had a worrying feeling about why that was. It would be a link between them, a deeper connection.

It would be a complication. An insurmountable one. Another *one*.

For some reason, every time Adam told himself that, his imagination veered off at a tangent, picturing their child. His and Maja's. A family of four. Five, if you included Leo. Six, if, as hoped, Danny returned... And what the hell was wrong with him?

Not only was he attracted to a Valkyrie, but now he was picturing a future with her? Because that could happen? Ever since he had met Maja, he had been unable to think straight where she was concerned. He had to sort that problem out fast, because he needed a clear head for the challenges ahead.

And right now, he needed to stop staring at her like a lovesick schoolboy and get some sleep. With that determined thought, Adam drew her into the crook of his good arm, settled her delicious weight close against his body and closed his eyes.

Chapter 10

Although Maja had initially been wary about the arrangement, they left Tarek in the care of Adam's housekeeper, a pleasant young woman named Sophie.

"He has so many new things going on in his life. Another new person may not be a good thing."

Sophie arrived as they were eating breakfast, and Leo greeted her with a volley of warning barks. This was his new home and she was an intruder. Clearly, he felt she should be evicted immediately.

Sophie knelt and, unfazed by the noisy welcome, stroked Leo's head. "Oh, isn't he sweet? I didn't know you were getting a dog, Mr. Lyon."

The brave guard dog instantly rolled over and invited her to tickle his belly. When she obliged, Leo became her devoted servant. Since she also turned out to be a fan of gaming, it wasn't long before she had captured Tarek's heart, as well.

"I think we can leave him without worrying to much about his well-being, don't you?" Adam had quirked a brow in Maja's direction.

Although this meeting was so important, she was having a hard time gathering her thoughts. Her mind insisted on returning to the events of the previous night. How could it be possible that sex with Adam kept getting better? That first time he had captured her body in a magical spell, but since then he had woven an enchantment that released new emotions, feelings she hadn't known existed. She was becoming more and more enraptured with him, the invisible threads that bound her to him growing stronger by the minute. Which meant that, when the time came, they would be harder to break.

Her only interactions with mortals had been on the battlefield, so she didn't know if this was normal. Some of the movies she watched with Tarek showed kissing and mild love scenes, but they didn't explain what the characters were feeling. It was frustrating not to know if she was the only person to ever feel this way. And to not know *what* she was feeling.

She was intensely aware of her every action in relation to his. Although she was comfortable around Adam now, that mindfulness extended to an appreciation of her body in relation to his. Of how he stood when he was close to her, his shoulder just brushing hers, his right hand occasionally touching her forearm.

While Adam treated such innocent interactions casually, Maja couldn't. She watched him in fascination, her eyes following the movements of his hands. Was she forever condemned to a state of aching arousal at the thought of those hands? Her lips felt bruised and swollen when she looked at his heartbreakingly sensual mouth. The memory of those lips anointing her skin, the scratch of his stubble on her tender flesh, his tongue tracing its determined, downward pathway made her quiver. Her nipples tightened painfully whenever she thought of that tongue probing the secret recesses of her flesh.

Now and then, when he spoke, she didn't hear the words he said because she was so lost in the erotic memory of his touch. And when that happened, Adam would give her a wicked smile to let her know he knew exactly where her thoughts were going.

Right now, she forced her thoughts in the direction of the coming meeting with Knight Valentine.

"Visible, or not?" she asked as they descended from the penthouse in Adam's private elevator.

"No matter how many times you ask me that question, I'm never going to tire of hearing it." He gave it some thought. "I think invisible will be a good way to do this. That way you can get a good look at Knight without having to interact with him. You can tell me what you really think of him after the meeting."

"Does he know you're coming?" They stepped out into the expensive marble lobby.

"No, I thought it would be a nice surprise if I just turned up."

Maja was getting better at interpreting Adam's moods. She knew this was one of those occasions when he meant the opposite of what he said. What was the human word for it? *"Sarcasm."*

Adam glanced down at her in surprise. "Pardon?"

"That was what you just did, wasn't it? You used sarcasm. You don't really think it will be a nice surprise for Knight if you turn up unannounced."

"You are getting better at this, Maja." He smiled at her as he held the door open so she could pass through. "We'll make a mortal of you yet."

The words jolted her, but she wasn't sure why. It was the fault of these strange new feelings. This one was like a tight little wire being twisted inside her chest. She wondered if it might be sorrow. But it would be foolish to feel regret that she couldn't be mortal. It would be mourning the loss of something she knew she could never have. Like a mortal wishing for a million dollars and then crying when it didn't materialize. Why would she waste her time on that? Surely she had enough problems?

They took a cab to the soaring black-windowed edifice called Valentine Tower. When they stepped out onto the busy sidewalk, Maja used the cloak of the crowds to use her powers and become invisible, although she remained at Adam's side. As she followed him through the revolving doors into a magnificent lobby, she became aware of a figure on the periphery of her vision. They were being followed.

She turned to look at the man who had walked into the building at the same time as them. Dressed all in black, he was tall and muscular. His shaved head gleamed in the overhead lights of the foyer. He made no move toward Adam, and she didn't know why she had gained the impression that he was following them. Except...

As she looked at him, he stared directly back at her and grinned.

He can see me!

As soon as the thought hit her, the man ducked his head, as if in acknowledgment of its truth, before walking away. It seemed his only reason for entering the building had been to let her know he was tailing them. Since Adam was already striding toward the reception desk, Maja had no time to do anything about the encounter except store it away to be dealt with later.

"Please let Knight Valentine know Adam Lyon is here to see him."

The polished young woman behind the counter gave him a smile that reminded Maja of a cat eyeing a bowl of cream. Maja got the impression she knew exactly who Adam was, even though he had said this was his first visit to Valentine Tower. Another new emotion assailed her. One that made her want to materialize and tell the woman to stop looking at Adam that way.

"Is Mr. Valentine expecting you?"

"No, but I'm sure he'll see me." Adam's smile provoked an even more annoying response, both from the woman and deep within Maja's chest. It was uncomfortable and she didn't like it. Adam had a devastating smile. How could she, who felt it rock her to the depths of her soul, blame anyone for being affected by it? Could this new feeling be *jealousy*? She must be wrong. Jealousy implied she had a claim on Adam, a right to this feeling of annoyance. She sighed. Life had been so much simpler before feelings.

"I'll call his secretary and see if he's available."

While Adam waited, Maja looked around the lobby. It had been designed to impress. The color scheme was black and silver, with concentric circles on the floor and walls. Three huge chandeliers of silver teardrops were suspended from the ceiling and one wall was a bank of screens, each showing a film highlighting the achievements of the Valentine Organization. Hotels, luxury apartment blocks, office buildings, leisure complexes, and sports arenas flashed onto the screen. Knight Valentine liked to advertise his successes to the world.

"Mr. Valentine will see you. Please take the elevator to the twenty-seventh floor. His secretary will meet you there."

Maja joined Adam in the elevator. Until now, she had never stopped to consider the mechanics of her invisibility. Once she had assumed her cover of concealment, she could interact with mortals if she chose. If she tried to touch Adam, he would be able to feel her. If she spoke, he would hear her voice. Since there were other people in the elevator, she decided against doing either of those things.

Odin had granted the Valkyries invisibility along with their great strength. It was a useful skill. It enabled the Valkyries to move around the mortal realm in search of the warrior souls they needed. On this occasion, it would allow Maja to observe the man Adam suspected of being responsible for these evil crimes.

Maja followed close behind as Knight's secretary escorted Adam down a long, featureless corridor and knocked before showing him into a large office. The man seated at the desk had been contemplating the view, but he swiveled his chair when Adam entered, turning to face his visitor.

As he smiled, Maja, entering the room just behind Adam, recoiled in shock. She had never felt such undiluted evil. It was coming off him in thick, oily waves.

Knight was of average height and slim build. His slicked back hair was dark and graying at the temples. Maja supposed his sharp, clever features were handsome, but she barely noticed them. Not when her attention was drawn to his eyes. Black as midnight, they seemed to draw every speck of light from the room into their depths. There was something very wrong about those eyes.

"It's been a long time." Knight gestured for Adam to take a seat on the opposite side of the desk.

Although Adam complied, Maja wanted to grab his arm and propel him away from this man. To yell at him to run away. The sense of malice in this room was so overwhelming, it made her feel nauseous. She was a Valkyrie; how could he, a mere mortal, stand it?

"Never long enough for me, Knight." Although the words were hostile, Adam's smile was pleasant. Yet she knew there was a world of painful memories behind his expression.

Maja searched her knowledge of the many beings who dwelled in Otherworld, wondering if Knight Valentine might not be mortal. Was he a demon determined to destroy mankind? A rogue vampire breaking free of the restraints of his leader? A phantom, lingering after his death to settle an old score? But no, he was a man. She was certain of it. Although he was human, he was more than that. Just as Maja herself had the body of a woman and superpowers, Knight, too, had something extra. She didn't know what it was, but she knew it was bad.

Knight displayed no anger at Adam's words. He had a curiously flat way of speaking, with very little rise and fall to his speech. It should have made him dull to listen to. Instead, because Maja sensed so much darkness in him, she wanted to hear every word. "And yet you are here. Why is that?"

"I've just returned from Syria." Adam indicated his

sling. "Had myself quite an adventure. I was shot by some of the Reaper's men."

Maja could see Adam watching Knight closely, looking for a reaction. There was none. "If that is the result of an encounter with the Reaper, you were lucky to get out alive. Why did you go there?"

"I was looking for Danny. He's gone missing out there," Adam said. "That's why I'm here. I was hoping you could use your contacts in Syria to help me find him."

Maja thought she saw something then. Like a ripple on the surface of a pond, just the faintest flicker disturbed Knight's practiced smile. It settled back into place almost immediately. "What makes you think I have contacts in Syria?"

"Don't you?" Adam fired the words back at him like a gunshot.

Knight laughed. It wasn't a pleasant sound. It sounded like someone had once described laughter to him and, never having heard it, he'd tried it out a few times while alone. Rough and crackly, it had a hoarse note to it that set her teeth on edge.

"I have contacts all over the world. Email me the details of where and when he went missing and I'll see what I can do."

Maja was growing tired of this. Knight wasn't going to give anything away, but she wanted to see that composure crack. Just a little. Adam had brought her along to observe, and she had done that. She had formed an opinion. This man was capable of any evil.

Now she stepped behind Knight and very gently blew in his ear.

* * *

Adam could feel all the old antagonism and frustration bubbling up inside him as he faced Knight across the shiny expanse of the other man's empty desk. Why had he ever thought this would work? He had been thirteen when his mother married Knight and he had never managed to get the better of his stepfather in an argument. Knight didn't do argument. Didn't do emotion. He just did *this*. Sat there calmly and didn't engage.

When Knight married his mother, he had systematically ruined Adam's life. The man sitting opposite him now was a sadist who had thought nothing of torturing a thirteen-year-old boy.

We both know it, yet you think you can look me in the eye and pretend it never happened.

There had been that brief glimmer when Adam had mentioned Knight's contacts in Syria. Like a snake's forked tongue flickering out, it had vanished as quickly as it had appeared. For the first time ever, Adam felt he had gotten to Knight. He had touched a nerve. But the other man had recovered now, and Adam didn't know how to press his advantage.

Because you don't have an advantage. This is Knight Valentine. He always has the upper hand.

Having asked Adam to email him the details of Danny's disappearance, Knight seemed to be signaling that the meeting was at an end. Until he momentarily closed his eyes and shivered.

Adam stared at him in surprise. It was the first time he had ever seen that facade slip. Okay, he hadn't been up close to Knight in the seven years since his mother's death. Maybe the man had developed a tic...

Just as Knight appeared to regain his composure, he suddenly raised a hand to his cheek, his eyes widening.

"Is everything okay?" Adam asked, the realization of what was going on beginning to dawn on him. He suspected Maja may have just caressed Knight's cheek.

"Yes." Although Knight answered with his usual composure, he turned his head as though searching out an unseen presence.

"We were discussing your contacts in Syria." Adam decided to try and push a little further while Knight was distracted. "The ones who work for the Reaper."

"I never said…" Adam had never heard Knight break off in the middle of a sentence. Never seen him get hastily to his feet. Certainly, never known him to raise a hand and ruffle his carefully styled hair. "I don't know what is going on here, but I think it's time you left."

Never known him to lose his cool.

Adam took his time. "I'd like to say it's been nice, but it never is."

"You'd better start running and finding yourself somewhere to hide, because you have no idea what you're up against." And there it was. For the first time, he saw it all. The full extent of the venom in Knight's soul was on display. It almost sent Adam reeling backward.

Adam was about to turn away without speaking when Knight's empty chair went scooting across the room. It was like a scene from a horror movie, but Adam knew that no poltergeist was responsible for that sudden movement. As Knight turned to look at the chair, his huge desk flipped over onto its side. Seconds later, each piece of priceless artwork was lifted from its place on the wall before being dropped on the floor. Filing cabinets flew open, spewing their contents into the air.

Knight made a move toward Adam as though recognizing that this mayhem was linked to him. "Make it stop."

His lips drew back in a snarl and Adam decided he almost preferred this side of him. At least there was no longer any pretense. All those years of suspecting that a malevolent spirit lurked beneath his stepfather's cool exterior. Now he knew he had been right. What he had never been able to understand was why his beautiful, sensitive mother had married this man. Belinda Lyon was not the sort of woman who would have married Knight for his money, so what had the attraction been? No matter how much Adam wondered about the reason behind their marriage, he supposed he would never discover the truth.

Knight took a threatening step toward Adam. As he did, he was lifted off his feet and held suspended an inch or two above the floor. As he clawed wildly at the invisible hand around his throat, his face darkened until it was almost purple. Mewling sounds issued from his throat and spittle formed on his lips.

"Maybe you're the one who doesn't know what he's up against." With a final look into those dead eyes, Adam walked out.

He heard the thud of Knight dropping to the floor and the sound of the door closing behind Maja. He half expected to hear Knight coming after him, or to encounter security on his way out, but he reached the elevator unchecked. When he stepped inside, he leaned against the mirrored wall and exhaled.

"Are you here, Maja?"

"Yes." Her voice was hesitant. "Did I do the wrong thing? He made me so angry... I've never felt like that before, and I reacted without thinking."

Adam gave it some thought. It wasn't the way he'd planned for the meeting to go, but it had worked in his favor. Maja had jolted Knight out of his usual composure. Although Adam had been under no illusion about the man he had come to confront, now all his suspicions were confirmed.

"No, it wasn't the wrong thing." He smiled. "I'd love to be a fly on the wall in that office right now. Does he think I did all of that through mind control? Or perhaps he thinks there is a rogue spirit following me around?" He felt an unfamiliar tightening in his throat. "Maybe he thought it was my mother come back to haunt him for the way he treated her when she was alive?"

He felt Maja's hand on his arm. Even though she wasn't visible, her touch soothed him and he felt some of the tension ease out of his muscles. As he exited the elevator, he glanced around the lobby. There was nothing unusual. Knight had clearly decided not to pursue this...yet.

Maja waited until they were a block away from Valentine Tower, and in the midst of a fast-flowing crowd, before materializing. She linked her arm through the crook of Adam's right elbow. "You were right about him. That man is toxic."

"He meant what he said about running and hiding. He will come after me," Adam said. "And that means Tarek is in danger. Knight is not the sort of guy to let the presence of a child stop him."

"We made a promise to Tarek that we would look after him. And that's what we'll do."

Glancing down at her, he saw the steely determination on Maja's face. Adam might not have much respect for the great god Odin, but he was thankful to him every time he saw that look on his daughter's face.

"Instead of sitting back and waiting for Knight to come to us, we have to find solid proof that he is behind the Reaper consortium. At present, we are working on a hunch and the circumstantial evidence of what Tarek overheard. If Knight is running this as a company, he isn't alone. As hard as it is to believe, he must have persuaded other people to join him in this sick venture. I have to figure out a way to get the names of his associates."

"Where would he keep that information?" Maja turned back to look at the still dominant outline of Valentine Tower. "Getting back into his office will be difficult for you, but I could do it."

"It won't be there. I know exactly where Knight keeps his valuables and his secrets, and it's not in his office." Adam felt a cold feeling of dread track its way down his spine. The day his mother had died, he had walked out of his stepfather's home and sworn he would never return. It looked like he was going to have to overturn that vow and walk back into Knight's Greenwich, Connecticut, mansion. Without an invitation.

Looking back at Maja, he felt his resolve harden as if a transfer of strength took place as they walked along that busy sidewalk. Adam knew his own strengths. He was a fighter. His determination and skill in business were legendary. Adam built up the Lyon brand by targeting failing businesses. Instead of closing them down, he brought them under his wing and made them thrive. His specialty was finding consumer discontent and turning that business into a success story. His loyalty to a cause was unswerving and his commitment to his employees and their rights won him accolades. But he was aware of his one weak point. Because it was also his greatest fear. Like the monster that lurked in the closet, Knight Valentine had assumed a larger-than-life persona in Adam's mind. The man who had dominated his teenage years had occupied a dark corner of his mind throughout his adult life.

Now, for the sake of the world, as well as his own sanity, he had to face him and defeat him. Looking into the endless blue of Maja's eyes, he felt he could do it. Today he had spoken to Knight without crumbling. That had been the first step. Now he was ready to destroy him…as long as he had Maja at his side.

Chapter 11

Over the following days and weeks, life settled into a routine. Tarek started school and Maja took him there each morning, collecting him at the end of the day when classes finished. It became their time. Although his anxiety at the change in his life occasionally showed through, his spirits remained high and he chatted about his teachers and his new friends. Maja worried about his reluctance to talk about his father, but Adam reasoned that it was still early. Having lost a parent at a young age, although in less dramatic circumstances, he sympathized with Tarek's silence.

"But I agree. It would do him good to open up about it." Maja wasn't sure if that was an admission. Did he wish he had opened up to someone about his own father's death? It was another reminder, if she needed one, that she knew very little about Adam. "If after he has settled into his new home and his new school you are still concerned, we can seek professional help."

Maja, having been thrust into an unexpected maternal role, found herself enjoying it. The responsibilities were huge, but so were the rewards. Having someone depend on her so completely was a new experience. Tarek had been through so much and she was determined to get this right for his sake. It wasn't easy. Not when he could fire a dozen questions at her, one after the other, without giving her time to think about the answers. Or when he could neatly trip her up with her own words. She quickly got used to dealing with the phrase "But you said…"

But she was falling in love with this little boy and this new life, and, when she stopped to examine the depth of her feelings, it frightened her. Despite his doctor's advice to the contrary, Adam returned to work almost immediately. It was a circumstance that left Maja feeling curiously bereft. Determined not to acknowledge, even to herself, how much she missed his company during the day, she decided to discover more of the mortal realm while he and Tarek were absent. Exploring the city on foot, she discovered a wealth of new experiences. And with each one, she fell a little more in love with this new world. A world that wasn't hers to love.

Shopping for clothes and other comforts she hadn't known existed became a daily delight. Department stores, coffee shops, food markets and outlets had her head spinning with the variety of wares on offer. She was conscious of the need to do something with her time. She had a new family and she wanted to care for them.

"I will cook tonight," she told Adam as he left for work on his second day back in the office.

He regarded her with a slightly wary expression. "You don't have to do that. We can eat out, or order in."

"I am a Valkyrie. One of my duties was to feed Odin's warriors."

"I guess you didn't do that on pizza or burgers?" he asked, referring to their recent diet of takeout food.

"No." She allowed her dignified facade to slip a little and gave him a teasing smile. "Although I am not sure if I will be able to get beached whale here in New York City."

He shuddered. "If you serve me beached whale..."

She laughed. "Go to your office, Mr. Lyon. Let me take care of your well-being."

He stared down at her for a moment, his expression becoming intent. She wondered what she had said to cause that look. It was as though he was seeing her for the first time, and his feelings were a revelation to him. It lasted only a second or two before he quickly brought the shutters down.

Maja had a feeling that traditional Viking fare would probably be okay with Adam, but it might not be popular with Tarek, who was rapidly developing a taste for fast food. She shrugged. He would soon learn to eat the hearty foods she intended to cook. Adam had given her a credit card, but she was still wary of it. Those machines asked too many questions that she couldn't answer. Instead, she snatched up a handful of the cash he had left her and stuffed it into her purse.

Leo pranced around her, begging to accompany her, but Maja had already learned the hard way that dogs were not welcome in food stores. Her only attempt to take him into one had resulted in a humiliating eviction for both her and Leo. Besides, Leo had already accompanied her on her morning walk to take Tarek to school, and he would go with her when she picked him up later.

"Your friend Sophie will be here soon." The little dog subsided into a pitiful heap.

When she reached the street, she headed in the direction of a farmer's market she had seen on one of her recent walks. She hadn't gone very far when a nagging sensation made her turn her head. The sidewalk was busy and, unsure what she was looking for, she scanned the faces of the people behind her. There was nothing that seemed out of place. But since she didn't *know* what she was looking for, that didn't chase away the feeling that something was wrong.

Shrugging her concerns away, she continued walking. What would Odin say if he knew one of his daughters could be so easily spooked? That after all her years of warrior training, she was paranoid enough to believe someone was right behind her? The Allfather was not a benevolent being. His response would not be kindly and reassuring.

He would have me whipped for my foolishness, and rightly so. I would be chastised for being not only the "rebellious one" but also the "imaginative one."

Yet the impression that she was being followed persisted, a sensation so real that she could sense eyes probing the back of her head, could even feel unwanted, unfamiliar breath touching her neck. It grew stronger with every step, piling on the tension until she wanted to scream. Not from fear. She was a Valkyrie and they didn't do cowardice. No, she wanted to cry out in rage and frustration.

If this was in her head, she wanted to get it out of there. If this was what having an imagination was like, she didn't want it. And if it wasn't all in her head, she wanted this unknown entity to fight fair, to show itself so she could deal with it her way. Lurking in shadows, blending into the crowd, stalking her... This way, there was nothing for her to fight. And fighting was what Maja did best.

"Scared yet, little Valkyrie?" The voice was close. Almost a whisper in her ear.

This time when she turned, she encountered the amused gaze of the man who had followed Adam into the lobby of Valentine Tower. He matched his strides to hers, walking alongside her as though they were together.

"No." She halted in her tracks, causing an obstruction to the people around her. *But you should be scared. You should be terrified.* She could kill him with an elbow to his throat or ribs, but she didn't think Adam would want her to draw attention to herself in that way.

Anyway, she wanted to know who this man was. How did he know she was a Valkyrie? And how had he been able to see her the other day when she had been invisible?

"Who are you?"

He grinned. "I work for your father."

That was what she had feared. Odin never ventured into the mortal world himself, but he sent his servants— the Valkyries and his warriors—into this realm to do his bidding.

"I don't know what you mean." She decided to act dumb in order to buy a little thinking time.

"I think you do. The Allfather's youngest daughter

has gone missing and there is a reward for the one who returns her to him." His eyes traveled over her body. "I have seen you many times in the palace of Gladsheim, but you never noticed me. The Valkyries are too high and mighty to look in the direction of a lesser being."

Maja let his words sink in. It seemed likely, from what he had said, that Odin remained unaware of her whereabouts. This man had recognized her and was following her in the hope of taking her back to Valhalla and claiming the reward from her father. Travel between Otherworld and the mortal realm wasn't easy, but it could be done. Access to the mortal realm could be gained through a series of portals. While some hardy adventurers used these as a means of traveling regularly between the two, most beings remained within their own worlds. Those in Otherworld had an awareness of the mortal realm, but humans remained blissfully unaware that another world existed. She didn't know why this man was here. There was a thriving interworldly black market.

"I was here on other business when I caught sight of you. A daughter of Odin, once seen, is not easily forgotten." His words confirmed her fears. She was distinctive.

Whatever circumstances had led to this encounter, if she could stop this man, she could stay here. Her only problem now was whether to try and convince him he was wrong, silence him or to kill him. She didn't know if she could trust him, and killing him would be messy.

She raised wide eyes to his face. "I really don't know what you're talking about."

She may as well exhaust the alternatives before committing murder. Mortals seemed to have very strict rules about that sort of thing. She had watched some news programs. Killing was definitely not popular.

"Don't try that with me. You are Maja, youngest and most favored daughter of Odin, mightiest of all the gods."

"Please stop harassing me..." She continued with her helpless, bewildered act, hoping it would work. It seemed less likely with every passing minute. "I don't know who you are."

"I am one of Odin's servants." His grin turned nasty. "But why don't we put this to the test? If you're not who I say you are, why don't you cry for help? Or better still, why not call the police?"

He had her and he knew it. Maja wasn't going to risk drawing attention to herself. She tried to figure this man out. He knew who she was, yet he didn't seem to know how much danger he was in. He was quite close to her, yet apparently unaware of the full extent of her strength. She figured that meant he fulfilled a menial role in her father's palace. He would have seen the Valkyries and heard of their legendary strength, but never actually witnessed it firsthand.

It was time for him to get his own demonstration.

She weighed her options. If she struck him a blow to his temple, the bridge of his nose or his throat, he would drop like a stone in the middle of this busy street. Maja could become invisible in the same instant that she felled him, but there was a chance that someone would remember seeing her with him. It was unlikely a witness would be able to lead anyone back to Adam, but she wasn't prepared to take the risk.

If she grabbed him, became invisible and tossed him under a vehicle it would be unfair to the driver. Throwing him from one of the tall buildings posed a similar problem. She didn't know what, or who, he would hit when he landed.

Clearly unaware that she was weighing her options for the best method of killing him, he grabbed her elbow, almost earning himself a lethal knee in the groin. He might have supernatural abilities of his own, but he would be no match for a Valkyrie. "You are coming back to Valhalla with me."

She wasn't going to persuade this man that she wasn't the person he sought, couldn't persuade him to leave her alone, and certainly couldn't trust him to protect her identity. If he walked away from her now, he could go straight to Odin and tell him where she was. They were close to a park and Maja decided her best approach would be to get him there. She didn't have the time or the inclination to persuade him, so she took off at a run, trusting that he would follow her. His shout of annoyance confirmed that he was right behind her. It would have been easy for Maja to outrun him, but she slowed her pace, dodging in and out of the people on the sidewalk, allowing her pursuer to stay with her.

She was seeking somewhere quiet as she ran through the busy streets. Eventually, she came to an area she didn't recognize and turned into a narrow opening between two buildings. There were Dumpsters lining the alleyway and, seizing the opportunity while it was deserted, she swung around and faced the man, who was close behind her.

"Does Odin know the details of your business here?"

His look of surprise told her she was right in her guess. He wasn't here on any legal matter. If Odin discovered that, his retribution would be terrible.

With a growl, the man lunged toward her. Using the element of surprise, and his forward momentum, Maja jerked her fist straight out. The punch caught him fully in the face. Without pausing, Maja hoisted him onto her shoulder and tipped him into the nearest Dumpster. He was going to have a bad headache when he woke up, but at least he wouldn't be able to find her.

Breathing a little faster than usual, Maja retraced her steps. She was confident she hadn't been seen. If the man was found before he regained consciousness, he wouldn't be identified, because he didn't belong in this world. There was nothing to link him to her. Okay, his presence on her tail was a worry, because it opened up the possibility of others arriving in this realm in search of her. But she would deal with that if and when it happened. Odin thought he had offered a reward for her safe return. In reality, he had placed a price on her head.

What she didn't understand was the peculiar effect of the incident. As she walked toward the market, her limbs began to shake and nausea washed over her. Both were unusual for her. She was physically and mentally strong. She had never experienced any ill effects following a fight. Although she tried to overcome the feelings, it didn't work and the discomfort lasted until she reached home.

Still feeling shaky, she unpacked her groceries. Then, irritated at her own weakness, she lay on her bed until the feeling passed.

"Maja, that was delicious." Adam sat back, having eaten a huge portion of the chicken stew she had served with homemade flatbread.

"You sound shocked." Maja's smile was teasing as she began to clear away the plates.

He returned the smile as he shook his head. "Pleasantly surprised."

"And Tarek's reward for eating my home-cooked food is ice cream for dessert."

Tarek grinned. "And I can eat it while I watch TV?"

Maja pursed her lips. "Okay. But one hour. No more."

Tarek jumped up from the table, taking Leo with him as he ran to his room.

Adam joined Maja, gathering up serving dishes and carrying them through to the kitchen. "You hardly ate anything." She usually had a healthy appetite. And now that he looked closely at her, he realized she appeared pale.

"I wasn't hungry." He got the feeling there was something more to it. She sighed, leaning against the counter as she looked at him. "I had a problem today."

He tensed. "Was it anything to do with Knight?" If that monster had threatened her...

"No. I was followed. The same man followed us when we went to Valentine Tower. I was invisible, but he could see me. We had so much else going on and I didn't think much of it at the time, so I forgot to tell you about it."

"Was this guy dressed all in black with a shaved head?" Why hadn't he warned her about the man he'd seen in Times Square? So much had happened since then, but it was no excuse.

Maja nodded. "He was from Otherworld."

"You spoke to him? My God, Maja. When I think of the danger you could have been in—"

She held up a hand, silencing him. "I dealt with him."

Adam exhaled sharply, not knowing whether to be relieved or outraged. He supposed one of the dangers of living with a Valkyrie was coming home to the unexpected.

"You'd better tell me all of it."

"My father has offered a reward for the person who takes me back to Valhalla. This man had come to claim me. I've become some sort of prize." She wrapped her arms around her waist as though trying to warm herself. "Of course, what no one, including my father, knows is that I have committed many crimes. Once I get back to Valhalla, I will be held accountable for them."

"Maja, they will only know of these so-called crimes if you tell them. Must you do that?"

She looked astounded at his words. "Are you suggesting that I should lie?"

"Not that exactly. But only you and I know what has really happened. I'm not going to tell anyone. If you keep quiet as well, how will Odin know?"

She was silent for a moment or two. "The Valkyries are taught to always tell the truth."

Adam could see he had planted a seed, so he decided to leave it at that. "What did you do with the guy who followed you today?"

"I knocked him out and threw him in a Dumpster." She peeped up at Adam through the fan of her long lashes. "You are not angry with me?"

"At least you didn't kill him."

"I considered it, but I didn't think you'd like it."

He supposed he should be shocked at the ease with which he could hear those words. His priorities had changed. Syria had changed him. He had come away from there with a secret that would rock the world…and he was trying to figure out the best way to deal with it. He was living with a Valkyrie. Going about his daily routine made him feel like a fraud. Day-to-day business no longer interested him. In meetings, his mind was preoccupied with the details of how to expose Knight Valentine for what he was. He dreaded news of another Reaper attack, feeling the weight of responsibility behind his knowledge. And the only person who could help him was Maja.

But she was more than his partner in bringing down Knight. As much as his mind was preoccupied with thoughts of the Reaper, they were focused on her. Adam had never seen himself in a relationship, had never believed that life was for him. He didn't need anyone to tell him why that was. The memory of his beautiful, fragile mother was too painful. Her marriage to Knight had been the worst kind of nightmare and Adam had been old enough to understand what he was witnessing. Knight had broken her, systematically crushing her like a butterfly beneath his heel. Adam had been old enough to know there were secrets in their marriage, dark secrets, that had led to her decline. When she died, she had been fighting an ongoing battle against her twin addictions to drugs and alcohol, and depression had held her in its tight clutches for many years.

He had been dealing with his own problems at the hands of his stepfather. Knight, determined to crush Adam almost from the first day of his marriage to his mother, had commenced a regime of psychological and emotional abuse that still haunted him. At the age of thirteen, Adam had gone from having a loving relationship with his father to being thrust into a nightmare with a man who deliberately designed ways to torture him. If Adam had a fear, Knight would exploit it. If Adam had a favorite belonging, Knight would destroy it. If Adam wanted something, Knight would promise it and then withhold it.

In public, Knight's behavior toward Belinda, Adam's mother, was impeccable. It was only her son, watching helplessly, who could see the gradual decline in her. A decline that became dramatic for no reason that Adam could explain.

Belinda Lyon's death had been a blessed relief. Having seen what one person could do to another in a relationship, Adam was never going there himself.

Now he had been unexpectedly thrust into a ready-made family. His pristine apartment had been invaded by other people. There was mess and noise and laughter and nowhere to hide. His ordered life had been turned upside down. And he liked it. He liked the fun, the jokes… He even liked the goddamn barking. He liked coming home to the smile in Maja's eyes and hearing about what Tarek had done at school. He liked it when the three of them curled up on the sofa and watched a movie together. He *really* liked it when Maja took his hand as they walked up the stairs to bed.

He drew her into his arms, enjoying the feel of her body against his. "Just don't make a habit of knocking people out and throwing them into Dumpsters."

"I won't." She pressed her face into the curve of his neck. "Unless other bounty hunters come from Other-world before I am ready to leave."

Adam found the subject of her leaving increasingly troubling. He knew it had to happen. He tested himself with that knowledge on a regular basis, steeling himself for the reality of it. Although his rational self knew it was coming, his emotional self was having a hard time dealing with it. Standing here, with Maja in his arms, her hair tickling his chin and her delicious scent invading his nostrils, he allowed himself a little daydream of forever. It was a screwed-up daydream. Because she was the only woman with whom forever really was impossible.

Maybe that was why his subconscious was taking this route? It was never going to happen, so tiny glimpses of might-have-been were safe. Maja would leave and Adam would return to safety and cynicism once more. His heart could retreat behind its iron-clad shield and he would be able to forget that it was ever in danger of being touched by a beautiful Valkyrie.

His life would never quite return to the way it had once been, of course. He had Tarek to care for now. Once Maja left, there would be the emotional fall out to deal with, and that shouldn't be underestimated. Tarek had bonded with Maja. He had already lost his parents. Losing her as well would be a huge blow, and Adam would have to handle it carefully. And, of course, he didn't know if, or when Danny would return. His brother might need care and support, whether physical or emotional, after his time in Syria. "I've been making some inquiries into Knight's plans. He is away visiting friends this weekend, which means he won't be going to his house in a town called Greenwich. It's a popular place for wealthy people to live and commute into New York to work." Although he didn't want to go back to the place where he had spent so many unhappy years, Adam knew Knight's secrets would be inside that elegant mansion. "I've checked with Sophie and she can stay overnight with Tarek on Saturday. She's promised to take him to a movie."

Maja laughed. "He may never want us to return." Her expression became serious again. "So we are going to go to this house of Knight's and break in to see if we can find any information about his partners?"

"That's the plan. Are you okay with it?"

He scanned her face. She really did look exhausted tonight. His Valkyrie had lost her glow. *Whoa.* Where did that thought come from? *His* Valkyrie? She wasn't his. She never could be.

She might be tired, but her familiar determination shone through her weariness as she nodded. "We have to stop him before he ruins any more lives."

Chapter 12

Valentine House was the largest waterfront property on the coastline between Greenwich and New York City, with incredible views across Long Island Sound. Although Adam had spent his early teenage years here, he had never taken the time to admire the beauty of the estate. His thoughts had always been on escape.

"If it hadn't been for Danny, I'd have run away." He had never said those words out loud and he surprised himself by saying them now to Maja. "I had to stay to look after him."

"What about your mother?"

"It's impossible to explain what happened with her. It was as if she became a wax model of herself. She looked the same, talked the same, but she was dead behind the eyes. I tried to talk to her once, but it was as if she didn't know who I was."

"Did Knight hurt you?" Maja asked.

They were viewing the property from the road. Not that there was much to see from this angle. Adam could just glimpse the four octagonal turrets that were a feature of the house. Rising above the roof as they did, their purpose was more than decorative; they provided an ideal position from which Knight's security guards could observe the whole area. The turrets were the only part of the house that was visible from the road. Everything else was hidden by the protective pine and beech forest that bordered the estate.

"Not physically. His methods were far subtler." Adam lowered the binoculars he had been using. "Knight is a sadistic villain." Could he give her an example? Talk about it to another person after all these years? He wouldn't know unless he tried. "I've always been scared of the dark. It stemmed from when I was very small and I'd gone down into the cellar of the house where we lived. The door had closed behind me, and I'd been stuck down there in the dark for more than an hour before my dad—my real dad—found me."

"No wonder you were scared." Maja gripped his hand.

"My mom understood and always let me have a night-light in my room. But when we moved in with Knight, he said I was too old for that nonsense and he refused to let me have one in my bedroom. Not only that, he insisted I should have blackout curtains so that my room was in total darkness."

Maja's hand tightened in his. "Hateful man."

"That wasn't all. When I couldn't sleep, he decided on his own form of aversion therapy." Adam felt his throat close at the memory. "He used to shut me in the cellar for hours at a time. He told me I would get used to it and overcome my fears. I never did."

"And your mother?" Maja's voice was hesitant. "She permitted this?"

"She had her own problems." He supposed it must be difficult for someone on the outside to understand why his mother hadn't come to his rescue. She'd been fighting her own battles. He wasn't sure his mother ever knew the full extent of Knight's abuse of her son, in the same way Adam never knew what was going on with Belinda. Danny was the only person who knew it all. By shielding his brother from the same treatment, Adam had drawn even more torture down on himself.

He supposed Knight believed he had broken the boy who hid in a corner of that cellar. He certainly hadn't expected to see Adam rise to become a business leader with an empire matching Knight's own. Adam's father had left him money, but he had made his inheritance work. And the perseverance and fire he brought to his business dealings had been forged out of a determination to ensure he was the only person who controlled his life.

Adam knew the layout of this estate better than anyone. Probably better than Knight himself. He had perfected the art of hiding away in its many nooks and crannies. It wasn't an easy place to get into without an invitation, but it could be done. Strolling up to the big double gates wasn't an option. Nor was scaling the eight-foot-high wall.

"We have to approach from the bay."

Maja looked horrified. "You know how you are afraid of the dark?" Adam nodded. "I don't like water."

He bit back a smile. Her Valkyrie training wouldn't allow her to admit to a fear, but it was written all over her face. The intrepid Valkyrie was scared.

He was glad to see her looking better. That curious fatigue had held her in its grip for a day or two, leaving her washed-out and pale. He had even found her resting once or twice, something he never thought he would see. On a normal day, Maja had more energy than an army platoon. Perhaps she was less invincible than she believed, and recent events had caught up with her. Today she appeared her usual radiant self.

"We don't have to swim. There is a point just along the bay where we can slip into the water and follow the edge of the shoreline until we come alongside the house. There is a blind spot where the security guards won't be able to see us. We can make our way through the trees and up to the house." He gave her a reassuring smile. "Only your feet will get wet."

She looked doubtful. "Promise?"

"Word of a Lyon."

When they reached the place Adam recognized, they removed their boots and socks and slid into the water. It was cold and Maja gave a little yelp of surprise as her bare soles connected with the slippery pebbles. Adam, who had used this method of sneaking on and off his stepfather's property many times, guessed his own feet had developed more of an immunity.

"You'll get used to it."

"If I don't, I'll make you warm my feet on parts of your body that don't like the cold." Her teeth chattered. "Word of a Valkyrie."

He laughed. "Let's go and find the names of the bad guys, so we know who we're dealing with."

By the time they were alongside the house, Maja could no longer feel her feet. Adam barely seemed to notice the cold as they paused, hunkering down below the level of the woodland that bordered the water's edge.

"If we keep going in this direction, we will come to the boathouse. There are steps nearby that lead down to the waterfront. Knight's guests sometimes swim here in the summer and that's how they access the water."

"Are they mad?" Maja shivered at the thought, not just because of the cold. The thought of striking out into these dark depths struck her as the ultimate act of foolishness.

"It's a pleasant experience. You should try it sometime."

Since it was never going to happen, she didn't answer. Let Adam cling to his eccentric mortal customs. She could tolerate his strange notions without having to engage in them.

"Once we reach the steps, we will be within sight of the house. Knight has security guarding the house 24/7." From his crouching position, Adam pointed upward. "This is the point where we have to climb up the bank. We will be hidden from view by the trees."

"If the place is so well guarded, how will we get into the house?"

"There is a way." His jaw clenched and she got the impression that he was momentarily looking back into the past. "It involves going through the cellar I told you about."

No matter where this led them, Maja wanted to make Knight Valentine pay for the pain in Adam's eyes when he said those words. She couldn't give him back the moments of his formative years his stepfather had stolen from him, but she wanted to see Knight suffer. She wanted to stop him harming anyone else through his Reaper alias, of course, but right now, this was about Adam. The man who thought he was too damaged to care for others. Why couldn't he see that the opposite was true? He cared too much. His love for his brother had taken him into a war zone without a thought for his own safety. His compassion for an orphaned child had led him to bring Tarek into his own life, even though that action had turned his regulated routine upside down.

And she knew he was afraid of allowing himself to get too close to her because of what that might mean. No matter how close their physical and emotional bond might be, he was frightened of looking into his heart and finding it wasn't as tough and unbending as he believed. Afraid of letting himself care because it couldn't last…and he didn't know how to cope with any more emotional damage.

"I'll be with you this time."

When he didn't answer, she wondered if she'd said the wrong thing. Then he nodded, dropping a brief kiss onto her temple, before cautiously lifting his head above the level of the bank and looking around.

"The trees are just a few feet away. You go first. You just need to scramble up here, make a dash for the woods and wait for me to join you."

"What about your injury?" Maja eyed the bank dubiously. Although it was only about six feet high, it was steep and the rocky surface looked slippery. Getting up it was likely to be an undignified scramble. For someone who had recently sustained a serious injury, it could result in a major setback.

"I'll be fine." Adam flexed his shoulder as if to prove it. His mobility had been improving steadily and he was using his left arm and shoulder more and more. Even so, Maja wasn't convinced.

"I think I should wait at the top so I can help you up."

"If you do that you will be out in the open and risk being seen," Adam said.

"Not if I'm invisible." She pulled her woolen hat down farther over her ears, tilting her chin at him at the same time.

"You are one stubborn Valkyrie, do you know that?"

"Yes. Odin always called me his obstinate daughter." Among other things. She often wondered why she was the Allfather's favorite daughter when she had so many traits he disliked.

Handing him her boots, she started to climb. She had been right, it wasn't easy. Gripping the grass at the top of the bank, she hauled herself up, trying to find a foothold on the smooth surface of the rock. Adam's view from below would be of her ass thrust outward as she bungled her way to the top. It didn't feel dignified.

When she reached the top, she leaned over and Adam passed her both pairs of boots. Stooping down, she gripped his right hand. Since she was so much stronger than him, she could have lifted him one-handed without letting him make any attempt at climbing. Deciding to allow him his dignity, she reined in her strength and simply supported him as he scaled the bank.

The trees offered seclusion and semidarkness. Once the two of them had slipped their socks and boots back on, Adam led the way toward the house. Pausing before they emerged from the shelter of the woodland, he ducked low behind the cover of a lilac bush. From their secluded vantage point, they could observe the house without being seen.

"It's magnificent."

Maja made the admission reluctantly. The house was

linked to Knight, and that meant it was tainted in her mind. Acknowledging its beauty felt wrong. Maja had once attended a feud between two warring factions of a noble French family. Her mission had taken her to a splendid chateau in the heart of the Loire valley. This three-story mansion reminded her of that grand structure. Its undulating swimming pool resembled the chateau's moat and its tennis courts mimicked the green fields. Like the chateau, this house had orchards and formal gardens.

"When Knight bought it, it was the most expensive piece of real estate in the country. I don't think he had even seen the place when he made an offer for it. All that mattered was the price tag. He needs to be seen to be the best at everything. That includes being the wealthiest and most powerful man in the world."

"What made him that way?" Maja asked. "I thought it wasn't possible for a human to be born evil."

Adam appeared surprised by the question. "I've never really given it much thought. While I agree that people are not born with the evil gene, I think some are more susceptible to it than others. If those people are then brought up in a cold, mercenary environment, they may become immune to empathy and find it easier to commit terrible acts. By all accounts, Knight's family was a strange one. He was an only child and his parents worshiped money and status."

"Surely there are many children raised in similar circumstances? I cannot believe they all go on to commit horrible crimes."

"You're right, of course. It takes a unique set of circumstances, and we may never know what they were in Knight's case." Adam's lips hardened. "And I'll confess, I don't really care. That bastard is killing innocent people and terrorizing the world, and he's doing it for money. And we are here to find the evidence of that. How he reached this point doesn't interest me."

Although Maja could understand Adam's point of view, she didn't share it. Her dislike of Knight was equally strong, but she couldn't help wondering about his background. Something had molded the man capable of such foul crimes. Her prolonged stay in the mortal realm had piqued her interest in humans. She thought back to Adam's meeting with Knight in the other man's office. A strong feeling had assailed her then. That sense that Knight was human…and more. What had happened to him that was over and above the normal mortal experience? Adam had talked about his environment. What if something—she wished she could be more specific—had taken advantage of his uncaring parents and cold upbringing? Her thoughts were too vague to follow them through to a conclusion. But since she and Adam had a difficult task ahead of them, Maja had no more time to spend on speculation.

"There are steps over there leading down to the cellar." Adam pointed to the side of the building.

"You said the house is closely guarded, so surely security is tight all over? How will we get in there?"

Adam reached into the pocket of his jeans and withdrew a bunch of keys. "With these."

"You have the keys to Knight's house?"

"They were among my mother's belongings when she died. I always meant to dispose of them, but I never got around to it. Now I'm glad I didn't." There was a curious note to Adam's voice, one Maja didn't like. It was somewhere between sorrow and triumph.

"Will they still work?"

Adam appeared to weigh the distance between their hiding place and the house. "There's only one way to find out."

Steep stone steps led down from the garden to the cellar, and they descended these swiftly, having managed to cross from the trees to the house without incident. There was a heavy door at the bottom of the stairs and Maja reached for the handle.

Adam forestalled her. "It will be locked."

He sensed her impatience as he tried several of the keys before he found the one that opened the door. It swung inward with a creak worthy of horror movie special effects. When they were fully inside the cellar, Adam peered around him into the pervading darkness. There was a smell of mildew, cleaning products and gasoline.

"Where now?" Although Maja spoke in a whisper, her voice sounded unnaturally loud.

"There is another set of stairs that leads to a storage area at the back of the kitchens. Once we are there, we can make our way to the corridor where Knight's study is located." Adam led the way across the gloomy basement, guiding Maja around a series of obstacles.

"What about his security guards? Do they patrol the house?"

"I'm hoping they won't. Knight has security cameras, but their focus is on the exterior and preventing anyone from approaching. Since we've done the hard part by getting in, I don't think the guards will be looking out for intruders inside the house." He turned to smile at her, just making out her features in the dim light. "But if they do come after us, I'm relying on you for backup."

"You can count on me."

It occurred to him that she was the only person he trusted to really mean that. Danny, the only other person with whom he had ever been close, had always been too young for their relationship to be on equal terms. Although the two brothers cared for each other, Adam had always been the one looking out for Danny. For the first time, he had someone who was there for him. Maja had his back. She had demonstrated that over and over. He examined the warm feeling that brought with it. He had always viewed himself as solitary, believing it to be a preference rather than his destiny. Now he wasn't so sure. It felt good to know he wasn't alone.

It was particularly reassuring here in this cellar, the place that had featured in so many of his nightmares. It was his own personal hell. He could still remember being pushed down the wooden stairs, still hear the sound of that door slamming, still feel the darkness wrapping its tentacles around him like a living thing as he curled up in a corner and wished for death. His fear of this place wasn't just pins and needles. It was daggers and razors.

Back then, fear had drained him of the ability to do anything. It hadn't just been this cellar. It had been the dozens of other things Knight had done to destroy the boy he had been. Fear had almost destroyed him. Even breathing had been hard, thwarting his ability to think straight.

Knight knew Danny was Adam's weakness. One day Adam came home from school and Knight met him in the driveway, his face serious. He told him Danny had fallen into the river, it didn't look good, they hadn't found his body... Choking back sobs, Adam had looked up at the house to see his brother waving at him from the playroom window. He had swung a wild punch, missed and fallen to his knees as Knight walked away laughing.

He had spent too much time over the years wondering why Knight treated him the way he had. All he could think was that Adam must have reminded Knight of his father.

Memories of minor cruelties came back to him. Being denied his dinner because of some imagined transgression was a feature of growing up in Knight's house. Adam could still remember being unable to sleep because of the twin torments of darkness and hunger. He had been old enough to have a strongly developed sense of right and wrong. He knew he was being treated unfairly.

Now, he was able to take those memories and use them as an energizer. In a curious way, they were part of his success story. Faced with the choice of fight or flight, Adam had fought, and he had done it successfully. Although he didn't let anything stand in his way, fairness was his watchword. The companies he took over were happy to have him in charge. Unlike Knight, Adam didn't tear down; he built up. He took over businesses and empowered the existing teams to succeed. With his keen eye for trends, Adam had run one of the first organizations to spot the potential of streaming music digitally; as a result, the Lyon brand had been ahead of the market. He was never going to thank Knight for giving him the chance to transform terror into action, but it felt like a victory over his torturer that he had emerged the man he was.

The door at the top of the wooden stairs was locked and another search among the keys, this time in semi-darkness, ensued. Maja, using invisibility as a cloak, emerged first. Once she had become visible and signaled that all was clear, Adam followed her.

They were in a storage area at the rear of the kitchen. The walls were lined with shelves and these were stacked with jars and cans containing every imaginable foodstuff. Adam paused to wonder why Knight still kept this amount of food in the house when he lived there alone. He supposed it was because his stepfather continued to entertain on a lavish scale. Appearances were what mattered to Knight. He had to be the best, had to win. The thought stuck with Adam almost as though it was an important thread in this whole nightmare.

He pointed out a door that led to the main corridor. This was the dangerous part. When they stepped into that corridor, they were in the heart of the house and exposing themselves to the possibility of discovery by one of Knight's security guards.

"Let me go first," Maja urged in a whisper. "If I'm invisible, I can take them by surprise and give you a chance to get away."

It made sense, even if it didn't suit Adam's sense of chivalry. He moved toward the door. "Once we are in the corridor, it's the third door on the right."

"Will we need a key?"

He shook his head. "The doors inside the house are never locked. With security guards monitoring the place, there is no need. And no one would ever dare go into Knight's study without his permission."

Opening the door a fraction, he glanced through the gap. The rich cream-and-gold decor of the corridor hadn't changed. He remembered the carpet, so thick it felt like it was gripping his ankles, and the tasteful paintings in their gilt-edged frames. Out of the corner of his eye, his glimpsed one of the crystal chandeliers.

"There's no one around."

Maja vanished and the door opened wider as she slipped through the gap. Adam followed her. Seconds later, he was inside Knight's study, his stepfather's sanctuary, and Maja was visible again. Although this room was serviceable, with its antique oak desk and bookshelves lining the walls, it had French windows with a view of the gardens that sloped down to the water's edge. There was a huge fireplace at one side of the room with a full set of tools.

Adam remembered that, on the few occasions he had been in this room in the past, Knight had made him clean the grate. His stepfather's argument had been that, although they had servants to do the job, it was an important life skill. Adam knew better. In his stepfather's eyes, he had never cleaned it well enough. Adam had spent hours on his knees in here, almost sobbing in frustration while Knight stood over him, finding fault with his efforts. He felt the wire-handled brush and the hot, soapy water that left his hands red and raw. Remembered the ache in his arms, the hard grate beneath his knees, and the dust in his nostrils.

You are not here to relive the past.

"He doesn't have a safe."

Knight's arrogance was going to work to their advantage. His conviction that no one would dare break into his home was so strong that he kept his private papers in his desk. It was made of solid oak, beautiful but functional. Its three drawers were locked, just as Adam had known they would be. He checked the room briefly for a key, but suspected it would be sitting safely inside Knight's breast pocket.

There was an ornate silver letter opener on the desktop and he tried to pry one of the drawers open with that, but only succeeded in scratching the polished wood.

"Let me try." Maja was clearly impatient to get into the desk.

He grinned at her. "If you get your hands on it, the whole desk will be a pile of firewood in seconds."

His eyes scanned the room and rested on the fireplace with its set of brass tools. Snatching up the heavy poker, he drove it into the drawer front, splintering the wood around the lock. When the drawer gave way, he repeated the process on the others, then cast the poker aside.

Each blow made a noise, and he hoped it wasn't loud enough to draw the attention of the security guards.

Once all three drawers were open, he removed the papers they contained and spread them on the desktop. He quickly discarded each of them as irrelevant.

Frustrated, he turned back to the desk. "There has to be something more."

Dropping to his knees, he checked beneath the desk, feeling for a hidden catch or compartment.

"Here." Maja beckoned him to the side of the desk. Adam's efforts with the poker had loosened the end panel.

"A concealed drawer. I remember Knight once boasting that he had paid a quarter of a million dollars for this desk at a German antiques fair. Now I know why."

There was only one item in the drawer. It was a plastic folder containing several printed spreadsheets. The top sheet contained a list of names and contact details. One name on the list jumped out at Adam.

He tapped a finger on the name, drawing Maja's attention to it. "Shepherd."

"Tarek said his father spoke to someone called Shepherd the night before he was killed."

Adam nodded. "If I'm right, the man Tarek's father called was General Rick Shepherd. He is the leader of the international task force that is hunting the Reaper."

"I don't understand. If Shepherd is hunting the Reaper, why would he kill Tarek's father for giving him his name?" Maja lifted a hand to her mouth as realization dawned. "Oh."

Adam felt his mouth thin into a grim line. "Exactly. The only reason I can think of is that Shepherd is in league with the Reaper." He pointed to a framed photograph on the mantel above the hated fireplace. It showed Knight shaking hands with another man. "It's not quite the conclusive proof we need. I'm hoping these spreadsheets will provide that. But that's a picture of Knight and Shepherd."

He placed the plastic folder in the back pocket of his jeans...just as a security guard walked through the door.

Chapter 13

The man who walked into the room was wearing a gun in a shoulder holster, but he didn't have time to draw it. He didn't have time to do anything before Adam punched him in the face and he dropped like a stone to the floor.

Maja was impressed. His reflexes had been faster than hers.

She had no time to offer her congratulations. Adam grabbed her hand and hauled her toward the French windows. They were locked, but Maja decided this was no time to fumble with keys. With one hard kick, she left the doors hanging from their frame as the two of them burst through and hit the grass at a run. She heard shouts behind them and shots rang out.

Realizing the direction they were headed, she gave Adam a sidelong look of horror. "I can't swim."

"It's time for your first lesson."

The grass sloped steeply down to a deck next to the boathouse. Still holding her hand, Adam launched himself from the wooden platform into the water. Maja was in midair when she realized this was something he must have done many times.

As the cold, dark water closed over her head, there wasn't much time for rational thought. *I am invincible.* It was worth a reminder. Because it sure as hell didn't feel that way right now. As shock drove the breath from her lungs and water replaced it, she felt sure this was the one thing that would destroy her invincibility. Although she knew there was no other way of escaping Knight's security guards—and she suspected now that Adam must have known all along this would be their escape route—she couldn't see any way of doing this. Not when she didn't even know which way was up anymore. She thrashed around, spluttering, kicking and holding on to Adam's hand like a lifeline.

"Keep still. I've got you." Adam's voice and his strong hands under her armpits as he pulled her to the surface went some way toward calming her fears. "Lie back and let me do the work."

Two opposing forces went to war within her. Part of her, the scared, irrational part, wanted to fight him, to try and get away. Another part, a deeper part, the one that felt connected to Adam, told her she could trust him despite her fears. That was the part she went with. Relaxing in his hold, she gave herself up and let him take over. It was a new sensation. Letting another person take charge wasn't Maja's way.

She felt Adam kicking out, propelling them along the shore in the same direction they had walked earlier. She heard more shots from the direction of the deck, and cringed each time in fear that Adam could be hit. Nothing happened. With every strong kick of Adam's legs, they were thrust further from the possibility of harm. Still trembling with shock and cold, with her throat raw from choking on the water she had swallowed, she was never going to call this a pleasant experience. But Adam was alive, so she had to consider it a positive one.

Adam kept going until they were out of sight of Valentine House. Then he kicked out strongly for the shore. Carrying Maja onto the pebbly beach, he sat on the stones and cradled her in his arms.

"I'm sorry." His breath hitched on the words.

She clung to him, her whole body shuddering. "I know why you did it."

"I couldn't think of any other way. If we'd stayed in the house or the grounds, they'd have shot us." He looked around. "We can't stay here. Even though we're no longer on Knight's property, they'll be looking for us."

There was no sign of Knight's men nearby, but she supposed it was only a matter of time before they caught up with them. They had seen them jump into the water and they knew which direction they had taken. The bank was less steep here than at the point they'd climbed earlier. Getting to their feet, they scrambled up it together, hampered by their wet clothing. Adam, who knew the area, quickly found the road that would lead them back to where they had left the car.

"I don't want to walk in plain sight, but we can go through these fields alongside the road. That way, we'll be hidden from view if Knight's guys come looking for us."

Maja decided it must be the effects of the water that were bringing on a renewal of the tiredness and nausea that had dogged her a few days previously. Just when she thought she had recovered, they came back with a vengeance. As she followed in Adam's wake, her whole body felt like it was made of lead. It was just as well they didn't encounter Knight's security guards, since she wouldn't have been able to lift a finger against them, let alone a fist or a foot.

There was a blanket in the trunk of the car and Adam withdrew it, wrapping it around her. "You look pale. Are you sure you're okay?" His face was a mask of concern.

"I think it's shock."

"Let's get you home."

She nodded, almost too weary to climb into the vehicle. *Home.* It was only a few short weeks since she had been scared of that elegant apartment. Now she did think of it as home. Although she suspected that had more to do with the man who lived there, and her new family, than anything else.

Adam was pleased his body had suffered no ill effects from their trip to Valentine House. Three days later, apart from some stiffness in his injured shoulder, he had never felt better. On this particular day, he had woken early, his mind on the spreadsheets they had retrieved from Knight's desk.

One of the sheets appeared to be a list of payments to someone called Berger. The payments were regular and the figures were eyewatering. *Berger?* The French word for *shepherd*? Adam's heart rate had kicked up a notch. He was certain these amounts would coincide with payments received by General Rick Shepherd.

Since scanning the contents, he had formulated and discarded several plans for next steps. Most of them centered around Shepherd, the man tasked with coordinating the Reaper hunt, the man Adam was now certain Tarek's father had called when he'd discovered the true nature of the world's most feared terrorist organization.

Shepherd was a four-star general and one of the most respected officers in the country. As soon as Adam had seen his name on the list of contacts he had found in Knight's study, his heart had sunk. He had suspected this all along. Now he had the confirmation he needed. It couldn't have been a coincidence that Tarek's father was killed the day after he'd called a man named Shepherd. The sorry truth was that the man the world trusted to bring down the Reaper was likely himself part of that consortium.

So not only do I have to get people to believe my story that Knight Valentine, billionaire businessman, is fronting a terrorist organization, I also have to convince them that a decorated war hero is in league with him, as well.

Turning his head, Adam noticed Maja was missing, and frowned. A faint sound drew his attention to the bathroom and he sat up, listening intently. There it was again. It was unmistakable. Throwing back the bedcovers, he rose and pulled on his underwear.

"Maja, are you okay?" He tapped lightly on the bathroom door.

A faint groan answered him. "I'm fine."

He hesitated. She clearly wasn't fine. So what did he do now? Respect her privacy, or go with his instincts and find out what was wrong?

"Can I come in?"

There was a moment's silence. "Yes. The door isn't locked."

As he entered, he paused in the doorway, taking in the scene. Clad in pajama pants and a camisole top, Maja was seated on the tile floor next to the commode. Her face was so pale it appeared translucent. As she tried to say something to him she winced and turned away. Leaning over the bowl, she clutched her stomach and retched.

Adam knelt beside her, pressing a hand to her forehead. Her temperature was normal. "Why didn't you tell me you were ill?"

She leaned her head against his shoulder gratefully. "With everything else that's been going on, it seemed like a trivial thing to bother you about. It's been happening every day. Just in the mornings. Then it goes away and I feel tired for the rest of the day."

The enormity of what she had just said hit him like a slap in the face.

"Maja." He spoke slowly. It was as if his brain was having difficulty processing his thoughts and translating them into speech. "This sounds a lot like morning sickness."

She nodded. "That's what I said. It only happens in the mornings."

"No." He tilted her chin up so she was looking at him. "Morning sickness is a very specific type of sickness. It's caused by a hormonal change that takes place in the bodies of women who are having a baby."

Her lips formed a soundless O as she stared at him. She looked about as stunned as a person could get without fainting. Then her eyes filled with tears.

"I'm sorry."

Although this had been at the back of his mind, Adam's initial reaction was one of disbelief. Could Fate be this cruel? That one time—the only time in his whole life he hadn't used protection—and this was the result? Two people from different dimensions now had to live with a consequence so huge it tilted both their worlds off course.

Even through his own feelings of shock, Adam was aware that how he reacted now was really important. Maja needed him. This was going to be hard on both of them, but what he said and did in the next few minutes would set the tone for how they got through it.

He took her hand. "I'm not."

The tears spilled over as she blinked. "Pardon?"

"I'm not sorry." He raised her hand to his lips. "I'll never be sorry we had that amazing night together, or the times that followed. And how can I be sorry we made a new life?"

Her lower lip wobbled and he could see her battling to get her emotions under control. She failed, and the next thing he knew his arms were full of weeping Valkyrie. It was some time later before she was coherent again.

"I'm scared." He could see how much it cost her to admit it.

"So am I." He reached for some toilet paper and dried her eyes. "But we're in this together. Every step of the way."

"What about Odin?" She looked around fearfully as though half expecting the mighty warrior god to be lurking in the shower cubicle.

"This is our baby. Odin can butt out." Perhaps saying it out loud would make it happen.

"You don't understand." Maja's voice was a fearful whisper. "This child is his grandchild. Living proof that a Valkyrie broke the code. Odin will never let that happen." She clutched his arm. "The Allfather will never let our child survive, Adam."

Her fear was palpable, communicating itself to Adam. He held her tighter against his chest. Before this instant, a baby might have been the last thing he wanted in his life. But this was his baby. His and Maja's. It was happening. The thought sent a new, unexpected thrill through him. Was it pleasure? Excitement? He didn't have time to examine it. All he knew for sure was nothing was going to threaten this child. Not Knight Valentine and his terrorist organization. Not a four-star general who was prepared to sell out his country for however many million dollars Knight was paying him each month. Not even a mighty Norse god with a mean streak.

Sitting on a cold floor in his underwear might not be the best place for the most momentous vow of his life, but Adam made it anyway. "Maja, I don't care who I have to fight. No one will harm our child."

It was real. Maja walked out of the doctor's office in something approaching a trance. The day after Adam had found her on the bathroom floor, eight weeks after the night they had spent together in Syria, it was official.

I'm having a baby.

Adam had arranged for her to see a female obstetrician, a partner of the doctor who had been treating his injured shoulder. Although Maja had told Adam her body was that of a mortal woman, she had gone into the initial consultation worried that Dr. Blake might notice something unusual. Her fears had been laid to rest. Although some of the questions and tests seemed intrusive to someone unused to discussing intimate details, the doctor had been pleasant and approachable. She had not denounced her patient as an otherworldly warrior woman. She had, however, confirmed that Maja was quite definitely pregnant.

Maja had been telling the truth when she told Adam she knew nothing about how her body worked. Since it was never going to happen to them, the Valkyries had no need to know about sex. That meant they also didn't need to know about pregnancy. Maja had never met anyone who had been pregnant. The Valkyries had been kept apart from other women at Asgard. She had never listened to stories of what it was like to carry a child or to give birth. She had never even held a baby in her arms. Tarek was the first child she had ever known.

If Dr. Blake had been taken aback at her patient's lack of knowledge, she had kept her surprise to herself. Talking to Maja and Adam together, she had explained what they could expect from the coming weeks and months, recommended books and websites, and told them to call her if they had any questions. They had made an appointment for an ultrasound scan during which they would be able to see an image of the baby.

I don't know how to feel about this.

The baby was on Maja's mind constantly, her feelings wavering between soaring elation and total devastation. Bitter, bittersweet. She wanted this child. And that frightened her more than anything else. The fierceness with which she wanted it was like a fever burning its way deeper into her with every passing minute. But

the fear of what this meant was a barrier to her feelings of joy.

Maja didn't know if a child had ever been born to
a Valkyrie. She couldn't believe it had ever happened.
She was fairly sure she was the first of Odin's daughters or stepdaughters to commit a misdemeanor of this
magnitude.

Adam had said he would not allow anything to harm
their child. And she believed him. He had said the words
with a conviction that would not be shaken.

But where does that leave me?

She didn't know how to approach that question. They
existed in different worlds. Worlds that had briefly and
magically collided. But they both knew she couldn't
stay here. So how did Adam see the future? Did he
picture her leaving their baby with him soon after its
birth? Because the illegitimate child of a Valkyrie had
no place in Valhalla.

Maja ran a hand over her still-flat stomach. *How can
I leave the child who already means so much to me?*

The answer was simple. She couldn't. Even if Adam
could keep his promise and ensure their child's safety
against Odin's wrath, what sort of future would there
be for a child who was half mortal, half Valkyrie? She
didn't know what the future held. All she knew for certain was that she would turn both worlds upside down
to ensure there was a future for her child.

Just as Adam had made a vow, this was Maja's. In
order to see it through, she had to stay alive. And that
meant she had to remain hidden from those seeking to
return her to Valhalla.

"Dr. Blake said the morning sickness will pass."
Adam watched her face closely as she nibbled on a

piece of dry toast, the only thing she felt able to eat before noon.

"But possibly not for some time." She set the toast aside and reached for a glass of water instead.

"We couldn't ask her about dropkicking bad guys, but I'm guessing that's banned." His voice was serious. "Or let me put it this way. It *is* banned."

"I read some of the information the doctor gave us on exercising, and it suggests continuing with your usual routine. Even if that is martial arts." She took a breath, guessing what his reaction to her next words would be. "Or kickboxing."

"Not a chance, Maja. I know what you are capable of. You don't have to tell me you can take on anyone and win, but you are not getting in a fight that might result in an injury to you or our baby." When she didn't answer, he moved closer to her, gripping her hands in his. "I feel bad enough that I made you jump in the water the other day. We're not taking any more chances with your safety. If you exercise, you do it in the gym, not face-to-face with a living, breathing, unpredictable opponent. Am I making myself clear?"

Maja wasn't sure how to respond. She wanted to be angry that he was taking over, telling her what to do. She was Odin's daughter. Was she going to bow to the will of a mortal? Yet part of her felt Adam's words enveloping her like a warm, protective blanket. And she liked it. The doctor had talked about pregnancy hormones. Maybe they were responsible for this desire to rest her head on his shoulder and let him take charge. Of everything.

Instead of objecting to his high-handedness, she simply nodded. "Yes, Adam." Changing the subject, she asked a question that had been bothering her. "What shall we tell Tarek?"

"I don't think we should tell him anything yet." It was clear Adam had also given it some thought. "He's still settling in at school. We'll give him this time to adjust before we drop this new bombshell on him."

"I'm worried about what it will do to him," Maja said. "On the surface, he's coping well, but he's been through so much. We're his family now that the adoption process has started, but he may feel a baby will push him out."

"It's our job to see that doesn't happen, even if we have to get professional help to do it." Adam dashed back the remains of his cup of coffee. "I've arranged for him to attend weekend classes at his Arabic school and to go to a mosque."

"Does Tarek remind you of Danny?"

The question was asked before she had time to think about it. She winced slightly at how it sounded—intrusive and abrupt. Adam rarely talked about his brother, but she knew he was on his mind all the time. He watched the news from Syria each day and emailed Edith Blair regularly for updates. Now and then, Maja would catch a faraway look on his face and she guessed he was thinking of the idealistic young man who had gone away to help, and gotten caught up in a war that wasn't his. She was surprised when Adam answered readily.

"In some ways he does. I think I was initially drawn to Tarek because he reminded me of Danny. They both have that smartness and determination to overcome their difficulties. And something more." He shook his head as if he was struggling to explain. "It sounds like a cliché, but it's a simple enjoyment of life. Something I was missing for so long."

The words struck Maja as odd, making it sound like he was no longer missing his own pleasure in life. Yet she didn't want to interrupt what he was saying by questioning him about what he meant.

"But I don't want Tarek to grow up thinking I brought him here to be a Danny substitute. Or out of pity. I love him and I'm proud to have him in my life."

"That's what he needs to know. From both of us." Bright tears stung the back of Maja's eyelids. These pregnancy hormones were a killer. "When we tell him about the baby, those are the first words he needs to hear."

"I suspect we will, then we need to follow the news with 'let's get pizza.'" Adam laughed, drawing her into his arms. "Tarek has adapted to some aspects of Western life remarkably quickly."

Maja leaned her forehead on his chest for several long, still moments, grounding herself in his warmth and delicious scent. When she lifted her head, she didn't want to break the ambience, didn't want to ask the next question. But there was no avoiding it. "And Knight? What happens next?"

"We've got the evidence that he was paying Shepherd, but we need more before we can take this to the authorities. You got me thinking when you asked about his background. I don't know how much it will help to have an insight into the mastermind behind the Reaper, but if we can understand his motives, maybe we can find his weakness and get more evidence. With that in mind, there is someone I need to talk to. Someone I haven't seen for a very long time."

Maja could sense he was subject to a torrent of conflicting emotions as he spoke. There was some residual anger in his eyes, but she could also see reluctance and a trace of pain. He didn't want to do this. Whoever he needed to see clearly aroused strong feelings in him.

"Who is this person?"

"My mother's aunt. Elvira was her only close relative at the time of her wedding to Knight. She hated and mistrusted Knight and caused a scandal by doing that dreaded thing and standing up during the wedding service—" Adam broke off with a smile before Maja could tell him she didn't know what he meant.

"It's a mortal thing," he explained. "There's a point in a marriage when the person performing the ceremony asks if anyone knows of a reason why the bride and groom shouldn't marry. It's always a tense moment and it has become a popular trope in films and books. You know, someone bursts in and dramatically spoils the wedding. Usually an ex-partner."

"And your mother's aunt did this during her wedding to Knight?" Maja liked the sound of Elvira already.

"Yes. Elvira got to her feet and denounced Knight in front of the hundreds of his socialite friends who were gathered at Valentine House for the occasion. I can't remember exactly what she said after all this time, but it was quite a speech. It even included a statement that Knight had sold his soul to the devil. Even though my mother and Elvira had been close until that point, it caused a rift between them that was never healed."

"I might not be Knight's biggest fan, but I can understand why that would happen." It was the sort of family split from which there could be no going back.

"I'd like to talk to Elvira. My mother married Knight

within weeks of my father's death. I was quite young and still grieving, but it seemed so strange, so callous. Yet my mother was almost in a trance. It was as if Knight had her under his spell and nothing was going to change her mind. How did Elvira get to a point where she hated him so much in such a short space of time? She was known to be a snob. Was it simply that Knight didn't come from old money—his family wasn't elite enough to suit Elvira's tastes—or was there more to it?"

Maja thought she could understand the storm of emotions she had sensed in Adam. If he talked to Elvira, he would have to speak of his mother. Adam was a complex tapestry, comprising many interwoven strands. She sensed that Belinda Lyon was the golden thread running through it. His mother completed the picture, so when you stood back you could see it all. But so far, no one had seen the whole image. Not even Adam. And he was frightened that, when he spoke to Elvira, the final stitches would be placed in the canvas. His tapestry would be complete.

"Can I come with you?"

He smiled. "I was hoping you would say that."

Chapter 14

"The book Dr. Blake gave me said sex is fine." Several days after her visit to the doctor, Maja had become a walking, talking pregnancy encyclopedia. She blushed. "If you want to."

"How can you even ask that question?" As they lay naked in bed, Adam drew her closer so she could feel his erection pulsing against her belly. "Surely you know by now that, with you, I *always* want to? Even when I'm not with you, when I'm walking down the street, when I'm in the middle of a high-powered meeting, taking a call from an overseas client, supposed to be one hundred percent focused on business…part of me is thinking about how much I want you."

It was more the look on his face than the words he spoke that instantly had her nipples hardening, her clit throbbing and her whole body thrumming in response to the blaze of need in his eyes.

He pressed his mouth against hers, parting her lips by flicking his tongue lightly over them. Wrapping an arm around her waist, he pulled her closer again and deepened the kiss. It was soft, yet there was a hint of the hunger that always burned between them. Heat infused her senses, sweeping over her body. It was addictive, a buzz tingling through her bloodstream, more powerful than any drug.

His hand was warm on her breast, cupping it gently. A new sensitivity made Maja shudder at his touch and press into his palm. Her nipple was hard, and ultraresponsive as his thumb rasped back and forth over the tip. It tightened even further, causing a feeling somewhere midway between pleasure and pain, until she murmured a soft protest and drew his head down to her.

The warmth of his mouth on her nipple was sweet torture. Rich sensation poured over her like cream and honey mingling in a heady concoction.

As if there was all the time in the world, he moved a hand down to part her thighs, slowly stroking a finger around her clitoris, causing it to swell and throb beneath his touch.

"Feels good." She wasn't sure the words were audible.

Adam must have caught the essence of what she was saying because he leaned on one elbow, watching her face as he pressed a finger inside her. Maja's flesh burned, clenching around the impalement.

"I want my cock inside you. So deep I can't tell where I end and you begin."

"Yes." She could barely pant out the words as she gripped his finger, grinding her hips against him. "I want that, too, Adam. So much."

"But first I want to watch as you come around my fingers. I want to be sure this feels okay."

Okay? If she had been capable of further speech, she'd have assured him it felt like perfection. Her inner muscles spasmed around his fingers as she lifted her hips in time with his pumping motion. Each thrust was heaven and hell. Rapture and torture. Each breath that left her lips was a moan of pleasure as she quickened her movements. The warning waves of her release started at her core and began to ripple outward. She tightened around him, arching her back and straining toward him.

Adam moved faster in smooth strokes as he buried his fingers inside her flesh. Each caress touched sensitive nerve endings and she cried out between attempts to draw enough air into her lungs. And then it hit. Savage and out of control. A ragged wail left her lips and she clung to Adam's shoulders as she was flung through a dark tunnel and out the other side into brilliant, blinding light. The violence of the sensations buffeting her body robbed her of any remaining breath as she tensed and shuddered through the storm.

She was still trembling as Adam turned her so she lay on her side with her back to him. His chin was pressed into the curve of her shoulder, his lips caressing the shell of her ear. "This is what we'll do when the baby gets bigger."

"Are we practicing?" Her breath hissed sharply as he pressed up against her tight entrance.

"Why not?" He pushed forward, opening and stretching her. "We may have to do it a lot to make sure we get it right."

He held her hips, cushioning her spine against the hard muscles of his chest and resting the back of her thighs on top of his as he eased into her. Maja could feel his heart pounding between her shoulder blades as his lips found the sensitive spot at the base of her neck. Excitement fizzed through her blood like bubbles in soda as she moved her hips in time with his.

The world narrowed to the point where their bodies joined, and the intensity built to a crescendo, vibrating through them, demanding release. Gasping, breathless moans issued from Maja's lips as Adam used the fingers of one hand to tease her nipples while the other circled her still-sensitized clit.

"Too much." She clawed at the sheets, squirming wildly against Adam's pelvis.

"Do you want me to stop?" His voice was a growl in her ear.

"Don't you dare."

Seconds later, she was convulsing again, gripping him tightly as another mindless orgasm tilted her world off course. With him buried deep inside her, holding her close against his heart, she felt the blistering heat of Adam's own climax as he murmured her name.

Later, when she turned to face him and lay in his arms, she wished she could smooth away the line of tension that pulled his brows together. Although she knew its cause, it worried her.

"What time do we need to set off?"

"Straight after we drop Tarek at school," Adam said. "The retirement home where Elvira lives is only an hour and a half away, so we will be there and back in time to pick him up again."

"Is she expecting us?"

"No." A flicker of a smile crossed his face. "Elvira is the most stubborn, contrary woman in the whole world.

With probably the nastiest tongue. If we turn up unannounced we retain the element of surprise and there's
less chance of her refusing to see us."

The Preserve was nothing like Adam's mental image
of a retirement home. It was more like a high-class
hotel. The concierge informed them that they would
find Ms. Perlman in the solarium where she would be
finishing coffee, having returned from her morning
round of golf.

Elvira hadn't changed. That was the first thought that
struck Adam. He hadn't seen her since he was thirteen,
but if he'd passed her in the street, he'd have known her
instantly. She was tall and stick thin, with piercing blue
eyes and strong features. As they approached her table,
Elvira glanced up from the newspaper she had been pe-
rusing and gave Adam a long, cold stare.

"Do you need money?" Her voice was perfectly
calm.

"No, but thank you for offering."

She gave a snort of laughter. "You'd better sit down."
She indicated a chair on the opposite side of the table
before turning a hard stare in Maja's direction. "Which
are you? A secretary or a gold digger?"

"Neither." Maja took the seat next to Adam. "But
I'm glad I was warned that you have a nasty tongue."

Elvira gave a single bark of laughter. "I like her," she
told Adam. "You should keep her."

"It's not that simple." He flicked a smile in Maja's
direction and caught her startled glance. "But we're not
here to talk about me."

"Why are you here? It's almost twenty years since
I last saw you."

"I want to ask you about Knight Valentine."

He didn't know what he'd expected Elvira's response to be. Anger, possibly. Outrage that he would bring up the subject of the man who'd been at the heart of the family rift. Even sadness.

Not fear. That was the last thing he expected to see. Yet for a moment or two, that was what he saw in the depths of her pale eyes. It shocked him. Somehow, he had never imagined Elvira would be capable of feeling afraid.

"No." She shook her head, and he heard a faint tremor in her voice. "You can go now."

"Elvira…" he lowered his voice "…this is important. We have reason to believe he is involved in something very bad, and I want to discover anything that I can use against him. You objected to his marriage to my mother very strenuously. You must know something. I need your help."

Her eyes scanned his face. He didn't know what she was looking for, and he wasn't sure what she found, but after a moment or two she pressed her lips together tightly. Giving a brief nod, she folded the newspaper and pressed a napkin to the corners of her mouth.

"Not here. We'll go to my room."

Her elegant, third floor room overlooked rolling hills and Elvira served coffee in bone china cups that seemed vaguely familiar to Adam. They made him think of his mother and he wondered if Elvira had used this set when he'd been a child. The thought stuck on a loop in his mind. *My mother could have drunk from this cup.* Why did it matter so much? He did know why. It just did.

Elvira took a seat in a wingback chair. "Let me be very clear about this. I don't want to talk about that man. I don't even want to think about him. I prefer to fool myself that he doesn't exist. But you are Belinda's son. I tried to help her and failed." A shadow crossed her face. "If I can help you, I'll do it. For her sake."

"Thank you." Adam was amazed at the depth of emotion in his voice. What was even more amazing was he didn't care his feelings were on show. If Elvira could talk openly about his mother, maybe he could, too.

"What do you want to know?"

"I don't remember much about the speech you made at their wedding. All I know is you spoke out about what a bad person he was and why my mother shouldn't marry him. I remember you said he'd sold his soul to the devil. Can you be specific about what you meant by that? Maybe give me some examples of the sort of dirty deals he'd done that made you use that expression?"

Elvira lifted her saucer from the table at her side and the cup rattled as her hand shook. Instead of taking a sip of her drink, she placed it down again. "You don't understand. I thought perhaps you did." Her gaze traveled from Adam's face to Maja's and back again. "When I said that, it wasn't a metaphor. Knight Valentine really did sell his soul to the devil."

Since Adam had been frozen into immobility by Elvira's words, Maja decided to take over his role and direct the conversation. "How did you learn of Knight's transaction with the devil?"

The question seemed to rouse Adam from his dazed state. "Surely you are not taking this seriously?" He scrubbed a hand over his face as though checking that he was awake. "Either of you?"

Elvira answered Maja's question as though Adam

hadn't spoken. "Adam's father, Robert, and Knight were best friends. Right through school and into adulthood. Although I found it difficult to believe, it was Robert who told me the story." She cast a wary glance in Adam's direction. "Just before he died."

"I can't believe I am listening to this." Adam got to his feet and went to the window, standing with his back to the room.

"Go on." Maja nodded to Elvira.

They had come to hear the truth, no matter how far-fetched or gruesome. She understood that it was easier for her to be open-minded about what Elvira was saying. She came from another world. A place inhabited by gods and demons. A realm in which werewolves fought vampires and the evil faerie king had just been overthrown. Pacts with Satan were rare, but they were not unheard of. Throughout history, there might have been only a handful of mortals who had taken the devil's hand and walked a dark, dangerous path at his side. But it had happened. As a child, she had listened wide-eyed to the stories. They never ended well.

"Robert told me that Knight always had this fiercely competitive streak. He said his family was odd. Knight once said he didn't know why his parents had a child, since they weren't interested in him. They just wanted an heir. Someone to carry the name." Although her hand still shook, Elvira managed to lift her cup to her lips and take a sip of her coffee. "Robert said it started as a game. Knight had to be the best at everything. It started with little things. They were practicing before a basketball game and Knight, who wasn't the best shooter, jokingly said, 'If I get this next shot, the devil can have my soul.'"

Maja cast a glance in Adam's direction. His shoulders were hunched and his head was bent. Everything about his stance spoke of despair. She leaned forward and gripped Elvira's hand. To her surprise the unyielding old woman returned her clasp gratefully.

"It became Knight's thing. His catchphrase. Anything they did, he would use the same words. When they played pool, he would say the devil could have his soul if he pocketed the next ball. The devil could have his soul if he flipped a coin and it came up heads. The curious thing was, every time Knight used that phrase, he got what he wanted."

Adam swung around. "So he's lucky. I don't like the guy any more than you do, but that doesn't mean he's in league with the devil."

"Do you want to hear this story, Adam?" Elvira had regained some of her strength and her voice was compelling.

After what appeared to be an internal battle, he gave a curt nod and returned to his seat.

"When he went into business, Knight was ruthless. Still is from what I hear. Robert told me he was seeing less of him at that time, but he met him for lunch. All Knight could talk of was this deal he was involved in. It was a make-or-break thing. And Knight said it again. 'If this deal goes through, the devil can have my soul.' Robert told me something about the way he said the words that time made him shiver." She gave Adam an uneasy look. "You father was not a man who scared easily."

"And the deal went through." Maja felt herself drawn into the story.

"The deal went through. It launched Knight as the

man he is today, the world's leading deal maker. The man who owns more luxury properties across the globe than any other. A brand name to be reckoned with. Robert didn't see him again for several months, but when he did, he was shocked at the change in him."

"Don't tell me. He had horns and a pointed tail?" Maja knew what Adam was doing. He was severely jolted and needed to stay in control. Nevertheless, his mocking tone introduced a discordant note that unsettled Elvira.

"I didn't ask you to come here and dredge up old memories." Her finger shook as she pointed toward the door. "Don't let it hit you on the way out."

Maja caught Adam's eye, conveying a message to him with her expression. *We are here to listen.* For a moment, their gazes locked. Strong brown eyes clashed briefly with hers. Then he relaxed, his body language changing. The tension left his frame and he nodded, acknowledging that he understood what she was attempting to communicate.

"I'm sorry," he said to Elvira. "I'm struggling to take this in, but that's no reason to behave like an ass. Please continue."

The outcome appeared to be in doubt for several seconds. Then she gave a tight-lipped nod. "Robert got a call from Knight out of the blue, asking if they could meet up. When they did, he was shocked at Knight's appearance. He said he looked thin and gaunt, like a man who was terrified. Over lunch, he told Robert he had made the worst mistake of his life. He had done something he couldn't undo. That deal he'd wanted so badly had looked like it was going to fall through at the last minute. Knight had used his old maxim, calling on the devil to see it through and offering his soul in return. The next day, everything was back on track. But Knight woke up that day and something within himself had changed. He said it felt like a part of him had gone missing. Like there was a giant hole in the center of his being."

"But he didn't talk about any specific interaction with the devil?" Maja asked. She was aware of Adam watching her intently as she spoke. "No vow of eternal servitude or pact signed in blood?"

"That was the exact question Robert asked. Knight laughed and said that wasn't how it worked. When Robert asked him how he knew, Knight told him what had happened the day after he'd signed the contract on his big deal. He was woken by an unusual sound in his bedroom. Lying still, he tried to figure out what it was. When he recognized it, his blood ran cold. It was breathing. Heavy and ragged, as though from someone who had run a long distance…or the panting of a wild animal. Of course, Knight thought someone had broken into his apartment. He was scared, but he kept a gun in the dresser at the side of his bed. As he slowly reached for the drawer, something moved across the room and he saw a figure coming toward him."

Elvira gulped down the remains of her coffee. She seemed to Maja to have crossed an invisible line. It was as if she was no longer here in the room with them. She had stepped back into the past.

"Knight saw a creature with the upper body of a man and the lower half of a goat. It had cloven feet, horns and eyes that glowed red in the darkness. If that wasn't bad enough, it was the tail, the awful pointed tail, swinging back and forth, that convinced him. The devil was in Knight's bedroom."

"Could it have been a dream?" Adam asked. "Brought on by Knight's insistence on using that expression about selling his soul?"

"That was what he hoped. He said he even tried a prayer as he lay there with his gaze fastened on the beast. As it moved toward him, he gave up hoping and praying and started screaming."

Elvira had started shaking again and Maja decided it was time for a break. "Shall I make more coffee?"

Both Adam and Elvira appeared grateful for the offer. As she gathered the cups together, Maja noticed a photograph in a silver frame on the table at Elvira's side. It was of a laughing young couple. The man could only have been Adam's father. The resemblance was striking. Which meant the slender woman with the cloud of dark hair must be Belinda Perlman, the woman who had married Robert Lyon and then Knight Valentine. Even in that picture, it was possible to see that Adam's mother had been incredibly beautiful. She had delicate features and an air of fragility. One woman and two friends who both loved her. Robert Lyon, the man in the picture, and Knight Valentine, the shadowy figure in the background. There had to be a story there.

When she returned with the coffee, she was pleased to observe that Adam and Elvira had been making conversation on neutral topics instead of staring into space as they had been when she left them. She knew from her interactions with the warriors who had joined Odin's army that mortals had a dread of the supernatural. They remained largely oblivious to the existence of Otherworld. Sometimes the two realms overlapped. Ghosts

were the most obvious example. Vampires and werewolves persisted in causing problems for those who
defended the borders of this mortal realm. Her own interaction with Adam was an example of how thin the
veil between the two worlds really was. Because Otherworld was hidden, with only occasional glimpses,
Maja could see why it was feared.

The devil, of course, was a whole other problem. He
was feared in both worlds. Satan was the angel who had
rebelled. Now, he was everyone's enemy. He had only
one mission. To destroy. When it came to humans, he
was prepared to achieve his ambition by killing or en-
slaving them.

With a fresh cup of coffee in her hand, Elvira was
ready to continue. "Knight knew he wasn't dreaming
when the devil spoke to him. Just two words. The same
two words every time. *Pay me.*"

"Every time?" Adam asked.

"He told Robert the beast came to him every night
from then on."

Chapter 15

It was like listening to the most ridiculously far-fetched fairy tale. Yet Adam could tell that Maja believed it. Elvira certainly did. And she was recounting a story that had been told to her by his father. Could he force his skepticism aside and open his mind to it? He had to try. Had to suspend belief and imagine that Knight had been visited every night by a horned being who was half man, half goat, because he had sold his soul to the devil.

"Robert said he did everything he could to put Knight's mind at rest. Told him he was working too hard, suggested he take a holiday, recommended he see a doctor who could give him something to help him sleep. Knight just laughed. The two men didn't meet again for several months. During the intervening time, Robert said the rise in Knight's fortunes was meteoric. Everything the man touched turned to gold."

Elvira drummed her fingers on the arm of her chair as she glanced at the picture in its silver frame. "By the time he saw Knight again, your father had met Belinda."

Adam followed the direction of Elvira's gaze. He hadn't seen that particular picture of his parents until today. Now he was glad he had come here, if only for that. It gave him a brief glimpse into who they had once been. Robert, big and strong, was staring at Belinda with such love it was obvious even through the lens of a camera. And it was good to see his mother looking happy instead of the sad, broken woman he remembered...

"When Robert did see Knight, it was only on social occasions with other people present. They barely got a chance to speak privately. Knight seemed happy and Robert assumed the strange dreams had ended. When he snatched a moment to ask him about it, Knight was flippant. He said his nocturnal visitor still showed up every night. Still uttered the same two words. *Pay me.* But he had laughed and said he thought it was worth it for the benefits." Elvira grimaced. *"Worth it.* Those were the words he used. He told Robert he was on the way to his first billion. That was the price of Knight Valentine's soul."

Adam supposed the story had value even though it couldn't be true in any literal sense. Knight had told Adam's father about it. It had taken a grip on his imagination. He truly believed he had a pact with the devil. That had to have screwed up his head. It explained why he thought he was indestructible. It also answered Maja's question about Knight's motives. She was right. He hadn't been born wicked, but had convinced himself that he was evil because of this imaginary pact. He had the perfect excuse. *The devil made me do it. The devil made me lock you in the cellar when you were a child. The devil made me drive your mother into an early grave. The devil made me create a terrorist organization as a front for wiping out my business rivals.*

"After that, Knight was so wrapped up in business, their friendship dwindled to nothing. They met now and then, but never in private. There wasn't another opportunity for the sort of confidences they'd previously enjoyed. If anything, Robert felt Knight was embarrassed by the things he'd told him. Years passed and Robert put it to the back of his mind. He assumed Knight had gotten counseling or other treatment for what must have been a delusion brought on by stress."

"But you didn't believe that," Maja said. "When you stood up to Knight at Belinda's wedding to him, you told everyone about his pact with the devil."

"No, I didn't believe it. For one simple reason. Knight Valentine always got everything he wanted in life." She took a deep breath and looked at the photograph again. "And what he wanted more than anything was Belinda."

Adam jerked as though an electric shock had been applied to his spine. "What are you suggesting?"

"I'm not suggesting anything. I'm telling you. As soon as Knight set eyes on your mother, he wanted her. She didn't feel the same. Not then. But soon after your father died her feelings changed." His aunt's eyes challenged him. "Knight Valentine gets what he wants."

"Elvira, this is nonsense. Are you trying to say that the devil killed my father so Knight could marry my mother?"

"Yes." That simple word hung in the air, cutting through any ambiguity or doubt. "And what's more, your father believed it. He told me all this as he lay dying. He begged me to take care of Belinda, and of you and Danny. He asked me to make sure she didn't marry Knight." She covered her face with her hands. "I let you all down."

Maja went to her and knelt before her chair, gripping her hands in her own. "You are one woman. You couldn't fight the devil."

Elvira raised a tear-streaked face. "At first, like you, I thought Robert's story was far-fetched. Then I saw how quickly Belinda fell under Knight's spell. I tried to dissuade her from marrying him. She'd always listened to me, but his hold over her was too strong. I decided I needed to do something drastic to stop the wedding. I wanted to denounce him publicly because I thought he wouldn't come after me that way, but I just made a fool of myself. And I lost Belinda. She refused to see me after that day. She wouldn't take my calls and my letters came back unopened. Oh, I know Knight was behind that. Belinda didn't have a malicious bone in her body. I should have done more, pushed harder. But I was a coward." Her voice trembled. "I feared what he could do, so I hid myself away. I'll admit it. I tried to pretend it wasn't happening."

"Did he come after you?" Maja asked.

"Not directly." Elvira's lips twisted into a half smile. "He didn't need to. I'd lost everything that mattered to me. Family. Friends. My reputation. I'd been written off as a crazy woman after my outburst at the wedding. But he sends me a warning now and then."

"What sort of warning?" Adam frowned. Knight took the time to threaten an old woman?

"The sort of things that would get me locked up if

I ever spoke of them to anyone. Fingernails scraping on my bedpost in the middle of the night. A demonic chuckle in my ear just as I'm dozing off to sleep. Glowing red eyes in a darkened corner of the room. Little reminders that Knight has friends in hot places." The smile was genuine this time. "I can read your thoughts, Adam. You're thinking you've wasted a morning on a crazy old woman. Hell, you only have my word that Robert told me that story. I could have made it all up."

Adam tried for a polite protest. "I wasn't—"

Elvira held up a hand, cutting across his words. "Don't worry. I'd be thinking the same thing in your place. But I have something that may persuade you."

Adam frowned, meeting Maja's eyes across the room. What proof could Elvira possible produce to convince him of the truth of something that must surely all be imagination?

Getting to her feet, Elvira went to a bureau under the window. Producing a key on a chain around her neck, she unlocked one of the drawers. "Your mother wrote me a letter from the nursing home where she was being cared for. It arrived the day after she died." She held the folded pages out to him. "Maybe Belinda's words will convince you where mine can't."

Although he remained perfectly still, Adam's reluctance to take Belinda's letter from Elvira was coming off him in waves. Maja felt his fear as though it was a black cloud descending on the room. And she understood its source. He didn't want to know what Knight had done to break his mother. He had been thirteen when she died, and Maja supposed that was the reason his father had told Elvira the story of Knight's pact with the devil instead of him. Robert would have reasoned that Adam was too young to be burdened with such a horrific tale. The part of him that took the burden of responsibility onto his own shoulders, that cared so deeply, was afraid of what he would find. The man who had traveled to Syria to find his brother was scared that the boy he had been could have done more. Even though he had been a child, subjected to his own nightmare at his stepfather's hands, he was weighed down with guilt at his mother's decline.

Maja wanted him to find the truth, and to do it he needed to read that letter.

She moved to sit next to him and took his hand. "Let's do this together."

He gave her a grateful look and nodded, holding out his other hand to Elvira. "I guess it's time."

The first thing that struck Maja was the precision of Belinda's handwriting. Adam smiled as he traced the first line with one fingertip.

"She was always such a perfectionist. My handwriting is untidy and she spent hours trying to get me to be neater. It was a losing battle."

The first few paragraphs contained a personal message to Elvira, an apology for the breakdown in their relationship. Without making any direct reference to Knight, Belinda implied that dark forces had been at work to keep them apart. She hoped Elvira would forgive her. There were splashes on the page. Belinda had shed tears as she wrote.

Maja rested her cheek lightly against Adam's upper arm as he read. She scanned the words with him, feeling the tension in his body as he followed his mother's final thoughts. Elvira returned to her seat and watched them, her hands gripping the arms of her chair so tightly that her knuckles gleamed white.

The next part of the letter developed into a story, and Maja supposed at first that Belinda's mind must have been wandering as she wrote.

"This is the story of a man who sold his soul and thought to gain riches in return. And he did. But what was the price? When the devil came for the debt, he asked a favor so great it brought the man to his knees, howling in pain.

"'Pay me.' They were the words the devil spoke in the darkness of the man's bedroom.

"The world is a dark place these days. The devil needed to call in the favor. Azrael, the Angel of Death, the one they call the Grim Reaper, was overworked. Death needed a helpmate.

"The woman in the corner of the room recoiled in dread as her husband's skin and muscle melted like candle wax and dripped from his body, and his blood boiled. She watched as all that was human about him was driven out with such force that he screamed and writhed on the floor, begging the devil to end his life rather than torture him this way. He died a thousand deaths that night, as his terrified wife looked on, helpless to do anything.

"When he rose, all that remained was a skeleton. The devil held out a black robe for him to cover his hideous appearance and handed him a scythe taller than himself, with a blade as sharp as a razor.

"'Join Death in his grim task. Find the ones whose time has run out and cut them down.'

"The devil's command echoed inside the woman's head. She thought she was going mad, but the foul-smelling smoke he left behind was a reminder that this was real.

"Silently, the man obeyed the devil's command. In the morning, his body was restored to normality. But each night he would assume his skeletal form once more and take up his robe and scythe to reap the souls of the dead alongside his grim master. He had sold his soul without questioning the detail of the contract. Now the devil was exacting his awful price.

"And that's my story, Elvira. When Death comes for me—maybe tonight, maybe tomorrow. Who knows the exact hour? I only know it will be soon—I will be the only woman to stare at that hooded figure and know she is looking into the blank eye sockets of her own husband."

Adam's own eyes were bleak, dark pools as he lifted them from the page and looked at Elvira. "She has been dead eleven years. If I hadn't come to you, would you ever have shown me this letter?"

"No." Elvira flinched as his expression hardened further. "Think about it, Adam. Your mother died in a nursing home. As far as the world was concerned, she was being treated for an affliction of the nerves. We know better, and so did most of her acquaintances. In addition to suffering from chronic depression, Belinda was addicted to alcohol and drugs. That was what Knight drove her to." Elvira pointed to the paper in his hand.

"That letter explains why. But no one would have believed what she was saying. They would have dismissed it as the sad ramblings of a confused mind. And if I'd brought that letter to you, that's what you would have done. You wouldn't have taken the time to listen to me and hear the rest of the story. Admit it."

Because Maja was still leaning against Adam, she could feel the tremor that ran through him. Could sense the conflict gripping him. Knew how close he was to walking out and turning his back on this. Because the truth was in danger of breaking him apart.

She also felt the moment he capitulated. The stiffness went out of his body and his breathing relaxed. Although she knew what it cost him, this was the man she knew. She understood his hurt and knew why he wanted to deny what he was hearing. But Adam was stronger and better than that. He was the bravest man she had ever met. And coming from a Valkyrie, that was quite an accolade. The only men Maja met were heroes, but Adam surpassed them all. He would not walk away from a difficult message, even if it tore him in two.

She heard his indrawn breath catch in his throat. "You're right, Elvira. Without a new chapter to this story, I wouldn't have come here today. If you'd told me your story of Knight's deal with the devil, I would have dismissed you as a bitter old woman." His expression was hard to read as he glanced down at the paper in his hand once more. "And even though it hurts me to admit it, if I'd read my mother's letter at all, I would have written it off as the ravings of the troubled mind of an addict."

"A new chapter?" Elvira sat up straighter. "What do you mean?"

Adam shook his head. "I think it's better if you don't know. The fewer people who are in danger the better. We are talking about the man who killed my father." His expression darkened as he spoke. "And who caused my mother's death, as well. I know what you are about to say, Elvira. You have borne this by yourself for almost twenty years, and now I'm taking over and making the decisions."

"Believe, me, Adam, I was going to say something far less polite." There was a snarl in Elvira's words.

He laughed, and although the sound was shaky, Maja was relieved to hear a trace of genuine amusement in there. "I promise we will come back and tell you how the story ends."

Evening had become Adam's favorite time. In the past, it had simply been an extension to his working day. An annoying interruption to his routine when other people stopped responding to messages and emails and didn't answer calls. Now he got it. He understood why people valued this part of the day.

It was a time to enjoy his new family. Maja sat curled up on the sofa next to him with her head resting on his shoulder. Adam kept his arm around her waist. He liked the feel of her close to him. Soon Tarek would be safely tucked up under his duvet with his furry bodyguard beneath his bed. This was their world. It belonged to the three of them...

Adam smiled and corrected himself. Five of them. Leo and the baby were part of this cozy bubble of theirs. If only they could keep the apartment door closed and stay this way forever.

Upon leaving Elvira's apartment the previous day,

Adam had heaved fresh air into his lungs, binging on it like a man rescued from drowning. The dramatic atmosphere had begun to stifle him, and with his promise that they would return and tell her the outcome of their fight against Knight, he had grabbed Maja's hand and left.

Adam still felt the grief of his father's death. He knew the trauma of his loss had made him the person he was today. He figured he was like a jigsaw puzzle. At the age of thirteen, all his pieces hadn't been in place. When Robert Lyon died, he took one of the pieces of his son's puzzle with him. Adam was incomplete without it. There were memories, private jokes, conversations...hundreds of moments in his life that he had shared with his father. No one else knew about them. There was no one else to turn to when something triggered a reminder. He had no one to go to with his silly questions, the ones his dad would always answer. There was no one to tell him silly jokes. He would never again hear that deep rumbling laugh... He had lost his hero as well as his parent.

His start in life had given him the perfect role model for the sort of father he wanted to be. The greatest gift his father had given him was his time. When his own child was born, Adam would be there for him or her in the same way. The love he already had for the unborn infant was an extension of everything he felt for Danny and Tarek. The same strength of emotion, the same urge to protect.

He had been older when his mother died, and watching her decline had been the hardest thing he had ever done. Belinda had been incredibly beautiful, but she appeared fragile. Looking back on her life before Knight,

Adam could see the difference, and it hurt him to know what had caused it. Her life with his father had been happy. She had been loved and nurtured. Adam had always suspected that the decline in her health, the depression, accompanied by her addiction, was caused by her unhappy second marriage. To find out he had been right—spectacularly so—gave him no satisfaction.

Would a stronger woman have walked out on Knight when the devil came to exact his price? Or did what she saw unhinge Belinda so that she couldn't leave? Adam hoped she hadn't stayed because of him and Danny. He didn't think that was the case. When Robert died, he'd left them well provided for, and Belinda must have known she could have gone to Elvira. He suspected that Belinda *couldn't* leave, no matter what she saw. For the same reason that she had married Knight in the first place. The same reason she didn't see how he was abusing her son. She was under his spell. She was one of the prizes Knight had been granted by his master.

Blackness clouded Adam's mind when he thought of Knight. The man whom, he now knew, was responsible for the deaths of both his parents. The man whose greed had forged a path of death and destruction, trampling on anyone who stood in his path.

No more.

Although they hadn't discussed the contents of his mother's letter any further, it had been hanging in the air between him and Maja ever since. Adam knew she had been giving him space, allowing him to digest the awful details of what he had read. It was part of that unique way she had of picking up on his mood. Now, as Tarek went to watch a TV program in his room—

part of his pre-bedtime routine—Adam felt it pressing down on him further.

He needed to feel Maja tight against him. He pulled her into his arms and, turning in his embrace, she molded her body to his. Her warmth and scent comforted him. Her heartbeat and breathing in time with his were exactly what he needed. When he found her lips opening beneath his, he lost himself in their sweetness, and some of the horror of his thoughts receded.

"I believe it." He rested his head forehead on hers.

"I know." He loved that he didn't need to say anything else. She picked up on the rhythm of his speech instantly.

"He is doing the devil's work and reaping souls at the same time." He gave a shaky laugh. "How arrogant do you have to be to call your organization after the Reaper when you *are* the Reaper?"

"He never thought anyone would find out," Maja said. "It was his private joke against the world."

"Elvira knew." Adam clenched his fists. "She must have been in hell all these years."

"You said it yourself. No one would have listened to her. Knight knew that. He was safe from Elvira." Maja took his hand. "But he's not safe from us."

"How can we fight him, Maja? He's the right-hand man of the Angel of Death."

"Aren't you forgetting something?" She laughed at his bemused expression. "I do the same job as the Reaper. I collect souls. We just obey different masters. I'm not afraid of Knight." Her brilliant smile lit her face. "He should be afraid of me."

"If we could just find a way to expose him. Elvira had the right idea. Exposing him publicly is the way to

hurt him. Knight is a narcissist who thrives on his reputation. If we can damage that, expose him as the brains
behind the Reaper, he's ruined. I can't even begin to
think of how we can do that, let alone show the world
the truth about his pact with the devil. I'd do it if I could,
but right now I can't think of a way to get close enough
to him to do anything. What we have still isn't enough.
If I published this story in one of my newspapers, it
would cause a stir, but it wouldn't ruin him."

"For now, let's concentrate on the first part. If we
can end the terrorism and the killings, we will have
achieved what we set out to do. While we are planning
that, we may also think of a way of exposing his deal
with Satan."

Adam shook his head. "I still can't get used to talking about it as reality. It's like we've stepped into a
nightmare."

"Not everything that has happened to us has been
bad," Maja reminded him.

"God, no." He pressed a hand to her stomach with a
smile. "And I won't let him detract from the best thing
that's happened to me."

Maja returned the smile, holding his hand in place
with her own. "What we need is a plan."

"You're right. Any plan would be better than the
big, fat nothing we have right now." Adam grimaced.

"We could use some reinforcements. A small army
would be useful."

"Sorry I can't oblige." Adam grimaced. "You are the
one with the warrior contacts."

"Unfortunately, I don't think Odin will allow my
sisters to come to our aid." The expression in her eyes

was shy as she raised them to his. "I liked the way you said our baby is the best thing that's happened to you."

He gazed down at her, drinking in the beauty of her features. How would he have dealt with this situation with Knight if she hadn't been here at his side? It was a silly question. Without Maja, Adam would be dead. She had saved his life and now she was dragging him through the most bizarre crisis he had ever experienced. His mind had already been opened by the arrival of a Valkyrie into his life. It had been flung even further open with the news that his stepfather had engaged in a pact with the devil. If that wasn't enough, he then had to contend with the information that Knight, in repayment of his debt, had entered into partnership with the Azrael, the Grim Reaper. All in all, for a man who didn't believe in the paranormal, Adam was having something of a wild initiation.

"Our baby is one part of the best thing that's happened to me," he said, enjoying the blush that stained her cheeks. "And here is another."

At that moment, Tarek emerged from his room to remind Maja that he needed to take something for show-and-tell the next day. It looked like persuading him that it couldn't be Leo might take some time. On reflection, Adam didn't know whether to be sorry or relieved that the moment of intimacy was lost. With every minute that passed he felt himself drawn to Maja. But nothing had changed.

A thought flitted through his head, futile and frustrating. *If only she could make me immortal...or I could make her human.*

If only one of them could break down the barriers and join the other's world. It wasn't going to happen.

They had more chance of Knight repenting and giving up his evil ways. Which meant each time Adam answered the powerful tug that was pulling him closer to Maja, he was making it harder for himself to break away when the time came for her to leave.

It didn't matter. He could tell himself that over and over. He could get it as a tattoo. Make it his ringtone. He was already in too deep. He was powerless to resist her. Which meant that as well as finding a way to expose Knight Valentine to the world, he was just going to have to find a way to make sure he didn't lose his family.

Chapter 16

The department store was busy and Tarek trailed behind Maja with a long-suffering expression. The video
game he wanted had been out of stock, and although
they had ordered it, as far as he was concerned the shopping expedition had lost its appeal.

Trailing around a busy store with a reluctant eight-
year-old in her wake was not Maja's idea of a pleasant
way to spend an afternoon, and she was about to suggest they leave when Tarek took her by surprise.

"Are you having a baby?"

"What makes you ask that?" She stalled for time.

"You are sick every morning." She had hoped she'd
hidden that from him. Clearly her attempts had failed.
"And you look at baby clothes. A lot. In catalogs. On
Adam's laptop. Here in the store."

"Would you mind if I was?"

Tarek appeared to give the matter some thought. "Will you send me back to Syria when the baby comes?"

"No." The words brought a lump to her throat. Ignoring the other shoppers around them, she stooped and wrapped her arms around him. "That will never happen. I love you, Tarek. So does Adam. Your home is here..." She wanted to finish the sentence by saying "with us" but she couldn't. There was no "us" and it would be unfair to give him false hope that she would be part of his life forever. "This is where you belong, and the baby will be a new brother or sister to you."

"In that case, I don't mind." He sounded cheerful. "If it's a boy, do you think you might call him Thor?"

"Probably not."

He sighed. "I thought you might say that. It's the name of my favorite character in the game we just ordered. Can we get ice cream on the way home?"

Once again, his resilience amazed her. Laughing, she took his hand and they made their way to the escalator. They were almost there when, out of the corner of her eye, Maja caught sight of something that made her pause. Two women were browsing through a pile of sale items, but they were watching Maja and Tarek.

Maja knew all the Valkyries.

Which made it almost laughable that these two would imagine that she wouldn't recognize them as they stood in the middle of a New York department store and pretended not to be following her. At least they had dressed in mortal clothing instead of their traditional garments. Maja thought back to her first encounter with Adam, when she had been clad in her Valkyrie attire. No wonder he had believed he was dreaming.

Aurora and Lotus were dryads who had joined the

a security guard, hundreds of people would have been killed that day."

"I wonder how Knight recruited these people," Maja murmured. "It's hard to believe they've all made a pact with Satan."

"Knight can be very persuasive. And looking down this list, I'd say we're not dealing with the nicest group of men and women. Although I have to agree. I don't imagine Knight has mentioned his silent partner. Even this little group would run screaming from the room if they knew they were dealing with the devil. They can turn a blind eye when it comes to killing and maiming innocent people for the sake of money, but add in horns and a tail and I'd imagine they would freak out." Adam flipped the top sheet over. "This next spreadsheet is interesting. It's a list of dates, past and future, each about six months apart."

Maja wrinkled her nose. "You find that interesting?"

He laughed. "Not in itself."

They had once again waited until Tarek was asleep before discussing the problem confronting them. Maja had told him that Tarek had figured out the news about the baby. When they'd sat him down and discussed it, he had surprised Adam by being mildly pleased. Apart from pushing strongly for a superhero name, and expressing a desire not to share a room, he had appeared unperturbed.

"You won't make me wear anything that says Big Brother, will you?" Tarek had directed a searching look at Maja. "There was a kid at school whose parents had a new baby, and his mom made him do that for a family picture. He was teased for days."

pers balanced on a woman's lap as, on a table close by, a full glass of champagne fizzed temptingly. The caption beneath the picture read No Rest for the Wicked. "As you can see, her location was Greenwich, Connecticut, USA. The time and date match this spreadsheet exactly."

"Greenwich? You think she was at Valentine House?" Maja asked. "That's where they meet?"

"I checked it out. None of the other people on this list have homes there, or any affiliation to the area. No reason to be there that I could discover. But Knight's house would be the obvious place to meet," Adam pointed out. "Knight controls the environment. You saw how difficult it is to get in. Security is rigid and privacy is guaranteed."

He went to another tab. "This is Alain Dubois, head of one of the top French retail companies. His chain of high-end clothing stores dominates the market. I've met him once or twice. The guy would sell his own grandmother if the price was right. A few hours before Suzanne was sharing her champagne picture, Alain was complaining about jet lag." Adam pointed to the screen. "Although his post is in French, the translation is straightforward. 'Transatlantic flights are the worst. Now facing a thirty-mile cab ride. But looking forward to catching up with friends in a beautiful, waterfront setting and a productive meeting.' Again, he shared his location. When he posted that, he was at JFK Airport."

"That doesn't prove they were at the same meeting," Maja said. "All it tells us is that he was in New York that day. We don't even know for sure that he went to Greenwich."

"No, it doesn't. Except Greenwich is about thirty

miles from JFK. And Suzanne and Charlie Hannon both 'liked' Alain's comment. Again, it proves nothing. But it gives me a gut feeling about their connection to each other. If nothing else, it says they were checking out each other's social media feed that day." He opened another tab. "Finally, we have the four-star general himself. Shepherd doesn't use social media."

Adam indicated a picture of a tall, straight-backed man with iron-gray hair descending the steps of a helicopter. He was dressed casually in jeans, leather jacket and distinctive blue-and-tan cowboy boots. "This was snapped at Westchester County Airport around the same time that Alain was arriving at JFK. You can see that the photograph was taken with a long-distance lens. It featured in an article written by a reporter who is highly critical of what he calls Shepherd's 'inactivity' over the Reaper. The article questioned what Shepherd was doing in New York when there had been a Reaper attack in Sweden the day before. Since Shepherd was appointed to lead the international force against the Reaper, there was strong feeling that he should at least have made an appearance at the scene." Adam shifted position so he was facing Maja again. "In case we were in any doubt about what we were up against, the guy who wrote that article was found dead the day after it was published."

"Didn't anyone ever connect his death to Shepherd or the Reaper?"

"He left a suicide note," Adam said. "Just as I'm sure I would when the time came."

Maja's hand crept into his. "That time will not come." Her voice shook slightly and Adam raised her fingers to his lips.

"This was what finally convinced me." He went back to Suzanne Sumner's picture. "Look here." He pointed to the top corner. Above the champagne glass, a man's crossed leg could be seen on the opposite side of the table. He was wearing jeans, and part of a distinctive blue-and-tan cowboy boot could also be seen.

"Adam." Maja raised wide eyes to his face. "You should be a detective."

He laughed. "Has Tarek been getting you to watch daytime TV with him?"

She nodded. "But none of those cops are as good as you."

"There are clues for some of the other dates, but none of them are as conclusive as this." Adam closed the lid of his laptop. "Of course, it only means something to us. To anyone else, including the authorities, it's meaningless." He pointed to the spreadsheet. "But it does give us the date of the next meeting."

Maja leaned over to read the information. "That's only two days from now."

"We have to act fast." He pushed a hand through his hair. "I run one of the biggest media organizations in the world. If we could get a recording of their meeting, I can broadcast it worldwide. That would stop them in their tracks. But getting past Knight's security? I'm struggling with the logistics of that."

Maja remained silent, but something about her expression intrigued him. It was just a little too innocent. "Maja, are you up to something?"

"No."

"I don't believe you."

She smiled, smoothing a hand over his chest. "I promise not to do anything you won't like."

Adam groaned. "So you *are* up to something?"

"I have an idea, but right now I don't even know if it will become a plan. Trust me, if it ever gets that far, I'll tell you."

He gazed into the endless blue of her eyes and nodded. "I'll trust you. But promise you'll tell me if this idea of yours starts to develop into action?"

Her expression became serious. "I think it will be obvious if that happens."

Adam took Maja's hand and led her into his dressing room. It was a large space lined with shelves and hanging rails. Adam had a lot of clothes. All of them were expensive. All of them had that delicious Adam smell.

"I've been considering having this space converted into a nursery. I thought we could talk to the designer together at the weekend."

The slight smile on his face changed to a look of astonishment as she started to cry.

"Maja, what have I said to upset you? I thought you'd be happy."

"I am happy. It's just..."

How could she explain it to him? He knew as well as she did how uncertain their future was. How could they consider something like a color scheme for a nursery when they didn't know where their baby would be living? Didn't Adam know her heart was breaking every time she thought about it? There didn't seem to be any way out of this dilemma. Every time she tried to focus, her thoughts became bricks in a wall, piling higher and higher and then tumbling down, burying her beneath their weight.

She wanted to stay here with Adam and their child.

And with Tarek. And Danny, if he returned. This felt like her home in a way Valhalla never had. She knew why that was. She loved Adam. Loved him with a certainty and fierceness that was never going away. Despite her tears, the admission made her heart soar. She, the hard-hearted Valkyrie, had succumbed to a range of emotions so vivid it was like she had hurled herself headlong into a rose garden. The color, scent and texture of her feelings for Adam were overwhelming.

But there were thorns. She knew he cared for her. Of course he did. He held her in his arms every night. There was no escaping the tenderness in his touch and in his eyes. But forever wasn't for them. And even if by some miracle they could wave a magic wand and make it happen, Maja didn't know if that was what Adam would choose. They were having a child together, but would he want her, that baby's mother, to be a part of his life? Would he prefer to look back on this as a sweet interlude? Or possibly not even that, since their time together would always be interwoven with the horror of the discoveries about Knight and the Reaper?

"Just...?" Adam prompted.

She took a deep breath. "What does this mean, Adam? How do you see our future unfolding?"

He took her hands, drawing her to him and running a palm along her spine. "I wish I could give you an exact answer to that question. Instead, I'm going to tell you how I hope our future looks. After we defeat Knight, we are going to come back here and live happily ever after. You, me, Tarek and—when he or she is ready to make an appearance—our baby."

Happily ever after? Maja knew what that would mean to her. It would mean they could live together just the

way they were now. It would mean Adam didn't need
any other women, because he had her. She blinked back
a fresh rush of tears. It would mean he loved her as
much as she loved him. She didn't know if she could
presume that much. But she suddenly knew that she
couldn't take half measures. If by some miracle she
found a way to stay in the mortal realm and raise her
baby here, she wasn't going to settle for anything less.

"Because you want our baby to have a family?"

Adam leaned back slightly so he could look at her
face. "Yes, I want our baby to have a family. I want our
baby to have all the things I had until my father died.
But if there was no baby, I would want you, Maja." Her
heart began to thud loudly at the warm look in his eyes.
"Because I love you."

Unable to speak, she made a little choking sound and
rose on the tips of her toes. Wrapping her arms around
his neck, she pressed her lips to his in a kiss that lasted
for a very long time.

"I hope that means you love me, too?" Adam murmured when he raised his head.

"More than you will ever know." What was it about
crying? It happened when she was sad *and* when she
was happy. She was going to blame baby hormones.
"But we don't know if I can stay here."

His arms tightened around her waist. "Maja, all I
know for sure is that, while there is breath in my body,
I will never let you go."

Chapter 17

Adam loved the feel of Maja's silken heat clasping him, her inner muscles tightening around him. The tiny gurgle she made as he thrust deeper into her. He was caught in a whirlwind of sensation, feeling it swirling around him, sinking into it, letting it tear him apart.

A day had passed since he told her he loved her, and he hadn't tired of the reality. He just wondered what had taken him so long.

Pleasure like this was once-in-a-lifetime. He knew that now. That was what made their lovemaking so sweet. She belonged to him. There were no barriers between them. Because he loved her, he would never stop needing her. The feelings she aroused in him were so powerful it felt like wildfire spreading through his bloodstream.

The emotional intensity of what he felt when they

made love was more extreme than the physical pleasure. Opening his heart to another person after years of believing it could never happen was a unique sensation. It had frightened him when he hadn't recognized it, made him feel vulnerable. Now he knew what it was—knew it was love and it was reciprocated—it thrilled him, taking his arousal to new heights.

He kissed her long and deep, drugging kisses that swept them further into rapture and had Maja writhing to press closer to him.

"Don't stop." The words came out in a ragged groan.

His hips jerked as she clenched around him, drawing him farther into her, holding him tighter as if she never wanted to let him go.

He slid a hand between their bodies, pressing the pad of his thumb against her clit, and Maja cried out, her whole body jerking wildly. Adam rolled his thumb, pressing the little bud, feeling it swell further.

"Oh, that feels so good." She lifted her legs, gripping his hips with her knees and arching her back as he pumped harder and faster.

She was so hot and wet, it was like she was stroking him with fire, possessing him with her tight muscles. Adam's cock throbbed and grew even thicker inside her, stretching her, opening her to him.

He watched her face, drinking in every tiny movement. Her eyes widened and her body tensed as he paused, buried fully inside her. Pulling back, he drank in the flare of pleasure in the depths of her eyes, giving in to the perfection of the moment before surrendering to the hunger tearing through him. With a thrust of his hips, he drove back into her, pushing into the tight clasp of her vagina. Each stroke was a new arousal, each thrust took him closer to perfection, each jerk of his erection pushed him closer to the edge of his control.

Locking his gaze on hers, he filled her, throbbing as he impaled her. The flames inside him burned brighter, searing his balls, scorching a path up his spine and triggering explosions along his nerve endings.

Maja tensed and cried out with her own climax as release erupted inside Adam in a wave of destructive rapture. It stripped everything from him. He had no energy, no breath, no senses and no thoughts. All that remained was this wild power overtaking him, storming through his veins, along his nerve endings like a thousand-volt electrical shock. Maja was shaking in his hold, gripping his shoulders tightly and crying out his name, as he continued to drive into her, riding the crest of the wave until they were both spent.

Gradually, the tremors stopped and Adam eased out of Maja, moving to lie at her side and wrapping his arms around her.

"This feels like a very decadent way to spend an afternoon." Maja stretched her arms above her head lazily.

Tarek and Sophie, with their shared love of gaming, had gone to a convention. Although Maja had made a halfhearted attempt to get Adam to accompany her on a walk in the park, he had dragged her off to bed almost as soon as the door closed behind the two.

"I am about to be even more decadent and go in search of coffee and cookies. Join me?" He reached for his boxer briefs and T-shirt, which were lying at the side of the bed.

"Luckily, since it would be bad for the baby, I have never succumbed to the mortal obsession for caffeine.

But cookies sound good." Maja also pulled on underwear and a T-shirt.

In the kitchen, Adam wrapped his arms around her and rested his chin on the top of her head. "As crazy as it seems to say , with everything that's going with Knight... I'm happy. I can't remember the last time I said that. I don't know if I've ever said it."

Maja lifted her head to look at him. The smile in her eyes corresponded with the one in his heart. Before she could say anything, there was an almighty crash and the sound of Leo howling in terror.

"What the...?"

Adam dashed into the entrance hall of the apartment, with Maja at his heels. The door was open and the whole area was filled with smoke. Standing in the center of the tiled space, an impressive figure placed her hands on her hips and glared at him. Leo, crouching low so that his belly touched the floor, bustled up to Maja, and she scooped him into her arms.

Adam recognized the woman's clothing. It was identical to the outfit Maja had been wearing when he first met her. This Valkyrie looked like Maja. Her hair was a darker shade of gold and her features, while still beautiful, were slightly harsher. This must be one of Maja's sisters.

"Here in the mortal realm, we have a custom you might want to try next time. It's called knocking." Adam closed the door as he spoke.

The frown that descended on her face was clearly intended to terrify him. In other circumstances, it might have worked. If it wasn't for pacts with the devil and Grim Reapers, he would have feared this apparition and her scowl. Now he had gone beyond terror and shock. He was in a state of supernatural overload.

"You dare address the daughter of Odin? Kneel before me, mortal, and tremble at my feet."

"Oh, stop being so dramatic." There was a note of amusement in Maja's voice. "Adam, I think it's time you were introduced to my sister. This is Brynhild."

It took some doing, but Maja persuaded Brynhild to join her in the sitting room.

"This is not a social call. Your hiding place was revealed to me by one of Odin's servants who saw you here. I am here to escort you to Valhalla."

Clearly threatening the man who had followed her, punching him and tipping him into a Dumpster had not been enough to deter him after all.

"Just listen to me, please?"

Beneath her fierce exterior, Brynhild had a kind heart, Maja knew. Possibly the kindest she had ever known. Although Brynhild's devotion to duty was legendary, Maja was hoping to tap in to the love she had for her sisters. Valkyries weren't supposed to have feelings, but Maja could see with hindsight just how deeply Brynhild cared for her siblings. She was the one who'd brought them up, taught them the skills they needed to survive, developed them into powerful warriors. She protected them from Odin's wrath, often at the expense of her own well-being.

Maja wasn't fooling herself. The magnitude of the task ahead of her was enormous. Asking Odin's devoted general to go against his wishes? Just the idea of it made her blood run cold. But she thought of the sister who had raised her. The sister who understood her. The sister who, even now, looked at her with affection. Maja knew she had to try. She pressed a hand to her stomach.

Not just for myself. For all of us.

Although she handed Leo to Adam and signaled for him to leave them, she was conscious of his presence just outside the room. The knowledge that he was there strengthened her resolve.

"Who is that mortal?" Brynhild's voice was outraged. "And why are you here with him? Interacting with him. In this state of undress. Maja, you know the Code..."

"His name is Adam Lyon." She took a steadying breath. "And he is the father of my unborn child."

Until that moment, Maja had never seen Brynhild at a loss for words. Her mouth opened, but nothing happened. When she tried again, a tiny croak emerged. In that instant, Maja felt sorry for her. She could almost read her sister's mind. The reputation of the Valkyries rested on Brynhild's shoulders. Odin might have conceived the idea of the female fighters who escorted the fallen to Valhalla, but Brynhild was the one who had built them into the elite force they were today. She was the one who would ultimately be blamed if they were disgraced.

"Sit down." Maja patted the place next to her on the sofa.

Moving mechanically, Brynhild obeyed. "This is my fault."

"What do you mean?"

"I should never have sent you to Warda. You were inexperienced. And this rebellious streak of yours was always there. Just like—" She broke off, appearing to think better of whatever she had been about to say.

"Just like?" Maja prompted.

Brynhild shook her head. "It doesn't matter. I should have known better. I am to blame."

Maja laughed. "This isn't about fault or blame. I'm having a baby. You are going to be an aunt. Can't we be happy about that?"

"You know we can't. The Allfather's rage will be like nothing we have ever seen." Brynhild took Maja's hand in her own. "I don't know if I can save you from it."

"Must you tell him?" It was a suggestion Adam had made, and it had taken a hold on Maja's newly discovered imagination.

There was that look again. Brynhild was stunned. Throughout her life, Maja had believed her sister was indestructible. Today she was discovering that Brynhild was just another woman. A woman who didn't always have the answers. It was quite an eye-opener.

"Deceive the Allfather? How can you suggest such a thing?"

"It's not deceiving him if you don't mention that you know where I am. If you take me back to Valhalla, he will have me and my unborn child killed." Maja paused and watched Brynhild's face as that information sank in. She saw the flare of emotion in the blue depths of her sister's eyes and relished it. That momentary lapse told her Brynhild would do all she could to prevent that. It told her she was right. Maja wasn't the only Valkyrie who could experience love. "While you think about it, there is something else with which I need your help."

"You don't think asking me to save you from Odin's rage when you are carrying a human child is enough?" Brynhild's lips curved into a smile.

Maja returned the smile with relief. Her sister was on

her side. Life had just gotten a little bit brighter. "This might score points with Odin. You know how much he loves mortals, and my plan involves helping humanity."

"You make it sound huge."

"It is." Maja bit her lip. Would Brynhild agree to her next request? "I need Adam here to help me explain."

Brynhild held up her hands in horror. "I cannot interact with a mortal."

"Brynhild, there is a consortium of humans posing as a terrorist organization, and Adam can prevent them from killing more people, but he needs our help."

"This is outside of the Valkyrie Code. You know our task is to escort the souls of the fallen to Valhalla. Interfering in mortal problems is not part of our job." Brynhild's expression was closed. This was the great general doing what she did best, refusing to be swayed from her position.

"The leader of this group is in league with the devil and he reaps souls on his master's behalf. He may be taking those intended for Valhalla." Maja didn't know if that was true. But she didn't know it wasn't... She saw the moment Brynhild wavered. "What harm can it do to listen? Odin will never know, and you may be able to save many brave warriors from the Reaper's scythe."

"Very well." The words were issued through a jaw that was clenched tight.

When Adam came into the room, Maja was pleased to see he had donned a pair of sweatpants. At least her sister's sense of decency would be appeased.

"You don't have any cause to love me." As he sat down and took Maja's hand, he spoke to Brynhild's averted face. "But we both love your sister, so I hope we can put aside our differences and do what's best for her."

Since there was no noticeable thaw in Brynhild's manner at his words, Maja decided to outline what they knew about Knight Valentine. Her sister listened in silence, speaking only when Maja had finished her explanation.

"Your plan is to unmask this group by—" Brynhild flapped a hand as though seeking the right words "—producing a moving picture with sound that reproduces their meeting? You will then distribute this throughout the world so that everyone can see exactly what they are doing?"

"Yes, but the problem will be getting past the security guards at Knight's house. It's heavily guarded. And of course, they are not going to conduct their meeting willingly if they know they are being filmed," Adam said.

"It seems you have set yourselves an impossible task." Brynhild had thawed slightly and was actually facing in Adam's general direction now.

"That would be the case." Maja looked from Adam to Brynhild. "If we didn't know a small army of people who can make themselves invisible."

Adam started to laugh. "This was the idea you had?"

She nodded. "Now you know why I didn't tell you. I needed Brynhild to come here so I could ask her to make it happen."

"Since I *am* here—" Brynhild's frosty tones cut across their conversation "—maybe someone could explain to me what you are talking about?"

"We can use a group of Valkyries to get past Knight's guards and into Valentine House. If we are invisible, we can hide in the room and film the meeting." She turned to Adam. "Maybe on cell phones?"

He nodded. "That would work. Even better is we use high-tech hand cameras and stream it live."

"I hate to interrupt your plans, but the Allfather will never allow this," Brynhild said.

"Does he need to know about it?" Maja asked. There. She had dared to say it. To suggest that Odin could be defied. Not once, but twice. Not only could Brynhild hide the fact that she knew where Maja was, but she could go a step further and help bring down Knight and the Reaper consortium. "Once it is done, there will be nothing he can do about it."

The question hung in the balance. She could see Brynhild weighing the two sides of the argument. She could choose to save human lives and defeat evil. Or she could do what she had always done and be Odin's loyal general, afraid to make a move without his approval.

"If I do this without his consent, his fury will move mountains." Brynhild's voice sounded different. Breathy and excited. That was the moment when Maja knew she was considering it.

"There will be other Valkyries involved. He can't kill us all," Maja said.

"He can't, can he?" A flicker of a smile crossed her sister's lips. Maja got the feeling she was thinking of other times when the Allfather's temper had moved mountains. Maja might be the only Valkyrie with a rebellious streak, but maybe Brynhild had a few scores to settle.

For the first time, she looked directly at Adam. "I will do this."

One of the most surprising things about the apartment being filled with Valkyries was the way Leo quickly became resigned to the situation. The little dog seemed to feel that if Adam and Maja were okay with this number of visitors, he should accept them, too. After sniffing around their feet in curiosity, he wandered off to Tarek's room and curled up on the rug.

Tarek was at school and the arrangement was for Sophie to collect him and take him out for dinner and to see a movie after he had done his homework. Adam had made the excuse that he and Maja were going to see his elderly aunt again.

"We will take you to see her one day." Adam had felt guilty about the lie and hoped he had done a good enough job of convincing Tarek.

Clearly, he had failed. The boy's bright eyes had scanned his face for a moment or two. "Will you tell me all about it when it's over?"

"What do you mean?"

"I know this is about the Reaper. That means you can't tell me now, but I'd like to know what happens when it's finished."

Adam recounted the conversation afterward to Maja. "Is he very perceptive because of what he's been through, do you think? Or is it something unique about him?"

"He's supersmart." She said it with a note of pride. "But he's also tuned in to you and me—what we're thinking and feeling—because he's scared of losing us the way he did his father. I hope he hasn't been worrying about this."

"It will be over soon."

And one way or another, it would. Adam had never given a thought to the future. If anyone had asked him, he would have said—vaguely—that if anything ever happened to him, Danny would inherit everything he had. He still hoped to find Danny, of course, but until recently, he'd had no other responsibilities, so no reason to care beyond that. Lately, the situation had changed. Last week Adam had met with his attorney and made a more formal arrangement. Now, he had ensured that Tarek would be taken care of. He was now his adopted son and Elvira and Sophie were named as the boy's legal guardians if anything should happen to Adam. It was more difficult to make provision for the unborn baby, mainly because Maja didn't officially exist. Instead, Adam had inserted a clause in his will bequeathing the bulk of his fortune to his children, including Tarek and any yet to be born. His attorney had agreed that the change was legal and had assured Adam that it would be upheld.

There were twelve Valkyries in the apartment, including Maja. These were the true daughters of Odin. Although they all looked alike, Adam was able to view them critically and decide that none of them were as beautiful as *his* Valkyrie. He knew, of course, that he didn't have a warrior princess fetish, but it was nice to have this confirmation. These blue-eyed blondes were all good to look at, but they didn't move him in any way. There was only one Valkyrie for him, and how he felt about her had nothing to do with her shield maiden status. His connection to Maja was about who she was inside. And who she was inside was perfect for him.

Although his visitors looked like a group of catwalk models, they acted more like a squad of GIs. Having abandoned their Valkyrie garb in favor of casual, human clothing, they were being briefed by Maja on what to expect when they reached Valentine House. Although they weren't quite standing at attention, there was nothing relaxed about their stance. Clearly, they had been told by Brynhild to interact as little as possible with Adam, since they treated him as if he was the one with the powers of invisibility.

He didn't like the feeling of being an outsider in his own home. Maja, obviously picking up on his discomfort, gave him a sympathetic smile once or twice and he shrugged in response. He would do whatever it took to end this. The disdain of a few Valkyries was nothing in comparison to what was at stake.

Whatever gets us through this day and out the other side with a recording of the Reaper meeting.

This plan of Maja's was all they had. Even if it didn't get them the recording they sought, it might shake up the Reaper consortium by letting them know someone was onto them.

When Adam mentioned the logistics of transporting a small army of shield maidens to Greenwich, Brynhild gave him a pitying look. "We are Valkyries. We will make our own arrangements."

Maja's older sister was beginning to seriously get on his nerves. Although her help on this mission was invaluable, Brynhild was determined to put Adam in his place. She never missed an opportunity to sneer at him, or remind him of his lowly status in comparison to her and her sisters. He got it. His parents were mortal; their father was a god. He wanted to point out that there was no comparison. He'd take Robert Lyon over a moody deity any day. But getting into a petty argument with Brynhild wasn't going to make the task ahead of them any easier. No matter how much it might feel like a good way to relieve some of the pressure cooker of emotions building inside him.

"The meeting is scheduled to start in three hours. Since I don't have the benefit of a winged horse, I'm going to head out to Greenwich now and watch the house as the members arrive."

Although he spoke to Maja, it was Brynhild who answered him. "Very well." She gave a dismissive wave.

Maja took Adam's hand as she faced her sister. "We will see you there."

"We?" Adam had an expensive heating system, but Brynhild's expression was doing its best to override it as she looked at their clasped hands. "You will come with us, Maja. You are a Valkyrie."

"I'm going with Adam." Maja's chin had that willful tilt to it. The one that always made him want to kiss her. He decided against it on this occasion.

It was a declaration. Maja was telling Brynhild loud and clear that she might be a Valkyrie, but her loyalties had changed. The atmosphere shifted in that instant. Adam saw a flicker of emotion in Brynhild's eyes. There was sadness, but it was followed by respect. He thought there was something more. Something that had stirred up memories Brynhild would have preferred to let lie.

She nodded. "You have made your decision and I will respect it."

Chapter 18

From their vantage point in the trees, Adam and Maja watched as the members of the Reaper consortium arrived at Valentine House. The security had been stepped up since their last visit; this time, they evaded guards and dodged new cameras before they reached a point from which they could view the house. Adam got no satisfaction from being right about this. Some of the most powerful men and women in the world had signed up to this alliance.

He wondered how Knight had recruited these people. It wasn't the sort of subject a person could ask over a business lunch. *"Hey, how would you like to make billions by joining me in a new venture? The catch? Well, we have to finance a terrorist organization that will commit atrocities as a front for wiping out our business rivals."* It needed just one slip—to ask one person

with a conscience who was willing to go to the police—
and Knight's cover would have been blown wide-open.

But he had clearly selected these people carefully.
Adam couldn't think of a nastier group. A conscience?
They couldn't raise one between them if they tried.
Adam had a reputation for ruthlessness, but each of
these people he observed made him look like a Boy
Scout.

Knight stood on the sweeping gravel drive, greet-
ing his guests. General Shepherd was the first to arrive. Adam felt a knot of cold, hard contempt tighten his
gullet as he watched the two men shake hands. Shepherd had been decorated for bravery. Had led his men
in action countless times. Served his country with loyalty and honor. At what point had he become *this* man?
Every day Shepherd had to look the leaders of the free
world and his fellow soldiers in the eye and tell them
he was no closer to finding the Reaper. Adam hoped
the words choked him. Even if they did, the sensation
was likely soothed by the thought of the billions he had
probably stashed in an offshore account.

Designer-clad Suzanne Sumner arrived next. Adam
had almost done business with her a few years ago. He
recalled her kittenish smile and relentless flirting. They
hid the venomous fangs of a snake. And that was probably unfair to snakes. He had pulled out of the deal when
he discovered one of Suzanne's companies used child
labor. She had proceeded to bad-mouth him, telling
anyone who would listen he was bitter because he had
made sexual advances and she had turned him down.

Charlie Hannon, a guy whom Adam was sure had
crawled out from under a rock, was next to emerge
from a cab. Adam had to fight the impulse to break his

cover so he could punch the self-satisfied grin from Hannon's face. The Englishman had made his money through internet porn and webcam services before moving into the more mainstream role of running a public relations firm. Now the lines had become blurred as Hannon himself regularly appeared on reality television programs, while managing the careers of some of the highest profile celebrities in the world.

Alain Dubois shared a ride with Donna Webb, founder of the world's second largest sportswear company. Adam bit back a smile. *Second* largest. He knew from experience how much she hated being reminded of that.

The final three were people he didn't know personally. A Saudi Arabian oil executive, an Italian hotel magnate and a Silicon Valley technology genius.

"They are all here." Adam watched as Knight followed the last of his guests inside the house.

"The meeting isn't scheduled to start for another hour," Maja said.

"It's lunchtime. I expect they'll eat first." Adam led her farther into the trees, finding the midpoint where they had arranged to meet Brynhild and the other Valkyries.

Maja shook her head. "They will be filling their stomachs and then planning mass murder?"

"That about sums it up. Knight might be the only one who made it formal, but each of those people is in league with the devil. The others just don't know it yet."

Adam and Maja had followed the same route they had taken the last time they had come to the house, following the shoreline until they reached the shelter of these trees. Because Adam was hampered by his inabil-

ity to become invisible, his task would be to coordinate
the activity of the Valkyries. He was frustrated at the
thought that he couldn't take part in the action, but he
had planned this carefully. He knew the layout of the
house and had directed Maja's sisters until they were
word perfect and could recite his directions back to him.

His concern was about Maja's role. Because of the
baby, Adam didn't want her involved at all, but she was
the only other person who had been inside the house.
She was also the only Valkyrie he really trusted to use
a camera. When he had given the others a training session in how to record a video on the tiny cameras he had
passed out, the results had ranged from poor to nonex-
istent. He was relying on Maja to get him the footage
they needed.

He had initially been worried that, although the
Valkyries would be invisible, the cameras would not.
How would that look? Twelve cameras floating around
Valentine House? There was no way that wouldn't
arouse attention, and he couldn't think of any way to
disguise them. Luckily, Maja had explained how it
worked.

"As long as the items we carry are small, they become invisible, too. If they didn't, our swords and daggers would give us away."

His lack of knowledge of all things paranormal had
let him down yet again. It made things a hell of a lot easier. The plan was for the Valkyries, all of them invisible,
to get into the house, each carrying a small backpack
containing the things they would need for this mission.
Their first task was to take out the security guards.

"You are under strict instructions to stay out of any

fighting. The baby comes first, remember?" he told Maja.

"You have told me that several times already."

"I thought it was worth another reminder." He knew his feisty Valkyrie only too well. If there was trouble, she would be in the thick of it.

Once the security guards were no longer a threat, Brynhild would lead her warriors into the meeting room. Maja, cloaked by invisibility, had sneaked over to the house and checked out the room where the meeting would be held. This was in a separate building from the main house. Situated near the pool, it was a single-story, purpose-built annex. Adam remembered Knight always used it for business meetings. It was comfortable and completely private.

On her return, she had confirmed that the room was already set up for a meeting. The six French windows were unlocked and three of these were open, affording a view of the gardens and the water beyond. It was a beautiful day and there was no reason to suppose anyone would lock the windows before the meeting started. To be absolutely sure, Maja had followed Adam's instructions and filled the locks with superglue, ensuring that the doors would remain open to admit the Valkyries.

Although all twelve of them would be in the room and filming, the focus was Maja. The others were there as her bodyguards. Since she was the most experienced, she was the one who was to film the meeting from start to finish, come what may.

Although Adam was near crazy with worry when he thought about Maja in close proximity to Knight, she reminded him that she would be invisible. Her pregnancy gave his fears for her safety an added edge, but the thought of the other Valkyries acting as her protectors helped calm his nerves.

Adam had configured the cameras so they would be live streaming their recordings to social media as they were filming. His job would be to use an electronic tablet to edit the stream and direct traffic to that site from other places. Adam had a vast social media presence. He would be able to use that to generate a huge amount of interest in the meeting, particularly once he mentioned the Reaper.

He still wasn't happy at the idea of sending Maja into that room without him, but Brynhild would be there. He had to have confidence in the Valkyrie leader's ability to take care of her sister. Anything else was unthinkable.

The Valkyries arrived with over an hour to spare before the meeting, and they talked through the plan one last time. Although Brynhild had no idea what Adam was talking about when it came to the technology, she had a clear grasp of her role. She would lead her sisters to overcome the security guards, while ensuring Maja's safety. They might not agree on anything else, but Adam and Brynhild were both focused on those twin outcomes. If they could ever be brought to see it, they were actually quite alike.

"I want you to do something for me." Maja had been waiting for the opportunity to get Brynhild alone.

"If this involves keeping any more secrets from the Allfather, I'm going to stop you right there."

"It's nothing like that. Did you ever find the warrior called the American Lion?" Maja cast a look over her shoulder to where Adam was crouched in the shrubs, watching the house from his hiding place.

"No, he has disappeared from my charts, much to Odin's annoyance. He really wanted that hero to join his army. Why do you ask?"

"I think I may know his identity." She threw another glance in Adam's direction. *Leave my brother out of this.* That was what he had said to her when they first met. But he was no closer to discovering Danny's whereabouts. And Brynhild might be able to help. "If I'm right, his name is Daniel Lyon and he is Adam's brother. Could you find out where he is, or what happened to him?"

"I'll see what I can do, but you know it isn't always simple."

"If you can try, I'd be grateful."

Brynhild followed the direction of Maja's gaze. "This thing with you and the mortal…it's serious, isn't it?"

"I love him."

There was genuine curiosity in Brynhild's expression. "How do you know?"

"Because I couldn't live without him." Maja didn't have to think about her answer. She continued before Brynhild could respond. "Do you think I don't know how much easier it would be *not* to love him? Loving Adam is hard. If there were ever two people who were not meant to be together, it's us. We come from separate worlds—our paths should never have crossed. The only things we have in common are an orphan and a dog. It would be so much easier if we could *not* love each other."

"So why don't you just stop it?"

"Because my first thought when I wake up in the morning is of Adam. Throughout the day, whenever I think of him, I smile. Every time I hear his voice, even if he's just talking on the phone to someone else, my heart skips a beat with pure joy. If he's not in the room, I glance up every time I hear a sound in case it's him coming through the door. When I go to bed at night, I hope I'll dream of him. If I say something that makes him laugh, I feel like I've won a prize." A smile trembled on her lips. "Those are a few of the reasons why I can't just switch off my love for him."

Brynhild was silent for a moment. "I didn't know it was like that."

"Nor did I. And although it is hard, I would not miss a minute."

"And you will have his child."

Maja straightened her spine. "Proudly. No matter what the Valkyrie Code says, I am not ashamed of loving Adam."

"Do you wonder if your child will inherit your magical abilities?"

Maja laughed. "If our child takes after Adam, he or she will be magical."

Before Brynhild could reply, Adam tapped his watch, signaling that it was time for them to move.

"Remember, the security guards are based in the turrets." He indicated the four towers, one at each corner of the house. "They will be watching the grounds for any signs of intruders, but they won't see you coming, of course."

He turned to Maja. "You remember how to use the camera?"

"Yes, Adam. Because you have shown me at least five times." She grinned mischievously. "And unlike my sisters, I have used a camera before. Tarek likes me to take photographs or videos of Leo while he is at school so he knows what his dog has been doing during the day."

He returned the smile. "I'm sorry. Was I being obsessive?"

"Maybe just a little." Ignoring her sisters, she stepped up close, enjoying the way his arms instantly closed around her. "I love you," she whispered.

"I love you more."

"Not possible." She pressed her cheek against his chest briefly before pulling reluctantly away.

She was aware of Adam and Brynhild staring at each other over the top of her head.

"Look after her." She had never heard that note in Adam's voice before. It was almost a plea.

"I intend to," Brynhild said.

Although they would get into the meeting room from the garden, they would have to go into the main house to access the turrets.

Maja led the way through the cellars using Adam's keys. Because the whole group was invisible, the only problem she could foresee was the point when they would emerge from the cellar into the storage area at the back of the kitchen. If Knight and his guests were dining here at Valentine House, someone must be cooking for them and serving their food. That meant the kitchen would be in use.

No one would see the twelve Valkyries, but they would notice if the door to the cellar suddenly opened. There was a possibility a witness might be spooked by that rather than believing it to be evidence of a break-in. But Maja didn't want to take a chance. She didn't want to do anything that would mean Knight might cancel his meeting. Today was the day they were going to expose him and his evil consortium. She was determined about that.

The second danger point was the door from the storage room into the main hall of the house. Once again, they risked someone watching the door. Brynhild was ready to move in and silence anyone who did notice anything.

Maja felt a fierce sense of pride at the way her sisters had responded to her call for help. She knew they were obeying Brynhild's orders, but any one of them could have gone to Odin and told him what was going on. Instead they had chosen to risk his anger and support her. Brynhild had made it clear to them that the Allfather knew nothing of this venture. Odin was likely to be pleased at the outcome, since he would welcome the downfall of a group that brought harm to the human race. He would not willfully cause bloodshed, even if it meant more warriors for his great army. But he would not be impressed to learn of his daughters' defiance.

Stealth wasn't usually a priority for the Valkyries. Their environment was the battlefield, where noise and fury were normal. When they used invisibility to disguise their intentions, they had no real need to be furtive. Now, despite their invisibility, they had to work together to keep their presence secret. For the first time, it felt like all of them were a team.

At the same time, Maja felt sad. Because no matter what happened here, she was no longer part of this. While she didn't want to be, she wished they could have reached this point without having to face the threat of Knight Valentine. This sense of sisterhood shouldn't have been so hard to achieve. And now that they had it, could it last when their number was about to be depleted by one? That shouldn't be Maja's problem, but they were still her sisters. She would always be a Valkyrie, even if she wasn't a practicing member of the team. It had taken a problem to bring them together. She'd have liked to know how things worked out for them in the future.

When they reached the stairs that led to the storage room at the back of the kitchen, Maja went first, with Brynhild following close behind. She didn't need Adam's reminders about taking care of herself. Nothing was going to stop her doing this, but she was going to be careful for the baby's sake. Using the key to open the door at the top of the steps, Maja slowly turned the handle. The storage area appeared different from the last time she had been here. Then the house had been empty. Now, she could hear noises coming from the kitchen, and the aroma of food filled the air.

Even so, the storage area was empty. Maja released a sigh of relief as she beckoned Brynhild forward. The others followed. The last Valkyrie to emerge from the cellar closed the door behind her.

It wasn't just the sounds and scents from the kitchen that made this visit different. Maja felt it as soon as she left the cellar. The whole atmosphere had changed. It wasn't about her. It was nothing to do with being here with her sisters instead of Adam. It wasn't pregnancy hormones. It wasn't nervousness about making sure she got the recording right.

This impression was like a bad smell. Once imprinted on the nostrils, it was immediately recognizable again. She knew exactly what it was. Knight Valentine was in this house, giving off his own unique air of evil. The devil had marked him, and no amount of expensive cologne could disguise the underlying aroma.

Maja reached for the next obstacle. Her fingers closed over the handle of the door that led to the main corridor. She told herself it was ridiculous for her heart to be pounding so loudly. Even if she opened that door and Knight was standing on the other side, he couldn't see her.

It didn't matter. She had an image of those eyes boring into her. How she had felt in his office, that sense of undiluted malice, came back to her, sharp and bright. Her nerves were jangling so wildly that she had to wait until she stopped shaking.

She had known this plan would involve seeing Knight. Yet being closer to him again brought the reality of what that meant into focus. This man had brought so much misery into Adam's life. Had caused him so much personal damage. She had to focus on the way Adam had risen above that. He was strong and good and true, despite the things Knight Valentine had done to him and his family. Maybe, in some ways, because of them.

Was that going to stop her being horribly afraid when she looked into Knight's dead eyes once more? No. Would it stop her from wanting to place her hands around his throat and squeeze until his face turned blue or his devilish master turned up to save him? Again, the answer to that question was a resounding negative.

Brynhild placed a hand on her shoulder, checking that she was okay, and Maja nodded. *I can do this.*

With a hand that no longer shook, she turned the handle and opened the door a fraction. A glimpse of the corridor revealed that it was deserted, and she beckoned her sisters through into that part of the house, closing the door behind them. Last time she had been here, she and Adam had followed the passage to the right and entered Knight's study. This time, they needed to turn left and into the main entrance hall. They would have to climb the sweeping central staircase to access the turrets.

As Maja placed her foot on the first stair, she heard a burst of laughter coming from a room to her left. There was a buzz of conversation emerging from that direction. Adam had sketched a plan showing them the layout of the house. Maja recalled it now. The noise was coming from the dining room. It sounded like lunch was proving to be an enjoyable occasion.

As the Valkyries began their ascent of the stairs, the dining room door opened and Knight stepped into the hall. Although she was invisible, Maja instinctively pressed her body tight against the wall. Aware of Brynhild's surprise at this reaction, she used her fingers either side of her head to mimic a pair of devil horns.

Brynhild looked down from her vantage point several stairs above Knight as he crossed the hall. Turning back to Maja, she grimaced. Maja released the breath she had been holding. It wasn't just her. Her sister could feel it, too. The aura of evil that hung about him was tangible.

When she had attacked Knight in his office, Maja hadn't known what he was. If she had, she might have thought twice about her daring behavior. Maybe not. Her impulsiveness had always been the subject of much eye rolling from Brynhild over the years.

But Knight didn't know what I was, either. She had scared him. His deal with the devil conferred some gifts upon him, but it didn't make him all-knowing. Right now, he was striding across his hall, calling impatiently for someone to bring more wine, unaware that twelve Valkyries were standing on his stairs. She used that knowledge to strengthen her resolve. *We know what he is now, but he still has no idea what he is up against.*

Chapter 19

The turrets were accessed through the attics. The Valkyries split into teams of three, each team taking one of the four turrets. Since Maja was under strict instructions not to take part in any fighting, she accompanied Brynhild and Eir, the two most experienced Valkyries.

They entered stealthily. It was a circular room with windows all the way around. The view across the gardens was spectacular. Maja could see why Knight had chosen this house. For a man who wanted to maintain his privacy, this was perfect. Nothing could move on those grounds without the people in these towers knowing about it. Unless, like Adam, you had grown up in this house and, as a frightened child, found hiding places and ways to avoid detection.

In addition to the view over the grounds, the turret also contained a bank of monitors showing images of the interior of the house. Maja recognized the staircase they had climbed to reach these attics, and the meeting room in the grounds. She noted with relief that the French windows were still open.

There were two men inside the circular room, and that fitted with the information Adam had given her. He said Knight employed sixteen security guards, working in two teams of eight. This was the day shift. The setup was identical in each turret.

Brynhild and Eir stepped forward in a concerted movement, grabbing the men from behind before they could move. Adam had been uncompromising in his instructions. No killing unless it was unavoidable. Brynhild had curled her lip slightly when he gave that order.

"No killing? How very mortal."

"I am mortal and proud of it. Not killing my fellow humans is what raises me above Knight Valentine and his terrorists," Adam replied.

"It would be so much easier if we could break their necks." Brynhild had placed her hands on her hips, prepared to argue.

"I'll tell their families that, shall I?" Adam had faced her, his own expression equally immovable. "Maybe I'll do it at the graveside." *This was more convenient than tying them up and gagging them.* "I'm sure they'll understand."

The unthinkable had happened— Brynhild had backed down. Which was why the Valkyries' backpacks contained rope and duct tape.

It was over in seconds. Moving with superhuman speed and strength, Brynhild and Eir had the two men trussed up like a pair of turkeys ready to be roasted. Adam had decided that leaving them in these rooms would be a bad idea. It was unlikely anyone would come up here, but he didn't want to take any chances. Brynhild picked up one of the security guards and tossed him over her shoulder as easily as if he had been a child. Eir did the same with the other.

One of the attic rooms was large and well ventilated, and they carried their captives to this space. The other Valkyries met them there and they deposited all eight inside. Maja found the key on the bunch Adam had given her and locked the door.

Extracting her cell phone from her backpack, she checked the time. "The meeting is scheduled to start in fifteen minutes. We need to get into position."

Firing off a quick message to Adam to let him know the first part of their mission had been successful, she replaced her phone and they made their way back down the stairs.

Once they were out of the house and crossing the garden toward the pool, the feeling of dread lightened. Maja knew it was because she was no longer as close to Knight. The air here was not contaminated by his poison. She thought of Belinda, Adam's beautiful, frail mother. No wonder she hadn't survived. Exposed to Knight's malevolence, up close to it every day, it must have been like standing within range of the heat from a blast furnace.

The Valkyries entered the meeting room. A central table occupied much of the space. One chair had been placed at the head of the table, with four others at each side. Bottles of water had been set in front of each chair, along with pads of paper and pens. There were also bowls of candy in the center of the table.

"I'll stand here." Maja took up a position at the far

end, directly opposite the head of the table. That was where she knew Knight would sit. She wanted to keep her eyes—and her camera—on him all the time. Every word, every expression, everything that would tell the world who he really was…she didn't want to miss anything.

Directing her sisters to their places, she explained what she wanted from them. One camera on each of the other consortium members. The other three Valkyries would have an overview of the meeting. Each camera's footage would be live streamed directly to Adam. This way, she hoped he would get everything he needed.

Adam. She thought of him waiting back there in the trees. He would be almost out of his mind with worry, wishing he was here with her, wishing he didn't have to put her through this. It was all made so much worse for him because it was *here*. This house, the scene of so many awful memories for him. The place that had clouded so much of his young life. He couldn't allow himself to hope that anything would go well here. Like Belinda, he had been exposed to the toxins that Knight gave off for so long it had affected his whole outlook. Everything had become so much worse now that he knew the truth. It was only now that he might finally be able to get the poison out of his system.

And with that thought, she felt an icy finger claw its way down her spine. Knight was approaching.

Impatience felt like a giant rodent sitting on his chest, gnawing at his flesh. The fibers of his woolen sweater felt like tiny razors scratching his arms, and Adam tugged the garment over his head, flinging it down on the damp grass. The birdsong was overloud, making the blood pound in his ears until he wanted to find something to cover his head. Overhead, sunlight breaking through the canopy of leaves was too bright, stinging his eyes like shards of glass, forcing him to bend his head and stare at the wet leaves between his bent knees. Behind him, the tree trunk against which he leaned pressed its gnarled knuckles into his spine, adding to the teeth-clenching, jaw-grinding, swearing-under-his-breath restlessness that spiraled higher with each passing second.

He spent most of the time staring at the blank screen of his tablet, telling himself Maja would be okay. She was a fighter. Before she met him, her life had been about going into combat zones and plucking warriors out of the middle of scenes of death and destruction. She was better equipped than he was to face Knight.

Adam's lectures didn't work. He wanted to be at her side, caring for her and protecting her. Skulking in a forest while the woman he loved placed herself in the line of fire? That didn't suit Adam's idea of chivalry. He could tell himself he had an important role to play in the fight, but it didn't feel right.

Right would be leading from the front. Right would be looking Knight in the eye while he brought him to his knees.

When his phone buzzed with a text from Maja, he allowed himself to breathe normally again for a few minutes. Then the tension ratcheted back up to stratospheric. The Valkyries would be on their way.

The silent screaming inside his head began again as he waited. Forcing himself to calm down, he concentrated on his breathing. Wasn't that what you were supposed to do? Trying to block out the negative thoughts, the images of what could go wrong, he kept his mind on each next inhalation.

Until an image appeared on the screen of his tablet, of Knight entering the meeting room.

"Maja, I love you." Adam whispered the words in the gloom of the forest. Even the birds stopped their singing and listened. Or maybe now that he had something to do, his irritation at every little sound was gone.

Adam watched as Knight checked out the room, moving around the table, pausing to straighten items on its surface. The quality of the recording was good. Inserting his headphones, Adam checked out the sound quality. Although there was no talking, Adam could hear Knight's footsteps, the rustle of paper and the scrape of water bottles.

He checked his signal and connection to the internet. He was logged in to the social media sites he would use to share the live stream of the video of the meeting. Everything was ready. The guards were patrolling the area around the house and grounds, but they hadn't penetrated this far into the trees.

As if in answer to a cue, he heard Knight's voice in his headphones.

"Come in. Sit down."

Adam switched from Maja's view to Brynhild's. She was facing one of the open French windows and, on Adam's screen, he saw the other eight members of the Reaper consortium enter the meeting room. He was pleasantly surprised by her technique. Her hand was steady and she got a good shot of each face as they took their seats. It would be easy for the police to identify them from these images.

Changing back to Maja's recording, he watched as

Knight took his seat at the head of the table. Adam had to get a grip on his emotions as he observed the smiling face of the man who had thrown his life into turmoil over and over. Now was not the time to let those feelings get the best of him. Defeating Knight would never wipe out the past, but it would help to redress the balance.

The group around the table got straight down to business. Adam listened carefully as he started to direct his social media followers to the live stream. There wasn't any specific mention of the Reaper in Knight's introduction, but there were references to recent successes.

"Our allies have delivered a high standard of service on every occasion, with the result that each of us has seen an unprecedented increase in profits." There was a ripple of agreement around the table. "We owe a debt of thanks, of course to the general—" Knight nodded to Shepherd, who was seated on his right "—for his hard work. He faces a difficult balancing act. Not only must he appease the international forces of law and order who are breathing down his neck, demanding results, he must also protect our allies from the risk of discovery."

"Come out and say it, you bastard." Adam muttered the words to the screen as he typed a commentary for his followers. "Instead of saying 'allies,' say 'terrorists.'"

"With that in mind, and before we discuss forthcoming projects, I have a recommendation to make." There was a ripple of interest around the table. Clearly, this was unexpected.

Adam checked the figures on his screen. People were beginning to follow the live stream. He had called it *Reaper Video* and encouraged his followers to watch. Although there were bemused comments asking what was going on, Adam's name and his own comments were maintaining interest. Adam Lyon, media mogul, had said the identity of the Reaper was about to be exposed live. Was it a scam? If it was, it was worth a few minutes to see how it panned out. If it wasn't...no one wanted to miss the final reveal.

"The general has been in touch with our allies in the Middle East. Given our recent triumphs and the increased focus on our ventures, they, and he, have requested an increase in their payment."

There was a momentary silence before Charlie Hannon leaned back in his seat, tapping a pencil on the table. The sound seemed unnaturally loud through Adam's headphones.

"How much?" The Englishman's voice was not encouraging.

"That would be a matter for negotiation."

Hannon cast a glance around the table. "I'm not denying that the general here does a good job of throwing the politicians off the scent. And we couldn't do this without the guys who plant the bombs and fire the bullets—"

Yes! Adam checked the live stream again. The number of people viewing the meeting was skyrocketing and, thanks to Adam's comments, *Reaper Video* was trending on other social media sites.

"—but I think we already pay enough."

A heated discussion ensued and it was clear that there were two distinct sides in the room. Those who felt the rewards they gained meant the general and the terrorists had earned a pay raise, and those who didn't want to part with any more cash.

After a few minutes, Knight intervened, his cool

tones cutting across the conversation. "My friends, in the interests of efficiency, may I suggest we put this to a vote? Just to remind you of our protocols… I will refrain from voting, but in the event of a tie, mine will be the final decision."

There was silence as Knight outlined the proposal again. "Raise your hand if you are in favor of an increase in the amount we pay to the general and our allies in the Middle East."

Four hands were raised and four remained down. Knight spoke again. "Since the final decision is mine, I vote that we increase the payments—"

"Hold it right there!" Charlie Hannon, who had voted against the increase, interrupted. "The general shouldn't be able to vote on this."

"He's right," Suzanne Sumner said. "It's a conflict of interest."

This was not what Adam wanted. A group of people fighting among themselves was not what he wanted his followers to see. He wanted the Reaper consortium to expose themselves by talking about their involvement in terrorism. He wanted to hear examples. Hard, cold facts.

The general slammed a hand on the table, bringing the argument to an abrupt end. Glaring at Charlie Hannon, he got to his feet. "Do you want to take a turn at doing my job, sonny? You want to negotiate with terrorists and murderers, then show up at the United Nations after the next Reaper attack and explain why nothing is happening?" His icy glare took in each person around the table. "Each one of us is the Reaper. We are all equal partners—maybe with Knight running the show—but I'm the one who gets my hands dirty. You get the benefits when your rivals topple after a terrorist attack. I don't have that. The least you bastards can do is pay me what I deserve."

Adam exhaled a long, relieved sigh. That was what he needed. The general might almost have been reading from a script. Adam checked the screen of his tablet. Within a few seconds of the military man's speech, social media was going crazy. Initial reactions ranged from disbelief—*was this for real?*—to outrage.

"Knight." Alain Dubois spoke in a slightly bored voice. "You're in charge here. You are the person who thought up the Reaper and recruited us all. The largest terrorist organization in the world is your master plan. Now can you please get this meeting back on track so that we can do what we came here for and plan our next attacks? I want to make some money from my investment in the Reaper."

"Guys…" Donna Webb held up her cell phone, drawing her companions' attention to its screen. "We have a bigger problem right now. I just got a message from my PA telling me to check out what's happening on the internet. I don't know how it's being done, but we're being filmed."

The room descended into chaos as the other members of the consortium checked their own cell phones. The awful truth began to dawn on them. They had been exposed. Their meeting had just been streamed live to hundreds of thousands, maybe millions, of viewers. While the others went into full-blown panic mode, Knight sat very still at the head of the table, his hands gripping the arms of his chair. He seemed to be staring at a point just past Maja's head. Fascinated, she continued to film him, wanting to capture his reaction—or lack of reaction—to what was going on.

"How can this be happening?" Suzanne Sumner's voice was high-pitched with fear. "There must be a hidden camera in here. Knight, didn't you check the place out? Can't you shut it down?"

"You were supposed to take care of security." The general seemed to have aged ten years. "That was the reason we came to your house. We trusted you."

"Get out." Knight didn't move as he spoke. His face remained expressionless. "All of you. Just leave."

There was a moment's hesitation. The snarl on Knight's lips as he turned the full force of his fury on his companions was truly terrifying. "Go...or suffer the consequences!"

The other eight members went from inactivity to an undignified scramble for the French window within seconds. Brynhild caught Maja's eye and jerked her head toward the exit. The message was clear. Should they leave? They had done what they came here to do. The Reaper consortium had been exposed. Adam had his recording.

Maja wavered. Yes, they had everything they needed, but something was going on with Knight. It was as if the air around him was beginning to boil.

Just a few more minutes.

Even though the toxic atmosphere was stifling her, she wanted to keep recording. To let the world see exactly who this man was. Brynhild gave a slight shrug, but the message in her body language was clear. She wasn't happy to stay.

Maja turned her attention back to Knight. His face was deathly pale, those soulless eyes bigger and darker than ever, as though all the light in the room was being drawn into their depths. The strangest illusion seemed to be taking place, almost as though a reflection of his face was overlaid on top of the original. There was just a hint of another image. It shifted and then disappeared so quickly that Maja was unsure if she had seen it at all.

Even though he couldn't see the Valkyries, Knight looked around the room as though he was aware of their presence. His expression was menacing, his lips drawing back in a grotesque snarl.

"Is this your doing, Adam Lyon?" His voice sounded different. Low and guttural, it rasped like a foul echo in the beautiful room. Although she knew he couldn't see her, he looked directly at Maja as he spoke. "You should have listened to me when I said you didn't know what you were dealing with."

Knight began to chant. Softly at first, then his voice gradually became louder. He was speaking a language Maja didn't recognize. The room filled with static and dark, swirling energy. Wisps of white mist began to curl up from the point where Knight's fingers gripped the chair.

"Maja." For the first time in her life Maja saw fear on Brynhild's face. "He is invoking a demon. We need to leave."

Maja nodded. They had seen enough. Was Knight summoning *any* demon? Or was he calling on a specific occult guide, one with the skills to help him in this situation? Maybe he was invoking the greatest of them all... the master to whom he had sold his soul? Would the devil himself answer a summons at will? Did Satan do house calls? Maja didn't think they should hang around waiting to find out.

She gestured toward the open French window, in-
dicating for the other Valkyries to go ahead of her. It
felt hard to leave. The air in the room was thick and
cloying. Something within it was pulling them back.
With each word Knight spoke, the sense of malice increased, stretching tighter like the skin of a drum. Maja
watched in relief as, one by one, her sisters left through
the French window.

Maja was the last to approach the welcome exit.
Fresh air greeted her like a kiss when she was within a
foot or two of escape. She turned to get a final look at
Knight, just as he rose from his seat. Crouching low,
his eyes gleaming red, he looked at her and smiled as
he licked his lips.

The cell phone slipped from Maja's hand as the window slammed closed, trapping her inside the meeting
room with the beast that was now inhabiting Knight
Valentine's body.

Chapter 20

Adam was running across the grass toward the house as soon as Knight began to chant. Why was Maja still inside the meeting room? It was all over. The Valkyries needed to get the hell out of there as fast as they could.

Why had he let her do this? Allowing her to head into that meeting without him had gone against every instinct he possessed. It wasn't about some macho gene that said he was a man and he had to be in charge. It was because Maja and their baby were the most precious things in the world to him, and he was handing them over to the devil.

It was also because this was his fight. It was Adam's life Knight had screwed up. He wanted to be the one to look into those shark eyes when the tables were turned.

Adam had seen the other members of the consortium leave the meeting room through the French windows.

Now, they were making their way across the garden toward the front of the house as he sprinted past them. They huddled together like a group of lost souls. Which, he decided, was exactly what they were. It didn't matter where they went now, or what they tried to do to cover their tracks. The authorities would deal with them. They would get what was coming.

He didn't have time to waste another thought on them. Didn't even have time to feel a flicker of satisfaction. As he rounded a corner of the house, his heart almost stopped. Brynhild, having abandoned her invisibility, saw him and ran across the grass toward him, her face a mask of terror.

"He has Maja. The demon could see her." She choked back a sob. "He is hurting her. We can hear her cries, but we can't get back in there."

The other Valkyries were trying everything they could to get the French windows of the meeting room open. Nothing they did—kicks, punches, even patio furniture thrown at the doors—made any impression. Something other than wood and glass was keeping the Valkyries out of that room.

There is superglue in those locks to stop them working; those doors shouldn't stay closed.

"Let me try." Adam stepped up to the door. "It's me he wants."

As soon as he touched the handle, the French window flew open. He stepped inside. Although Brynhild pressed close behind him, attempting to follow, she was forced back again by the window slamming in her face. Her cry of fury was drowned out by a hoarse cackle from within the room.

Adam's blood froze as he took in the scene. Knight

was seated in the chair at the head of the table. His face was vampire pale and his eyes had lost their dark sheen. Instead they glowed from within. Red sparks danced in their depths. His bloodless lips were drawn back in a terrifying smile. Whatever demon he had summoned was inside him, but the man still retained control. This was Knight Valentine, but supercharged. Scarier than any demon.

Maja was curled in a fetal position at his feet. She wasn't moving. As Adam took a step toward her, Knight raised a hand. "I wouldn't."

"If you've hurt her..."

Knight's laughter was like fingernails on a chalkboard. "What will you do? Pay me back? I'd like to see you try."

"Let her go, Knight. This is between you and me."

"You've made it more than that." Knight's voice was petulant as he held up his cell phone. "You've made sure it is between me and the whole world."

"You did that yourself." The words came out before he could stop them.

Knight's foot connected with Maja's ribs in retaliation and she cried out. Relief, fury and fear stormed through Adam in equal measures. Relief that she was still alive. Fury at himself for provoking Knight. Fear, because if anything happened to her...

"Take it out on me, not her, you coward." He took a step closer to Knight, his fists clenched.

"Why would I do that, when it's so much more fun this way?"

He knew why Knight had called upon this demon. He didn't want to relinquish control, but Adam knew that deep down his stepfather was a coward. He needed this boost to his psyche and his strength. He wanted to know he could defeat Adam in spectacular style, rather than risk a fair fight. The glowing eyes, the rasping voice, the ability to keep the Valkyries out—they were all part of the show.

"What happened to the man who wanted to be the best in his own right?"

"Stalling for time, Lyon? Are you scared? The way you used to be when you went into the cellar?" Knight's smile widened.

"My dad used to talk about his best friend. An honorable guy. A guy who fought fair, never took a cheap shot and always paid his way." Adam was making this up as he went along. Robert Lyon had never spoken to him about his friendship with Knight. But when he was fighting for his life, and Maja's, Adam guessed a few liberties with the truth were permissible.

"Your father was a loser."

"The sort of loser you used to be? The sort who could look in the mirror and like what he saw? Would you like your reflection now, Knight?" Adam looked at the antique mirror on the wall. "Shall we find out?"

"My reflection hasn't changed." Even though the words were confident, the snarl wavered. "I'm not playing your games."

"But you like games, Knight. You like to be the best at them." Adam wasn't sure if Maja could hear him. If she could, he hoped she knew what he was doing. *Hang in there. I'm here for you. We can do this...together.* "Remember how you used to say the devil could have your soul if only you could make that shot, sink that pool ball, make that money?"

"My deal with the devil was the best I ever made."

"If that's true, and you truly believe it hasn't changed you—that you are still the same guy my dad knew—you won't be afraid to take a look in that mirror." Adam tried out a smile to go with the words. "The Knight Valentine who was my dad's best friend would never back down from a challenge."

"You think your pathetic mind games will work on me? That I'll be scared of what I see in the mirror? You think I can't look at my own reflection and live with what I've done?"

"Prove it."

Knight got to his feet and moved toward him. At the same time, Adam saw Maja press her hands to the floor as she attempted to get to her knees. His heart gave a thud of gratitude. His brave Valkyrie knew what he was trying to do. Could a demon multitask? Was the one inside Knight strong enough to pit its wits against Adam while still keeping those French windows locked against the Valkyries? There was only one way to find out. And to do it, Adam had to keep Knight's attention focused on him.

Side by side, the two men moved toward the mirror. Being so much shorter, Knight came up only to Adam's shoulder. It meant he not only couldn't see as much of his own reflection, but he also couldn't see as much of the room behind him.

"What am I supposed to be looking at?" Knight's voice was mocking. "Are you expecting me to be shocked because my face is pale and my eyes are glowing?"

"What is the name of the demon inside you?" Adam tried not to fix his attention on what was going on behind them.

The abrupt change of subject brought a slight frown to Knight's brow. *Damn.* Adam didn't want to make him too suspicious. "Why do you want to know?" The gravelly note in his voice was more pronounced.

Behind him, Adam was aware of Maja crawling toward the French windows. Was she going so slowly because she didn't want to alert Knight to what she was doing, or because she was badly hurt? His head was spinning at the notion that she could be injured and he couldn't go to her. It felt like a giant hand had been thrust into his chest and was slowly drawing out his heart inch by painful inch.

What if she tried the handle and couldn't open the French window? If the demon's power was still too great for her and the other Valkyries together to override, what then? Adam had no plan B. This was it. This was all he had.

That's why you have to make this one work.

"Because I prefer to talk to the puppet master rather than the puppet."

Knight's fist, powered by the full force of the demon's strength, connected with Adam's jaw. Even though he was expecting the blow, it rocked his head back. That whole seeing-stars thing was a myth. It was more like being underwater. Everything became blurred, including sound.

Knight was talking, but the words came to him as though spoken in a wind tunnel. Adam caught the most important ones: *"...impertinent jerk with a death wish..."*

Maja had reached the window. Adam had to buy her enough time to try and get it open. He swung at Knight's stomach. It was like punching a brick wall.

Pain shot up from his knuckles through his wrist and flared into his elbow. He barely had time to register the shock before Knight grabbed him by the neck, pinning him against the wall. Dark spots appeared before Adam's eyes as he clawed at the hand around his throat.

"What do you think you're doing?"

Adam was on the verge of blacking out. No matter how hard he fought for his next breath, he couldn't draw even a gasp into his lungs. As blackness invaded the edges of his vision, he saw Maja scrabbling to get the French window open. His senses became supercharged. He could hear Brynhild yelling encouragement from the other side of the door.

Knight, becoming aware of what was happening, swung around, a growl issuing from his lips. He released Adam, who slid to the floor, gulping in air. As Knight dashed across the room, Maja used both hands to pull on the handle, and Brynhild crashed through the window with the other Valkyries behind her.

The demon fought like—well, he fought like a demon—but eleven Valkyries would have been a match for the devil himself. Knight disappeared under a blonde onslaught.

Staggering to his feet, Adam lurched to where Knight had placed his cell phone on the table. With fingers that felt like they belonged to someone else, he called 911.

"I need police and paramedics. Yes, it's an emergency."

He gave the operator the details as he stumbled across to where Maja was sitting propped against the wall. Stooping low, he managed to lift her into his arms. Without speaking, she linked her fingers around his neck and rested her head against his chest.

Slowly, Adam carried her outside and sat on the grass with her cradled in his lap, until he heard the sound of sirens.

Brynhild placed a hand on Adam's shoulder. "We have to go before your mortal authorities arrive. Knight is still alive...but only just."

"Thank you." His voice was gruff with emotion.

She bent her head to kiss Maja's cheek. "You were right. We both love her." The Valkyries disappeared and Adam and Maja were left alone as the emergency vehicles appeared.

When Maja spoke, her voice was so quiet he had to lower his head to catch the words. "You fought a demon for me, but you never did find out its name."

"I didn't need to." He pressed his lips to her temple. "There was a demon inside his body, but the thing I feared the most was the man called Knight Valentine."

Maja tried to focus on a part of her body that wasn't experiencing pain. It was no good. There wasn't one. As soon as he was alone with her, Knight, his strength enhanced by the demon within him, had launched into an attack so ferocious she thought she was going to die. No amount of Valkyrie training had prepared her for it. It didn't matter how hard she tried to fight back; the onslaught was relentless. Though vaguely aware of Brynhild and the other Valkyries desperately trying to get back inside to help her, she'd found her only thought had been to protect the baby.

When Adam arrived, she had been barely conscious. Even so, her first emotion had been relief that he was there. It had been swiftly followed by fear. Adam was a mortal. He had no defense against the demon residing inside Knight's body. If Maja, with her strength and Valkyrie training, could be so easily defeated, Adam would be crushed like a moth between a careless thumb and finger.

She didn't know how she had dragged herself to the French window. The memory was a blur. All she could remember was the overwhelming feeling of joy as Brynhild rushed into the room. After that, the only thing she could remember was Adam's arms around her.

Now, as she lay in the hospital bed, one thought persisted. Her whole body was a mass of bruises. An initial examination had reveal that she had two broken ribs and a fractured wrist. That diagnosis didn't tell her the most important thing. She pressed a hand to her stomach.

"Dr. Blake will be here any minute." Adam, interpreting her thoughts, took hold of her uninjured hand.

"What if…?"

"No." He shook his head, and she could sense how hard it was for him to say it. It was hurting him as much as her. "Let's not do 'what if.' Not yet. Let's hear what the doctor has to say."

Maja leaned closer and rested her head on his shoulder, feeling the tension of his muscles beneath her cheek. They stayed that way until Dr. Blake arrived. Her manner was brisk. Clearly, she knew that was what they needed.

"I'm going to conduct a pelvic ultrasound examination. That should show us if, and how, this attack has affected the baby." An orderly wheeled a trolley into the room. "This is the machine I'll use."

When the orderly had left, she looked from Maja to Adam, her expression grave. "Your injuries are serious, Maja. It will also allow me to diagnose a potential miscarriage."

Maja tightened her grip on Adam's hand. That was the word she hadn't wanted to say. Hadn't even wanted to think. It was what had sustained her through the attack. *Stay alive. Protect the baby.* She had used her fear to keep her focused. Initially trying to fight back, when she realized she was up against a superior power, she had used her own strength to defend herself, curling up and shielding her abdomen and pelvis. Had she done enough? That metal wand the doctor was holding in her gloved hands was about to reveal the truth.

"I thought an ultrasound was done abdominally?" Adam's question surprised Maja. She had believed she was the only one who had been obsessively reading all the literature.

"Normally it is," Dr. Blake said. "But this is an early ultrasound and doing it this way will produce a clearer picture." She gave them a reassuring smile. "Don't worry, it's perfectly safe. There is no risk to either Maja or the baby."

The feeling was mildly intrusive rather than uncomfortable, and Maja watched the screen, feeling as though her heart didn't dare risk its next beat. She wanted to look at the doctor's face for a clue to what was happening, but it was too daunting. What if she caught a glimpse of something she wasn't meant to see? A frown or a pursed lip? Adam kept a hand on her shoulder and her whole world seemed focused on the grainy image before her eyes and the warmth of his fingers through her hospital gown.

Dr. Blake pointed to the screen. "This black area here is your uterus, Maja." She turned her head and smiled.

"And this—" she pointed to what looked to Maja to be a gray blob inside the larger black area "—is your baby. You can just about see his or her limbs developing."

Maja wanted to say something, but she burst into tears instead. It wasn't a good move. The action caused pain to rip through her injured ribs and she gasped, clutching her uninjured arm around herself in a defensive gesture. Doing her best to stem the flow of tears, she gazed at the screen in wonder. There it was. Their baby. She and Adam hadn't been the only ones fighting Knight in that meeting room. The tiny life inside her had survived, as well.

The emotions welling up inside her felt like a dam threatening to burst. The tears came again, less violent this time. Tears of pure joy. This baby was going to be okay. She knew it in that instant. Like its parents, it was going to be a fighter...and a survivor.

"Can you see the heart?"

Dr. Blake nodded. "It's very clear." She pointed. "You baby's heart is beating normally. Everything else is fine as well. If you come into my office in two weeks, we can repeat this procedure, and by then we will be able to hear the heart as well as see it."

Even though the movement caused her more pain, Maja turned her head to look at Adam. There were tears in his eyes as he bent his head to kiss her.

Dr. Blake removed the probe. "Now, both of you need to get your injuries checked out. Then I believe the police are waiting to speak to you."

Adam had repeated his story about half a dozen times to different agencies. Now he was telling it again to two officers, one male, one female, from the Department of Homeland Security.

"Explain to me again how your girlfriend—" the woman, Agent Glenn, who was clearly senior to her partner, consulted her notes "—Miss, er...?"

This was what he had tried to avoid. Given that she didn't actually exist as a mortal, too much scrutiny of Maja could give them a problem. "Odin." Maja would hate it, but it was the first word that came into his head. "Maja Odin. She's Scandinavian."

"Okay. Just explain one more time how Miss Odin came to be inside Mr. Valentine's meeting room."

"She was looking for me."

Once he had been checked over, Adam had not been admitted to the hospital. His jaw wasn't broken, and although his throat had taken a beating, there was no lasting damage there, either. All he wanted to do now was getting back to Maja's bedside. These interviews were formalities. He knew that. So did these expressionless people opposite him. They had the video evidence from that meeting. They had all the members of the Reaper consortium in custody, including Knight Valentine. Although whether Knight would survive the injuries inflicted on him by Maja's sisters was not a foregone conclusion. The live-streaming of the meeting had been illegal, but Adam knew as well as Agent Glenn did that her investigation into that wasn't going anywhere.

"You didn't arrive at Valentine House together?" Agent Glenn asked.

"No. It's well known that my stepfather and I don't get along. I was going to Valentine House to confront him. When Maja found out what I was planning, she followed me with the intention of trying to stop me." Adam was surprised at the ease with which he had come up with the story, and the calm way he was able to deliver the lies. But he could hardly tell the truth. Valkyries, deals with the devil, the Grim Reaper and demons? He didn't want his child's only experience of its father to be visiting a secure mental facility.

"That doesn't explain how Miss Odin came to be in the meeting room with Mr. Valentine and his associates."

"I'm sure Maja already told you this herself." *Because we concocted this story together.* "She couldn't find me in the house or grounds, so she went into the meeting room. When Knight and his colleagues arrived, she was scared that she was trespassing. Knight is a scary guy." Adam fingered his jaw reminiscently. *You should see him in action.* "So she hid behind one of the potted palms. When she realized what they were discussing, she started to film the meeting."

"And you live streamed it?" Agent Glenn, double-checked her notes.

"She live streamed it." Adam guessed they had ways of checking that, so he decided to keep it factual. "I was on the grounds of the house, making my way to her. When I saw what she was doing, I shared the recording digitally."

"Wasn't that a little...unheroic of you?" Agent Glenn gave a disapproving cough. "Your girlfriend was trapped in a room with a group of dangerous criminals. In the time it took to share that recording, you could have called the police."

"You think I don't regret that now?" Adam gave her

back look for look. *Unheroic?* She could tell that to his aching knuckles.

"What I'm having a hard time understanding is who tied up Mr. Valentine's security guards and locked them in the attic, and who beat Mr. Valentine to a pulp while you and your girlfriend escaped." Agent Glenn peered at him. "Both you and Miss Odin are pretty vague about that."

"Probably because we were fighting for our lives at the time." Adam came back at her with a touch of acidity. "Have you asked Mr. Valentine or his security guards these questions?"

"Mr. Valentine is not able to answer questions. It's possible he may never be able to do so." Adam wanted to ask a few questions about that, but he got the feeling Agent Glenn wasn't the type to be forthcoming with answers. "And none of his security guards saw their attackers."

"So we're not the only ones who can't answer your questions about these mystery assailants?"

"No." She seemed disappointed at the admission. "But they overpowered eight guards without a fight, and the attack on Mr. Valentine was delivered by a number of people in a particularly ferocious manner."

Good. Adam might have a few issues with Brynhild, but if he ever saw her again, he would enjoy thanking her all over again.

"The doctors have no idea how he survived," Agent Glenn continued. "He must be incredibly strong to have put up any kind of fight, but he's waning fast now."

Adam wasn't going to enlighten her about what had really happened. It was the demon inside Knight that had done the fighting, but he guessed it had made a quick getaway when it realized the Valkyries were winning. He might not be an expert in the paranormal, but even Adam could guess that demons weren't renowned for their loyalty. As for the devil, would the deal still stand now Knight was no longer able to pay his dues?

Agent Glenn closed her notebook and got to her feet. "If you remember anything else, particularly about these mysterious vigilantes, please get in touch, Mr. Lyon."

Her voice wasn't hopeful. And she was right not to indulge in any false confidence. *We gave you the Reaper; what more do you want?*

Intense weariness overcame Adam as he watched them walk away. But he knew the perfect cure for that. With a smile, he walked along the corridor to Maja's room.

Chapter 21

Tarek had made Maja a "get well soon" card and he and Sophie had brought her flowers and cookies. Dr. Blake had said Maja could go home the following day, as long as she promised to rest, and Sophie was staying in the apartment until then. Once Tarek was satisfied that Maja would recover from her injuries, he began to plan a marathon gaming fest for the duration of Sophie's stay.

Sophie grinned in response to Adam's rolled eyes. "I enjoy playing games with him. Honestly."

"Remind me to give you a pay raise." He escorted them to a cab and watched as they departed.

When he returned to Maja's room, she was half sitting, half reclining, propped against her pillows with her eyes closed. Adam paused just inside the door, watching her.

He was overwhelmed by the strength of the connection that drew him to her. It was always the same. Her beauty hurt his heart. But Adam had seen many beautiful women. Maja's physical characteristics couldn't account for a yearning so fervent it made him tremble. Was it stronger because his life had been so dark before she had come along to brighten it? Had this burning intensity been caused by two worlds colliding? He didn't know the reasons, and he didn't care. It just *was*. That was all that mattered.

Adam had found out early, and learned the hard way, that life was cruel. Those lessons had encased his heart in steel. They had focused his mind, making him ambitious and determined. For a long time, hatred and fear had been his driving forces.

Maja had dissolved his pain. She had given him a different reason to be resolute, and a new focus. Money, power, ambition, all the things that had once mattered, were nothing now. The only reward he wanted was her smile. His riches were her happiness. His goal for the future was to stay wrapped in her love.

He had proved over and over that he could do anything if he put his mind to it. Now there was only one thing on his mind. A future with his family.

"I know you're there." She didn't open her eyes, but a slight smile lifted the corners of her mouth.

"I want to kiss you, but I'm scared of hurting you," Adam said, as he pulled a chair up as close to the bed as he could get.

"I'll risk it." Just when he thought he couldn't feel any more emotion, she opened her eyes and his heart did a backward somersault.

Even though her lips were bruised and swollen, Maja's smile made it all okay again. All the hours of interviews, of reliving the horror of what they'd been through, of trying to convince people who blatantly didn't believe him that he was one of the good guys, faded away as he gently touched his lips to hers.

"Our baby is alive." Her whisper was filled with wonder. "Knight tried to destroy another part of your family, but this time he failed."

Adam lightly placed a hand on her stomach. "We made ourselves a fighter."

He was still overawed by the memory of the images they had seen on that screen. Of the life that had started in the midst of chaos, violence and confusion. When he had been at his lowest ebb, searching for Danny but not finding any trace of him. Injured, scared and confused, he had found Maja and they had made this new life. With every fiber of his being, he vowed to nurture that tiny person. He hadn't been able to protect Danny, but he would devote everything he had, everything he was, to ensuring that nothing ever harmed this baby.

"He takes after his parents."

"He?" He cocked an inquiring brow at her.

"Or she." Maja placed her hand over his. "But I think it's a boy."

"Do Valkyries do intuition?"

She shook her head. "It's just a feeling."

They remained still for some time, Maja resting her head against his shoulder. Although neither of them spoke of it, he knew they were thinking the same thing. Knight had been neutralized, the Reaper had been brought down, but there were still some hefty roadblocks in their way.

When the door opened, Adam expected to see a

nurse. Instead, Brynhild stepped into the room with her usual, confident stride.

She approached the bed, her brilliant eyes scanning Maja's face. "You look like someone who has danced with the devil."

Adam winced. "No matter how grateful I am to you for saving our lives, can we dispense with the dark humor?"

Brynhild raised her brows. "I am a Valkyrie. I don't do humor."

He held up a hand. "I forgot."

"I came to see how you are, and to tell you what happened when Odin discovered what we had done." Brynhild took a seat on the opposite side of the bed from Adam. Clad in jeans and a hooded sweatshirt, she still managed to maintain an air of authority. Adam imagined she was an unstoppable force as the Valkyrie leader.

"Did you tell him?" Maja asked.

"Of course."

Adam recalled what Maja had said. The Valkyries couldn't lie. Even when he had suggested omission or telling a half-truth, the concepts had been alien to Maja. He wondered briefly what it would be like to live in that world. Would life be better if truth always prevailed? His own world had been rocked recently when hidden secrets had been revealed. Maybe there was something to be said for absolute clarity.

"Was his anger very bad?" Maja's eyes were round with anticipation.

"It was one of the worst rages I have seen. The whole of Gladsheim and beyond shook with its force."

Maja bit her lip. "I'm sorry."

"It burned itself out eventually." Brynhild smiled. "And I am still alive. You were right—even in his fury, Odin saw that he couldn't condemn his finest Valkyries, including their leader, to death."

Maja swallowed. "Did he issue a pardon?"

"To all except one." Brynhild's voice lacked emotion and Adam decided that was probably the best way. If she'd done this with drama and sympathy, it would have been harder for Maja to hear. Cold, hard facts— the Valkyrie way—might sound harsh, but they were quicker and easier to listen to. "When he learned of your other crimes, he could not spare you, Maja."

"So he knows it all?"

"He knows what I told him." Was Adam imagining it, or did Brynhild look ever-so-slightly guilty? He definitely didn't imagine the quick glance she cast over her shoulder. "I said due to your inexperience, you had made an error of judgment and interacted with a mortal man while leading your first mission."

"You didn't mention the rest of it?" Maja reached for Adam's hand. "That I saved Adam's life? Our relationship...the baby...?"

There was no mistaking it. Brynhild, fearsome Valkyrie general, was blushing like a naughty schoolgirl. "I may have skimmed over some of the details."

"What did he say?" Adam could barely get the words out, he was breathing so hard.

"For once, the Allfather was lost for words." Brynhild gave a reminiscent smile. "I don't think that has ever happened before. He said he always knew that this day would come. Then he asked what I thought should happen to a Valkyrie who had broken the Code in such a manner. I pretended to give it some thought, although in reality I had already prepared what I wanted to say. I told him that although your crime was serious, your innocence was a mitigating circumstance. However, if you were pardoned, it could send a message to the other Valkyrie, suggesting that such a violation of the Code was not taken seriously."

"You urged Odin not to pardon me?" Maja voice was barely a whisper. "You, my own sister, deprived me of my freedom?"

"I did, but it is not as bad as it sounds. I suggested a punishment other than execution. And Odin took my advice." Her voice became formal. "I am here as the messenger of Odin, father of the gods. You, Maja, Valkyrie and shield maiden, are henceforth banished from Otherworld and cast out from the presence of the Allfather. From this moment on, your Valkyrie powers, including your immortality, are revoked and you are condemned to live out the rest of your days as a mortal woman."

Maja blinked, her grip on Adam's hand tightening. "That is my punishment? I am to become human?"

"It is decreed and cannot be reversed." Brynhild's expression was wary as she looked from Maja to Adam. "I thought you would like it. Was I wrong?"

Maja choked back a sob, lifting Adam's hand to her cheek. "You weren't wrong."

"How can I ever thank you, Brynhild?" He wanted to hug her, but he got the feeling her response could be a death punch to his larynx.

Her eyes blazed blue Valkyrie fire. "By taking care of my little sister."

Adam nodded. "That's my plan." He bent closer to Maja. "You know what this means?"

"We can take Tarek to Florida?"

"I was thinking more that I can finally ask you to marry me—" her expression of surprise was followed by a rosy blush "—but we can do Tarek's Florida vacation, as well."

"Before I leave, there is one more thing." Brynhild's voice dragged him back to reality. "Maja asked me to find out what I could about the man called Daniel Lyon."

Maja's blush faded as she turned to look at Adam. "I didn't tell you because there wasn't time with everything else that was happening. Brynhild consults the Norns to discover where the bravest and strongest fighters will be, and I thought she might be able to use her charts to discover where your brother is."

Adam's heart gave a thud of anticipation so violent it felt like it was trying to escape from his chest. After all this time, all the fruitless searching and disappointment, was he finally going to find out where Danny was?

"I'm afraid it is not good news." Brynhild's calm voice plowed on, cutting through the turmoil of his thoughts. "Daniel Lyon was killed in Syria two years ago."

The words were like a knife to his heart, an organ that had already been subject to considerable mistreatment in the last twenty-four hours. But Adam couldn't simply accept what he was hearing. He owed Danny more than that. A horrible image intruded into his mind. What if Brynhild was wrong and Danny wasn't dead? What if he should one day lie injured in the red Syrian dirt, calling his brother's name, but Adam was no longer searching for him because he listened now and believed Danny *was* dead?

"How can I be sure we are talking about the same Daniel Lyon?"

"I am talking about your brother," Brynhild said. "The man who had more heart and feeling for his fellow humans from the day of his birth than most men acquire through a lifetime of interaction."

"Did you tell her this?" Adam turned to Maja. Even as he asked the question, he knew he had never described Danny in those terms to her. Yet Brynhild had described his brother's personality to perfection.

"No." Maja's eyes were sympathetic, as if she could sense his distress. "I simply asked Brynhild to help find your brother."

"How did he die?" The words were easier than he expected. Finally, he had questions, even if they were not the ones he wanted to ask.

"He met a group of men. They tricked him into believing they shared his beliefs, but in reality, they were vicious mercenaries. Their numbers were depleted and they hoped to persuade Daniel to join them. He accompanied them to a town where they carried out some appalling atrocities. Daniel was horrified and fled. His aim was to get to the peacekeeping forces in the area and report what he had seen. The mercenaries captured and killed him before he could reach the peacekeepers."

"I don't understand." Maja sat up straighter in her agitation. "Odin sought the American Lion, one of the bravest fighters ever known. I went to Warda in search of him. It was Adam's brother, Daniel Lyon."

"Daniel was not the American Lion," Brynhild said. "It is most confusing. My charts show me that the man we seek is still alive. He is now in America."

Maja's cry of surprise drew Adam's attention back

to her. "Don't you see?" Her eyes were shining as she looked at him. "*You* are the American Lion."

He shook his head. "I'm not a warrior."

"You are the bravest man I have ever known. You saved Tarek from the Reaper without sparing a thought for your own safety. Then you brought him here and gave him a home. You fought Knight Valentine and saved so many lives." A smile trembled on her lips. "And you rescued me. You made me into a person with real feelings, hopes and dreams."

Brynhild nodded. "Maja is right. Bravery takes many forms. It does not have to be courage in battle. The valor you have displayed is greater than that of many of the fighters who now reside in the great hall of Valhalla."

Adam quirked a brow at her. "If you think you are going to drag me off to Valhalla just as your sister is able to stay here…"

Brynhild shook her head. "I can only claim the souls of those who die in conflict."

Adam raised Maja's hand to his lips. "If that means I must live a peaceful life from now on, you and I are taking our family to a new home in the country as soon as you leave this hospital."

"I must go." The sheepish look returned to Brynhild's face. "I told the Allfather after I delivered your sentence I would never speak to you again."

"Could that be another of those things about which he doesn't need to know the full details?" Maja asked.

Brynhild smiled. "I think there may be more of those in the future." She surprised Adam by holding out her hand. When he took it, her grip almost brought him to his knees. "I can show you on a map where they buried your brother's body."

"Thank you." He held the door open for her. "I meant what I said. I will take care of her."

She nodded. "I know you will."

Was this it? Was it all finally over? Knight was defeated. Odin had not condemned her to death. She could live in the mortal realm. She was free to bring up her child as a human. It felt like a giant knot had been undone inside Maja's stomach. And yet...

Apart from one brief comment about asking her to marry him, Adam hadn't referred to the future at all. Now, as they traveled from the hospital in Greenwich back to the apartment, he gazed out of the cab window and seemed unaware of her presence. If anything, his thoughts appeared a million miles away. Could his mind be back on business so soon after the momentous events they had endured? It certainly looked that way.

A few days ago, all she had wanted was to be able to stay here with him. To be able to raise their child together. Now, she wanted more. After all they had been through together, she didn't want half measures. *I want everything.*

Could she say that to him? Explain that she wanted reassurances about the future? She knew he loved her, but after everything that had happened, she needed to feel his arms around her as he told her he would never let her go.

The apartment was curiously quiet when they stepped inside. "Where is Tarek? He should be home from school by now." Maja turned to Adam with a furrowed brow. "And Leo? Why isn't he here?"

In response, he swung her up into his arms, carrying

her up the stairs to the master suite. "I asked Sophie to take them out. To give us some peace."

"I'm fine. I really don't need peace…" The words of protest died on her lips as they entered the room. Beautiful arrangements of white roses lined the walls and filled every surface.

"I wanted it to be special, but I thought you'd want to keep it private because of the bruises." Carefully, he set her on her feet and went down on one knee. Withdrawing a small, square box from the inside pocket of his jacket, he opened it. Sunlight glinted on diamonds.

"What are you doing?" The blaze of love in his eyes almost tilted her off balance. She might not know the details of human courtship rituals, but she had a feeling she might be in the middle of one. If so, she needed clarification about her role.

Adam started to laugh. "I should have realized I would have to provide a commentary. This is what mortals do, Maja. When a man loves a woman and wants to spend the rest of his life with her, he asks her to marry him. It's customary to give a ring as a sign that the couple have made a promise to marry."

"And the kneeling?" Maja studied him with her head on one side.

"A sign of respect and humility." His eyes twinkled. "Although most men don't have to explain it to their partners."

"I understand. You can continue now."

"Thank you." His lips twitched as though he was suppressing a smile. "Maja, when our worlds collided, something unique happened. We created a new world. Our own world. From now on, within that world is the only place I want to be. With you. Wherever you go,

I'll walk beside you. Whatever you do, I'll support you. Every dream you have, I'll make it come true." His eyes were bright with the same tears that stung her own eyelids. "Because I love you, and I want you to be my wife."

Maja placed a hand on his shoulder. "What do I do now?"

"You give me your answer."

"Oh. My answer is yes. Yes, please." As she tugged at his shoulder to get him to stand, Maja was relieved that she didn't have to rein in her strength. She was no longer stronger than Adam, and she liked it that way. Liked this new imbalance. Loved it when he placed the ring on her finger—it seemed to matter which one—then swung her up into his arms and kissed her until her head spun.

"What happens next?" she asked, when she was able to catch her breath.

"Next, I explain to you how a wedding works, then we get married as soon as we can. Since you don't have any identifying documents, I'll have to pull a few more of those strings that confused you when we first came to America." His smile shone brighter than the diamonds on her finger. "But once that's done, you will be Mrs. Lyon."

Maja shook her head in amazement. "I will be a real person."

Adam held her close. "You always were. I thought you were my fantasy, but it turned out you were my reality all the time."

Epilogue

Daniel Lyon's baptism was a quiet affair, attended only by close family and friends. After the ceremony, they went back to the four-bedroom cabin on the waterfront plot in suburban New York.

Elvira looked around her in surprise at the homey rooms with their bright rugs and comfortable furnishings. "This is not the sort of place in which I pictured you living."

Adam grinned. "It's temporary. We are having a new home built closer to the lake. Although Maja has made me promise it will not be a monument to the glass and chrome industries."

Elvira looked across the room at where Maja, holding her baby son on one arm, was getting a soft drink for Tarek, while talking to Sophie and Brynhild. "Who is she, Adam?"

He raised a brow. "She's my wife, Elvira."

"Oh, very well. Be mysterious if you must. Don't think it hasn't escaped my attention that Knight was captured just after you came to see me. And at his trial, they said he claimed he was severely beaten by a group of beautiful blonde women. From the details he gave, he could almost have been describing Maja and her sisters."

"Delirium." Adam poured her a glass of champagne as he spoke. "The man was unhinged *and* he had just been attacked. He wasn't expected to live."

"But he did live. He's alive in his prison cell after being found guilty of murder and using weapons of mass destruction." Elvira's eyes were probing his face. "Was letting him live all part of your plan?"

"I don't understand."

"Come now, Adam. Let's not play games. Sooner or later the devil will come for Knight. It might have been easier on him if he'd died." Elvira's expression was bleak. "Satan doesn't like failure."

"I hadn't thought beyond neutralizing the threat." It was true. Making sure the Reaper consortium couldn't do any more harm had been his only goal.

And the world had felt like a better place recently. Adam wasn't going to claim responsibility for a change in the global climate, but the imprisonment of terrorists seemed to have signaled a fresh approach among world leaders. There was a new sense of international responsibility.

In his own life, Adam felt renewed. Taking a step back from business had been a huge relief. The man who once thought the office was all there was had discovered it was only a minor part of his life. He had his priorities right now. His family came first.

"But if I'm honest, I'd have preferred him dead. Maja still has nightmares about him. Even here, in our own little corner of paradise, she worries about security and makes me sleep with a gun in the drawer next to my bed."

He didn't add that it was a major personality change for a Valkyrie. Odin had made Maja human, but part of the price of that had been fear.

"What now?" Elvira's voice drew his attention back to her.

"Are you asking if I'm going to continue being a inter-worldly vigilante?" He laughed. "The answer is a resounding no. This was a one-time-only mission. Coming to terms with Danny's passing is taking time. I have a new Daniel in my life now, and two sons to care for. From now on, I am living a quiet life in the country with my wife and family."

"That sounds like a good ambition to have." She nodded approvingly.

Later, when Daniel was sleeping in his crib and Elvira had left, Sophie took Tarek out to play on the lawn.

"I'm glad to have this time alone with you," Maja told Brynhild. "There is something I have wanted to ask you."

"Is it about how I managed to get away so I could be here today?" Brynhild's smile encompassed both Adam and Maja. "I told the Allfather I was spending time organizing my maps and charts."

Although Maja smiled, Adam was surprised to see a touch of nervousness on her face. "That was not what I wanted to know." She took a breath. "When you came to see me in the hospital to tell me how Odin reacted to the news that I had broken the Valkyrie Code, you said something that intrigued me. You said he told you that he always knew this day would come. What did he mean by that?"

"Yes." Maja kept her gaze fixed on her sister's face. "Does this have something to do with Freyja? Is it the reason why our mother never loved me?"

Adam sat up straighter. "What is this? You've never spoken to me about your mother."

Maja seemed to drag her eyes away from Brynhild with an effort. "There are twelve true Valkyries. We are the daughters of Odin and his wife, Freyja. I am the youngest. But our mother never cared for me the way she loved my sisters."

"You don't know that," Brynhild said. "She is not a demonstrative woman."

Maja's smile was sad. "I do know it. Throughout my entire life, she has scarcely looked at me, let alone spoken to me. Although Freyja is close to her other daughters, she and I are barely acquaintances."

"You are Odin's favorite. Perhaps she felt it was necessary to redress the balance."

"Perhaps. But if there is something more, you can tell me now. I won't be returning to Valhalla," Maja said. "If there is a scandal in my past that affected Freyja's attitude to me, it no longer needs to remain hidden."

Brynhild appeared to consider the matter for a minute. Then she gave a decisive nod. "I always believed you should have been told the truth. You are not Freyja's daughter."

Adam was watching Maja's reaction for signs of hurt, but she remained calm. It was as if Brynhild was confirming something she already knew. "Who was my mother?"

"She was a Dryad named Tansey. She was the first of the new Valkyries. Odin fell in love with her at first sight. It was a difficult time. Freyja felt her position was threatened, particularly when there was a baby on the way." Brynhild smiled reminiscently. "And Tansey was very strong-willed and rebellious. It is easy to see where you get your stubborn streak from."

"What happened to her?"

Brynhild's expression softened. Despite her protestations that she didn't do feelings, now and then the Valkyrie leader displayed her gentler side. "Tansey died soon after you were born. Odin went to Freyja and begged her forgiveness. She agreed to raise you as her child on one condition. All future new Valkyries must be given the status of stepdaughter. That would put them out of reach of Odin's roving eye."

"So Freyja tolerated me but couldn't love me. And Odin favored me because I reminded him of my mother." Maja shook her head. "Yet no one told me. I lived with the scolds and the frowns. I was always the bad Valkyrie. I was told I was a rebel, a troublemaker, that I couldn't be trusted to lead an expedition on my own. But no one ever told me why."

"We thought we could teach you to conform," Brynhild said.

"But you didn't understand me. You didn't love me for who I was." Maja spoke with quiet dignity. "I only got that acceptance when I came to the mortal realm. Adam was the first person who saw the real me."

"I'm sorry." Brynhild's expression was pained.

"It wasn't your fault. It was the life we were forced to live."

Adam moved away, leaving the two sisters alone

as they embraced. They didn't know when, or even if, Brynhild would be able to return. He owed Maja's sister a lot. Thanks to her, his brother now had a grave next to his parents in their family plot. Getting Danny's body home from Syria had not been an easy task, but Adam had applied his usual hardheadedness to the task. It helped that he was now the man who had turned the spotlight on the Reaper consortium. Although an air of mystery hung over how he had achieved that, it had given him some leverage with the authorities.

Dusk was falling, leaching the color from the sky as he went into the kitchen and looked out over the lake.

He opened the sliding glass door and called to Tarek and Sophie. It was time for Tarek to come in for his bath. Although there was some good-natured grumbling from him about this arrangement, the boy said goodbye to Sophie and went to the bathroom.

When Sophie and Brynhild had gone, Adam went around the house, locking the doors and closing the drapes. Although they were miles from anywhere, that was another of Knight's legacies. Maja worried that they were vulnerable if it wasn't done properly.

"All done?" Maja was feeding the baby when he returned to the family room.

"All safe." He sat next to her on the sofa, placing an arm around her shoulders.

"It was good to see other people today, but this is what I like best." She leaned against him. "Just us."

He nodded. "Our family of four."

Maja woke with a start, her eyes straining into the darkened corners of the room. Was it a dream that had wakened her? It wasn't the baby. Daniel was sleeping peacefully in the crib he occupied next to the bed.

She lay still, hoping it was nothing. Knowing there had been something. A faint noise reached her ears. Midway between a growl and a whimper. She had never heard Leo make that sound before.

Getting out of bed, she slipped on a robe. She called the little dog's name as she made her way through the darkened house, but there was no response.

When she reached the kitchen, she paused. The sliding glass door was partly open, the drape that covered it drawn back.

A cold feeling of dread seized her. There was no way Adam would have left this door unlocked. His nightly routine was precise and unfailing. He checked every door and window, locking them and closing the drapes.

She had half turned to call Adam's name when a movement caught her eye. Illuminated by the light from the exhaust hood over the oven, it was a reflection in the glass window of a figure in the kitchen behind her.

If Maja hadn't seen it and dodged the blow, the baseball bat the man swung would have caved in the back of her skull. Instead, it caught her on the shoulder, bringing her to her knees.

Maja lifted her head and found herself staring down the barrel of a pistol. Behind it, Knight Valentine's eyes glittered coldly. Halfway between the man he had been and the Grim Reaper he had become, he wore a hooded cloak pulled up over his skull-like face.

An unpleasant smell pervaded her clean kitchen. It was the scent of unwashed bodies, blocked drains and something more. Like the residual smoky smell after a match had been struck. It was the aroma of hatred.

"Did you think it was over?"

Knight attempted a smile, but there was something very wrong with his face. Maja guessed it was from the beating he had been given by her sisters.

"I thought it was over for you." Even from her kneeling position, she remained defiant. "You stood trial and were found guilty of the terrible crimes you committed."

"You must have forgotten that I have powerful friends."

As Knight spoke, Maja could see he was a wreck, a mere shell of a man. His cloak fell back, revealing that his body was skin and bone, fitted oddly back together after being broken in so many places. His face was gray, the skin stretched tightly over his skull, giving him a skeletal appearance. Even his once-thick hair had thinned.

How had he escaped? Could that powerful friend he spoke of be the devil? Maja couldn't see any other way this walking corpse could get out of a high-security prison without satanic intervention.

We were right to be scared. The locking of doors and hiding of weapons—that was my intuition telling us he would come for us one day.

That day was here.

Maja's thoughts were divided between what was happening here and what was in the other rooms in the house. Adam and Daniel were sleeping peacefully in one room, Tarek in another. Protecting her family was uppermost in her mind.

"And you have a new baby. Another Lyon to continue the name." Knight's lips twisted. "How nice."

This was not going to happen. The man who had destroyed Adam's family once wasn't taking away what they had now.

As Maja contemplated her options, it seemed Leo was thinking the same thing. The little dog, who must have been hiding beneath the kitchen table, launched himself at Knight's ankle with his teeth bared.

Maja used the distraction to throw herself forward. She heard a gunshot and braced for the impact.

It didn't happen.

As she hit the floor, taking Knight with her, she looked up and saw Adam standing in the doorway between the kitchen and the hall in classic combat stance. His legs were apart, arms extended, and he held the gun he had just fired in his right hand, with his left hand supporting it.

Maja took a moment to register what had just happened. It wasn't Knight's gun that had been fired. Adam had killed Knight before his stepfather could shoot.

Shakily, she got to her feet.

As she moved toward Adam, Maja felt something leave the room. The smell was gone and the pervading sense of menace lifted. Her home was free from evil once more. She looked down at Knight's body and thought she could see peace on his face. She saw the man he must once have been.

"How did you know he was here?"

"I woke and you weren't there. When I came to find you and heard you talking to someone, I went back and got the gun."

He placed the weapon on the counter and she walked into his arms. They clung to each other.

"It's really over." Adam smoothed her hair back from

her brow. "It never felt like it while he was still alive. I always thought the devil wouldn't let him go."

"Or Knight wouldn't let the devil go. He didn't exist without his master. He couldn't be the best unless he had the devil at his side." She shivered and pressed her face into his chest.

"I need to get the police out here. Hopefully, they can deal with this before Tarek wakes up."

Maja nodded. A soft wail from along the corridor made her smile. "Real life."

"Our life." He kissed her.

"I'll go and see to Daniel. In the meantime—" she pointed at Leo "—you need to thank the real hero of the night."Adam watched her as she walked away from him. He never tired of looking at her, not since the moment she had burst in on him that day in Warda. She was his fantasy come to life.

And now they really did have forever.

* * * * *

Sharon Ashwood is a novelist, desk jockey and enthusiast for the weird and spooky. She has an English literature degree but works as a finance geek. Interests include growing her to-be-read pile and playing with the toy graveyard on her desk. Sharon is the winner of the 2011 RITA® Award for Best Paranormal Romance. She lives in the Pacific Northwest and is owned by the Demon Lord of Kitty Badness.

Books by Sharon Ashwood

Harlequin Nocturne

Possessed by a Warrior
Possessed by an Immortal
Possessed by a Wolf
Possessed by the Fallen
Enchanted Warrior
Enchanted Guardian
Royal Enchantment
Enchanter Redeemed

ENCHANTER REDEEMED

———

SHARON ASHWOOD

This is for all you readers who like
a bit of magic and romance in your stories,
preferably at the same time.

Prologue

Merlin had destroyed the world as he knew it. The question was what to do next.

As with many disasters, the beginning had been innocent enough. He'd lived in the kingdom of Camelot as the enchanter to King Arthur. Those were eventful years—someone was *always* trying to murder the king, antagonize a dragon or start a war. Often it was his rival in magic, Morgan LaFaye, who wanted Arthur's crown for herself. In nearly every case, the first person Arthur called was Merlin, whether for magic, for advice or even just to complain. In that brief, wonderful time, the solitary enchanter had been part of a community. He'd had friends and drinking partners. He'd even kept pets.

Not that things were perfect. In those days demons roamed the mortal realms, causing untold suffering to everyone in their path. The witches, fae and human lords formed an alliance under Camelot's banner to cast the demons out. Thousands of soldiers massed to do battle, but it was Merlin's magic they counted on for victory. Merlin delivered and they won, but at a terrible cost. As a side effect of his final spell, the fae suffered irreparable damage and fled to nurse their wounds. In a parting shot, the fae swore to return and wreak vengeance on King Arthur and all of humankind.

No one knew when this attack would come. So, once again, Camelot turned to Merlin for answers. With a heavy heart, he summoned all the knights of Camelot to the Church of the Holy Well and put them into an enchanted sleep. For centuries they lay upon their tombs as stone statues, set to awaken when it was time to fight once more.

Centuries rolled by, and Merlin wandered many enchanted lands in search of a cure for the fae. Meanwhile, the Medievaland theme park bought the Church of the Holy Well and the stone knights and shipped them all to Carlyle, Washington, as a tourist attraction. In the process, many of Arthur's knights were sold as museum pieces and curiosities.

When Merlin returned to the mortal realms, no one knew where the knights of the famous Round Table had gone. Camelot was in ruins. The fae—who had chosen Morgan LaFaye as their new and wicked queen—picked this moment to return, seeking vengeance. And, just in case his day wasn't bad enough, the demons were back—including his ex.

Chapter 1

Sorcerer, enchanter, wizard, witch, warlock—they were all job descriptions that were synonymous with "idiot." A person could be born of witch stock and blessed or cursed with natural talents, but it was lunacy to make magic a profession.

This raised the question of precisely why Merlin Ambrosius had been a professional enchanter for over two thousand years and had earned the laughable title of Merlin the Wise. By most standards, he was the most powerful magic user in the land, but that wasn't always an advantage. While Regular Joe Enchanter might have a bad day and blow up his cauldron, Merlin had ripped the souls out of the entire fae race. Merlin the Wise? Not so much.

And now here he was, about to peer through a portal torn through time and space to spy on the scariest creepy-crawlies to ever sprout horns.

His workshop was on the top level of an old warehouse, while the bottom floor was occupied by an automotive repair shop. It was a good arrangement, since Merlin preferred to work at night when the employees had gone home and wouldn't be tempted to ask about funny smells, indoor hailstorms or a flock of flying toads. Today, though, the shop was shut and he had the place to himself. This was a definite bonus, even if it meant getting up before noon. Superstar wizard or not, stalking demons on a sunny afternoon was slightly less terrifying than on a dark and stormy night.

The ritual circle was drawn in chalk in the middle of the floor and the scant furniture pushed aside. The curtains were pulled, softening the light. Empty space yawned up to the rafters, the shadows untouched by the dozen sweet-scented candles flickering in the draft. A hush blanketed the room. Merlin sat cross-legged in the middle of the circle, his comfortable jeans and faded T-shirt at odds with the solemnity of the magic. The truth was, ritual robes didn't matter. Only strength of will and focus would help with this kind of work—which was, in effect, eavesdropping.

Merlin needed information. Specifically, he needed to know what Camelot's enemies had been doing in recent months, because rumors were flying on the magical grapevine, blog sites and social media accounts—not to mention Camelot's spy network. On one hand, there were the fae. They had been far too quiet since the autumn—no attacks, no gratuitous death threats, no random monsters unleashed to trample a city—and the silence was making everyone nervous.

On the other hand, the demon courts were stirring. Arthur, with Merlin's help, had thrown the hellspawn back into the Abyss during Camelot's glory days. But no banishment lasted forever and sooner or later the demons would try to return. Was that what was going on?

He cupped his scrying stone in the palms of his hands, willing answers to flow his way. The stone was cool, smooth and heavy and he concentrated until it was the only object filling his senses. Popular culture loved the image of a wizard with a crystal ball, but to tune into Radio Demon, dark red agate was best. The good stuff was rare, and Merlin had searched for centuries for a flawless globe the size of a small pumpkin. When he'd finally found what he wanted, it had cost enough gold to purchase a small country, but it had been one of his go-to tools ever since.

He spoke a word, and the solid rock dissolved into a cloud of dark gray streaked like a bloody sunset. He still held a hard sphere, but it was like a bubble now. Inside was a window into a complex web of realities that included Faery, the Forest Sauvage, the Crystal Mountains and many more separate but connected realms. He nudged the vision until he was staring into the demon territory called the Abyss.

The mist parted and Merlin had a view of two figures. It wasn't the best angle—he was somewhere above and to the left—but that was an advantage. Spy holes were unpredictable and he had no desire to get caught. Grumpy demons had sent the last unlucky eavesdropper home in a soup bowl.

At first he could only see two figures talking, but a quick shake of the ball fixed the audio.

"What do you mean, you were summoned?" asked the taller of the two in a scholarly accent. He was dressed in a well-tailored suit, his head bald and his black beard neatly clipped. He would have looked at home in any metropolitan city except for the claws, pointy teeth and yellow eyes slitted like a goat's. Merlin knew this demon's name was Tenebrius. They'd had uneasy dealings before.

"I know," replied the other demon, who called himself Gorm. He was small, about the size of a large cat or a smallish monkey, and his leathery skin reminded Merlin of an old shoe. "In these days of computers and binge television, who bothers to summon a demon? But there I was in a chalk circle just like the old days. Talk about retro."

"Don't try to be funny," said Tenebrius, narrowing his eyes. "Who was it?"

"LaFaye. You know, the Queen of Faery?"

The image of Tenebrius stiffened. So did Merlin. Morgan LaFaye had caused most of Camelot's headaches until she'd been imprisoned. She shouldn't have been able to summon so much as pizza delivery from inside her enchanted jail.

"What does *she* want?" asked Tenebrius with obvious caution. He was staring at Gorm with something between suspicion and—was that envy?

Gorm shrugged. "Power. Freedom. King Arthur's head on a platter."

Tenebrius looked down his nose and clasped his hands behind his back, resembling a supercilious butler. "The usual, you mean."

"She is a queen locked up and separated from her people."

Tenebrius snorted, releasing a cloud of smoke from his nostrils. "She rose to power by trading on the fae's grievance against Camelot. I'd hardly call that a good qualification for a leader. They're better off without her, even if they have lost their souls."

And that summed up the damage caused by the spell Merlin had used to banish the demons. Gone was the fae's love of beauty, their laughter, their art. Now they were emotionless automatons sworn to take vengeance on Camelot and feast on the life energy of mortals. Old, familiar guilt gnawed inside him, no less sharp for all the centuries that had passed.

Gorm frowned. "Her Majesty has a grievance."

"Don't we all?" Tenebrius examined his claws. "Do you trust her?"

"Would you trust someone who summoned one of us?"

Tenebrius rolled his slitted eyes. "But why *you*? Was her magic so weakened by prison that she was forced to grab the first demon she came to?"

"Uh—" Gorm started to look up, as if sensing Merlin's intense interest in the conversation, but was distracted a moment later.

"Who's grabbing whom?" came a third and very female voice.

Merlin all but dropped the ball, his mouth suddenly desert dry. The image warped and churned until he forced it back into focus—and then wished he hadn't. Vivian swam into view. She looked as good as she had the last time they'd wrestled between her silken sheets. Scholars claimed demons were made of energy and therefore had no true physical form, yet there was no question that Vivian was exquisite. She was tall and slender but curvaceous in ways that were hard to achieve except as a fantasy art centerfold. A thick river of blue-black hair hung to her knees and framed a heart-shaped face set with enormous violet eyes. Warm toffee skin—bountifully visible despite her glittering armor—stirred dangerous, even disturbing, memories. Beyond Vivian's inhuman loveliness, her demon ancestry showed in the long, black, feline tail that twitched behind her.

Ex-lovers were tricky things. Demon ex-lovers were a whole new level of dangerous. Merlin still wanted to devour her one lick at a time. *Merlin the very, very Unwise.* He closed his eyes, hoping she'd disappear. Unfortunately, when he looked again, she was still there. Then he cursed the loss of those two seconds when he might have been gazing at her. Vivian had been *his*, his pleasure and poison and his personal drug of choice. He'd moved on, but she'd never completely left his bloodstream.

"Gorm got himself summoned," said Tenebrius.

"Who was the lucky enchanter?" Vivian asked. She gave a lush smile with dainty, feline fangs.

"The Queen of Faery."

"Oh," said Vivian, quickly losing the grin, "her. It's almost tempting to give the fae their souls again. Then they'd get rid of LaFaye themselves."

Tenebrius gave her a sly look. "You don't think the situation presents some interesting opportunities?"

Merlin wondered what he meant by that, but Gorm interrupted. "Is it even possible to restore their souls?"

"Theoretically," said Vivian. "Everything's possible with us."

"But we could do it?" Gorm persisted.

Tenebrius shrugged. "The spell came from a demon to begin with. Therefore, demon magic could reverse it."

By all the riches of the goblin kings! Merlin sat frozen. Hope rose, wild and shattering, and he squeezed the ball so that his hands would not shake. He had searched and searched for a means to fix the fae, but had found nothing. Then again, he'd been searching among healers and wielders of the Light, not hellspawn. Demons corrupted and destroyed. They did not improve.

And yet Tenebrius had just said that the demons could provide a cure. Impossible. Brilliant. Amazing. Merlin struggled to control his breath. How was he going to get his hands on a demon-crafted cure? Because it was immediately, solidly obvious that he had to, whatever the cost.

His gaze went from Tenebrius back to the she-demon again. At the sight of her sumptuous body, things—possibly his survival instincts—shriveled in terror while other bits and pieces heated with a toxic mix of panic and desire. Any involvement with demons was an appallingly bad move. Sex was beyond stupid, but he'd been there and done that and insanely lusted for more.

Vivian wanted him dead, and some of her reasons were justified. To begin with, he'd stolen from her. The battle spell that had gone so horribly wrong had come from her grimoire—the great and horrible book of magic that rested on a bone pedestal in her chambers. Maybe she had the power to help the fae—but that would mean facing her again. Now, there was a terrifying idea.

The door behind Merlin banged open with a loud crack. "Hey, you busy?"

Startled out of deep concentration, Merlin jumped, dropping the globe. With a curse, he snatched it up.

"Oops. Sorry, dude." The new voice seemed to ring in the rafters, blaringly loud against the profound silence of the magical circle. A corner of Merlin's brain identified the speaker as his student, Clary Greene, but the rest of him was teetering on the edge of panic. When he righted the globe, the swirling clouds parted inside the stone once more. He peered until the image of the room grew crisp. Three demon faces stared back at him with murderous expressions.

Merlin said something much stronger than "oops."

Vivian's eyes began to glow. "Merlin!" she snarled, his name trailing into a feline hiss that spoke of unfinished business.

Merlin quickly set the agate ball on the floor and sprang away, colliding with Clary's slight form. His student's pixie-like features crumpled in confusion. "What's going on?"

"Duck!" he ordered, grabbing her shoulder and pushing her to the floor.

Bolts of power blasted from the agate globe in rainbow colors, arcing in jagged lightning all through the room. With three demons firing at once, it looked like an otherworldly octopus, its tentacles grabbing objects and zapping them to showers of ash. Merlin's bookshelf exploded, burning pages filling the air as if he was trapped in an apocalyptic snow globe.

"Making friends again?" Clary asked, flicking ash from her shaggy blond head. Her words were flippant, but her face was tense.

"Stay low. They're demons."

Clary's witch-green eyes went wide. She was Vivian's opposite—a lean, fair tomboy with more attitude than magical talent. She was also everything that Vivian was not—honest, kind, thoughtful and far too good to be in Merlin's life. She was a drink of clean water to a man parched by his own excesses, an innocent despite what she believed about herself. Everything about her had beckoned, woman to man, but he'd kept their relationship professional. It was bad enough that she had begged him to teach her magic. He should have refused. Nothing good came to anyone who lingered near him.

And right now lingering was not an option.

"Move," he snapped, forcing her to creep backward one step at a time. The slow pace was nerve-racking, but it gave him a moment to weave a protective spell around them both.

He was just in time. Lightning fried his worktable, shattering a row of orderly glass vials, and then his bicycle sizzled and warped into a piece of futuristic sculpture. Merlin scowled as the seat burst into flame. Maybe he should rethink the slow and steady approach.

Vivian's clear voice rang from the agate globe. "Curse you, Merlin Ambrosius. I vow that you shall not escape me, but shall suffer due vengeance for what you have done!"

"What did you do?" Clary whispered. "She's really mad."

"Not now," Merlin muttered. Not ever, if he had a choice.

He sprang at the agate ball, intending to break the connection between his workshop and the demon realm with a well-placed bolt of his own. Before he was halfway there, a purple tentacle of energy lashed out and fastened on his chest. A blaze of pain sang through him, fierce as a sword stroke. He thrust out a hand, warping the stream of power away before his heart stopped.

Then Clary cast her own counter spell, just the way he'd taught her. The blow struck, but only clipped the edge of the stone ball, rolling it outside the containment of the ritual circle. Merlin pounced, but the damage was done. Once outside the circle, the demons were free to cross over into his world. As he groped on the floor for the agate, Vivian's armored boots appeared in his field of view. He looked up and up her long legs to her shapely body and finally to her furious eyes.

"Who is this witch?" Vivian pointed a claw-tipped finger at Clary. Her long black tail swished back and forth, leaving an arc in the ashes coating the floor.

"Darling. Sweetheart. She's my student," he said in calming tones as he got to his feet, still clutching the stone. The agate sparked with the demons' power, as if he held a heavy ball of pure electricity.

"Does she know what you really are?" Anger twisted Vivian's beautiful face. "Or should I say, does she have any idea how low you will stoop for power?"

Clearly, the demon was still mad that he'd stolen her spell. Or, more likely, she was furious that he'd left their bed without a word—but there had been no choice, under the circumstances. It was that or hand Camelot and everybody else over to the hellspawn.

Vivian's furious form was just a projection of energy—half in her own world and half in his—and yet Merlin took a cautious step back. "Clary is only a student, Vivian. I can promise you that much."

"I'm standing right here," Clary snapped.

It was the wrong tone to take with an angry demon. Vivian flicked a bolt of power from her fingertips that hurled Clary against the wall. To Merlin's horror, the young witch stuck there, suspended above the floor like a butterfly on a pin. Clary grabbed at her chest, tearing at the zipper of her leather jacket as if she needed air.

"Enough!" Merlin roared. "She is nothing to you."

"But she is something to you. I can smell it!"

"She's under my protection." He lashed out, breaking Vivian's hold.

The demoness rounded on him, fixing him with those hypnotic violet eyes. Her predatory beauty held him for a split second too long. As Clary crumpled to the floor, Vivian's claws slashed at the girl, leaving long, red tracks soaking through the sleeve of thin burgundy leather. Vivian snarled, showing fangs. In moments, Clary would be dead—and for no reason other than because she'd interrupted his ritual.

Desperation knotted Merlin's chest. He lifted the agate globe, infusing it with his power. Part of him screamed to stop, to guard his own interests, but the fever of his grief and guilt was too strong. With a howl, he smashed the globe to the floor. It exploded into a thousand shards, taking most of his earthly wealth with it. Vivian shrieked—a high, pained banshee wail—and vanished with a pop of air pressure that left his ears ringing. A heavy stink of burning amber hung in the air, borne on wisps of purple smoke. Clary began to cough, a racking, bubbling gasp of sound.

Merlin fell to his knees at her side. "It's over."

He put an arm around the young woman, helping her to sit up. The warm, slender weight of her seemed painfully fragile. Witches were mortal, as easily broken as ordinary humans, and Clary's face had drained of color. He touched her cheek with the back of his hand to find her skin was cold.

His stomach clenched with panic. "How badly are you hurt?"

She didn't answer. She wasn't breathing anymore.

Chapter 2

Clary jolted awake. Power surged through her body, painful and suffocating. Her spine arched into it—or maybe away from it, she wasn't sure. Merlin had one hand on her side and the other on her chest, using his magic like a defibrillator. The sensation hammered her from the inside while every hair on her body stood straight up. When he released her, she sagged in relief. A drifting sensation took over, as if she were a feather in an updraft.

Merlin's fingers went to her neck, checking for a pulse. His hands were hot from working spells, the touch firm yet gentle. In her weakened state, Clary shivered slightly, wanting to bare her throat in surrender. She was a sucker for dark, broody masculinity, and he projected it like a beacon. All the same, Clary sucked in a breath before he got any big ideas about mouth-to-mouth. If Merlin was going to kiss her, she wanted wine and soft music, not blood and the dirty workshop floor.

Another bolt of power, more pain, another pulse check. Clary managed a moan, and she heard the sharp intake of Merlin's breath. His hand withdrew from her pulse point as she forced her eyes open. He was staring down at her with his peculiar amber eyes, dark brows furrowed in concern. She was used to him prickly, arrogant or sarcastic, but not this. She'd never seen that oddly vulnerable expression before—but it quickly fled as their gazes met.

"You're alive." He said it like a fact, any softness gone.

"Yup." Clary pushed herself up on her elbows. She hurt all over. "What was that?"

"A demon."

"I got that much." Clary held up her arm, peering through the rents in her jacket where the demon's claws had slashed. Merlin's zap of power had stopped the bleeding, but the deep scratches were red, puffy and hurt like blazes.

"Demon claws are toxic."

"Got that, too."

"I can put a salve on the wound, but you'd be smart to have Tamsin look at it," Merlin said. "Your sister is a better healer than I am."

"She's better than anybody." Clary said it with the automatic loyalty of a little sister, but it was true. "She's got a better bedside manner, too."

Merlin raised a brow, his natural arrogance back in place. "Just be glad you're alive."

She studied Merlin, acutely aware of how much magic he'd used to shut Vivian down. He looked like a man in his early thirties, but there was no telling how old he actually was. He was lean-faced with permanent stubble and dark hair that curled at his collar. At first glance, he looked like a radical arts professor or dot-com squillionaire contemplating his next disruptive innovation. It took a second look to notice the muscular physique hidden by the comfortable clothes. Merlin had a way of sliding under most radars, but Clary never underestimated the power he could pluck out of thin air. She was witch born, a member of the Shadow-ring Coven, but he was light-years beyond their strongest warlocks.

That strength was like catnip to her—although she'd never, ever admit that out loud. "What were you doing?" she demanded, struggling the rest of the way to a sitting position.

"A surveillance ritual." His face tensed as if afraid to reveal too much. "There've been rumors of demon activity in the Forest Sauvage."

The forest lay at the junction of several supernatural realms. "Demons show up there anyway, don't they?"

"One or two of the strongest hellspawn can leave the Abyss, but only for brief periods. It's not a regular occurrence. Yet Arthur's spies report a demon has been meeting with the fae generals on multiple occasions."

"You want to know what they're up to," she murmured, a horrible awareness of what she'd interrupted settling in. Gawd, how stupid was she? It was a wonder Merlin hadn't kicked her out of his workshop after her first lesson. He would have to now.

"I was summoning information through a scrying portal. The conversation was growing interesting when you arrived." His tone was precise and growing colder with every syllable. Now that the crisis was over, he was getting angry.

Clary pressed a hand to her pounding head. "They heard me come in?"

"Yes."

She cringed inwardly, but lifted her head, refusing to let her mortification show. "Then Babe-a-licious with the tail showed up."

"Yes." There was no mistaking the frost in his tone now. "Vivian. Do you have any idea how dangerous she is?"

"She tried to kill me." Clary's insides hollowed as the words sank home. *Dear goddess, she did kill me!* And Merlin had brought her back before a second had passed—but it had happened. Her witch's senses had felt it happen. The realization left her light-headed.

"She doesn't get to have you," he said in a low voice.

Their gazes locked, and something twisted in Clary's chest. She'd been hurt on Merlin's watch, and he was furious. No, what she saw in his eyes was more than icy anger. It was a heated, primal possessiveness that came from a far different Merlin than she knew. Clary's breath stopped. Surely she was misreading the situation. Death and zapping had scrambled her thoughts. "What happened when you smashed the stone?"

"The demon returned to where she came from."

"Will she come back?"

"If she does, it will be for me. She won't bother you. You were incidental."

Clary might have been insulted, but she was barely listening now. The events of the past few minutes fell over her like a shadow, pushing everything else, even Merlin, aside. She'd felt death coming like a cold, black vortex. She began to shake, her mind scrambling to get away from a memory of gathering darkness. She drew her knees into her chest, hugging them. "I shouldn't have walked in on you."

"No, you shouldn't have," he said in a voice filled with the same mix of ice and fire. "You'd be a better student of magic if you paid attention to the world around you. That would include door wards."

Tears stung behind her eyelids. Trust Merlin to use death as a teachable moment. "You could be sympathetic. At least a little."

He made a noise that wasn't quite a snort. "You asked me to teach you proper magic and not the baby food the covens use. If you want warm and fuzzy, get a rabbit. Real magic is deadly."

Clary took a shuddering breath. "No kidding."

He was relentless. "Today your carelessness cost me a valuable tool."

She sighed her resentment. "I'll get you a new stone."

"You can't. There was only one like it, and now I'm blind to what the demons are doing."

Abruptly, he stood and crossed the room to kick a shard of agate against the wall. It bounced with a savage clatter. Clary got to her feet, her knees wobbling. Merlin was right about her needing Tamsin's medical help. She braced her hand against the wall so she'd stop weaving. "I'm sorry."

He spun and stormed back to her in one motion, moving so fast she barely knew what was happening. He took her by the shoulders, the grip rough. "Don't *ever* do that again!"

And then his mouth crushed hers in a hard, angry kiss. Clary gasped in surprise, but there was no air, only him, and only his need. She rose slowly onto her toes, the gesture both surrender and a desire to hold her own. She'd been kissed many times before, but never consumed this way. His lips were greedy and hot with that same confusing array of emotions she'd seen a moment ago. Anger. Fear. Possession. Protectiveness.

Volatile. That was the word she'd so often used in her own head when thinking about him. Volatile, though he kept himself on a very short chain. Right now that chain had slipped.

And she liked it. Head spinning, she leaned back against the wall, trapped between the plaster and the hard muscle of his chest. Now that the first shock was past, she moved her mouth under his, returning the kiss. Hot breath fanned against her cheek, sending tingles down her spine. She'd never understood the stories about danger sparking desire until this moment, but now she was soaring, lust a hot wire lighting up her whole frame. Being alive was very, very good.

Merlin had braced his hands on either side of her head, but now he stroked them down her body in a long, slow caress. It was a languid movement as if he was measuring and memorizing her every curve. Clary let her arms drift up to link behind his neck.

"I think I'll skip the fuzzy bunny and keep you instead," she murmured.

The effect of her words was electric. He stepped out of her embrace as unexpectedly as he'd entered it, pushing a hand through his hair. "We can't do this." He turned away as if he needed to regain control.

After being killed, revived, scolded and ravished, Clary was getting whiplash. "Why not?" she asked through clenched teeth.

"Vivian."

"She was angry," Clary conceded. "Did you and she have a, um, thing?"

He made a noise like a strangling bear. "She is everything unholy."

Yup, Viv was an ex. For some reason, that sparked her temper in a way nothing else had. Clary wiped her mouth on her sleeve.

"I said you were incidental to her." His voice had gone cold again. "Let's keep it that way. Touching you was a mistake."

"A mistake?"

Merlin faced her, frowning at her sarcastic tone. "Yes."

"So Vivian is a jealous mean girl," Clary snapped. "That's not my problem, and I'm not a mistake. I don't deserve that kind of disrespect."

And yet she did. She was a screwup, a talentless hack of a witch and not much better with her personal life. She'd just proven it all over again by bursting in where she wasn't wanted. The knowledge scalded her, but it also raised her defenses. It was one thing to reject her as a magician, but he'd just rejected her as a woman.

"Don't be difficult," he replied.

"Don't be an idiot. I'm a person, not an error." She'd never spoken to Merlin like this, but she'd never been this upset. She didn't care if he had a point.

Clary pushed away from the wall. Merlin took a step forward as if to support her, but she wasn't dizzy now. Anger had cleared her head and set her pulse speeding at a quick march. Her whole body sang with pain, but she stalked toward the door on perfectly steady feet.

"Clary!" Merlin said, his tone thick with irritation. "Come back here."

"Don't talk to me right now. And don't come after me." Clary slammed the workshop door behind her, taking the steps down to the main level of the warehouse at a run. She didn't look back.

When she reached the street a minute later, the late May sunshine seemed strange. There was no darkness, no storms and certainly no demons. Sparrows flitted through the last blossoms of the cherry trees lining the streets, and a senior couple walked matching Scottie dogs in the leaf-dappled shade. It was the perfect day for a cross-country bike ride, the kind that might take her fifty or sixty miles. Clary shook her head, feeling as if she was suddenly in the wrong movie.

She started walking, the residue of her anger still hot in her veins. Merlin's workshop was at the edge of Carlyle's bustling downtown and a twenty-minute walk from her sister's apartment. If Clary went for a visit, she could get her throbbing arm checked and complain to Tamsin about men at the same time.

Tamsin would be sympathetic for sure. Clary was the baby of the family and her uncertain talent upset a cartload of familial expectations, but she was an accomplished computer programmer and was making a new career as a social media consultant for Medievaland. Tamsin would tell her she was doing fine, which was exactly what she needed right now.

The social media job had been a stroke of luck, something she'd pitched to Camelot when she'd moved across the country to study with Merlin. In fact, she was his first student in a hundred years because she'd refused to take no for an answer the moment she'd found out her big sister had met the man. In her imagination he'd been the ultimate enchanter, a rebel prince of the magical world. He'd turned out to be short-tempered and demanding, arrogant and aloof. She'd been crushed.

It wasn't that Merlin was a bad teacher—he was fabulous. He drilled her remorselessly, showing her three or four ways to launch a spell until they found one that worked for her. Fighting spells, spying spells, portals, wards—he taught far more practical application than theory and approached every lesson with resolute patience. Her skills had leaped forward. It was just that he was so very *Merlin*.

Clary swore under her breath. You'd think he could have put a sign on the door to keep visitors out. Sure, she'd dropped by unexpectedly with a question about the homework he'd given her and, yes, there had been a ward she disarmed to walk in, but he *always* had a ward on the door. Sometimes he put them there just to test her. How was she to know he'd be chatting with hellspawn?

And as for the rest, why was she surprised? It had been a kiss in the moment, a rare moment of compassion from a very dark horse. Merlin was the greatest enchanter in written history. She was so far down the food chain she wasn't even on the menu. There would never be anything more between them, however much that one embrace made her imagination explode.

She ground her teeth. Maybe she should have stuck with computers. At least software didn't have claws. At least it didn't kiss her and then shut down the moment with a wall of ice.

Clary's thoughts scattered as she neared Tamsin's street. This block was lined with low-rise storefronts featuring a drugstore, a used-clothing exchange and a place that still sold vinyl records. The neighborhood was like a small town where shopkeepers greeted their customers by name and residents knew which child belonged to which mother. Normally, she enjoyed the relaxed atmosphere, but she was starting to feel sick again. Whatever fury she'd been running on was draining fast. There was a café with a few outdoor tables, and she sat down on one of the ornate metal chairs. She rested her head on her good hand and cradled her injured arm in her lap. *I should call Tamsin*, she thought, but the pocket with her phone seemed miles away.

Her heart was hammering, perspiration clammy on her skin. It took her a moment to recognize the sensation as raw, primal fear. But why? She was out of danger now, wasn't she? Hadn't Merlin said Clary herself was of no interest to the demons? And yet, it felt as if something was looking over her shoulder. She jerked around, but saw nothing except a passerby startled by Clary's frown.

The sudden motion sent spikes of pain up her arm. She pushed up the torn sleeve of her jacket to see the scratches were swelling now. She touched the pink skin and discovered it was hot. Infection. Wonderful. No wonder she felt queasy. She slumped in the chair, aware of the clatter and bustle of the coffee shop though it seemed far, far in the distance.

She fished her phone out and set it on the table, realizing she'd have to dial it left-handed because the fingers of her injured hand had gone numb. Clary had managed to punch the code that unlocked it when a wave of pain struck her. It was like the shock of power Merlin had administered, but on steroids.

Clary hunched over the table, robbed of the breath even to cry out. A white haze swallowed the world around her, turning everything to static. Sound vanished, a high, thin hum filling her brain. She began to shake—not a ladylike trembling, either. Her head lolled back as her jerking knees rattled the table. All at once she was on the ground, her cheek pressed to the gritty sidewalk.

Blackness.

Hands gathered her up. Voices distant and muffled as if she was underwater. She was in the chair again, the cold metal beneath the seat of her jeans. Hard to stay in the chair because her limbs were like spaghetti.

"Miss? Miss?"

There was a sound like a bubble popping, and she could see and hear again.

"By the Abyss!" Clary gasped as the world smacked her like cold water. Sounds, colors, smells all seemed out of control. Clary blinked, wiping her eyes with the back of her good hand.

"Can we call someone for you?" asked a voice.

Clary squinted, recognizing the square, pleasant face of the woman who ran the coffee shop. She searched for the woman's name, but it was gone. "Huh?"

"You passed out," the woman said slowly and carefully. "You might have had a seizure."

Goddess! She should probably be in the hospital, but then she'd have to explain the claw marks. Clary looked around. Her phone was still on the table. "Tamsin," she said but couldn't manage more. A wave of disorientation swamped her. Her voice sounded wrong, but she wasn't sure why.

"Tamsin who lives in the apartment building down the street?" the woman asked.

Clary nodded, afraid to speak again.

"She ordered a birthday cake for the weekend. I have her number." The woman bustled back inside.

Clary closed her eyes. Whose birthday was it? The name bobbed just out of reach of her thoughts. Facts and memories receded, as if her consciousness was a balloon that had come untethered. When she opened her eyes again, she caught sight of her reflection in the café window and froze.

Her face was familiar, and it was not. *So this is what it's like to be human.*

Clary's thoughts swerved. *What the blazes?*

She'd recognized the voice in her head. Cold needles of fear crept up her body, turning her fingers and nose so cold it felt like January. Something had been watching her, and now she knew it was Vivian.

Or what's left of me after Merlin smashed his precious globe. Immortals are hard to kill, but I was vulnerable when he did that. I needed a safe harbor and your body was empty for a split second before he brought you back. Hope you don't mind a roomie.

Clary sat up straight, fighting a sudden urge to scream. Her head, seemingly of its own accord, turned back to her reflection. She took in the mop of shaggy blond hair, the ragged, bloody clothes and her wide, frightened eyes.

It's not the body I'm used to, but beggars can't be choosers. Still, we need to do something about the wardrobe.

Chapter 3

Surely it had all been a horrible hallucination. The next morning found Clary sitting at her sister's kitchen table, a cup of black coffee before her. Everything seemed normal, and Clary felt as loved and cared for as Tamsin could manage. She'd slept in her sister's tiny second bedroom and still had a crick in her spine from the lumpy futon.

"How are you feeling?" Tamsin asked, putting a hand over Clary's. Gawain, Tamsin's soon-to-be husband, had already left for the day and the two women were alone. Normally, Clary would have been disappointed. She liked Gawain, and he'd spent almost as much time teaching her self-defense as Merlin had spent teaching her magic—if there was to be a fight with the fae, she needed to be ready. But today she wanted alone time with her sister.

Clary looked up from staring into her cup. Like Clary, Tamsin was green-eyed and fair-haired, her long locks pinned up in a messy bun. The similarity in coloring was deceptive. Tamsin was actually a stepsister who had joined the family when Clary's mom had married a second time. They had all been lucky—Stacy, the eldest, and Clary, the youngest, had readily accepted their new middle sister. Tamsin was easy to love and Clary adored her. She'd been the gentle hand that had led Clary through a rebellious adolescence when their mother had all but given up in despair.

"My wound feels better," Clary answered, pulling up her sleeve.

Tamsin angled Clary's arm for a better look. Besides working as Medievaland's historian, Tamsin's magical specialty was healing. After a round of smelly ointments and ritual, the wounds on Clary's arm were now just scratches, as if Clary had lost an argument with an alley cat.

"I've met demons, but I've never treated any injuries they caused before now. I never knew they had poisoned claws," Tamsin said, releasing Clary's arm.

"Do you think that's what caused the seizure?" Clary sipped her coffee, welcoming the caffeine as it hit her bloodstream. She hadn't said anything about the hallucinations. She'd stopped hearing that voice in her head by the time Tamsin had finished doctoring her, and decided to keep the crazy to herself. "Maybe the infection was messing with my brain?"

She could hear the pleading in her voice. She felt okay now, and desperately wanted to put yesterday behind her.

"I'd bet the two are connected." Tamsin picked up

Clary's hand again. It was a comforting gesture, but Clary could feel the faint tingle of Tamsin's magic course through her. Tamsin leaned forward and kissed her forehead as if Clary was a little girl again. The gesture salved Clary's hurts the way no medicine could.

"You're still not a hundred percent," Tamsin said, "but I don't detect any lingering damage. Take it easy for a few days."

"I'm supposed to be at Medievaland today."

"In the office?"

It was a reasonable assumption. Clary handled pretty much all of Medievaland's online presence. Since King Arthur and a handful of his knights had awakened to join the modern world, they'd become famous for the mock tourneys hosted by the theme park. The knights now had a rapidly expanding fan base, which Clary fed with judicious tidbits of insider knowledge—none of which included the fact that they were born centuries ago and had returned to save humanity from soul-sucking fae monsters. She tried to keep things upbeat.

However, today's activities weren't about posts and blogs. "Merlin's doing the special effects at today's show and he wants a second pair of hands."

Tamsin frowned. "You should call in sick. Obviously, he'd understand."

"Maybe, maybe not. I broke his ball."

Tamsin arched an eyebrow. "Just one of them?"

Clary grimaced. "Crystal—stone—ball. His spy camera to the demon realms. He had to smash it to save me from Vivian." She was feeling more than a little guilty about that.

"Yeah," Tamsin replied, drawing the word out. "Those stones are expensive and rare."

"He said it was one of a kind."

"Are you sure you're still his student?"

Clary pulled her smartphone from the pocket of the boho-style dress Tamsin had loaned her to replace her bloodstained clothes. It was pink and flowery and nothing like what she usually wore. She held the phone up as if it was evidence. "I'm scheduled to be there at noon. He sent a text to confirm."

"That's probably his way of checking on you. You had a near death by demon, then a seizure." Tamsin had that frozen look that said she wasn't happy but was trying to be polite about it. "I think you can skip a session."

"Normally, I'd welcome a day off, but as you say, I cost him a piece of expensive equipment. Showing up is the least I can do."

"You feel guilty."

"Pretty much."

Clary's mind immediately went to the kiss. Her cheeks heated at the memory, and she looked away from her sister. Merlin's behavior was just one more strange thing to add to the list of yesterday's weirdness.

"What else happened besides the demon who attacked you?" Tamsin asked. She'd always been able to read Clary's expressions.

Clary rose from the table. "I need to get ready to go." She suddenly didn't want to talk anymore.

Tamsin—still protesting—drove her to Medievaland. They parked and passed a long line at the gate that proved the summer tourist rush was beginning. The weather promised to be warm, so the steady stream of paying customers would only increase as midday approached. And why not? Medievaland, with its jousts and feasts and rides and games, was good family fun.

Clary and Tamsin passed the turnstile and pushed through the knot of visitors milling at the information booth. A herald rode by on a milk-white mare, shouting directions to Friar Ambrose's delicatessen and the noon show at the bandstand. To the right was the market area crowded with merchants selling all manner of handcrafts and snack foods; to the left the traditional arcade that led off to the rides, where the Dragon's Tail— a roller coaster that challenged even Clary's daredevil instincts—swirled high above the crowds. Tamsin's destination was the Church of the Holy Well, the one truly medieval structure in the park. It had been moved, along with the stone knights, from the south of England and turned into the museum where Tamsin worked.

The two women stopped when they reached a fork in the path. "You're absolutely sure you feel up to this?" asked Tamsin. "No headaches or weakness?"

"I feel fine," Clary protested, and that much was almost true. "As if there was anything on the planet that could withstand your healing!"

"Then, be brave, little witchling." Tamsin gave her a hug. "I'll check on you in a few hours."

Clary laughed at her childhood nickname. "You're such a big sister."

Tamsin made a face and left, heading toward the ancient church ahead. Feeling content for the first time since before barging into Merlin's workshop, Clary took the path to the tourney grounds.

Jousting and other events took place in an amphitheater, where the audience could get a good view of the armored horsemen doing battle. Behind the large structure were the stables, changing rooms and other service buildings. As Clary hurried in that direction, she could hear the stampede of hooves and the crash of lance on shield. The crowd roared and applauded, which meant someone had scored a good hit. After a glance at her phone to check the time, she picked up her pace, ignoring the hawkers selling T-shirts and ball caps.

When she reached the change rooms, she grabbed a long blue gown out of her locker and quickly put it on. All the employees at Medievaland dressed the part, and by the time she was done, she'd added a long belt of glittering—if fake—jewels and pinned her hair under a fluttering white veil. Then she headed for the amphitheater, where she was to meet the enchanter in one of the high boxes that overlooked the field.

Nerves made Clary's breath come faster. She was here because, despite yesterday, she still wanted Merlin as her teacher. She wanted to be an effective witch, ready to fight fae or demons or whatever threat darkened Camelot's door. She wanted to belong here like Tamsin did. Still, she had to admit she'd come for other reasons, too. She needed to bury the anger between her and Merlin. He'd been a jerk, but she'd burst in on him. He could have handled everything better, but she'd resorted to a tantrum. Neither had been at their best with dying and exes and all.

And—here, she mentally shied away just a little— they had kissed. She had to face him with her head held high and not reveal how much more she desired. Sometimes attitude was all a person had.

When she saw Merlin, her step slowed so she could take in the sight. He wore long robes of deep blue and carried a tall staff of knobby wood. With his lean face and unusual amber eyes, he carried the fantasy-wizard costume well. Very well, and with the kind of brooding intensity that teased something low in her belly. He was gazing at the tourney ground, a thoughtful frown on his face.

"Hi," she said.

He looked up, his expression startled for an instant before it settled into his habitual reserve. "How are you feeling?"

"Fine," she said, sounding as defensive as she suddenly felt. "I can work."

A long moment passed in which Merlin studied her, his expression closed. "Do you remember what you're supposed to do?" he asked.

If he was trying to keep her at a distance, it was working. All at once, Clary felt exposed in her feminine dress, the light breeze tugging and touching in ways that didn't happen with her usual denim and leather. She wanted to say again how sorry she was for yesterday's mistake, but the words died under his cool stare. His mood felt like punishment, but whether it was for himself or for her, she couldn't say. It took a moment to get her lips to move. "Yes, I know what to do."

"Good." He turned back to the amphitheater. The packed dirt field had been cleared, ready for the next event. "Keep to the script, regardless of what else you might see. I'm raising the bar a notch for today's show."

Clary swallowed. The show would be grunt work for Merlin, but for her it would be tricky. She tried not to think about the time she'd accidentally teleported a moose into her hotel room. *Be brave, little witchling.* "I'm ready."

Merlin gave a signal, and the voice of the announcer boomed through the public address system. "Lords and ladies, honored guests of Medievaland, welcome to this afternoon's main event. This is the moment of dread, the true test of bravery and the battle you've all been waiting for—Medievaland's courageous knights versus the enchanter Merlin's monsters!"

The audience roared its approval. The gates at the far end of the amphitheater swung open, and the knights rode in two by two—Gawain and Hector, then Beaumains and Percival, and finally Owen and Palomedes. They parted, each pair splitting left and right to form a colorful double line. The last to appear was King Arthur, resplendent in blue and gold and riding a huge bay stallion. The amphitheater rumbled with enthusiastically stamping feet as the knights took up their position flanking the king.

Two musicians with long golden trumpets blew a fanfare, silencing the crowd. Merlin turned to Clary and gave a nod. She braced herself. She'd practiced this spell hundreds of times and now she recited the words of the spell exactly as he'd taught her. Then she released her power. With relief, she felt the magic shape itself, swirling until it solidified into an enormous black wolf. It bounded toward Palomedes, jaws open to reveal a lot of drool and fangs.

"Nice," said Merlin.

He didn't give praise often, so Clary felt her cheeks warm with pleasure. Far below, Palomedes did battle with the illusion to the obvious pleasure of the paying guests. But that was only the first of many monsters, and Clary set about creating the next. A quick sideways glance showed Merlin had begun an incantation of his own. Clary wondered what it would be, but quickly pushed the thought away. She couldn't get distracted.

With exquisite care, she wove the next spell bit by bit, checking and double-checking each element she added.

Seriously? said the voice in her head—the same voice that had plagued her at the café. *This isn't brain surgery.*

Startled, Clary released her power an instant too early and it bobbled wildly. Then—without knowing how she did it—she reached out and patted it back into shape. Except it was the wrong shape. She'd planned on one oversize lion. Instead, two flightless raptors straight out of the Jurassic era popped into existence and began charging the knights at lightning speed. Clary stared at them in dismay. *What did you make me do?*

I upped your game. You should be grateful.

Stop it! Go away! You're a hallucination! At least she'd hoped Vivian's voice had been the product of her infected wound.

The voice in her head gave a wry snort. *Do you feel feverish?*

No, Clary felt physically fine. Better than ever, in fact—which meant even worse trouble. "Why are you doing this?"

She didn't realize she'd spoken out loud until Merlin gave her a quick glance. "Keep going." Then he turned back to his long, intricate spell.

The show must go on. With a flick of Clary's wrist, the demon summoned not one lion, but a whole pride. All at once, the knights were extremely busy.

Vivian! Clary protested. She wanted to round on the demon, glare at her, maybe punch her. Except it was impossible when the opposition was inside her head. *What do you want?*

Vivian's gaze—in the form of Clary's eyeballs—

turned to Merlin. *He took something from me and walked away.*

An ominous feeling gripped Clary as if she'd just stumbled upon an unquiet grave. *What?*

Vivian didn't answer. She was watching Merlin work, and Clary had a front-row seat to the demon's emotions. They weren't as deep or complicated as human feelings, but they were uncomfortably frank. Vivian liked everything about Merlin, from the straight line of his nose to the angle of his jaw. There was also distinct disappointment about how much of his body the robes concealed.

An image of Merlin, his hair longer and his clothes absent, flicked across Clary's mental screen. The vignette revealed a lot of long, lean muscle and tanned limbs. Clary's skin heated, suddenly too tight as her own desire melded with the demon's.

I know his secrets, the demon mused. *You wouldn't worship him half so much if you knew the truth.*

Clary struggled, now barely aware of the spectacle below. *It's none of my business.*

He's your flawed hero, your rebel prince. Of course you're curious.

With horror, she realized Vivian was quoting her own thoughts. Fury pounded against Clary's temples. This hopeless attraction was her own affair, buried where it couldn't embarrass her.

Don't bother, said Vivian. *He thinks you belong to him, but that is a far cry from passion.*

Clary's nails bit into her palms. *And what's he to you?*

Another sweep of eyes, another rush of need. It was all Clary could do to keep her hands at her sides and not reach out to touch the enchanter's warm skin. *Merlin Ambrosius was my soul mate, the one who filled the empty places in my heart.*

Was the demon lovesick? Clary wondered with astonishment. She shifted uncomfortably, suddenly hot and weak with their mingled need.

No. Vivian flexed her power—which Clary felt in a sudden head rush. *I'm here to take my revenge.*

He'll stop you. Clary dug her nails into her palms, using the pain to focus. *I'll stop you. I'll tell him you're here.*

Really? And you think there would be no consequences?

I don't care what he does to me as long as he stops you.

Vivian laughed, a low, husky sound that belonged on a phone sex hotline. *Oh, very good, but I'm not done with you yet. On the other hand, I have no use for your sister.*

Clary's lungs stopped working. Tamsin! She didn't need the demon to say more. If Clary gave Vivian away, Tamsin would suffer.

Sorry it has to be her, Vivian drawled, *but you don't have a vast selection of loved ones to choose from.*

That stung more than Clary liked. *Leave her out of this!*

But this is revenge, remember? Before I'm done, Merlin will wish he were dead. And if you don't do exactly as I say, little witchling, so will you.

Chapter 4

Merlin's lips moved over silent words as he worked his spell. A faint glimmer sparked in the cloudless sky above the auditorium. It would look like nothing to one of the cheering spectators that crammed the seats, just a random flash of light, but to Merlin it was hard-won success. He'd practiced the spell the way a musician learned a piece from memory, going over and over each element until they formed part of his instincts. It was the way he taught Clary: ritual, rinse, repeat. The drill wasn't just for the sake of perfectionism—it was as much for safety. With this amount of powerful magic in play, he couldn't afford to stumble.

Which was why he couldn't think about Clary, for all he felt her gaze on him. Her attention was like the heat of the sun, and all the more tangible because of his own disquiet. If only he hadn't kissed her, because now he could not deny how she made him feel. He might have immense skill, knowledge and power beyond the fantasies of mortal men, but he was still flesh and blood. She was a happiness he wanted but could not have—and for an instant, he'd forgotten that last part.

His control had slipped after witnessing her death and revival. Still, that was no excuse. His enemies were too dangerous for a junior witch who was just beginning to master her talents. He had no right to draw their attention to Clary. At the very least, he had to be careful until he was sure Vivian was safely locked back in the Abyss. The demoness was definitely the jealous type.

So he ignored his student, keeping his focus on the spell. It was tricky but, unlike women, it followed a pattern of logic he understood. With the force of one driving a spike deep into bedrock, he fixed the silver glimmer to the canopy of the sky. From there it spun, growing larger and larger into a disk of shimmering light. If his thrust had been too great or too feeble, the swirl would have wobbled and collapsed, but this was as perfect as a whirling top. The momentum of the magic formed a tunnel between worlds, splitting open a passage between the mortal realm and the enchanted worlds beyond.

The perfection of the spell eased Merlin's temper. The silver bled to a blue deeper than the surrounding sky. The audience cheered in anticipation, believing they watched a special effect none of Medievaland's competition could copy. In a way they did, because no other theme park could boast a guest appearance by a real live dragon.

With a lazy flap of wings, Rukon Shadow Wing floated through Merlin's portal. A smile split Merlin's face at the sight and he allowed the pleasant tiredness that followed a well-cast spell to claim him. Portals took a lot of energy, but they were worth the effort for a sight like this.

The great male dragon flew low enough that Merlin caught the scent of musk and cinders as the wings blotted out the sun. The dragon's green head was long and narrow, the sinuous neck twisting to survey the ground below. As it turned, the light caught the bony ridge of spikes that traced its spine to the tip of its snakelike tail.

Rukon's head bobbed toward Merlin in acknowledgment. The dragon's visits were made in exchange for Camelot's assistance last autumn, when Arthur and Guinevere had freed Rukon's mate. Plus, preening before a crowd of unsuspecting humans seemed to amuse the beast no end.

It was only then, with the spell complete, that he could risk a good look at Clary. Her face was flushed with effort, her eyes wide with what looked like shock. Stomach tense, he followed her gaze to the field below.

Clary's illusions sometimes had a mind of their own, but normally they were forms without substance, as dangerous as a puff of smoke. As long as they showed off the knights and their shiny swords, what else mattered? So he hadn't paid much attention when triple the number of required monsters appeared from thin air. Apparently, that had been a mistake.

A lion raked its claws across the flank of Sir Palomedes's steed. The horse screamed, rearing up to reveal a bloody gash. Surprised, the knight struggled to keep his seat, but the terrified horse threw him and bolted for the stables. Horror gut-punched Merlin, and he grabbed the cold metal railing before him. Illusions didn't draw blood. Something was very wrong, and now the lions were circling Palomedes.

Merlin shot a glance at Clary, who had raised her hands and seemed poised to begin another spell. He grabbed her wrist. "Stop!"

She rounded on him. "I can't!"

Her voice held a sharp edge of panic that clutched at Merlin's instincts. She'd gone from flushed to bone-white, her lips trembling with panic. Normally, he made students fix their own problems—it was the best way to learn—but lives were at stake. Right now he had to take charge. He pointed to the bench at the back of the space. "Sit down!"

"I need to make it stop!" Tears stood in her green eyes. Her distress tugged at him, sharp as any beast's fang, but until everyone was safe, he couldn't afford pity. Not even for her.

He thrust her toward the seat. "Sit down and don't touch anything. Whatever you do, don't use magic."

She collapsed so hard the bench squeaked against the concrete. "It's not my fault."

"I don't care." Blame could come later. He needed solutions now.

Merlin turned back to the chaos below. The wolf Clary had conjured was gone, the magic of the illusion spent. That was what was supposed to happen—and it was the only normal thing that *had* happened. The far-too-real lions were only part of the problem. There were a pair of prehistoric creatures straight from night-mare, and one of them had Beaumains cornered. The knight's blade ran red with blood, and so did his sword arm. Merlin's thoughts scrambled in confusion. What the blazes had Clary done?

The audience sensed something was wrong. A strained silence had fallen over the amphitheater, as if every spectator held his breath. The show was supposed to be make-believe, but the fearful whinnies of the horses were all too real. Then shadow fell over the field once again as the dragon flew another loop in the sky. Merlin looked up to see Rukon peering back, the slitted pupils of the huge topaz eyes wide with interest.

The lioness crouched, the motion of her hindquarters making it plain she was about to spring at Palomedes's throat. The sight jerked Merlin back to life. He summoned a shimmering ball of lightning to his hand and hurled it. It struck the lioness square in the back with a flash of pure white brilliance. Air rushed in a thunderclap as the creature burst into a cloud of tiny black scraps that looked like bats. They arrowed upward in a chorus of shrill cries.

Merlin's breath stuck in his chest. The cloud of flying darkness said this was demon magic. Rukon recognized it, too, for the dragon released a stream of blinding, blue-white fire that wiped the flapping shadows from the sky. The spectacle of a fire-breathing dragon changed the somber mood in an instant. The crowd erupted in a collective gasp of wonder and glee. Cries of "Whoa!" and "Go, Merlin!" drowned out the sounds of battle.

But Merlin was just getting started. He scanned the field, giving an involuntary wince at the sight of the dinosaurs. The raptors pranced around Beaumains like naked chickens sizing up a worm. One bled but seemed oblivious to the wound, a primitive need to kill stronger even than pain. Merlin's chest tightened with apprehension as Beaumains stumbled, his own injuries obvious.

Merlin's next fire bolt split in midair to target the two raptors. The fireballs struck the earth with a *thwump* and crackle that fried both monsters to ash. This time nothing flew out of the smoldering ruins. Demons were hard to kill, but enough raw power did the trick. Without sparing the time or energy for satisfaction, he turned his attention back to Palomedes and the circling lions.

Clary—ignoring his orders as usual—was back at Merlin's elbow in time to see Palomedes swing his blade at a shaggy-maned beast. The knight's sword sliced into the lion's hide, driving deep into the massive shoulder. The great cat roared, but the sound twisted into an unholy shriek as the beast dissolved into a flurry of blackness. Merlin flinched, every reflex recoiling at the sight.

"What just happened?" Clary demanded, her voice rising as she pointed at the sight. "Are those crows? Bats?"

"Demon magic does that," Merlin replied, giving her a hard look. "The filth break apart and reform as some other monster."

Her expression raised the hair along his arms, though he couldn't say why. The scowl was Clary's—he'd seen it often enough during their lessons—but there was something else, too. And then the look was gone, leaving him wondering if the battle with Vivian had left him paranoid.

Above, Rukon banked and turned to pass over the field once more. The wind in his huge wings rumbled like rippling thunder. Merlin gathered himself, every movement deliberate, and returned his attention to the lions. He hurled another ball of lightning that smashed into the pride and sent dirt fountaining into the air. One by one, the great cats burst into flurries of squeaking shreds of blackness. They swirled upward in a spiral, no doubt preparing to meld into some other, more horrific creature. Merlin searched for a fresh spell, something powerful enough to prevent a demonic attack on the crowd of innocent humans. Was this what the hellspawn had wanted all along? A means to infect this world with their evil?

If so, they had forgotten about dragons. A blast from Rukon's flame scoured the bats from the sky. Merlin felt the clean heat on his upturned face, fanned by the stroke of Rukon's wings. The stink of charcoal tickled his nose, but not before he caught a distinctive whiff of spice and sulfur. *Vivian.*

Then every thought was driven from his head by the roar of the crowd. They were on their feet, stamping and howling appreciation as the unprecedented spectacle wound to a new close. As if on cue, Rukon looped upward, climbing toward the open portal with another flourish of flame. The dragon rose with seemingly weightless ease and was soon swallowed by the azure sky of the Crystal Mountains. But his long neck curved backward for a last glance at Merlin. It didn't take magic to read the message written in Rukon's topaz eyes: *be careful*. And then the portal sealed with the efficiency of an invisible zipper, and the dragon was gone.

Merlin gripped Clary's arm, holding her at his side while they stepped forward to take their bow. He was carefully blind to the knights below, acting as if their wounds and bewildered fury were all part of the entertainment. They'd finished the show. No one was dead and the demon magic dispelled. The audience was none the wiser. The only thing left was to exit the stage—and then he could start asking hard questions.

After three standing ovations, the audience finally let them leave. By then, Merlin's temper was at a new peak. He dragged Clary into the corridor that led to the locker room, striding at top speed.

"Slow down!" Digging in her heels, she tried to wrench free of his grip.

He stopped, but didn't let go as he turned to face her. The harsh overhead lights bleached the color from her face, adding to the shadows beneath her eyes. He crushed a rising panic that told him she was in trouble. "Very well."

She blew out a long breath, but otherwise seemed tongue-tied.

He let his voice drop to something near a growl. "Let's take this slowly. Start talking."

She was shuddering as if plunged into Arctic waters. "I don't know what to say."

"Velociraptors? Really?"

"I didn't mean to! I—" She broke off, her face flushed with confusion. She looked as if she couldn't decide what to say.

Merlin's chest tightened with foreboding. "If you didn't mean it, then why did it happen?"

Clary sucked in a breath as if he'd struck her. The sound was loud in the echoing corridor.

Her expression gut-punched him. "What did Tamsin say about your wound?"

"She thinks it's okay." She pulled up her sleeve to show her arm. "It doesn't look like much now. She fixed it."

And yet Clary had started casting random spells far beyond her level of skill. That didn't say *fixed* to him.

Her gaze turned to him, now empty of everything but fear and pleading. The look broke him.

Like a man in a dream, Merlin reached out, stroking her cheek with his fingertips. They came away wet with her frightened tears. For that, he would have cheerfully sent every demon back to the Abyss all over again. As the pounding of his heart slowed, anger caught up with him, along with a profound sense of awe. Something had given Clary immense, even stunning, power. Demons were the obvious answer, but how?

Clary was the least talented student he'd ever taught. Could a mere scratch have changed everything? He really didn't know. Demon magic followed different rules—if you could apply rules to its chaotic nature—and not even Merlin the Wise understood every last nuance. A hard knot of worry gathered in his chest. He could not resist the urge to touch her, brushing back a wisp of hair that was falling in her eyes.

Somehow that innocent gesture turned into an embrace. He'd sworn to himself that wouldn't happen again, but her lips were against his, soft and uncertain. The first kiss ended, her breath warm and a little too fast against his face. It had been a long time since he'd allowed himself this kind of intimacy—not just physical need, but with emotion attached. Everything around him—the concrete walls, the dull roar of the crowd—fell away, leaving only this woman and her haunted gaze. It was plain she was seeking reassurance, someone to catch her and put her on her feet again. If he was a better man, he'd be a little less literal about the catching part, but he couldn't seem to take his hands from her waist.

Her fingers curled in the fabric of his costume. "What are you doing?"

This unguarded, vulnerable side of her destroyed his equilibrium. "Making certain you're well."

He pushed back the veil of her costume and tangled his fingers in her shaggy blond hair. She tilted her head, studying him from beneath her lashes. "You can't tell anything by kissing me." And yet she looked afraid that he might find something.

He released her, but didn't back away. Her eyes were their usual color, like new leaves in the golden light of May. Her skin glowed the same delicate cream, her mouth still invited him—and yet something was different. It prickled against a sense that had no name.

She put one hand on his sleeve, the lines of her face going tight. "Tell me what I should do."

He couldn't answer. He didn't know how to put his uneasiness into words.

The moment ended when a door slammed behind him. Heavy footsteps marched their way. Clary took a short, sharp breath.

"Merlin!" came a booming voice that rang against the concrete walls.

Merlin turned to see Arthur Pendragon, still in full armor, closing the distance between them. The king's russet hair was brushed back from a face dominated by pale blue and furious eyes. He came to a stop just feet away, chain mail rattling with the sudden halt. His fingers tapped once on the helmet clutched under his arm. "What happened? My knights were injured, two of them badly."

Arthur's gaze went from Merlin to Clary, demanding answers.

Silently, Merlin stepped between them, blocking the king's view.

Chapter 5

Merlin never protected me that way, Vivian commented inside Clary's head, her tone haughty. *I never needed it.*

No doubt the comment was meant as an insult, but Clary didn't care. One look at Arthur's scowl said she needed all the protection she could get, and one of the few people who could face Arthur down was Merlin. The king and the enchanter had a long, if sometimes volatile, friendship.

"How are Beaumains and Palomedes?" Merlin asked.

"They will survive," the king replied. "Fortunately, Tamsin was working at the church today and could come in minutes."

"That's good news," said Merlin.

Clary literally gulped, wondering how bad the wounds might be. Her stomach felt like ice.

Don't worry, said Vivian. *Those wounds are clean. I don't bother with poison when simple fangs and claws will do.*

Why do it at all? Clary shrieked inside her head, but as she peered around Merlin's straight back at the king, she understood. Arthur was furious. Of the hundred and fifty knights of the Round Table, only a handful had awakened in the modern era. They were his friends, the only familiar faces from his old life, and they were all he had to fight the armies of the fae. What better way to pit Arthur against Merlin than threatening his men?

"You put my knights in danger," said the king in a low, rasping voice.

"That was not our intent." Merlin shifted, blotting out her view of Arthur's flushed face.

"Perhaps it was not yours, but I know the script of the show." The king's tone rose, sharp with anger. "Your student was responsible."

Again, people were talking as if Clary wasn't there. Her temper stirred, but she didn't dare protest when this was her fault.

"There was a mistake," said Merlin with icy calm.

"A mistake?" Arthur snarled. "If it was not for Tamsin, Beaumains would never hold a sword again!"

Clary squeezed her eyes shut, heartsick. Beaumains was a good friend—cheerful, kind and almost like a brother. He *would* be an in-law once Gawain and Tamsin married, since he was Gawain's youngest sibling. And her hands had cast the spell that had nearly killed him. The knowledge made her stomach roll.

"I want answers." Arthur's demand gave no room to refuse.

"We all do," Merlin said evenly. "I will find the cause of what happened."

Clary fell back a step. Answers were the one thing she needed and the last thing she could ask for. The demon inside her was still, and yet she could almost hear it snicker. Clary took another step, this time toward the exit to the locker rooms. The distance gave her a view of the two men. Arthur had one finger planted on Merlin's chest. The king's expression was thunderous, but Merlin's was like stone.

Merlin looked at her, moving only his head. "Go get changed and I'll meet you at the concession stand. Don't leave until we've talked."

Cringing with guilt, Clary wasted no time making her retreat. She'd put Merlin at odds with his king. She'd put the knights in danger. If that wasn't bad enough, she was hiding the vengeful demon behind it all. She was a coward—but Vivian had threatened her sister. What was she supposed to do?

Frustration made her move quickly. It took less than five minutes to change and walk to the concession stand, where happy throngs of tourists were buying Knightly Nachos and Jalapeño Dragon Fries by the bucket. Clary stood beside the booth with the straws and napkins, watching the path for Merlin's approach. Normally, she'd be tweeting or posting pictures from the afternoon's show, but she wanted to hide instead. Even the smell of the food, usually so tempting, turned her stomach.

The familiarity of the place oppressed her, too, as if Medievaland itself knew what she'd done. So many of her hopes and dreams were tied up in the place. She'd spilled blood on this earth during her endless sparring matches with Gawain. There had been countless midnight practices with Merlin on the tourney ground, throwing balls of energy until she hit the target. He'd drilled her mercilessly, not just in illusions but in portals and farseeing, summoning and casting. The big empty grounds had been perfect for the messes she'd inevitably made. Merlin never seemed to care, but just made her do the spells over and over and over…

She didn't notice the couple approach until it was too late. They were both in their teens, the boy tall and rangy and the girl with a short afro and ebony skin. "Are you Clary Greene?" the boy asked with an infectious smile.

Clary managed to nod.

"We saw you with the wizard today. That show rocked."

"Would you?" the girl asked, handing her a program and a pen decorated with moons and stars.

"Sure." Clary took the pen and paper and managed what she hoped was a friendly smile. She didn't want to celebrate her role in the show, much less take a bow for something that was actually a disaster. Still, she couldn't confess to launching homicidal demon constructs. Those conversations never ended well, even with other witches.

Vivian's amusement hit her like heartburn. Grinding her teeth, Clary braced the program against the side of the booth and started to write, then blinked. Rather than her own name, she'd scrawled an elaborate rune. *Well,* sighed the demon, *you can't blame me. No one's ever asked for my autograph before.*

That's not a spell that will harm the girl? Clary demanded.

And injure my first human fan? Goodness me, no. I haven't had this kind of adoration since I was revered as a goddess, and that was simply ages ago. I'm feeling generous.

After a moment of confusion, Clary scrawled her name beside the rune and handed the pen and paper back to the girl.

"Cool!" the girl said, peering at the scribble. "Thanks a lot!"

Clary barely noticed them leave, directing her thoughts inward instead. *Don't do things like that! You'll give us away.*

Do you care that much for my safety? The words dripped with sarcasm.

Don't play games. Clary shifted, finding a patch of deeper shade. *You've already threatened to harm Tamsin if you're found out.*

Do you think I'd blame you for something I did?

You're a demon. Isn't that the kind of thing demons do? I care for my sister too much to risk it.

You do care for your sister. I can feel it like a warm fire in your soul. The sarcasm was gone. *And you care for Merlin, though that is a very different fire.*

Merlin had kissed Clary right after the show—she hadn't had time to take that in before now, and the memory made her palms grow damp. It hadn't been the angry, frustrated kiss he'd demanded from her after the ritual—this time his touch had been gentle, as if meant to comfort. She'd never seen that side of him before, and it left her a little shaken, almost humbled. Merlin the Wise never dropped his guard.

Oh, for pity's sake, haven't you ever had a lover before? Vivian sounded irritated.

Sure. Clary stiffened. *Lots.*

Why aren't you with one of them? Vivian's curiosity was a tangible thing. *Surely there is a better fit for the likes of you.*

Yeah, well, the witches have an expression. They didn't waft my wand.

There was a beat of blessed silence where Clary was free to watch the hot dog–munching public come and go. A warm breeze rippled through the maple trees, promising a pleasant evening. Then Vivian broke into her thoughts again. *Why not? Why weren't they enough?*

Clary's temper stirred. *None of your business. You're not my BFF.*

To her surprise, Vivian fell quiet again without a fight. Still, Clary could feel her presence like a dull toothache. There was something wistful about her mood, as if beneath her contempt was a childlike confusion about human relationships. That didn't make Vivian any less dangerous or passionate. Rather, it was more like being trapped in an elevator with a toddler— a toddler armed with a flamethrower.

She saw Merlin striding toward her. He was still wearing his enchanter's robes and drawing stares from the crowd. His face was stony.

"Come with me," he said, grabbing her arm and pulling her into the stream of pedestrians.

"What's going on?" she asked, tension swarming through her. "Is everyone okay? How mad is the king? Am I fired?"

"You're not fired yet, but unless we get out of sight that may change." As he spoke, patches of color flushed his high cheekbones. "The only reason you're not in the king's custody is because I've promised to investigate this afternoon's events. If I don't find satisfactory answers, we're both in trouble."

He was putting himself on the line for her. Clary felt Vivian's twinge of satisfaction, followed by the image of Tamsin's face. A plain warning.

Clary pulled out of Merlin's grasp. "You don't need to do this for me."

"You're my student. I know what you're capable of, and none of that should have happened." He glared down at her. "It doesn't make sense."

"Sorry that offends you." She wanted to get away, to put as much distance between Merlin and Vivian's revenge as she could. And yet one look at his face said he wasn't letting her leave his sight.

"You put everyone, especially yourself, at risk." He put an arm around her shoulder, propelling through the exit and into the parking lot. It might look like an affectionate gesture, but Clary felt the steel in his arm. "I can't let this slide."

He led her to a four-door black SUV, one of Camelot's vehicles. Merlin himself didn't own a car, more often using magic to travel, but after a show he often drove to conserve energy. He pulled the robes over his head and threw the costume in the backseat. He was left wearing jeans and a black T-shirt.

Clary folded her arms. "So what do you intend to do?"

"Go for coffee." He opened the passenger door, releasing warm air that smelled vaguely horsey. One of the knights must have driven the car right after jousting practice. "You and I need to talk."

He drove to Mandala Books, which had a coffee shop and bakery in the back. The merger of the two businesses—and of the old Victorian houses that contained them—had been recently completed and the scent of new paint and sawdust still lingered in the air. Nimueh, the fae Lady of the Lake, was still a silent partner in the business, but she and Sir Lancelot du Lac rarely visited anymore. Most of their time was spent in the Forest Sauvage, keeping watch on the prison of Morgan LaFaye.

Merlin chose a table far in the back of the café, where they had some privacy. A server brought black coffee and a cinnamon bun before Merlin had to ask, which said something about how often he went there. Clary ordered a London Fog and looked around the place. It had wooden floors and pine tables with checkered cloths, geraniums in the window boxes and chandeliers made from old mason jars. An enticing view of the bookstore peeped through the archway that joined the two buildings. It was homey and simple.

"This doesn't seem like your kind of place," she said to Merlin as the waitress set the vanilla tea latté before her.

He shrugged. "Nimueh placed powerful protections around it, which makes it safe. Plus, they have an excellent bakery."

She watched him take a huge bite of the cinnamon bun. She'd never pegged Merlin as having a sweet tooth. Usually he was all about vitamins and lean protein. "That thing has enough calories to feed a small village."

He shrugged. "I burned it off during the show. Fireballs take energy."

She looked away, her mind's eye fixed on memories of lightning and dragon fire. "Why did you protect me from Arthur?"

"I need to understand what happened." He washed the pastry down with coffee, his shoulders easing a little. "Tell me what you experienced when you cast those spells."

She could feel Vivian come alert inside her, and so she chose her words with care. "The show started okay.

The spell that made the wolf worked normally. Then the next one had a mind of its own and then—I can barely remember."

He studied her through critical eyes. "You're holding something back."

"So are you," Clary retorted. It was a random strike, but the fleeting alarm in his expression said she'd struck home. She sucked in a breath. "Trust works both ways, doesn't it? There was more to that ritual you did than you're saying."

"I told you already. I was conducting surveillance on the demons, which you interrupted." He made a face. "A demon has been sighted in the Forest Sauvage in the company of the fae. The king and I wish to know why."

"Did you learn anything?" Clary sensed Vivian's interest and wished she hadn't asked.

"Perhaps."

"What?"

"Nothing that concerns you."

"I got hurt. That makes it my concern." Clary pushed her tea away. More than anything, she wanted to demand he evict the demon from inside her head. Despite Vivian's threats, the need for privacy was like a maddening itch.

Don't, warned Vivian. *If he knows I'm here, he will do his best to destroy me. Your mortal form is too fragile to withstand such an assault.*

How long are you going to keep this up? Clary demanded.

As I said, you are too weak a vessel for an open fight. I will have to take him by surprise. Therefore, I need you until that moment.

Clary's lips parted in surprise. She had to say something—this was unbearable.

Remember your sister.

Clary let loose a sob, but covered her mouth. Merlin was looking at her, a furrow creasing his brow.

But the demon chose to drive her point home. Paralysis crept from Clary's tongue all the way to her lungs. When she tried to inhale, nothing happened. A fiery pain spread through her chest. Clary strained, starting to choke. *Please! Please let me go!* Fear clawed at her insides until Vivian suddenly released her. Clary dissolved into a spluttering fit of coughing. Merlin jumped up, making the dishes rattle. He bent over her, patting her back until she stopped. "Did you choke?"

She nodded, mopping her eyes with a napkin. "Something stuck in my throat."

"Perhaps an explanation you aren't telling me?" he asked, sliding back into his chair. Now that the crisis was over, he was once again cool and professional. "You have a secret and I want an answer. I suspect they are exactly the same thing."

And Clary was almost certain whatever he wasn't telling her contained the answers to her predicament. They were in a deadlock. Merlin had dirty laundry—dirty, demonic laundry.

"If you hate demons so much, why did you have one as a girlfriend?"

Merlin's face was like stone. And now, the one time Clary wanted the demon to chime in, Vivian was mute. Okay, then. Apparently, there was a juicy story there.

He leaned forward, fixing her with his amber eyes. "Are you going to help me?" he asked softly.

Clary had to tell him something, so she gave him the merest sliver of truth. "What if Tamsin didn't cure everything? What if there is a lingering demon poison that affected my magic?"

She felt Vivian's claws prick the inside of her mind, threatening to shred her from the inside out, but Clary stood her ground. The demon needed her alive for the moment, and she hadn't given away the whole truth. They had to compromise to get through this.

Merlin's face remained still, but his eyes closed as if in thanks. "That's possible."

"Can you test for something like that?"

"Sort of." His face fell as he put money for their coffee on the table.

"Just sort of?"

"There are one or two methods that do not harm the subject." He looked uncomfortable.

"You're such a romantic," Clary said, and then gripped the edge of the table, blackness nibbling at the edge of her vision. Her heart drummed in her ears, leaving her hot and weak.

Merlin circled the table, kneeling beside her. "What's wrong? You've gone pale."

Clary struggled to answer, and this time it wasn't the demon who froze her tongue. It was the horrific realization it hadn't been her that had spoken. *You're such a romantic.* That had been Vivian's thought, Vivian's words. She was losing control to the demon.

Clary met Merlin's eyes, holding his gaze and willing him to understand all the things she couldn't say. A crease formed between his brows, and he put a hand to her cheek, his palm cool against her fevered skin. Slowly, his thumb stroked her cheekbone, the gesture offering her a shred of comfort.

"Help me," she begged.

Chapter 6

Merlin's hand covered hers. "Of course."

Clary closed her eyes, not able to meet his gaze any longer. She concentrated on the feel of his touch and the long, strong fingers wrapping around hers. She was being split in two, but he was a solid anchor. "Okay," she whispered.

"Come." Merlin's hands were gentle as he pulled her to her feet. "Let's take care of this."

Clary followed him to the car. "Where are we going?"

"To your sister's."

"Tamsin's?" she asked in horror. The last thing she wanted was to put Vivian and her sister in the same room.

Merlin shot her a curious look as they got into the SUV. He started the engine. "Is there a problem with that?"

Vivian's claws dug into Clary's mind, sharp as any physical pain but far more frightening. Somehow she knew whatever injuries the demoness might cause to her mind and soul would never heal. She cleared her throat. "Tamsin's done what she can already."

Merlin pulled away from the curb into Carlyle's afternoon rush. "Maybe, maybe not. I have an idea she can help me with."

"She won't have time. She'll still be at Medievaland, healing the knights."

"I already asked her to meet us at her place when she's finished." He gave her an inscrutable glance. "We talked before I met you at the concession stand."

Defeated, Clary sank back into the leather seat of the SUV. How was she going to keep Vivian in check? Even if there was a cure for her demon problem, surely Vivian would fight back.

You're quite right, little witch, but let's not get ahead of ourselves. Your lovely sister hasn't had a patient quite like you and me before.

And she'd failed to detect Vivian's presence once. There was every chance she'd miss it again.

Just so. If Merlin trusts her healing skills to find me, her failure will work in my favor.

Clary understood. After all, Vivian wanted to catch Merlin by surprise. However, if Tamsin made a correct diagnosis... Clary dropped that train of thought, already feeling a wave of nausea clog her throat. There was no way to win. She stared at the passing streets, scrambling for an answer where no one got hurt.

When they arrived at Tamsin's door, the smell of tomato sauce filled the apartment hallway. Her sister answered Merlin's knock, a wooden spoon in her hand.

"It's Gawain's favorite dinner," Tamsin said in explanation. "He'll be home soon and after today, we all want comfort food."

"Aren't you tired?" Clary asked, noting the dark circles under her sister's eyes. "You must have just got home."

She followed her into the kitchen. Tamsin moved the pot of sauce and turned off the burner, her movements brisk. "Of course I'm tired, but I just did the cleanup. I didn't fight."

Then she turned to face Clary, fear tightening her jaw. "I've seen demon-born monsters before. What were you doing?"

Clary took a step back. She could see the picture forming in Tamsin's head—Gawain, brave knight and love of her life, perishing in the jaws of Clary's creation. Tamsin's future destroyed by her hapless kid sister. The scene wasn't far off the mark.

"I'm sorry," Clary said softly. "In perfect honesty, I don't know exactly how that happened." *And for all our sakes,* she willed her sister, *don't look deeper.*

Emotions cycled through Tamsin's expression. Anger. Fear. Compassion. The last was the worst because it was so familiar. Once again, Clary was the weak magical link in the family. The only difference now was that her incompetence had hurt their friends.

Tamsin licked her lips, seeming to come to a decision. "Go have a seat in the living room. Send Merlin in here so I can talk to him."

Clary's first instinct was to object on principle. As the youngest child, she'd been shut out of adult conversations too often. This time, though, she'd be keeping

Vivian out of earshot. Clary did as she was told and turned on the TV to make eavesdropping impossible.

You think you're being clever, Vivian sneered.

Yes. Clary changed the channel to a home renovation show. She didn't care about fascia boards and roof tiles, but the shirtless construction guys were cute.

Vivian snorted, but her attention drifted to the show. *Do humans truly have to rely on teams of physical workers to keep the rain off their heads?*

Clary rolled her eyes at the demon's appalled tone. *Pretty much. When you don't have magic powers, you need helping hands. That's how this world works.*

And sometimes the magically gifted needed help, too. When Tamsin and Merlin reappeared, her sister was holding a clay goblet filled with steaming brew. Clary turned off the TV and accepted the cup. The mixture smelled of woodlands and flowers, more like a herbal tea than a strong medicinal. Nevertheless, Vivian's interest zeroed in on it with laser focus.

"What is it?" Clary asked.

With a weary sigh, Tamsin sank into Gawain's oversize leather chair. "Just drink it."

Merlin sat on the sofa to Clary's left, putting her between the two of them. His expression was, as usual, guarded and cool. "It will stimulate the body's natural healing and help the infection pass from your system."

Clary took another sniff. "There are raspberry leaves in here."

Raspberry? Vivian scoffed. *That's supposed to stop me?*

Clary looked up at her sister, who folded her arms. "Drink up," Tamsin said.

Clary lifted the goblet, feeling the steam against her cheeks.

Wait! Vivian demanded. *There has to be something else in there. Something she's not saying.*

Clary—and the demoness—studied Tamsin for answers, but her sister's expression gave nothing away. And, concentrating as she was, Clary didn't feel the needle Merlin stabbed into her thigh until it was too late. Brew splashed as she dropped the goblet in surprise. It thunked to the carpet and rolled to Tamsin's feet.

What was that? Vivian shrieked. Clary felt the slash of claws, but they were already blunted, rendered harmless by whatever had been in the needle.

With a shaking hand, her sister picked up the goblet and set it on the coffee table. "I'm sorry, little witchling. We had to do it."

Clary watched her sister with an open mouth, too surprised for any deeper emotion, then spun to face Merlin, who still held the hypodermic. He glanced at it, and it dissolved into smoke.

"You tricked me!" she said, accusing them both.

"Apologies," he said. "We had no way of knowing if this lingering infection of yours might try something."

Bewildered, Clary glanced down at the stain on the carpet.

"It was just Pixie Forest blend from the local tea shop," said Tamsin, not meeting Clary's eyes. "The most it was going to do was make you sleepy."

Betrayal stung almost as much as the fiery sensation crawling up her leg. They didn't trust her to take whatever cure they offered. Worse, they saw her as a genuine threat that had to be managed. Her mind understood, but her heart hurt.

"Then what was in the shot?" she asked, her voice gone rough.

The pain had reached her belly. Vivian howled—or maybe it was her. Clary doubled over, clutching her middle. Merlin steadied her with firm hands, easing her back onto the couch. "It will put whatever you have to sleep. It might interfere with your powers for a time, but the trade-off in safety will be worthwhile."

Merlin the Wise always knows what's best, said Vivian in a sarcastic snarl.

But he spoke the truth. Clary could feel Vivian draining away, disappearing to somewhere too deep inside for Clary to detect. She wanted to test for the demon's presence, poking around as she would for a sore tooth, but her thoughts scattered. The pain rippling through her was like wave after wave of fire.

At the same time, that feeling of being watched was finally gone. "There was a demon's voice talking in my head," she gasped. "It was Vivian."

"I suspected something like that." His face unreadable, Merlin stroked a hand over her bowed head just once, more apology in his gesture than his words. "Demon essence leaves echoes behind. Demons are energy and Vivian was caught between worlds. It's not surprising that a bit of her touched you during the ritual."

Sure, during the part where she blew into messy demon bits as the portal closed. Clearly, those bits had tried to reassemble themselves inside Clary.

"Witches are vulnerable because demons can attach themselves to another person's magic." Despite Merlin's closed expression, his voice was gentle. "It's serious, Clary. It can drive people mad."

"How long will this cure last?"

Tamsin knelt before her, pressing a damp cloth to Clary's face. It was wonderfully cool. "It's hard to say, but it should hold until the infection leaves your system."

"She'll come back. She's more than just an echo."

"Hush," Tamsin murmured, putting a hand to Clary's face. "We don't know that yet."

Clary wanted to argue, but her head was pounding now. A tide of sickness rose up, swamping every other consideration. She jumped up, pushing past her sister, and ran for the bathroom.

The only good thing was that she hadn't had much to eat. Too bad whatever drug Merlin had given her didn't care if her stomach was empty. At some point, she locked the door to keep Tamsin out. Her sister might be a healer, but Clary needed privacy more than soothing words. After a while, Tamsin's anxious voice faded and Clary slumped on the cold tile in peace.

What was she going to do? If the cure wasn't permanent, she'd be back in the same hopeless place the moment Vivian woke up. Except it would be worse. Vivian would be furious, and Tamsin would be in even more danger. Merlin would be vulnerable, because now he believed Clary was, if not cured, at least inert.

She needed to get away, far away, to someplace where Tamsin and Merlin would be safe. Her own Shadowring Coven was on the opposite coast of the continent. Better yet, she could go to a circle of witches where she didn't know anyone and there would be no friends or family Vivian could use as hostages. The moment she formed that thought, it became her plan. It was clear, simple and the right thing to do.

Clary already hated the idea. It made sense, but she craved emotional comfort, too. She'd always been the independent misfit, whistling her way through scrape after scrape, and yet home had always been there. So had her sisters. Cutting herself off wouldn't be easy.

She heard Merlin's voice, muffled by the door and distance to the next room. Tamsin replied. The words weren't clear, but her sister's concern was evident. Clary didn't have much time before someone was knocking on the door again. If they stopped her before she got away, it would be twice as hard to leave them behind.

Eventually, Clary got to her feet. Pain made her knees wobble as she stood. She drank some water, then stole some mouthwash to get the vile taste out of her mouth. Finally, she looked in the mirror, confirming she looked as awful as she felt.

Slowly, she opened the bathroom door. Merlin and her sister were in the living room down the hall, their view of her blocked by the angle of the wall. To Clary's left, just a few steps away, was the apartment door. A glance told her that Tamsin hadn't locked it when they'd come in.

Years of teenage misbehavior had made her an expert at sneaking out. Clary slipped away, silently shutting the door behind her. Since she didn't carry a purse, she still had her keys, wallet and phone in her pockets. Nothing was left behind at her sister's place. All she had to do was make it home to pack a suitcase, and she'd leave town. A quick mental check told her Vivian was still gone.

Clary ran down the apartment stairs, not bothering with the elevator. The exit emptied into the parking lot, and she strode across the sunny pavement with renewed confidence. And nearly ended up a speedbump for Gawain's motorcycle.

Oh, hell! She jumped back, plastering a smile on her face and waving brightly. The Scottish knight waved back, used to her coming and going. That would only buy her minutes at best. The instant he opened the door and mentioned that he'd seen her, the search would be on.

Clary slipped out of sight and ran. Now going straight home wasn't an option. In fact, all the places she knew—Tamsin's, her own apartment, Medievaland, Merlin's place—were bound to be under Merlin's magical surveillance. She wasn't sure what to do. Maybe head to the bus station and catch a ride out of town?

She entered an alley that crept between a gas station and a pub. It was smelly and narrow, the brickwork on either side black with age and dirt. Patches of straggling grass grew under rusted downspouts. Clary looked over her shoulder even though she'd barely taken two steps into the confined space. But that was stupid. She was a witch with a demon on board. That made her like a bomb in an action-adventure movie, one that had to be dumped in an ocean or shot into outer space before it nuked the free world. She could blast any mugger to smithereens.

Squaring her shoulders, Clary pushed on. It was broad daylight, and she could tell this alley was a shortcut to the main road ahead. Going this way would put distance between herself and well-meaning friends.

Halfway across, she heard music from a window above. It was an ordinary pop tune, barely worth remembering, but someone with an exceptional voice was singing along with the words. *That* was special.

The sound vanished as quickly as it had come, but Clary paused just long enough to look up. There were curtains and knickknacks in the second-floor windows, and the sash of one was pushed up. That had to be where the voice had come from. There was only one kind of being that could sing so beautifully—a fae.

Despite the lovely song, Clary drew back. The soul-sucking monsters found witches especially tasty. She spun on her heel, ready to run, but a figure dropped from the window right into her path. The male rose from his crouch as if this was a perfectly normal way to say hello. He was tall and slender, casually dressed but for an elaborately tooled belt of green leather. A long, silver-handed knife hung at his hip. He sniffed the air, as if confirming it was she who had smelled so tasty.

"Great," Clary muttered under her breath.

"Where are you going, my girl?" asked the fae. He had dark olive skin that showed off the bright green of his eyes. His long, white hair was pulled back to reveal a fine-boned face that would have put him on the front of any fashion magazine.

"I'm going past you." Clary raised her hands, ready to weave a spell that would hurl the fae into the next block. Except no power flowed through her body, ready to shape to her will.

She was helpless. Merlin had warned her that the injection might mess with her magic, but she hadn't expected this.

The fae must have seen her confusion, because he burst into a cruel laugh.

Chapter 7

Panic made Clary stagger back. Her magic had never been brilliant, but it was as much a part of her as sight or hearing. She clenched her fists, fighting a need to scream. Her struggle seemed to amuse the fae even more. Or maybe amusement was the wrong word. While fae had no feelings, they still seemed to enjoy tormenting their prey.

"Who are you, pretty boy?" Clary demanded, mostly to make him stop sniggering.

"I am Laren of the Green Towers." He waved a hand at the alley. "Or perhaps I should say the back streets. The hunting is far better here."

By hunting, he meant stealing the life essence of mortals. Drinking mortal souls restored a fae's emotions, their love of beauty and ability to create—but only for a short while. Those addicted to the rush left a trail of dead or mindless victims in their wake. At least Laren appeared physically healthy, which meant he hadn't been a soul-eater for long.

"What happened to your witch's tricks?" he taunted.

"I'm on a cleanse." She shifted her feet, bracing to run. Fae were incredibly strong despite their slight appearance. Unless Clary found a weapon, she'd lose the fight before it began.

"Afraid to face me, wench?" Laren glided forward, his steps silent. His intent, predatory posture reminded her of the velociraptor's.

"The name's Clary. I'd stay and brawl, but my calendar's full."

She spun and ran, pumping her legs for all she was worth. She'd made it past a row of garbage cans before Laren tackled her to the ground, his arms wrapped around her waist. Apparently, the fae were as fast as they were strong.

Clary's knees exploded with pain as she fell, the fae's weight driving her into the ground. She raised her arms to protect her face, but not before a blur of gravel and straggling weeds filled her view. Her lungs emptied in a rush. Stunned, she lay helpless as Laren flipped her over and straddled her waist.

It was then she met his eyes. They were green like her own, but a vibrant shade unlike any mortal's. And they were utterly, chillingly void of feeling. The loss of his soul had turned him into something alien. She might as well have been pinned by a shark.

Terror flooded her, robbing the last shreds of her strength. She had no magic and no weapon. She drew in a shaking breath, fighting down the urge to wail.

His lips drew back from his teeth in a mockery of a

smile. "What a pretty thing you are." He placed a fingertip between her eyes and traced downward, over the tip of her nose and the bow of her lips. "You will be delicious."

Clary shuddered at the naked hunger in his face. It promised a brutal end, and a primitive instinct to live took over. She twisted beneath him, arching her back against his weight. Laren pushed her down again, but not before the knife in his belt caught her eye, its silver hilt gleaming in the alley's muted sunlight. A fae hunter would need such a thing to finish his victims. It taunted her, promising death or just maybe deliverance.

She widened her eyes, letting all her fear show. Laren's nostrils flared as if scenting her distress. His knees tightened against her hips and he grabbed her jaw, using one hand to pin her head in place. That was all he needed to control her. Compared with his strength, her arms might have been helplessly beating wings.

Or not. Clary plucked the knife from its scabbard with a quick hiss of steel on leather and drove it toward his ribs. It would have worked, if not for fae reflexes. He twisted with the agility of a cat, his free hand clamping around her wrist in an iron grip.

A chilling sound of regret escaped his lips. "Very good. I see I'm growing careless." He peeled the knife from her fingers and tossed it just out of reach. Clary heard it fall with a ping of metal on stone. Clearly, he wasn't a warrior obsessed with keeping his blades in perfect condition.

Then he bent over her again, the smell of his skin and sweat far too intimate. He grabbed her jaw once more, forcing her mouth open with bruising insistence. "Give yourself to me," he whispered. "Give me your joy and tears and hope." His lips sealed over hers.

The assault on her soul was far, far worse than she had ever imagined. It felt as if her insides were being torn through her throat, leaving an icy vacuum behind. She pushed against his chest, but he was solid as granite. Her hands fumbled to his face, poking and clawing and finally to his hair, but nothing made him flinch. Sight and sound vanished, leaving only an unholy pain. Finally, Clary screamed, but Laren drank that down along with everything else.

Then something hurled him back. Clary collapsed backward, hitting her head on a sharp rock. The universe swam for an instant before she rolled to her side to see Merlin standing over Laren. She expected Merlin to pound the fae into a pulp, shock him with thunderbolts—something—but the enchanter stood poised and unmoving, a look of naked curiosity on his face.

Then she realized that the fae writhed on the ground in agony, his grinding moans like nothing she'd ever heard. Taking no chances, Clary fumbled for the knife he'd thrown aside and staggered to her feet, using the filthy wall for support. Slowly she approached, the long blade gripped in one hand.

Laren's eyes had rolled back into his head until only the whites showed. Foam coated his lips and he trembled with long, violent spasms. Merlin's face was grim as he took her by the shoulders and turned her to face him, scanning her slowly from head to the scuffed toes of her shoes. He squeezed her gently, angling his arms as if for a reckless moment he might decide to pull her close. After an odd hesitation, he let his hands fall away. "Thank the gods you're all right," he said quietly.

For an instant, she saw possessive anger storm over Merlin's face, lighting his odd amber eyes. The primitive heat stirred an answering call deep in her core. Her response was as inevitable as the autumn flight of birds—or perhaps the rage of earthquakes. It was that deep and mesmerizing.

And then the heat in Merlin's eyes was gone, buried again—but this time she saw the effort it took him to hide it, as if it was growing harder to smother. *But why does he care about me, especially after the trouble I've caused?* Not that she'd let him see her doubt. That would leave her cracked open like an egg dropped from its nest to the pavement below. And this wasn't the time for confessions, anyway. She'd just about had her soul snatched. After a long moment, she stepped back, heaving a long breath. She was grateful he'd come and angry he'd stolen her power, and she didn't have the strength to deal with either of those things right then.

Instead, she pointed at the fae writhing at their feet. "What happened to him?"

"I'm not certain, but my first guess would be indigestion," Merlin replied drily.

A slightly hysterical laugh escaped Clary. Her world wavered and she gripped Merlin's arm. Humor aside, the enchanter's remark made no sense, but the evidence was before her eyes. Still, how could her life energy be toxic to a fae? It was ludicrous, and just a little embarrassing.

She opened her mouth to say so just as she passed out.

Clary woke up in an unfamiliar bedroom. After jerking into a sitting position, she pressed a hand to her aching head and found a lump where she'd hit the pavement. An involuntary groan escaped her as she blinked the room into focus. She was clothed and lying on a king-size bed. One wall of the room was exposed brick, the floor wide planks of hardwood sanded to a soft sheen. Another wall was a balcony with a view of the sun fading over the distant hills. This had to be one of those trendy lofts in the downtown's converted warehouses. The furniture was plain but top quality, the bed linens definitely not from a big box store. Whose place was this?

She swung her feet off the bed and took a second look around. The room was nice, but the clutter said a real person lived there. A bookshelf spawned stacks of books around it, like seedlings around a tree. Unfolded laundry was heaped in a chair and spilled over onto the floor.

Slowly, Clary bent and pulled on her shoes, which someone had removed and left beside the bed. Her head throbbed with the change in angle, but it was manageable. When she stood, she caught sight of the T-shirt on the floor by the closet. It was black with a faded logo of a metal rock band, and she'd last seen it stretched over Merlin's chest. Was this his place? It looked too—she searched for the word—normal.

She left the bedroom, curiosity in full flood. The room opened directly into the main living area, and she caught an impression of more wood, brick and large windows hung with plants. "Anybody home?" Clary called.

Merlin appeared around the corner. "Ah, you're up." His usual mask was firmly in place—cool and slightly amused, as if the world were a movie and he'd already seen the credits. The only clue to his mood was the vertical pleat between his brows.

"Do you live here?" she asked.

He nodded, sipping from a glass of something green. "How are you feeling?"

"Not sure yet." She wrinkled her nose. His drink smelled like lawn clippings. "Is that brew from the Fabrien Spell Scrolls?"

One corner of his mouth quirked. "It's wheat grass from my juicer. Want some?"

Clary shuddered. "Not unless we're going for a true exorcism. Why am I here?"

"Medical observation. You've been through a lot in the past few days." His eyes were thoughtful as he sipped his disgusting drink. "Why did you run from your sister's place? Imagine my surprise when Gawain lumbered in to announce he'd seen you crossing the parking lot."

She looked away. "I'm putting everyone in danger."

"The danger won't vanish with a change in location. You'll just take it somewhere else."

Clary heaved a breath. "Vivian wants revenge on you, and she threatened Tamsin so I would cooperate. We're dealing with more than a slight touch of possession." There, she'd said it. She watched Merlin's face for a reaction.

To her disappointment, he just shrugged, hard to read as ever. "That's Vivian."

"I'm serious."

"I know." For an instant, his composure slipped and she saw lines of tension bracket his mouth. "I suspected as much about halfway through the show at Medievaland. Not even demons are typically that skilled at conjuring, but she is."

"Why didn't you say something?" Her tone grew sharp.

He tossed back the rest of the wheat grass, making a face as he swallowed. "What would Vivian have done if I'd confronted her?"

Clary swallowed, not liking the truth. "She'd have lashed out."

"And that would not have ended well for anybody, especially you."

Clary buried her face in her hands. Of course Merlin had figured it out. He'd just kept his cards hidden from his ex-lover. She hated him for it, but knew her life depended on his skills. "Vivian will come back, you know."

Merlin put a hand on her shoulder and gave it a gentle squeeze. "Yes, but now we have time to figure out a solution."

Clary caught the scent of him: clean soap and cotton and the faint spice of herbs. She realized how familiar it had become to her and how badly she'd come to crave it. She was as addicted as the soul-craving fae. She turned her face away, needing to keep her wits about her. Nothing had changed just because he'd rescued her again. "I can't stay here."

"You're too vulnerable to leave. Your magic doesn't even work."

Her stomach tightened as she struggled between needing Merlin and wanting to punch him. "You took it!" She pulled away from his touch. "You could have asked permission."

"And what would Vivian have said? We've already had that conversation."

Clary all but growled. "You're right."

"Of course I am, which is why you're staying here. Tamsin is getting some things from your apartment." Merlin waved a hand. "Shall I show you around?"

Reluctantly, Clary nodded. She wanted to know what Merlin's home said about him. The kitchen was large and sunny, the dining room dominated by a farm table big enough to seat a dozen people. Instead of dishes, it was covered by a scatter of books and an expensive-looking laptop. In the corner was a telescope with a stand. Another balcony ran on this side of the suite, this time with a view of the downtown. They stepped out to watch the purpling dusk and leaned on the black iron rail, side by side.

"Are you working on a project?" Clary asked with a backward glance at the books on the table.

"Always."

The reply didn't give her much to work with, but she persevered. "What?"

Merlin looked up at the dusky sky. "I'm searching for a cure for the fae. It's my one goal. You saw up close what they've become."

"Yes." She shuddered, feeling again the fae's power draining her soul.

He waited a moment as if to let the memory take full effect. "That's my doing."

The simple statement said so much. Everyone knew the story of how Merlin defeated the demons at the expense of the fae. His battle spell had broken the magic of the witches, too, but at least they had eventually recovered. The accident, in truth an unexpected side effect, had defined him. Many still hated him for it, saying the disaster was a punishment for his pride.

He turned so his back was to the view. He frowned. "Did I tell you that during the ritual one of the demons said their magic could cure the fae?"

The revelation was so unexpected, Clary's mouth dropped open. "Really?"

"I will find out how."

There was no conceit in him now, just a quiet determination. He had vast power, the ear of a king and centuries of wisdom. None of it had helped him until this one thread of hope had come his way. She reached out, brushing his arm with her fingertips. He finally met her gaze, and she finally understood the deep sense of responsibility he carried. It left no room for anything else. No joy, no plans of his own. All those emotions he locked away.

"If you find the cure," she said slowly, "it will erase what happened."

"No," he said, sounding tired now. "It won't erase the past, but it will make the future something I can live with."

His words had brought an ache to the back of her throat. She let her hand drop, suddenly overwhelmed with the need to touch more of him, but uncertain if that would be welcome. "How are you going to get this cure?"

"Come with me." He pushed away from the balcony, leading the way back inside.

The rest of the condominium consisted of a small library, the usual storage closets and a guest bedroom. He paused at the door to the bedroom, holding up a hand to indicate Clary should stay where she was. He opened the door slowly, revealing a small chamber with the bed pushed against the far wall. An elaborate spell circle was chalked on the remainder of the floor. She'd been Merlin's student long enough to recognize the containment spell that would keep just about anything within the boundary of the chalked lines.

Laren of the Green Towers hunched in the middle of spell circle. The fae had his knees drawn up to his chest as if cold, his expression pure misery. Clary didn't care if he wasn't happy about captivity. This was the creature who had tried to devour her soul.

She rounded on Merlin. "What's he doing here?"

Chapter 8

Laren cowered at the sound of Clary's voice, curling in on himself like a frightened child. Nothing about his posture reminded her of the fae who'd attacked her in the alley, and she glared at Merlin, silently demanding an explanation.

"He is not who he was," Merlin replied, his voice almost colorless. "Or perhaps I should say he's someone he hasn't been for a long time."

"No." Laren began to rock, lowering his forehead to his knees. "I cannot be what I was. I remember it all and there is no hope of going back."

Clary was utterly mystified. "I don't get it."

"He tasted your life essence," said Merlin. "Not a lot, but enough that it reversed the spell."

She swore under her breath. "Demon essence to reverse a demon spell."

And it was in her, whether Vivian was contained by Merlin's potion or not. Apparently, it was mixing with her own life force sufficiently to roofie a hungry fae. If Clary needed more proof that she was in trouble, this was it. Her temples throbbed. "Is he okay?"

"Laren's soul has returned to him," said Merlin. "But as he says, he remembers everything."

She closed her eyes, only able to guess at what a fae might have done after a thousand years without a conscience. With no sense of beauty, no joy or natural desire, novelty was everything to his kind. That typically involved bloodshed, or a taste for mortal souls. Now he had to face what he had done.

He began to softly sob. It was the sound of a heart breaking.

Clary's breath was jagged. She looked up into Merlin's face. For once, his mask had slipped and Laren's pain was mirrored in the lines around his eyes and mouth. She could hear his words once more: *You saw up close what the fae have become. That's my doing.*

This was Merlin's nightmare, almost as bad for him as it was for the fae. It didn't take magic to know he blamed himself for every crime, every ounce of suffering his spell had unleashed.

Laren raised his head, his green eyes fierce with grief. He knelt facing Clary and beat a fist to his chest, a gesture of anger turned inward. "My offense against you cannot be forgiven."

She heard Merlin's intake of breath, a sharp, painful rasp. As terrible as it was, the sound freed something inside her. She took a step toward the circle.

"Clary!" Merlin's warning was sharp.

She held up a hand, palm out. "I'm fine."

She hoped that was true. Laren was still kneeling, head bowed and arms loose at his sides. He made her think of a prisoner awaiting execution. She walked up to the edge of the circle, her toes almost touching the chalk lines. The fae lifted his head. His long, white hair had come loose and hid most of his face, but she could see the tracks of tears down his cheeks. The sight hurt something deep inside her.

"None of this should have happened to you," she said. "You didn't deserve it. Nobody did."

He blinked, his mouth drawn tight. "But I..."

"I know," she said. She couldn't ignore what he'd done, but then, she couldn't blame him, either. Judging him was beyond any wisdom she had, so she didn't try.

He hung his head again, releasing his breath as if speech deserted him. Clary bit her lip. The chalk circle was there to keep Laren contained, but every instinct told her there was no need for that now. The fae was no longer a danger. She stepped across, ignoring Merlin's noise of protest, and knelt to face Laren. She took his hands. They were unresisting and almost lifeless. She squeezed them gently. "If you need forgiveness for what you did to me, I forgive you. I'm not sure it shouldn't be the other way around, though, for bringing you such anguish when you tasted my soul."

His head came up, seemingly startled. Their eyes met, and this time she saw how beautiful his were, filled with warmth and energy. He had a soul now, and in that moment she fully understood what the faery people had lost. A throb of grief ached in her chest.

"I am infinitely grateful to you for walking across my path," he said softly. "The miracle you brought demands a price, but I gladly pay it. You have saved me from doing more harm in this world."

Warm wetness touched her face, and she realized she'd begun to cry. With a tentative smile, Laren brushed them away. "Be at peace. I am whole again, thanks to you."

Without thinking what she did, Clary embraced him. "Welcome back, Laren."

Merlin cleared his throat. Clary looked up to see him leaning against the doorframe, arms crossed over his chest. His expression was neutral except when he turned to Laren. Then his eyes narrowed the slightest degree. "I hate to end this touching scene, but there are practical matters to discuss."

Laren rose and bowed deeply to the enchanter. "I am in your debt for sparing my life. Ask whatever service I may perform in your name."

Merlin frowned. "You owe me nothing." He gestured toward the chalk circle, and Clary felt the spell that bound it drop away.

"Come sit with us, Laren of the Green Towers," Merlin asked formally. "Will you accept food and drink?"

"I shall, with thanks."

The rituals of hospitality had power among the fae, and sharing a meal was an act of friendship. As long as Laren was under Merlin's roof, neither would harm the other. Clary got to her feet, following them out of the room.

"Do you know if any of the fae are in communication with the queen?" Merlin asked.

"Queen Morgan LaFaye is held prisoner by the Lady of the Lake, deep in the Forest Sauvage," Laren replied. "How could any of my people contact the queen?"

It was a good question, Clary thought as they settled in Merlin's living room. The comfortable chairs were a deep forest green that complemented the natural wood floor and fieldstone fireplace.

"I have it on good authority that LaFaye is summoning demons to her prison," Merlin announced. "In addition, one of the hellspawn is meeting with generals among the fae army. She could be directing her lieutenants that way."

Laren sat up, surprise sharpening his features. "That explains many rumors I have heard."

"What rumors?"

"That there is an alliance between the demons and fae against Camelot. I gave it no credit until now. It seems utterly unnatural."

"That may not matter," said Merlin. "Not if there is greed. LaFaye was always lavish with her promises."

Laren lowered his gaze, not meeting Merlin's eyes. "There is another rumor that says time alone should have healed the fae. Why didn't that happen?"

Clary answered, because this was one fun fact she knew. "LaFaye kept the wounds fresh with her own magic."

Fury lit his face. "Is this true? How do you know?"

"There is a small contingent of fae who are friends of Camelot," said Merlin. "They healed or escaped the spell's effects altogether. They know the truth."

"Why would the queen do such a thing?" Laren demanded.

"Tell me this: What does she promise her armies of fae when she asks them to invade the human world?" asked Merlin.

Laren turned pale, his fingers curling into fists. "An

abundance of mortal souls for the taking. If we were cured, her promise would have no power."

"Exactly."

"Perhaps you are to blame for the original spell that injured us, Merlin Ambrosius, but our queen has made herself our jailer." Laren rose, pacing the room. "Where are these other fae you speak of? Surely they work to free our kin?"

"They have formed an alliance." Merlin rose, as well. "I'll make a call and let them know you're here, if you wish to join with them."

Laren's face filled with a defiant hope. "Please."

Despite Merlin's confident tone, the business of introducing a stranger to the close-knit resistance was hardly simple. Many of the fae had tragic histories, and the risk of betrayal was too great. However, in the end, a meeting was arranged and Merlin took Laren to meet his contact. Clary remained behind at Merlin's insistence, under observation even if she was the only one in the condominium.

After saying a heartfelt goodbye to Laren, she took a shower, stole a clean T-shirt from Merlin's drift of unfolded laundry and settled at the dining room table. With the beginnings of a plan, she opened the laptop and hacked through Merlin's password—Wiz123—in less than ten minutes. He might be light-years ahead in magic, but she knew math and computers, not to mention basic internet security.

She ignored Merlin's files and opened a blank spreadsheet, typing in the rudiments of a formula. If a taste of demon essence cured one fae, how much would it take to cure all the fae? In their natural form—that is, not muddled up inside Clary—demons were raw energy, so how would one begin to disperse that energy? Could it be converted into a beam of light? Sent over Wi-Fi? Atomized and spritzed? Clary fiddled with mathematical models, but there were too many unknowns to get very far. She was still heads-down with the problem when Merlin returned.

"I see you've made yourself at home." He dropped his keys on the table and raised an eyebrow.

"How did the meeting go?" she asked, still intent on the laptop's screen.

"Perfectly. Laren is among friends. You needn't worry on his account."

A knot of tension unwound under Clary's ribs. "Good."

"That's my computer."

"Your password sucks," she said, wishing her complexion didn't show every blush. "I'm trying to figure out a way to rain demon essence on the Kingdom of Faery. I'll donate it myself if I can figure out a way to do it."

His lips curled into the shadow of a smile. "A generous offer, but I doubt one demon, even Vivian, would go far enough. We need to think bigger."

He'd said *we*. Relieved, Clary stopped typing and turned in her chair to face him. "How?"

The slight smile faded. "I don't know." He put one hand on the table and leaned down, brushing his lips against her cheek. "But I'm infinitely grateful that you tried."

She froze, surprised by his gesture. For once, he'd reached out without something incredibly bad—death, monsters, murderous fae—having crossed their path moments before. Her pulse pounded double time.

He began to rise, but Clary caught his arm, pulling him closer. "You're not in this alone anymore. You know that, right?"

As soon as she said it, the words felt ridiculous. Why would he care if his student—one whose failures were bound to get him in trouble—was in his corner? She hadn't even come up with a good theory for the cure on paper, and that was stuff she was good at. Clary let go of his arm, folding her hands in her lap. She was so far out of her depth, she'd lost sight of the shore.

"Clary," he said softly. He was looking at her intently, his expression speculative as if he was seeing her for the first time.

Heat burned up her neck, over her ears and flamed across her cheeks. There was no hope of pretending she didn't care what he thought of her, and yet she tried. She turned her face away. "Yeah?"

He put two fingers under her chin and turned her face toward him. "I work alone for a reason."

"I know," she said quickly, still avoiding his eyes.

"It's not always a very good reason, but I've lived a long time and it's not always easy to change."

She had to look at him then. His expression was serious, but something had shifted beneath it, the way a pond thawed under the surface layer of ice. It gave her back a little of her swagger. "So?"

He nodded to the computer. "You have skills I don't. I may need your help before this is over."

Her face went numb with shock. He was actually letting her a step closer into his world. "I know there was a compliment somewhere in that statement."

He leaned closer. "You were a model of compassion with your would-be murderer. You could try giving me a break."

"Will you forgive me for breaking your crystal ball?"

"Agate."

"Whatever."

"Is there a good reason why I should?" Merlin's voice was hoarse, but it wasn't with anger or his usual arrogance. All at once, the mood shifted to something far more risky.

Clary curled her fingers in the front of his shirt and pulled him closer until their lips were a hairbreadth apart. His breath fanned her face as she tilted her head slightly, finding the best angle to kiss. He tasted like coffee and chocolate as if he'd had refreshments at the meeting. Clary suddenly realized she hadn't eaten for hours, but it was a fleeting thought. She was hungry in a lot of different ways.

She kissed him again, and this time he responded. Nervous energy pulsed through her. What was she doing? She never let anyone get this close, not when it mattered. That was why all those past boyfriends had never worked out. So why was she throwing herself at Merlin? He terrified her. He didn't just *matter*; she'd crossed the continent to be near him, even if it was as a lowly student.

There was no denying the need burning low in her belly. It was her own desire, but the volume was cranked to a pitch she'd never experienced before. Their lips were locked, but her hands were in motion, trailing down his back and over the curve of his jeans.

Merlin broke the kiss, but did not pull away. His amber eyes were just visible under the sweep of his lashes, but she could feel him studying her. He was breathing hard, almost panting. "What are you doing?" he asked.

"Shall I draw you a map?"

A shudder ran through him, and it was a moment before she realized he was laughing. "I think I can find my way."

"Men never want maps."

"It ruins the process of discovery."

Then Merlin took charge of the kiss, teasing the seam of her lips until they parted. His hands curved around her cheeks, holding her with firm gentleness as if she were a piece of precious sculpture. Then they brushed her neck as he traced her jaw with kisses. It was a slow exploration, but it was not tentative. He simply refused to be rushed.

Fear suddenly blanked Clary's mind as if she'd unwittingly stepped off a cliff. She hadn't imagined this, hadn't expected it. And then, as if an updraft caught her, she surrendered to joy. This was a turning point, and it was good. She'd wanted Merlin for so long, and now here he was in her arms. In the midst of so much bad luck, it was a surprising gift. Heat climbed up her cheeks all over again, a sign of her excitement and an unexpected bashfulness.

Clary's blood thundered so hard in her ears, it took a moment before she realized there was a steady pounding on the door.

"Merlin!" bellowed the angry voice of King Arthur. "Answer me! I know you're in there."

Chapter 9

Morgan LaFaye, Queen of Faery, felt Laren of the Green Towers slip from her grasp. It was a slight sensation, barely a tickle, but the predatory part of her mind was ever on the alert for threats. The fae were hers. *Hers.* She'd seized their throne in the aftermath of Merlin's ridiculous blunder and had guarded it since. Morgan had used her magic to keep the fae damaged, hungry, obedient as long as she supplied them with mortal souls. She'd found an easy road to power—why not make it last?

Especially when *easy* was in short supply. She rose from her throne in the white tower that imprisoned her—it was really just a chair, but it was a throne if she said it was—and swept to the window. The view of mountains and lakes was stunning, but it gave the queen no pleasure. *I lost something of mine this day.*

Every time one of the fae regained his or her soul, it stole a tiny bit of Morgan's queenship. Worst of all had been the loss of her jailer, Nimueh, the famous Lady of the Lake. The fae enchantress had rediscovered her soul and her extra-shiny knight, Sir Lancelot du Lac, right before locking Morgan up. The two lovebirds were still camped outside the tower, making certain their prisoner remained secure. The tower's magic ensured she never lacked for the necessities of life, but she was bored, lonely and helpless.

She hadn't felt this way for a very long time, but it wasn't the first occasion. Just before the demon wars, when she had still been part of Camelot's court, Arthur had commanded there be a winter feast, and all the guests wore white. Morgan knew she was beautiful, and that night she'd shone like the evening star. Merlin had been there, too, handsome and laughing and for once dressed in all the finery his rank decreed. They were rivals, Morgan and Merlin, each proud of their magic and forever vying to outdo the other. Merlin did it to win Arthur's regard and she did it to spite them both, but that night had been different. They had flirted—or she thought they had. At the very least, they had danced and drank and exchanged quips like sparring lovers, right up until Arthur had invited them to play a game.

"I say we play a kissing game," she'd said to Merlin. "I dare you to tell us the name of the lady you love, or else kiss me in forfeit. I warn you, I'll invoke a charm to make sure you tell the truth."

Merlin had bowed. "Madam, I do not play games that might touch on a lady's reputation."

In hindsight, she should have left the matter there, but her pride had been wounded.

"Don't be a cold-blooded codfish," she'd said, giving his arm a playful slap. "Are you sure it's not me, and you're simply embarrassed to draw attention to a hopeless *amour*?"

That brought the laughter of the courtiers, and even Arthur.

Merlin had bowed again. "I will shovel the stables, kiss the lowliest chambermaid and ply my magic in the village square before engaging in a game that will only bring dishonor."

The courtiers had applauded his arrogant, insulting words, saying that he won the match by adhering to the rules of chivalry. Which meant Morgan had not. The wretched magic-monger had embarrassed her in front of the entire court of Camelot, and she had been teased without mercy for weeks thereafter. She felt then as she did now, cast adrift by those who were lesser than she.

If Morgan had been attracted to Merlin that night, it was for the very last time. Their rivalry had turned to something worse until finally he'd helped the Lady of the Lake put her in this tower prison. He would pay for that.

And her revenge would come soon. She'd struggled against Nimueh's enchantments, finally punching a hole just big enough to work her summoning circle. Demons were scum, but they could be very useful messengers.

She felt her visitor arrive before she saw him. His presence was like a pressure between her shoulder blades. Fear tingled. Demons might be scum, but they were also deadly. Nevertheless, she turned to face the new arrival with a gracious smile.

"To what do I owe this pleasure?" she asked. "It must be important since I didn't invite you."

Tenebrius regarded her with his yellow, goat-slitted eyes. Today he was dressed in scarlet robes, his claws crusted with tiny gemstones that winked as he wiggled his fingers in a tiny wave. "But you would have eventually. I just saved you the trouble."

He never used her title as queen, so she also dispensed with false courtesy. Why bother? They'd never liked each other one bit. "What do you want today, hellspawn?"

"We have a deal. I assist in your escape and you free me and my followers from the bonds of the Abyss."

"I know this," she said, growing irritable. "I offered you the deal, if you recall."

He shifted his weight, but did not move. He might have invited himself in, but he couldn't step outside the summoning circle she'd drawn on the floor. Morgan folded her hands, doing her best to look regal. It was hard when one had been wearing the same gown for so many months. The dark folds had gone ragged, like the feathers of a storm-tossed crow.

When she said nothing more, his brows flexed downward into an inky V. "Then why are you dealing with that pustule, Gorm?"

"Ah." She waved a careless hand. "I'm surprised you heard about that."

"He is less than discreet."

That was a problem—one she might need Tenebrius to solve. She spoke a word and the summoning circle released the demon. Morgan indicated a pair of chairs that sat before an empty fireplace. "Sit. Tell me all."

The demon reclined in a majestic sprawl of red silk. "What can Gorm do that I cannot?"

"His involvement bothers you." The temptation

to needle Tenebrius until he bled—figuratively, of course—brought Morgan to the edge of her seat.

He stroked his long, black mustaches with glittering claws. "Please answer my question."

She bridled, but she wasn't stupid. Nothing could jeopardize her endgame. "I've known Gorm for many years. He invented spells to make horses lose their shoes, and carts their wheels. When foundries and factories covered the lands, he devised ways to foul their gears. Even from exile in the Abyss, he delights in making the works of humanity crumble."

"So?"

"So, I wanted to know what he was working on these days," she said, doing her best to sound reasonable. "Now that Arthur is in the modern world, he is vulnerable to Gorm's brand of chaos in new and interesting ways."

"Arthur." Tenebrius sighed and rubbed his forehead. "It is always Arthur with you. Retribution, magic swords, blah, blah. Isn't the crown of Faery good enough for you?"

She clenched her teeth in aggravation, but was forced to loosen them to speak. "I should have been Queen of Camelot. The crown rightfully belonged to my kin. He stole it with the help of that interfering mountebank, Merlin. In truth, I think I hate Merlin worse than the king."

The demon nodded in a way that said he'd heard it all before. "Right. So you asked Gorm over for tea."

Morgan sat back, her temper simmering. She hated having to explain herself. She also hated the shabby room, her aching boredom and the fact that the only creatures who would talk to her had to be summoned from the Abyss. But then, no one said conquering the world was a popularity contest.

"Gorm promises a unique means of attack," she said. "One that will cripple Camelot while opening the door for demons to return to the mortal realms."

Tenebrius sat forward, his strange eyes lighting with interest. "Really? What is it?"

"Something technical," she said dismissively. "Something very Gorm. I don't understand the specifics, but it's modern and he promises that it will work."

"And why did I not know of this?"

"You would have been informed the moment construction began on his spell. He said there are ingredients he needs that are in your keeping. He will also need both our powers to fuel it. The three of us will need to work together."

She hated the notion of working with demons, of her magic touching theirs. It was a fall from grace, but she told herself it was also a means of recovering her power.

The demon crossed his legs. "And how does this escapade of Gorm's coincide with your plans for escape from this tower?"

"There will be a test run," she said with a shrug. "If it succeeds in providing a safe means of escape from the Abyss, you will take it at once and free me."

Even if the demons abandoned Morgan then and there, she'd escape in the resulting confusion. Besides, she was certain Arthur and his flunkies would perish trying to defend their precious humans. It was a perfect plan.

"Interesting," Tenebrius mused.

Morgan could see the conflict behind the demon's languid pose. It was no secret that he preferred Arthur to Morgan, at least on a personal level. But she was offering him freedom while Arthur's war—and Arthur's enchanter—had banished the demons from the mortal realms. She watched his face, seeing the moment self-interest conquered his personal inclinations.

"There is a complication," he said.

Her stomach dropped. "What?"

"Gorm was prattling to me about his visit to you. We were overheard."

"By whom?" Her voice was shrill. She had too much riding on this plan to risk interference.

"Vivian. She is a friend, but she has a history with Merlin, who was listening, as well."

As he spoke, Morgan rose and began to pace. Her steps grew quicker as he explained what had happened with the ritual and the scrying ball and Merlin's foolish student.

"Vivian is gravely injured," he finally said. "Trapped between realms."

The Queen of Faery spun to face the demon. "If she knows anything she should not…"

"Don't fret," he said with a wicked smile. "Who but Vivian is better positioned to be our informant inside Camelot's court?"

"Very well," Morgan said. "But make certain she's on our side. If she's not, you know what to do."

Clary jumped at the pounding on the door, her green eyes widening at the sound of Arthur's voice. "Why is he here?"

Merlin clenched his jaw, his mind still fixed on the taste of Clary's lips. They reminded him of sun-warmed cherries, ripe and sweet and begging to be devoured. It took an act of will to shift his attention to the rattling door.

"Give me a minute!" he shouted, the angry snap in his words unmistakable.

The pounding stopped, but he could still feel Arthur's impatience like a physical pressure. Though he didn't want to admit it, he'd put off another encounter with Arthur. The king had legitimate concerns, but Merlin loathed explaining himself to someone who barely understood magic.

He'd rather be interrogating—or whatever he was doing with Clary. His actions had something to do with the scene with Laren, the sight of her holding him, her forgiveness, her generosity and the trust she'd shown the moment she'd crossed into the circle that held the fae. He'd never seen the likes of that before in all the centuries of his life. Clary was special.

He finally released his grip on her waist and stepped back, still holding one of her hands. The absence of her body against his made him annoyed all over again.

"What does the king want now?" Clary whispered, clearly nervous.

Merlin frowned, aware that he hadn't been able to protect her from Vivian—not well enough to keep her out of this bizarre situation. The very least he could do was keep her safe from Arthur's temper. "Go to the bedroom and close the door. Don't come out until I give you the all clear."

She nodded solemnly, but neither of them moved. He heard Arthur's impatient shuffling outside. That wasn't due so much to supersonic wizard ears as to Arthur making a point. Monarchs didn't enjoy waiting.

Merlin took a reluctant step back, finally releasing her slim palm. With contact finally broken, they both regained their wits a little. Clary shook herself and went to the bedroom, but kept her gaze locked with his until she shut the door. Slightly dazed, Merlin went to answer the knock. When he opened the door, a small green suitcase sat in the hall. No doubt it contained the clothes Tamsin had packed for Clary. Merlin set it inside, wishing the delivery was the only reason for Arthur's visit but knowing he wouldn't be so lucky.

He stepped into the hall, folded his arms and looked around. Arthur had wandered down the corridor toward the elevator and was now pacing from one wall to the other like an agitated cat.

Merlin frowned. He'd been on the cusp of something wonderful with Clary. From the first moment she'd burst into his world, with her wayward magic and smart mouth, he'd wanted her. He'd meant to teach her, protect her and launch her career as a witch, but never to give in to desire. Not with an innocent—and yet he yearned to break his own rules. For all her attitude, she was a loving, forgiving woman and much, much more than he deserved. Her generous heart had saved Laren as much as any cure.

Merlin took a deep breath and let it out slowly. As for him, how often had he said nothing good came of knowing Merlin the Wise? Maybe this interruption had saved both of them from a step they'd regret. Surely it had.

Or had it? He couldn't tell at the moment, and he wouldn't get peace and quiet to figure it out for a while. Right now he had to deal with an angry king.

Arthur leaned against the wall next to the elevators. "Well?" he demanded. "What have you discovered?"

Merlin's thoughts flashed to Clary's lips, her smooth, slender neck and the promising softness of her curves. "Many things, Your Majesty."

Chapter 10

Arthur's eyebrows rose in question.

"Perhaps this is not the place to discuss them," Merlin suggested. "It would be helpful to have the queen present and a few of your closest advisers."

"What of Clary?"

Merlin pulled the door closed behind him, letting the lock click into place. "She is safely confined for the moment. Tamsin and I leashed her magic as a precaution."

Arthur visibly relaxed. "Good."

"None of this is her fault, you know," Merlin said.

"You don't need to defend her."

"I do." Merlin's voice was flat.

"I realize she's your student."

"She is also Tamsin's sister, your dedicated employee and a faithful member of your court." Merlin struggled to keep his tone quiet, but it was a losing battle. All at once, he'd lost the capacity to hide what he felt.

Arthur held up his hands in a placating gesture. "Fair enough. She's Gwen's friend, too, but after what I saw today, I want assurances it's safe to let her near my wife."

That much, Merlin could accept. After literally centuries of waiting, the queen carried Camelot's heir. Her term was near, and everyone was on baby watch.

"Where shall we go?" Merlin asked, mostly to change the topic.

"My place, if you care to take us there," Arthur suggested. "Perceval drove me here, but I sent him on his way. The lad cannot distinguish city traffic from a battlefield melee."

"No wonder you look green."

"He attempted to parallel park. Please return me to my home, where I can pour myself a drink."

Merlin allowed himself a smile. With one hand, he sketched an arc in the air before them. White light trailed behind his fingers, showing the gesture's path and the outline of a door in space and time. The glow brightened, rays of blue and green flowing into the arc's center. When it was filled, the light growing almost solid, the brightness changed course and began to dissipate like a morning mist. What was left behind was a window into Arthur's apartment. The two men stepped through and Merlin closed the portal with a wave of his hand. The spell allowed them to enter silently and unobserved, and for a moment he paused to take in the scene.

Queen Guinevere sat in an easy chair with her feet propped on a stool. Her hands rested protectively over her burgeoning stomach, but she'd lost none of the lively energy that made the queen the beating heart of Camelot's court. Beaumains, his arm in a sling, sat next to Gawain on the couch. All three were watching baseball.

"Where did you come from?" Gwen asked.

"Just passing by," Merlin returned with a smile. "How are you feeling?"

She grinned. "Like a beached whale. Cheer me up."

He summoned a carnation from thin air and presented it to her with a flourish. The queen took it and held it to her nose. "Thank you. You are gallant as always. Have some birthday cake. Tamsin brought it over for Beaumains. I think he's finally reached drinking age."

That brought a general laugh. Gawain's youngest brother was in his early twenties, but had a melting smile that would make him look boyish forever. Merlin accepted a slice of cake, which was chocolate and very good.

"How fares Palomedes?" Merlin asked.

"Resting," Gawain replied as he switched off the TV. "He will fight again, but he will carry the scars from that encounter with the lions."

Merlin heard the edge in the knight's words and didn't blame him. As one of the senior knights, Gawain's job was to protect his own.

Arthur sat on the stool and gathered the queen's feet in his lap. He set about gently massaging them. "Merlin says he has news."

Gwen's blue eyes turned his way. "About Clary?"

"In part."

Her gaze grew troubled. "I'm counting on you to look after her."

Merlin gave her a nod, not able to find the right words. He had failed Clary the moment Vivian put one demonic toe in this world. He put down his plate of cake, his appetite gone. "There are rumors that the hellspawn are in league with the fae."

"Which hellspawn?" asked Gawain.

"Tenebrius, for one," Merlin replied.

"That makes no sense," Arthur said. "When LaFaye challenged us to a tourney just before she was imprisoned, Tenebrius clearly disliked her. He judged in our favor and awarded the prize to me."

"You never claimed the prize," said Gawain. "Can you use that to your advantage?"

"If it were only that simple," Arthur muttered under his breath. "We are speaking of hellspawn."

The knights fell deathly silent, their faces drawn. These men had fought in the first demon wars, and all remembered the horrors. But as little as he wanted to darken the shadows already gathering around them, Merlin had to tell the truth. So he did, relaying everything he'd learned from the ritual to the discovery of an unexpected cure to the information Laren had provided. The only thing he glossed over was the growing heat between himself and Clary. That was nobody's business but theirs.

Beaumains was the first to speak. "Of all of this, the news of Morgan LaFaye's involvement worries me the most."

"If there is a danger she might escape," Arthur replied, "we should send word to the goblins to gather their armies."

"And the Charmed Beasts of the Forest Sauvage," Gwen added. "They are our eyes and ears."

Merlin listened with growing unease. All the suggestions were sensible, but no countermeasure would be enough if Morgan truly slipped her leash. Merlin's spell to bring the Round Table forward in time hadn't worked as well as he'd hoped, and only a handful of knights had awakened from their stone effigies. Modern humans didn't believe in magic, and even if they did, there was no reason to believe they'd follow a king who earned his living in an amusement park. And if that was not discouraging enough, every accord with the hidden world, including the goblins, pixies, witches and even the fae who still retained their souls agreed that the magical realm had to stay hidden. Humans had a bad habit of burning things and people they didn't understand, and breaking the accords meant war with the few allies Camelot had left.

The only real answer was to turn the fae armies against Morgan, and that meant a widespread cure that would restore their souls. But although he had found the beginnings of a solution, Merlin—even with Clary's help—had a long way to go.

"I have a question." Gwen's soft voice interrupted his thoughts. "Who is more powerful—the demons or LaFaye?"

"In the magical realms, demons are the darkness where fae are the light," Merlin said. "They should be in balance, except LaFaye has changed the equilibrium of magic by bargaining with the hellspawn. She risks much by trusting in that pact."

"Good riddance," Beaumains said hopefully.

Merlin frowned. "Don't be so quick to hope she is the loser. Once the demons demanded all earthly powers to kneel before them."

"We would not," Arthur said simply. "But that refusal began the war."

Merlin remembered how it had started. He'd been standing on the balcony of his tower at Camelot, a shiver up his spine telling him magic was afoot. The morning had taken on an unearthly quiet as if the land held its breath. The first visible sign of what was to come was his pet raven flapping against the iron-gray sky. The bird had been arrowing toward him, its panicked caw a warning of approaching doom.

Then Merlin had caught the scent of rain. That would have been innocent enough, but the cold March sky had seemed to crumple, going from the flat gray of early spring to billowing charcoal clouds in the span of a heartbeat. Thunder ground through the heavens like an avalanche, and then the deluge had begun. Suddenly, rain danced on the edge of the stone balcony, on the slate roofs and the cobbled courtyard. In an instant Merlin was drenched, with the sodden raven landing in a heap in his arms. No birds flew in that rain—the force of it was too hard.

It churned the fields and the forest for months on end, and then the summer came with brutal heat. No crops were harvested that year. The winter took what supplies remained. Disease and hunger cut like twin scythes. The mortals had to surrender, or they had to fight and win. Failure would mean the certain death of thousands upon thousands of innocents. That was when Arthur had asked Merlin to lend his battle magic, whatever the cost.

In the face of the destruction of the land and its people, what could Merlin do but agree?

Vivian opened her eyes and then squinted as a bright light flared in her face.

"Ah, you're awake," said Tenebrius, allowing the flame at his fingertip to go out. "I was beginning to wonder if you were already snuffed."

His goat-slitted eyes were impatient as if she'd delayed mealtime. Vivian frowned and sat up, taking in her own opulent bedchamber. Demons might be made of energy, but they all chose a physical form and concrete environment to dwell in. This month she'd chosen the Hollywood interpretation of an exotic pleasure palace just in case she got the chance to drag Merlin back to her lair. For all his cool swagger, he could be flustered if one knew how.

She swung her legs over the edge of her scarlet silk bed. "How did you bring me back? I was stuck inside that pathetically incompetent witch, and then Merlin knocked me cold."

"I know," Tenebrius said drily. "As demonic possessions go, that was a poor effort. You barely qualified as a guilty conscience."

Vivian rose, her feline tail swishing with temper. "I was injured. It was a dreadful experience, trapped in all those complicated human emotions." She drew the last word out for effect.

She stomped to and fro for a moment. "I felt like a spider swimming in syrup. I was about to come down with a case of stomach ulcers. Or poetry."

"My, but you had a narrow escape."

She ignored his sarcasm, focusing on that ridiculous fae, Laren. She'd been paralyzed inside Clary, but she'd heard every weepy word of his tale. She turned to the other demon. "Is it true some of our leaders are working with LaFaye? Are you?"

His smile was sly, which was as good as an emphatic yes. "If I told you, I would have to kill you."

Her hands fisted. "I thought you hated LaFaye."

"Arthur and your ex-lover cast us out of the mortal realms."

"So? Everyone would have, given half a chance."

"The Queen of Faery is willing to help us return to our former glory."

"And you believe her?"

He waggled a hand in a so-so gesture.

"How will she do it from inside a prison?"

"A plan of Gorm's. I'm not sure if it will work yet, though from what I hear the modern age offers some interesting opportunities. It will release us from the Abyss."

Vivian rolled her eyes. "If you'd mentioned this before, I might have kept my eyes open while I was in the mortal realms. Now I'm back here, as stuck as I was before."

There was a beat of uncomfortable silence that raised the hair on her neck. If she didn't know better, she'd think Tenebrius was embarrassed.

"You're still trapped," he finally said. "You're there, and you're here. You split when Merlin broke his scrying ball."

"What?" Vivian stilled, only the tip of her tail tap-tapping against the floor. "How do you know?"

"I saw it happen."

"I feel fine."

"You're numb. You can't feel it because the energetic bond between your two halves is nearly severed."

"How? That should not have happened. The bond should be strong."

He shrugged. "An accident, I suppose. You won't last like this, Vivian."

She slumped down on the edge of the bed, her normal grace lost. Horror crawled through her, bushing her tail. She looked up at the other demon's pinched expression. "But I'm immortal."

"Not like this, you aren't." Sadness filled his eyes, but like everything else with demons, it was hardly trustworthy. "The only thing keeping you alive is the witch's natural strength."

It was a death sentence. It was impossible. It was unfair.

"Then get the rest of me back," she said, her voice quiet. "Make me whole."

Once upon a time, Merlin would have hugged her and tried to soothe her distress. Even Clary seemed to weep for her would-be assassins. Why was no one here for her? Vivian slammed down on her sudden yearning to return to the mortal world. She didn't need mortal sympathy. Weakness wasn't the demon way.

"I can't make you whole again," said Tenebrius. "The most I could do was to summon your consciousness for a brief period. You will wake up inside your witch. There is no coming home, Vivian."

Her chin jerked up. Her mind scrambled with the idea of a finite life, of actually dying.

"Is that the truth?" she whispered. "Do not play tricks with me. Not about this."

"I am sorry." This time he did look genuinely regretful.

The first shock past, her temper flared. "So, you brought me here to pronounce my death sentence. Anything else?"

"Help me wreak havoc on his precious Camelot. Make the most of the time you have left."

"How?" Vivian narrowed her eyes.

"Be my informant. You have a front-row seat to Arthur's court."

Vivian considered. "I want vengeance on Merlin."

"You can't kill him yet. He's your source of information."

"Your source, you mean." She watched Tenebrius's goat-slitted eyes go cold and knew she was courting trouble.

"LaFaye ordered me to kill you. I told her you'd work for her instead."

That would happen about the same time Vivian took up crochet. "Very well," she lied. "I'll be your spy. Then I'll kill him."

"A good choice. I'll be in touch." Tenebrius reached out one clawed hand and touched her forehead.

Vivian woke for a second time, but in a different bed. She had a fuzzy recollection of lying down for a nap when Merlin left with Arthur, and then a bizarre dream about...

That wasn't a dream.

Groggy, Vivian pushed herself upright and dragged a hand through her hair—short, fair hair and not her thick cascade of blue-black locks. She was back in Clary's body, but their positions had been reversed. Now she was completely in control, and the witch's consciousness was a tiny spark buried deep inside. Triumph swelled inside her. Her newfound freedom was undoubtedly Tenebrius's handiwork. A parting gift, perhaps?

She closed her eyes, shutting out the room around her. Dying? It made no sense. She felt strong, clear-headed and filled with purpose. Could he have been mistaken? She didn't think so—Tenebrius might lie to her, but not about this. All the same, his information might not be complete. He didn't say how long her demise would take. Months? Years? A mortal lifetime?

And yet now every second was made precious just because their number could be measured. Tears pricked at the backs of her eyes. Demons didn't cry, but a death sentence was a good excuse to make an exception.

Vivian rose, in sole control of this body for the first time. She stretched out one arm, then the other, feeling the delicacy of the bones and muscles. By mortal standards, the witch was fit, but Vivian would need to be careful. Such bodies were easily broken.

And now she was stuck in one. Who was responsible for this? Merlin. Always Merlin. She'd shared her treasury of scrolls and grimoires, which was why he knew about that cursed battle spell. She'd shown him the many realms of the known world, from the Crystal Mountains to the grim wonder of the Abyss and its silent, barren lakes. She had unlocked his magic and made him a great enchanter. Most significant, at least to her, they had lain together.

Still, he'd betrayed her. He would pay for that, and she wasn't going to let the opportunity slip, whatever Tenebrius wanted. What was he going to do, kill her?

The first step in her plan was to clean herself up. The little witch needed a lesson in style. After a long, hot shower, Vivian contemplated her clothing options. She had a vague memory of a suitcase arriving. Once she located it, she undid the zipper and stared inside. A rising sensation of dismay brought heat to her cheeks. Most of the clothes looked as if they belonged on a boy. She'd seen pictures of current fashion—the Abyss was far away, but advertising had an astonishing reach. Clary could have done so much better, with a splash of red and some body-conscious styling. She knew the girl was savvy about clothes and had all but dressed Queen Guinevere during her first weeks in the modern age. She was just too self-conscious to take her own advice.

Vivian snorted and tipped the suitcase upside down, rummaging through the piles Tamsin had carefully folded. A handful of dog-eared paperbacks fell out, and she pushed them out of the way to better see the fashion options. She finally selected slim-legged black slacks and a spaghetti-strapped top in white. It had a low-cut back that showed off a bit of skin. Vivian dressed and stood in front of the mirror on the back of the bedroom door. Clary's figure was far less dramatic than what she was used to, but she could work with it.

Vivian reached out, touching her reflection fingertip to fingertip. For an instant the image in the glass wavered, showing her own dark-haired features before breaking apart like a mirage. Vivian gave a superstitious shudder and turned back to Clary's clothes.

The only interesting shoes were high-heeled sandals, but walking in them would take practice. The girl had no tail, and that ruined Vivian's sense of balance. She opted instead to paint Clary's toenails a vivid scarlet called The Devil Made Me Do It. Who said demons had no sense of humor?

With her toes still wet, she padded to Merlin's expansive kitchen to see what she could cook up. For a man who lived alone—and ate a lot of home delivery, judging by the menus on top of the microwave—he had a lot of pots and pans. Vivian quickly figured out why. One set was for cooking food, the nicer one with copper bottoms was for cooking spells. She selected a double boiler and set it on the stove.

A trip to the pantry revealed row upon row of glass jars filled with herbs, ground minerals and dried bits of things most humans would never willingly touch. She gathered what she wanted and began to measure out ingredients. It was a painstaking, exacting process but she only needed enough to make a single dose.

Once everything was measured and sifted, she added a generous splash of Chardonnay she found in the fridge. Then she began heating it all gently, stirring as she began a lilting chant. The trick was never to let the mixture overheat.

As Vivian had told Clary, she had to take Merlin by surprise. He had to be vulnerable, unguarded and un-suspecting—essentially opposite to his default mood. This potion would put him in the right condition for her plan to work.

As the chant ended, she lifted the mixture from the heat and poured it into a mug to cool. For the final in-gredient, Vivian pricked her finger with a kitchen knife and let a drop fall into the brew. She stirred it in, wrin-kling her nose at the scent of the steam. Love potions were powerful, but they tasted like swamp water. How was she going to get him to drink it?

Vivian's gaze fell on the unwashed dishes in the sink. Among the usual mugs and plates were the cast metal pieces of the wheatgrass juicer. A tray of the bright green grass sat on the wide windowsill, looking like a misplaced fragment of a meadow. Vivian found Clary's memory of the pungent juice Merlin had been drinking. That would cover the smell and taste of just about anything.

She rinsed off the juicer and, after a few false starts, reassembled it. It was a hand-cranked model that clamped to the wooden butcher's block that topped the island counter. A few minutes later the apartment smelled of freshly mown lawn. Now all she needed was to make it appealing to someone besides a sheep.

Fortunately, there was a fully stocked bar and a cupboard dedicated to organic juices. She mixed a selection in a glass pitcher, added the wheat grass and poured herself a glass. Then she added her love potion to what remained and mixed it thoroughly with a wooden spoon. By the time Merlin had unlocked the front door, she was washing the dishes while sipping the frothy green concoction.

"I didn't mean to take so long," he said, leaning against the archway that led to the kitchen. "What do you have there?"

Vivian leaned on the counter, careful to mimic the way Clary moved—a little bit awkward, a little bit defiant. The mortal had a way of leading with her chin as if expecting a fight. "I got bored waiting. I've been experimenting to see if there's a way to make that stuff drinkable."

She nodded at the flat of grass, which was missing a few more tufts than it had been twenty minutes ago. Merlin followed her gaze, oblivious to who she truly was. He was thinking like a mortal, mistaking the physical body for the person who lived inside it. Unless she made an obvious blunder, he'd never guess that she wasn't Clary.

Merlin picked up the glass pitcher and sniffed it. "What's in this?"

"Call it a smoothie," she said lightly. "There's strawberry and apple juice, coconut milk, a few other things. Try it if you like."

She sipped her glass as he poured an inch into another tumbler and tasted it with the air of someone being polite. Then he paused, glass at his lips. Vivian tensed when he raised his eyebrows.

Then he smiled. "This is actually pretty good."

"Then help yourself," she said, turning back to the sink and rinsing plates. It was good to keep her hands busy and her face hidden so she didn't accidentally give herself away. She heard him top up his glass as she scrubbed the last of the cereal bowls. "So, what did Arthur have to say?"

He told her, eventually grabbing a towel to dry. Vivian's chest tightened as she listened, imagining the war that would devastate the mortal realms. It was not as if she had a fondness for humans, much less for Arthur and his court. It was just that it was nice in the kitchen, with the soap suds and companionable conversation. She'd missed having Merlin around and wanted the moment to last a little while longer.

"Is that everything that needs a wash?" she asked, looking around.

"Don't forget this," he said, holding up the empty pitcher. There was nothing left in it but green scum.

"You drank all that?" she asked in genuine surprise. The drink was okay, but not exactly ambrosia.

"Arguing with Arthur is thirsty work. Sorry, I didn't mean to hog it."

"That's okay." She sank the pitcher in the dishpan, doing a quick mental calculation. The normal dose of that potion was a few spoonfuls, not the whole batch. How long would it be before it took effect?

Chapter 11

Vivian had barely finished the thought before his hands snaked around her waist from behind. He pulled her tight to his chest, fitting his body to the curve of her spine. "That pitcher needs to soak," he murmured in her ear.

She couldn't help herself. She shivered as if they were the most erotic words in any mortal tongue. It was his voice—low and rough with intent—or the sudden nervous tension in his hands.

He turned her around with slow, careful movements. She complied, ending up with her back to the sink and her soapy hands pressed against the wall of his chest. The room was suddenly silent except for the sound of bubbles popping in the sink.

Merlin cradled her face, his thumbs stroking over her cheekbones with an urgent gentleness she remembered with piercing clarity. He'd done that to her, but not this way. Back then he'd been fascinated but his touch had possessed none of this protective tenderness.

He truly cared for the little witch, then. Jealousy tore at Vivian's insides. She'd inspired many things—fear, adoration and even terror—but never love. In the end Merlin had stolen her spell and left her behind.

He moved one hand, trailing his fingertips over her lips. Vivian's fists clenched in his shirt, leaving dark, wet handprints in their wake. She had come here for revenge, and the unusual softness in his amber eyes—softness he felt for another woman, but never her—would make it oh, so easy.

His lips touched hers, startling a gasp from deep in her core. She hadn't taken the potion but her limbs trembled almost as much as his. Anticipation hammered like a second pulse, demanding satisfaction.

The next kiss was almost brutal, a taking that left no doubt what he wanted. The edge of the counter dug into her back, damp puddles of water soaking into her shirt. But the only thing that mattered was his hunger. The potion was taking full effect, blotting out reason and conscience. Vivian knew how to mix it well—every demon did. There were few more effective tools for sowing trouble among unsuspecting victims.

Except his desire stirred hers, especially in this frail human body. Clary had wanted this, and so nothing lingered to block the need crackling through her. Vivian's core throbbed, making her rise on her toes to meet his embrace. He hitched her up to sit on the counter and spread her knees so he could stand even closer. She dug her fingers into his dark hair, bending over to take charge of the kiss. His short beard prickled just as she remembered it, but now the memory was clouded with want. This might be her revenge, but nothing said she couldn't enjoy it.

His mouth was hot and velvety, tasting of the drink she'd made. He captured her tongue, teasing with his teeth as she sucked and nibbled in turn. Warm breath fanned her skin, bringing every nerve ending to life. Her hand slid down his front, finding his jeans and the hard evidence that her potion had worked.

All at once there were too many clothes between them. He was so close, his body pressed against hers. She locked her legs around his waist, shifting so that he bore her weight. "Take me to the bedroom," she murmured in his ear.

He needed no urging. Moments later they were both on the bed. He pulled off his shirt, the gesture showing off the muscles of his chest. Most forgot that Merlin was skilled with sword and spear, but it showed now in the flow and curve of solid flesh. Vivian swallowed, realizing that she was actually drooling.

She fell back against the pillows and spread her arms. "Come get me."

Merlin's chest rose and fell with quick, shallow gasps. He grabbed the front of her shirt and tore it in a single, swift wrench. Vivian squeaked and then chuckled, amused and gratified by his eagerness. The pupils of his eyes were huge as he bent to run his tongue along her breastbone in a long, warm line that cooled with his breath. She arched into it, luxuriating in his attention. This body couldn't purr, but she wanted to.

With a deft twist of his fingers, he undid the front clasp of Clary's bra. It sprang apart, letting the weight of her breasts fall free. He moaned, the sound wrenching her core. His mouth fell to one nipple while his hand closed over the other, and all at once Vivian's senses were swamped. Sparks of electricity seemed to shoot from the heat of Merlin's mouth straight to her belly, firing her need as he sucked. Her nails—pathetic, short, human nails—dug into his shoulders, clawing her response into his skin.

Having sex with him was every bit as good as she remembered, and every bit as immediate. Her teeth found his shoulder, and she bit down, claiming him until she tasted the copper salt of blood. He did no more than flinch, the urgency of the potion riding him hard.

She did not notice when her pants disappeared, but she heard the growl of relief when Merlin let loose his zipper. He was full and ready, the sight of him making her slick with need and a little afraid. She drew up her knees but he pinned her down, caging her limbs with his.

Merlin's amber gaze held her, his pupils blown to twice their normal size. They had always reminded Vivian of a hawk's steady gaze, the predator in him plain in this one feature. Yes, he was loyal and loving to those he claimed, but he could be equally cold, and even more lethal. Vivian had seen and recognized that trait as one of her own. What would he do if he caught her hiding here, inside his lovely little protégée? What would he do once the potion wore off?

Would Vivian let him live long enough to find out? She held his gaze a little longer, counting down the moments until that decision had to be made. It was a thrill to teeter on this knife's edge, the throb of her body answering the merciless lust in his eyes.

He used his knee to part her legs, then thrust a hand

against her core. She jumped at the pressure. She was already slick and throbbing, protected only by the flimsy fabric of her panties. Heat flared beneath her skin, raising a pink flush across her pale flesh. Her breasts ached with every beat of her pulse, the nipples tight, burning nubs. His thumb flicked at her cleft, nearly making her come.

With a word of magic, he tore away the last scrap of fabric that covered her. She was naked and entirely his. His next kiss bruised her with its heat but Vivian didn't care. It said something about Merlin's strength of will that he had not taken her with simple brute force, even if the potion left little room for anything but blunt desire.

He drove into her with slow precision, the length and breadth of him drawing a moan from her. All at once, there was nothing but the sensation of fullness, stretching, of surrendering to a pulse that had suddenly gone wild. For an instant Vivian quailed. Sex had never been like this before. The fragility of this body, its deep vulnerability, thrilled her. She felt naked in ways that had no words.

It also left her without a single defense.

When Merlin drew back, even halfway, she was bereft, digging her fingers into his shoulders to make him stay. And then he was back, thrusting deep. And again. And again. Sensation fluttered and exploded, winding her belly tighter and tighter with need. She began to whimper, her head pressed deep into the pillow.

There were some rewards for being a puny, helpless human. Vivian closed her eyes as deep pulses of desire tore through her. Her mouth fell open on a cry as the pulses turned into a shattering cataclysm inside her. She cried out, cresting again as she felt the hot explosion of

Merlin's seed inside her. It should have ended there, but he thrust on and on, her body shuddering with pleasure at each push as the power of the spell she'd woven into the potion spun its own climax. It had been a robust work of craftsmanship.

Finally, everything went still as if they'd rung a perfect, pure note.

Vivian panted, hot tears sliding from the corners of her eyes. The savage gnawing of desire had ceased, but a different kind of ache had settled into her. She'd always understood simple, mindless need and had been prepared for it, but this mortal lovemaking had transformed lust into complicated emotions. She'd come for revenge. Now she was tangled in doubt.

Merlin rolled to the side in a profound slumber, his limbs settling in perfect relaxation. Within seconds a soft snore escaped him. An irrational stab of fury shot through her. How dare he sleep, when she was here to be adored?

Wait—why did that matter? She needed to settle down and focus on her plan. Enjoying the effects of the potion was one thing—demons enjoyed pleasure as much as the next sentient entity—but she was there for a reason. Slowly, Vivian stretched, waking her limbs one by one. Despite her roiling thoughts, satisfaction sang through her. Her body was sore and still slightly aroused, but she couldn't remember ever feeling this relaxed. No wonder humans bred like rabbits.

She rose to her elbow, looking down on Merlin's sleeping face. He looked younger this way, relaxed and peaceful. With one finger, she lightly traced the straight line of his nose, the bow of his upper lip and the fullness of the lower.

Vivian smiled to herself. Merlin had his tribe's dark hair and even features. They had lived in the ancient kingdom of Mercia, fending off the invading Romans with spear and spell. They'd lost, of course. Merlin's mother—matriarch, warrior and druidess, had charged her son with saving the land for her people. Eventually, Merlin had found Arthur and tried to fulfill that promise through Camelot's king.

Vivian had watched it all, year after year, wondering where the story would end. It had been fun right up until Merlin had betrayed her trust. Vivian lifted her finger from his lips, her mood suddenly somber.

This deeply unconscious, his enchanter's powers could not alert him to danger. Vivian had achieved what she wanted with the potion—he was finally at his most vulnerable. She had only to pluck a knife from the block in the kitchen, or one of the blades she'd seen among the heap of Merlin's clothes. He wore such things the way a woman wore jewelry, selecting each one to suit his mood that day. Weapons would be easy to find. Or she could choose poison, or suffocation or even another spell.

She'd expected this moment to feel triumphant, but instead a gray sadness filled her like poisonous fog. She sank down on the bed, Merlin's warmth against her side. She sighed, then her own breathing quieted, leaving only his light snore to fill the room.

I'm dying. She'd managed to put it out of her mind for hours, but now the idea pressed in again, blackening what was left of her serenity. Even a demon could grasp the irony of a death sentence on the same day she'd discovered this kind of pleasurable intimacy. Was this the mortal state? How did they survive the strain of it?

Well, clearly they didn't, which was the point. Vivian pressed a hand to her forehead, wondering if she was about to experience her first headache.

I just had mortal sex. And it rocked my world. It had reached inside her to places she rarely noticed. There had been unfamiliar nuances of emotion involved, but she hadn't minded that so much. They had made the event memorable, maybe even meaningful. Absurdly, she was glad her first time as a mortal had been with Merlin. Someone important to her. Someone who had changed the course of her life, even if she loathed him for it.

It certainly made the prospect of ending his life seem less satisfying. She sighed again, rolling over so that she could rest her head on his shoulder. They fit together well. If she killed him, they would never lie together like this again, and that seemed a shame.

Vivian stared up at the ceiling, more confused than she had ever been in her long existence. Should she simply spy for Tenebrius and LaFaye instead?

Merlin awoke with a jolt, sitting upright before he was fully conscious. He was vaguely aware of a warm body in the bed, but his first thought was for the magical residue clouding his brain. It was like a hangover, the bad kind that came from mixing drinks on a hot day that involved too much greasy food and no sleep. The light made his eyeballs burn and he squeezed them shut as he groped for some clue as to what had led to this moment.

He rewound his memory. Arthur. Talking to the knights. Returning home. Clary and the jug of wheatgrass. Soapy water. *Oh.* There was a reason he was completely naked. He forced his eyes open and turned to look at the other person in the bed. Clary looked deliciously tousled. She had a blanket pulled up to her chin, but he could see the slope of a pale shoulder that promised a garden of delights below. Random snatches of memory told him what they'd done and that he'd enjoyed it very much. In fact, he hadn't had so much fun since... That thought stopped him cold. *By the ashes of the ancient gods!*

Her green eyes were wide and cautious, searching his face for clues to what he was thinking. Fury began crawling through him, but he reined it in. He'd already lost what little dignity he had that day. "You drugged me." He kept the words neutral, just a statement of fact, and watched her reaction.

She bit her lip, but it looked more like laughter than contrition. "What makes you say that?"

"Love potions are nothing new. I know the aftertaste. I got that recipe from an old girlfriend." The urge to rage and scream surged through him, but tantrums would get him nowhere. Neither would magic, if his suspicions were correct. He'd learned long ago to never start a spell battle he wasn't guaranteed to win.

Now that he was angry, his thoughts were clearing fast. He studied Clary's expression, her eyes, the way she held her hands, and they were familiar. But they were not Clary. His stomach dropped, dread certainty rising. "Under ordinary circumstances, you wouldn't need a potion to get me into your bed. But neither the circumstances nor the people are what they seem."

"Oh?" She rose to her knees, her expression still intent. There was no bashfulness, no embarrassment.

Just concern about what he'd do next. It was the kind of poise Clary had never possessed.

Until someone else possessed her. His hand snapped out, catching her wrist. "Why did you do it?"

"Why do you think?" After a moment's hesitation, the mask dropped and Merlin's skin pebbled with a sudden chill. The bones and flesh were the same, but the spirit behind the eyes transformed. A fierce, proud fire lit her face as she dropped the blanket, abandoning all modesty. It took every ounce of Merlin's will not to savor the sight she offered.

His fingers closed tighter around her wrist until she winced and he remembered whose body this was. He released her and she sank back on her heels, amusement lurking at the corners of her lips.

"I don't believe you merely wanted the pleasure of my company," he said drily.

"Are you certain?" Her gaze raked him up and down, at once appreciative and mocking. "You have certain, uh, attributes that I remembered fondly all these years."

Merlin swore under his breath. He'd already tried the best treatment he knew for possession by a powerful demon. At least it was the one cure that wouldn't kill the host. "We both know very well that you want me dead. You weren't exactly restrained about telling the world."

Her gaze went dagger-sharp. "And yet you gave me such an enthusiastic welcome."

Despite a rush of chagrin, Merlin's scalp prickled with dread.

"Hello, Vivian." He gave an unfriendly smile. "What have you done with Clary?"

Chapter 12

"Your little witch is safe," Vivian said. "She's slumbering the same way you put me to sleep. We simply changed places."

Relief unclenched Merlin's fists, but only for a moment. He wondered how the demon had managed the switch, but then, this was Vivian. She was every bit his equal in power, not to mention cunning. He gave a reluctant nod. "And then you slipped me the potion, knowing that I would trust Clary."

"Mmm-hmm." Vivian lay back on the thick pillows, slowly stretching. "She was the perfect Trojan filly."

And he had been so besotted with her that he, the greatest enchanter in the human realms, hadn't bothered to check his drink for potions. Lust had made a fool of him. "Why do it?"

"Revenge. I swore to kill you, remember?" She cast

him a sidelong look, a glint of emerald from under her long lashes.

"And I won't kill you?"

The threat would have carried more weight if they hadn't just made love. Merlin tried to convince his body that the luscious, naked female mere feet away was a monster, but it wasn't easy. Parts of him refused to be convinced. He jumped off the bed and snatched a pair of pants out of the laundry basket. Her amused chuckle brought unwelcome heat to his ears.

"Hide, o mighty wizard," Vivian drawled. "You can't kill this body without snuffing your pet witch."

He pulled on a shirt, unsuccessfully ignoring the naked woman lolling on his bed. She'd turned on her stomach and was facing his way now, chin in her hands and feet kicking in the air. As good as she looked, the gleam in her eyes was more predatory than flirtatious.

Merlin shrugged, striving for casual. "Speaking of snuffing, why didn't you murder me when you finally had the chance?"

"I like to play with my food."

Her smile was slow, a good imitation of her usual feline grin, but it lacked conviction. There were few beings in any realm—mortal, fae or the demonic Abyss—who would see that crack in her armor, but Merlin knew Vivian too well. He made careful note of it. There would be precious few weaknesses he could use against her.

He tucked in his shirt, feeling slightly better now that he wasn't on display. "Let Clary go, Vivian. Go home and leave us alone."

Her chin jerked up. "Are you sure that's what you want? If I leave, you'll never see me again."

"Since you're here to kill me, it's hard to see the downside to your absence."

"Oh, really?" The heat in her stare nearly unraveled his self-possession. "I doubt you've enjoyed yourself so much since you ran away from my bed."

"I didn't run. I left."

"Once you've gone hellspawn, the rest is like cold oatmeal." Her grin spread wider this time. "Admit it, Merlin. You missed me."

"Oatmeal is rarely homicidal." He leaned against the dresser, crossing his bare feet at the ankles. He was outwardly calm, but inside his guts were in a knot. She was right about one thing—demons understood lust like no one else. Memories of their potion-induced gymnastics, however confused, made his pulse jump.

She chuckled low in her throat, no doubt sensing his discomfort. "You thought you had me, didn't you? You thought a mere injection could put me in chains?"

Merlin said nothing, hating her so deeply that he tasted it like bile. How was he going to make her leave without harming Clary?

"Oh, my poor little half-druid monster, how long have you been watching your sweet student and wanting this?" Vivian rose to her knees and spread her arms wide, displaying her body. "A bit skinny, don't you think? But then, not everyone can be me."

Fury jerked him from his slouch. He grabbed a clean shirt and threw it at her. "Put some clothes on!"

Vivian snatched it from the air. "Have you turned prudish, grandfather?"

She chuckled as she pulled the shirt over her head. The sound seemed to crawl over his skin, reviving memories of a different bed and Vivian in a different body. Merlin shifted, his nerves on alert.

"Is that better?" Vivian asked in mocking tone. The shirt fell halfway down her thighs and bore a faded logo of pouting lips and a lolling tongue.

"Whatever." Soft shadows had stolen over the room as daylight failed. What should have been intimate was suddenly claustrophobic. He made a move for the door, but her voice stopped him in his tracks.

"You can't be so proper if you're lusting after your students. Just like I seduced you, or have you forgotten?"

Not likely. "Don't go there, Vivian."

"Why not?" she purred. "Guilty conscience?"

Maybe. He'd wanted Clary since they'd first met, but he'd resisted an entanglement. At least he had right up until she'd been all but dying in his arms. He hadn't kissed her until then, but that had opened a floodgate of emotion he hadn't been able to close.

He glared at the impostor in his bed. "You're right that I want her. That's why your potion worked so well."

Vivian's face scrunched as if she smelled something bad. "Why her? She's weak."

That was where Vivian was wrong. Clary had nearly died at Laren's hands, but she'd held the fae while he wept in shame and grief. "You'd never understand."

The dying light blurred Vivian's features, making her look impossibly young in that oversize shirt. "Explain it to me," she asked softly, sliding off the bed and padding toward him.

"You'll take whatever I say and make it a weapon."

"But say I don't." There was a hint of uncertainty

in her eyes that gave him pause. Vivian was never uncertain.

"If I tell you, will you leave?" he asked.

"No." She stepped closer, putting both palms against his chest. "But I do want to know."

The pressure of her hands felt completely ordinary, but his skin still crept at the touch. His first instinct was to back away, but rejecting her out of hand would not be wise. She was too proud to accept another rebuff, even from him, and wounded pride meant payback.

Her fingertips dug into his shirt, reminding him they should be claws. "We used to have lots of discussions. We would talk for hours," she said softly. It nearly sounded like a plea. "Remember?"

Of course he remembered those conversations. For all their intelligence and prodigious powers, demons were almost childlike when it came to matters of the heart. Complex emotions baffled and repelled them, but unlike most demons, Vivian was curious. Merlin had found himself trying to explain why guilt and rage could be confused in the mortal mind, or how anger at another could become hatred of oneself, or a thousand other conundrums. In the end he'd become just as confused and fascinated by the vagaries of the human heart.

Vivian searched his face through Clary's witch-green eyes. By her expression, she saw the truth. He didn't want to speak that way with her ever again. Not after the way their affair had ended, and not now that Vivian held the woman he wanted hostage in her own body.

"Did you ever care for me?" she asked, a faint smile playing on her lips.

Trust Vivian to wonder. "In my own way," he said, knowing it was a poor answer.

She pulled her hands from his chest and took a step back. "If I asked what that meant, would you tell me?"

Merlin hesitated, unsure what to say because there was no single answer. He'd begun his time with her as a student, then as a lover and then as a thief and traitor. During that time he'd learned what demons truly were, and they'd shown him the darkness inside his soul. How could he love that? And yet there had been a time...

It began in a town that clung to the towering cliffs above the white-capped Mediterranean Sea. He'd been far from his birthplace, wandering in search of knowledge, pleasure and easy money. The fledgling Roman Empire had seemed like the place for a strapping young man to find all three. Sadly, all he'd gotten for his trouble so far was sore feet and bruises from a dozen tavern brawls. But that, he'd told himself, was all part of the adventure.

One hot summer day he came upon a shady olive grove and stretched out in the long, cool grass. The blades tickled his cheek as the breeze ruffled through it, and he closed his eyes and wished for a jug of wine to ease his dry throat. Then he let his thoughts drift away like early morning mist. The sun was much lower in the sky when he woke again to find restless fingers combing through his hair. Merlin sat up with a start to find a hooded figure crouched beside him. He put a hand to his brow, still feeling the brush of what had been decidedly feminine fingertips.

"Who are you?" he asked, unsure if his visitor would answer. The soft gray robes looked like something a priestess would wear, and he'd heard of virgins sworn to shun the company of men. He'd just started to spin an interesting fantasy when she spoke.

"I am called Vivian." Her low, throaty voice seemed to smoke with sensuality. Though her features were hidden, he was certain she was a carnal goddess, figuratively speaking. "You are sleeping in my grove."

"Yours?" He looked around, but there were none of the fine stone villas he'd seen in these parts. There wasn't even a shepherd's hut. "Where is your dwelling?"

"It is both near and far, Merlin Ambrosius."

He sucked in a breath, surprise banishing his pleasant daydreams. "How do you know my name?"

"I know your name and the name of Brida the Druidess, who gave you life."

The odds of anyone knowing him this far from home were infinitesimal unless, of course, there was magic involved. Suspicion cramped his shoulders. He was new to the ways of enchantment, but he already recognized how little of it was innocent. This woman—whoever she was—could not be trusted. Merlin slowly rose to his feet, watching the hooded form as he might a wild animal. No sudden movements. No taking his eyes from her. Ready to run.

She rose with him, proving to be almost his height. "My knowledge troubles you."

"What do you want?"

"I can give you much," she said with a casual wave of her hand.

A long staff appeared in her hand. At the top was an intricate cap of metalwork that held a frosted white stone in filigreed claws. Merlin eyed it, knowing it was a true wizard's staff worth more than his entire village back home. Such objects held immense power, enough to launch him from obscurity to the right hand of kings.

He itched to grip the polished rosewood and fold it to his chest the way a young girl clutched her doll. But even an obscure bumpkin of a hedge wizard knew nothing so precious came without a price.

"Why?" he asked, so shocked that his voice was nearly lifeless.

"We've been watching you from the cradle. We've been watching for signs of greatness."

A surprised laugh burst from his lips. "Any luck?"

She went very still. It was impossible to see her face beneath the hood, but he got the impression she wasn't pleased by his laugh. Fear prickled along his skin, responding to an instinct he only half understood.

"You are a disappointment to your people," she said. "Your mother trained you well to follow in her tradition, but your magic is weak. You have not led your tribe to greatness, or even safety. Invaders will come from this faraway land and crush your people into the dust of history."

Her words burned, as had his mother's, but he knew the simple truth. "I'm not a war leader. I'm not even as good a magician as my mother."

"No, you're not. You are barely wizard enough to amuse children at the midsummer festival. You ran away to find your fortune because of the disappointment you saw in every eye, from the chieftain down to the lowest goatherd."

Shame itched along every nerve, begging to be soothed by some spark of promise—but that would never come. He simply wasn't that talented. She rested the butt of the staff in the thick grass, clearly tired of holding it out to a fool who wouldn't take it. Merlin clenched his fists, straining not to grab it and rewrite his future.

The robes shifted as if their occupant was casually leaning on one hip. "I know what's holding you back, young Merlin. You have more power than all the Druids in the western islands, but your magic works a different way. They cannot teach you the way I can."

His mouth went dry. He worked his throat a moment before words would form. "What are you saying?"

"Let me teach you. I understand you. I can make you fulfill the promise of your birth."

He'd been born to the greatest Druidess in all the kingdoms of Britain and yet his power produced as much bang as a soggy drum skin. Her promise wasn't so much temptation as an offer of survival—or so his pride told him. A thousand clamoring needs brushed aside all his caution.

She understood him. No one at home had ever done so much.

And then she pushed back the hood. Her hair was a lustrous blue-black and her eyes a violet he'd never seen before. It was the shade of dusk just before the night. Merlin swallowed hard. He'd been a favorite of the ladies all the way across Gaul and Germania, and now here in these sun-baked lands. He'd seen his share of feminine beauty, and yet he could not stop staring at her face. Vivian wasn't pretty or even beautiful—she was a true goddess.

She held out a hand. "Come with me."

Some shred of sanity reared up. "I still don't understand why."

"Let's just say I took an interest because of your father."

Merlin stilled. "No one knows who my father was."

She wiggled her fingers, urging him to follow. "I'll tell you someday."

It was more than anyone else could offer. He finally

took her hand, finding comfort in the soft, warm press of her palm. He should have known it would go horribly wrong in the end. Nothing came without a price.

Merlin stared down at her now, recognizing the same glint in her eyes. It didn't matter that they were green, or a different shape, or that she was fair instead of dark. Vivian was what she was. A change of form wouldn't alter her essential nature. Better to ask a crow to sing like a canary.

But she had changed his life. Nothing had been the same since that day in the south of Italy. Vivian had taken a foolish youth and made him wise. Along the way she'd set the stage for Camelot's destruction and pointed him toward the precipice. He'd done the rest himself because, all else aside, she was an excellent teacher. After all, she'd made him understand his true nature—as little as he'd wanted those answers. But now? She was inhabiting the body of the woman he loved and threatening his life.

So why ask if he cared for her? She had never asked such a thing before.

Merlin narrowed his eyes. "Get out of her, Vivian."

Her grin was carnivorous. "What if I said I wanted to stay with you?"

"You, of anyone, should know that nothing good comes of being with me."

"Ah, you blame yourself for that spell in ways no one but me can guess. Before you take me back, you will have to forgive yourself."

"That day will never come."

With that, he turned and left the bedroom, desperate for air and even more desperate for a plan.

Chapter 13

Of course, Vivian followed Merlin from the bedroom like a lethal shadow. Even without looking, he was aware of how her steps glided like a cat's. It was the opposite of Clary's brisk tread.

Clary. The thought of her made him frantic, but he couldn't let Vivian see that. Dismay was catnip to a demon.

He stopped in the living room, bowing his head in thought. Resentment twisted inside him. Revenge he could understand—he'd wronged Vivian in ways that were hard to forgive—but by taking a body, she was hurting an innocent woman.

"Your residence is charming," the demon said from behind him. Her voice was casual as if she'd dropped by for coffee. "The light reminds me of the place we first met. Perhaps it has something to do with being near the ocean."

Merlin felt the heat rise to his face as rage scattered his thoughts. She had to go. Vivian had taught him a lot, but he'd had a few centuries to find tricks of his own. He turned to face her, bracing his feet on the pine floor. The natural decor—bare wood, plants and stone—was more than a decorating choice. Druid magic came from life energy, and he could feel the traces of that force through his bare soles. He began to draw it into his core.

One corner of her mouth quirked up. "Do you really think you can overpower me?"

"I promise I will never underestimate you."

"That's almost a compliment."

She drew closer, threads from the ragged hem of the shirt fluttering around her thighs. The next moment she stood close enough that her toes brushed his, the contact oddly intimate. She smelled like Clary's shampoo and the soft musk of Clary's skin. Memories of Vivian tangled with the present, weaving lust and anger and a fierce protectiveness into emotions he couldn't understand.

He bent his head so their faces almost touched. "Are you really going to kill me?"

Her lids lowered, the sweep of her lashes anything but demure. "I told you I play with my food."

The worst thing was, he understood the impulse. There was a part of her that was very like a buried part of him, and that intrigued and appalled him at the same time. They were both black-hearted. The only redeeming quality he had was that he understood why that was wrong.

He kissed her forehead lightly. "Stop this, Vivian. Go home."

She tilted her face up to him, catching his lips with

hers. "And miss humbling you? I don't think so. I paid a high price to be here. Higher than you will ever know."

He wondered what that price was, but then her fingers slipped beneath his shirt to caress his bare back. Wondering took a backseat to more basic sensations. His breath sucked in and she chuckled low in her throat.

"How much humbling is enough?" he asked, his thumb stroking the clean line of her jaw. He'd almost gathered enough power. Almost.

"I'll let you know."

His hand closed, for the briefest instant, around the fragile architecture of her throat. He drew it away at once, too aware of what he might be tempted to do. Instead, he kissed her back, finding the hem of her shirt and the soft skin beneath. He stroked her then, firm and gentle as he slid his fingers lower to explore the sensitive places he knew brought the best results.

She nearly came right then, but he pulled back. She cursed softly, the look in her eyes frustrated and demanding. She stretched, rising on her toes to lock her lips to his, taking him without quarter.

It was then he unleashed his spell, releasing all the power he'd gathered and knocking Vivian back into oblivion. Maybe turnabout wasn't fair play, but Clary needed a fighting chance. Her body sagged in his arms, suddenly limp. She sighed softly, the bloom of sensual pleasure turning her cheeks rosy. He gathered her up, carrying her back to the bedroom and settling her beneath the comforter. She breathed gently, kiss-swollen lips parted as if she'd fallen into a natural doze.

He prayed it would be Clary who woke up, but at the very least this gave him a moment to think.

He slipped out of the bedroom, closing the door

softly behind him, and retreated to the guest bedroom.
The smudged outline of the chalk circle remained on
the floor. He stepped over it, the scene between Laren
and Clary replaying in his mind as he entered the en
suite bathroom and turned on the shower to warm up.
If Vivian was the perfect demon seductress, Clary em-
bodied everything he valued among the mortals—live-
liness and humor, loyal affection and a kindness that
lit the world wherever it could be found. She made him
believe in fabled beasts that housed the humbled soul
of a prince.

That he, someday, might be worth redemption.

Merlin shed his clothes and stared into the mirror
over the tiny bathroom sink. He and Vivian were too
well matched to survive an actual fight, and he couldn't
risk hurting the very woman he meant to save. The
only positive was that Vivian, vain and self-protec-
tive, would be equally careful as long as she intended
to stick around and make his life a misery. The situation might have been amusing, like something out of
a broad, tasteless comedy, except it was unimaginably
dangerous. Between them, they could break the world.
They could break Clary.

He needed ideas, and a shower, even a fast one, always helped him think. He stepped under the stream
of steaming water, grateful to ease the tension from his
muscles. It wasn't just frustration knotting his shoulders—that potion had left toxins behind. Since waking,
he'd felt like a bundle of aches. The shower was deliciously hot until a blast of cold announced someone else
was using up the heated water. Merlin yelped, the spray
pounding in his face as he fumbled with the controls.
He slammed off the water, dripping and bad-tempered.

"Vivian!" he roared, because only a demon would leave a man in a freezing shower. Grabbing a towel for modesty, he stormed toward the master bathroom.

But when he flung open the door, it was Clary who emerged from the cloud of steam, wrapped tight in a white cotton robe. Her irritated expression left no doubt who was ascendant. She stabbed him in the chest with a forefinger. "What was that?"

"What?" he asked defensively.

"I like a romp as much as the next girl," she bit out, a blush flaming up her cheekbones, "but that was uninvited."

Yes, this was Clary.

"The potion wasn't my idea." He gripped his towel tighter. To be fair, they needed to talk, but he wanted to dry off first.

"That was revenge sex. I *hate* revenge sex."

"What was I supposed to do?" He flipped wet hair out of his eyes and grabbed the robe he'd left on the back of the master bathroom door. He rarely used it, but today seemed like an excellent time to start. "Vivian would cheerfully kill us both if the mood struck her."

"I don't know about that."

The uncertainty in her voice sent a cold finger down his spine. He finished knotting the tie of his robe and turned to face her. "Of course she would. You don't know her like I do."

"Maybe, maybe not." Clary's eyes were dark with anger. "Now that I've been stuffed in the basement of my own skull, I know what it feels like. Don't do it again."

Merlin felt his jaw drop. "So what—"

She cut him off with a slice of her hand. "You two

need to work things out like grown-up wizards. I refuse to be in the middle anymore."

Clary pushed past him and stalked into the bedroom, slamming the door behind her.

Clary sank onto the edge of the bed, then sprang up almost at once and began rummaging through her clothes. She rarely dressed with modesty in mind, but this time she chose plain black slacks and a white blouse that buttoned at the neck and cuffs. She wanted to look the opposite of Vivian.

When she bent to slip on low-heeled boots, she could feel aches in unfamiliar places. Vivian's possession had blurred the details, but she knew what had happened. She straightened, brushing the creases from her pant legs, and studied herself in the mirror. She looked composed and businesslike, the way she would going to a job interview.

Her calm features hid a storm of turmoil inside. The sexual encounter she'd just had was bone-shattering, extreme, simply *more* than she'd had with any other man. Vivian's complete lack of inhibition was part of it. Merlin himself was—she searched for the right term and came up empty. Highly experienced. Enthusiastic. A textbook of hormonal fantasy. But she categorically refused to participate in bedtime gymnastics from the backseat of her own brain. She wasn't Vivian's plaything.

No, Clary Greene would not be used or drugged or knocked out again. She wasn't a meal for the fae or a convenient container for stray demons. If sheer annoyance could lock hellspawn in the deepest, darkest recesses of her mind, Clary had it covered. Vivian was toast—and so was Merlin if he tried stabbing her with any more concoctions that messed with her magic. If that was getting rescued, it was too hazardous by half.

She was looking after herself from now on, thank you very much. Of course, that made no sense because she was still infested by a crazed hellspawn, but she'd deal with that once her blood pressure came back to planet earth.

She was combing her damp hair when a phone pinged. She looked around to see Merlin's smartphone sitting on top of his dresser. It pinged twice more in short order. Whoever was texting him was insistent, and in her current mood the piercing sound tempted her to smash the phone to splinters. She crossed the room in two strides and snatched it up.

The texts were from K. Art. As the social media co-ordinator at Medievaland, she knew that was King Arthur. There were three messages, and they were short, probably because Arthur couldn't type to save his life.

Do not update.

Malediction ware beware. Tisthelan.

Going darke.

Darke? Tisthelan? Clary squinted at the phone, momentarily distracted by the strange spelling. Once in a while olde tyme English slipped into whatever the knights wrote, which made the actual content hard to figure out. Malediction ware? Did he mean malware? It was hard to tell with medieval people. She was pretty sure Perceval still believed there was a teeny tiny angel inside the motherboard. Of course, after you've met a talking dragon, everything was relative.

With the phone in hand, Clary went in search of Merlin and interpretation. He was brooding over a mug of tea and looked up at her with an expression reminiscent of a sad golden retriever. He was as confused and hurt as she was, but she wasn't ready to talk about demon sex quite yet. If ever. That would have to fester until she was good and ready to rip that bandage off. Significantly, she noted there was no wheatgrass in sight.

She held up the phone so he could read the screen. "Does this make any sense to you?"

"No." He took the phone and set it on the counter, saying nothing about the fact she was snooping on his phone. "Should it?"

When she didn't answer, he poured her a mug of tea and slid it along the countertop. His wary look said he expected another round of their previous argument.

"Going dark sounds serious," she said. "With or without the *e*. It's like he's been hacked or something."

"You're the computer expert."

"You're the Arthur expert. Could he be in trouble?"

By way of reply, Merlin crossed to the table, set down his tea and opened his laptop. It came to life with a faint beep.

"Wait," Clary said. "Does your software automatically update?"

"Of course. It's more secure that way."

His face fell as he connected the dots to Arthur's first message. He dove for the keyboard, but not quickly enough. A low, malevolent chuckle sounded from the laptop's tiny speakers. A spark flew from the power connector, singeing Merlin's fingers as he reached for it. Clary's breath caught as she sensed Vivian stirring to life, but rather than triumph, the demon seemed to be as puzzled as she was.

"My computer's possessed," Merlin said in affront.

Clary had heard that before, but never so convincingly. With a swipe of her boot heel, she kicked the cord out of the wall socket. It wouldn't help immediately, but the battery had to run down sometime. "Have you tried hitting Escape?"

Merlin shot her a withering look just before a cloud of green fog rolled out of the screen. Merlin jumped back, staying well clear as the cloud hovered over the table. It shimmered a moment, sparkling and bobbing like a bad special effect.

"What by all the coven's pointy hats?" she muttered, circling the table.

The cloud seemed to dissipate, though the laughter kept going. At first, she thought the manifestation had been harmless, but then saw the green goop eating its way through Merlin's books and papers. With an oath, he grabbed a jar of powder from his spell cupboard and began sprinkling it over the mess. The green goop bubbled and hissed, which was bad enough, but then it seemed to coalesce into something with clumsy tentacles. It tried to lift itself by crawling up the neck of the study lamp.

Merlin slammed it with a fireball, scorching the table, but the goo sizzled until it was no more than smoke. Clary slid the balcony door open to get rid of the stink of rotting fish.

"That's malware all right," she said under her breath.

"It was trying to manifest," Merlin replied.

But whatever that was didn't belong in the mortal realms. "Was that a demon?"

Not quite, Vivian replied. *Nevertheless, they are testing your electronic highways to see if they are safe for us to travel. We are made of energy, after all.*

Did you know about this? Clary demanded, deeply unhappy that her visitor was awake.

The modern age offers some interesting opportunities. Vivian's tone sounded oddly detached. *That is what Tenebrius told me. This is Gorm's plan to bring us from the Abyss.*

Before she could reply, the screen of the laptop bulged, a green and glowing hand stretching toward Merlin with grasping fingers. The enchanter looked down his nose at the apparition. "Seriously?"

The laughter was suddenly drowned out by a cacophony of voices, crackling static, scraps of music and what sounded like tearing sheets of metal. It grew and grew as the TV switched on to a football game at full volume, then a radio and then a stereo playing jazz. The hand was conducting like a demented maestro. Sparks fountained from the overhead fixture, and a car alarm sounded from the street below. It was only a matter of time before something caught on fire.

"Did I mention how much I hate demons?" Merlin grumbled with disgust.

Clary stalked toward the laptop, approaching it from behind as Merlin stayed just out of reach of the grasping hand. Though it had no eyes, it seemed to be able to track his every movement. Clary clenched her teeth, fighting the panic welling inside her. When she was just within reach, she jabbed at the laptop, hoping to slam it closed.

But the hand snaked around, faster than she could follow. It closed on her wrist with a grip like ice, startling a cry from her lips.

The grip was so cold that Clary's muscles jumped in protest. She staggered back, pulling away with all her weight, but the fingers squeezed tighter. For a glowing green hand made of static, its strength was terrifying. She was aware of Merlin reacting, grabbing the lamp and swinging it at the laptop, but he seemed far away. Her senses were filled with the demon's chill touch and a mounting agony that rose like spears of ice through her gut. She doubled over, her captured wrist twisting painfully.

"Clary!" Merlin snapped, worry sharpening her name into a command. When she didn't respond, he dropped the lamp and clasped her face in his hands and tipped her face up to his, but her vision blurred. Somewhere in the back of her mind, it occurred to her that his attempt to smash the screen must have failed.

"Clary?"

Chapter 14

Clary's consciousness slipped as if the present was a slick surface. Gravity—or the demon's power—pulled her into an inky pool to drown.

Wherever it was, whatever state she fell into, there was no air. Her lungs began to burn as her throat spasmed, every scrap of her flesh suddenly on fire. She caught a glimpse of a cave—no, it was a room made of stone. A marble bowl on a long pillar stood in the middle like a great big birdbath, and it was filled with green fire. Merlin was staring back at her, but it wasn't the Merlin she knew. He was younger, his expression filled with determination and eagerness. This wasn't the master enchanter at work—he was still a student.

Student-Merlin reached out toward the fire with one hand, the other holding up a gem. He began to chant, and as he did the green fire leaped from the bowl to the gem in a perfect arc of light. His expression grew triumphant, his eyes almost wild with the vision of possibility. Clearly, this was a breakthrough, though Clary had no idea what it meant.

She was seeing the past through Vivian's eyes, but even as that thought took hold, the vision began to melt away. It wasn't a simple fade to black, but a wholesale destruction that began at one edge and ate across, like a photograph held in a flame. If this was Vivian's memory—her life flashing before Clary's eyes—the demonic force from the computer was destroying them both.

Vivian shrieked in rage. *No, no, you shall not take my existence from me!*

Then the only thing that mattered was survival. Clary choked, unable to take a breath. Her lungs ached, seeming to fold themselves inside out as they struggled for air. Merlin's power flared, heating the air as his spell sizzled around the laptop in a corona of electricity, but it had no effect. Clary fell to her knees, dangling from the apparition's clutch. She was starved for air. Consciousness ebbed as black fuzzed the edges of her vision. Vivian held on one second longer and unleashed every ounce of power she had. Lightning flared around Clary's hand, frying the demon's fingers.

Suddenly free, Clary dropped to the floor. Breath surged down her abused windpipe in a loud, sawing gasp, but she was on her feet in an instant. Her head spun but she grabbed the black plastic of the laptop's lid and slammed it closed. A moment later the laptop went silent, only a weak wisp of smoke leaking from the edges.

It was in sleep mode.

"Well," said Clary, her face numb with shock. "That happened. I hope you do regular backups."

She looked around to see the table was scorched, the books and papers fried or covered in demon goo. Merlin picked himself up off the floor, his expression an odd mix of wariness and relief. "Are you okay?"

"I think so." She examined her hand, which was pink and tender from the discharge of power. At least it wasn't blistering. Vivian had saved her life, and Clary was reluctant to tell Merlin she was back just so he could zap her again. Maybe that was stupid, or maybe she had to find a resolution that didn't put her in the middle of their war.

"That was an excellent fireball," he replied, pulling a leather satchel from the mess of belongings scattered around the room. He pushed the laptop into it and buckled the flap closed. "That thing would have destroyed us all given a chance."

"Didn't it just want a way into this world?" Clary sank into a chair. She wanted comfort—a hug, a pat on the back, something—but the air between them was still tense. Clearly, they weren't ready to touch each other yet.

"If the demons reach our world, Camelot will be their first target. We banished them, after all." He frowned. "I haven't seen that trick before. It was a clever one."

Clary imagined the choking sensation again, the sharp panic just before the lightning speared through her. She shuddered. Merlin set the satchel down and put his hands on her shoulders for a second before dropping them. The gesture was still awkward, but it was filled with concern. "You did well."

"Yeah?" It was Vivian who had done well.

His eyes were dark with worry, but there was humor, too. "Yeah."

Clary felt for the demon's presence, but she had retreated, leaving behind an impression of strong annoyance. Odd as it might seem, Vivian showed signs of jealousy. "That thing in the computer wasn't a normal hellspawn, was it?"

Merlin shrugged. "It was energy with only a primitive consciousness. Demon essence, as opposed to an individual demon. My guess is that was the advance guard, and it had two functions—to test the plan, and to kill as many knights as possible."

That was an image Clary didn't need in her dreams.

When she didn't reply, he took a step back. "I'm going to take the laptop to my workshop and destroy it there." It made sense. Destructive magic was messy, and hostile residue wasn't something a person wanted in their home. Nor was this the kind of job Merlin would trust to anyone else.

"Do you want me to come?" she asked.

"No. Stay here." He took another cautious step away, probably wondering if or when Vivian would make a return visit. "Can I trust you to sit quietly for an hour?"

"Yes." She tried not to sound offended.

Afraid of a little witchling? Vivian's voice was faint, but it had lost none of its bite.

Clary ignored her. A sudden thought had popped out of her subconscious. "Tisthelan."

Merlin gave her a blank look. "What?"

"In Arthur's message. *Tis the LAN.* All of Camelot's files are on a local area network."

Merlin didn't look any wiser.

"Look." Clary hitched forward on her seat. "If demons are energy and want to get onto the great electronic highway, where do they start? There's endless streams of data, networks, wireless transmissions, cables, you name it. If they wanted to target the knights in particular, finding Camelot's LAN would be the perfect point of entry. From there, they could jump to individual devices and the people using them."

Merlin glared at his laptop case. "The vile thing came for me. Did I mention how much I loathe demons?"

"We have to get the word out. No email, no blogging, no gaming. No one touches any devices or the internet."

He nodded. "I will. I'll find a landline to call from. Be sure to take your own advice."

He touched her chin lightly, brushing it with his thumb. It seemed an unconscious gesture, but an uncomfortable silence followed. A few days ago they'd been master and student, not lovers. And not engaged in—whatever this three-way relationship was. It was beyond awkward.

Merlin turned away, picking up the satchel and heading for the door. "Don't go out and don't let anyone in."

Clary followed him into the living room and folded her arms. "Aren't you going to lock me in with unbreakable wards or something?"

Merlin opened the door to the outside corridor and then paused, looking back with one eyebrow arched. "Would you trust me again if I did?"

It was an excellent point. She'd hate him for it.

So would I. I would make him pay.

"And no cooking, okay?" he said. The door clicked shut like a punchline.

Clary flopped onto the couch, depression hitting her

like a wall. *Did I mention how much I loathe demons?* Illogical as it might be, she found it hard not to take the statement personally when she had Vivian inside her.

Her hand still smarted as if she'd dunked it in too-hot water. Apparently, shooting lightning bolts had its price. So did everything else that had happened that day—or days. She wasn't even certain how long she'd been in Merlin's suite. A glance out the window said it was growing dark. Since it was nearly summer, that meant it was evening. She didn't feel tired. She was too jittery for that.

No cooking? Vivian asked, not so distant anymore. *He's joking about my potion? He's grown cocky.*

Clary pressed her face into her hands, wondering for the hundredth time how she ended up with a high-maintenance demon inside her head. Not only was that weird to begin with, it was also evolving in a strange way. She'd started out paralyzed with terror, and she was still terrified, but she was also exasperated. It was also like having a cranky roommate that wouldn't shut up.

Why aren't you grateful I've chosen you for my vessel?

"I don't know where to start with that one."

I saved your life. You owe me everything.

"You keep borrowing my body without asking, so shut up."

I made us have excellent sex.

"You had sex. I got to watch."

Just as well. Merlin is too much for a mere wisp of a mortal like you.

Clary gave a strangled cough. "Oh, yeah? What's the matter, scared he'll fall for me instead?"

The demoness gave a low, growling hiss. Vivian seemed to loathe Merlin, but that glimpse of memory

Clary had seen told a different tale. Vivian had been proud of her student.

It tried to take my memory, Vivian said, changing the subject.

"Did it mean to?"

I don't know. The sullen admission seemed dragged from deep inside the demon. *This is not my plot. I was invited to participate, but I had other priorities.*

Something told Clary that was a problem. "How did the other demons take that?"

Vivian seemed to consider her answer. *Tenebrius said that he would be in touch. I did not think he would send a disembodied hand to do the touching on his behalf.*

"That seems ominous."

Agreed. I would not be surprised if I was the target just as much as Merlin.

So the bad-guy demons weren't just nuking Camelot's tech toys so that they could invade Earth, but they might just be gunning for the creature cohabiting her skull. "Y'know, I think I miss the days when I was just a no-talent witch with a hopeless crush on my instructor." Which would have been around forty-eight hours ago.

You must admit I keep boredom from the doorstep.

There was a light rapping at the door. Clary straightened, recalling Merlin's orders not to let anyone in. Then she went to see who it was, because no one told Clary what to do.

Queen Guinevere waited outside. Clary froze. "Gwen!"

They were good friends—had been ever since Clary helped the queen adjust after she'd awakened in the modern age. For all her rank and importance to Camelot's future, Gwen was very much her own person. Clary had recognized a kindred spirit on the spot.

The queen stepped forward, one hand on her baby bump. "His Highness needs me to sit down."

Clary sensed Vivian's instant interest in the baby. *New life.*

"Please, come in," Clary said a beat too late. Gwen was already in one of the easy chairs. "What brings you here?"

"I know you're supposed to be in quarantine or something," Gwen replied, opening her shoulder bag and pulling out an ebook reader, "but you're the computer genius. This won't switch on."

Clary all but snatched the device out of the queen's hand. "You don't need that right now."

"But I do," Gwen said earnestly. "All my books are on there and I've got nothing but time to read. I was in the middle of a really good mystery when the battery died and it won't charge back up."

Clary's mouth had gone dry, picturing Gwen fighting off a possessed device. "How did you get here?"

"In a car. I know how to drive."

Of course she did. Clary had died a thousand deaths coaching her for the road test.

"About my books," Gwen prompted her.

"Can't you get paperback copies for now?"

Gwen shrugged, rubbing her stomach. "When you can't move, it's hard to go hunting through bookstores. I want my fix as fast as technology can deliver it."

The life is strong, Vivian all but purred.

Alarm trickled through Clary's chest, kicking up her pulse. The demons hated Arthur, and Gwen carried his heir. Was Vivian's interest a threat? "Didn't Arthur tell you to stay away from computers?"

"Of course. He drove Excalibur through his monitor earlier this afternoon. Apparently it began talking to him. At first I thought he'd just triggered that talking assistant thing and panicked. It turns out it really was possessed."

"Um, yeah." Clary imagined the scene all too well.

"But that has nothing to do with my ebook reader. My books are already loaded." Gwen's brow furrowed. "Can you fix it?"

Reluctantly, Clary turned the device over to examine it. "It could be the battery died for good, or maybe a connection is broken."

A healthy baby means a strong future for the kings of Camelot and their people. LaFaye's invasion would destroy it.

Vivian's words were filled with emotion, but it was impossible to tell if it was happiness or anger. Clary's hands stopped in their exploration of the ports and buttons. Her fingers still ached from blasting scorch marks in the dining room table, and all she could think about was her friend and the innocent baby just a few feet away.

"I think this is beyond repair." It was a lie, but Clary wasn't sorry. "Just stop by a bookstore on the way home."

"You've barely looked at it," Gwen said reproachfully.

"Do you really want to risk your safety—the baby's safety—on the fact that the wireless switch is off?"

Gwen's blue eyes narrowed. "I would never risk my baby. I'm not an idiot, and I have a library card."

"Then why are you here?"

Gwen's chin tilted so that she looked up at Clary, her expression stern. "You're in trouble, I can tell. You don't sound like yourself."

Clary's chest squeezed, a sudden sharp ache of affection. "You mean the ebook reader was just an excuse to come?"

Gwen lifted a shoulder. "I really do want to finish that story." Her smile belied the words.

"Thank you." Clary couldn't help a smile, however weak. "Arthur will be furious with you for coming."

"Arthur's always furious. It's his default setting, right next to fussing over my health. I wish he'd take up golf." The words were fond, tinged with just a little exasperation. "I needed to make sure you were okay."

"What if I wasn't?"

"You would never harm me or this child. I know you too well."

She is foolish, Vivian said. *She does not know me. She did not see the green hand. She does not know how the others would use a baby.*

Clary squeezed Gwen's hand, loving her friend and wishing she had never come. "You need to go."

"Are you sure?" Gwen looked sad. "I'd hoped for some girl talk."

"I'll come by later with an armload of books." It was another lie. She was too aware of Vivian staring through her eyes at the fair-haired queen and her unborn young. It was like Vivian wanted to drink them in.

They are fresh life. I have not seen it through the eyes of mortality before.

Something in Vivian's tone confused Clary as if the words meant more than she understood. Gwen seemed to sense her tension, because she rose to go. "Please be all right, Clary. I need my friends."

Her eyes had lost none of their warmth, but they considered Clary as if seeing her for the first time. Normally, they hugged, but neither of them moved. Without a word, Gwen turned and left, abandoning her device on the coffee table. Vivian watched her every move.

In the stark silence that followed, Clary swore under her breath. Was Vivian a danger to Gwen? Were the demons chasing Vivian a threat to those around her?

You need to go.

Clary decided the words weren't just for the queen.

Chapter 15

Clary grabbed the bag of clothes Tamsin had brought her and repacked the few items she'd spread around the bedroom. She zipped it back up with a decisive rasp of metal and put her hands on her hips. Packing was easy. The next steps would be hard.

You don't trust me around the queen. The demon gave a restless sigh.

"Ya think?" Clary grumbled.

Demons do not have children in mortal fashion unless there is a mortal mother to give it life.

"That's reassuring. I'd hate to encounter a hellspawn in the terrible twos." Clary's sarcasm was automatic, and yet she'd heard the longing in Vivian's voice. Was it possible to have maternal instinct when your species couldn't reproduce? "So where do little demons come from?"

We come to awareness from within the collective force of demon energy. We call that force the essence. That is what powered the attack on the computer. It was a waste, using a finite resource for such a thing.

Clary heard Vivian's anger and was curious. "The essence is finite?"

The essence came to be when the world was young, but we do not know how or where. Some say there is a distant homeland for the demons. Others say that we were made of the fire at the core of the world. The only certainty is that the Abyss is not the place where the essence was born, and that is why we are a dying people. There is nothing to replenish us.

It was the longest speech the demoness had made, and for the first time Clary heard the teacher in her. It would have been intriguing if she'd had time for a history lesson. Unfortunately, Vivian was trying to kill Merlin and using Clary's body to do it. And then there was the suspicion Vivian's pals weren't such good pals at the moment.

"I need to get out of here," Clary said.

Vivian didn't seem to mind the sudden change in topic. *I wouldn't recommend it, little fool. These are dangerous times.*

"Says the malign entity taking over my brain."

You make it sound as if there was effort involved.

"Not making me feel warm and fuzzy about your presence here."

And what do you plan to do about that, witchling?

That was the question. Ever since first meeting the knights of Camelot, Clary had wanted to help in their battle against Morgan LaFaye. Now she was infected by the enemy, a liability instead of an ally.

And whatever Vivian said, Clary had felt her interest in Gwen's baby. Clary didn't understand demons, but Vivian definitely wanted to hold that child in her arms. The only thing she could do to help Camelot and its queen—and Clary's best friend—was to get Vivian out of there. She could walk away, just as she'd decided to do back in Tamsin's bathroom.

"Do I still have command over my own two feet?"

Is it any wonder that you are a pathetic little witchling? Do you really think you're going to save the world by asking that kind of question? If you're going to fly in the face of all logic and common sense, seize the opportunity by the throat. Don't ask permission.

"Not helping, pussycat."

If you do manage to escape, what makes you think Merlin won't find you and drag you back home by the ear?

"Because your pride wouldn't allow it."

Vivian fell silent at that. Seizing the opportunity as instructed, Clary grabbed her bag and left.

Clary might not be an expert witch, but she'd had ample experience running away as a teenager. Renting a car or buying a bus ticket required showing ID that could be traced. Hitchhiking could be dangerous. Bicycles, however, could go long distances and were largely anonymous to most people. She was an avid recreational rider—who wouldn't be with so much gorgeous scenery around Carlyle?—and had a decent road bike at her apartment along with a stash of cash. She retrieved both, stuffing her backpack with necessities, and was out of town within the hour.

But the day had taken its toll. Determination got her as far as a cash-only motel two towns away, where she slept despite the dirty room and dubious lock on the door. It was the end of the next day before she reached the outskirts of Seattle, every muscle in her body begging for rest.

Vivian sniffed. *You contain an entity possessed of staggering power, and yet you sink to this primitive mode of transport. I'm unsure whether to be amused or embarrassed.*

"I'm sure you could sprout bat wings and fly, but I think someone would notice."

Isn't shock and awe the point of power?

"Only if you equate power with being blown to smithereens by paranoid security forces."

Modern mortals are no fun.

"They have their own problems." And if Camelot had its way, the supernatural world would not be added to the mix. Merlin had told her about the accords. Species who couldn't compete with the humans—the sasquatches and merfolk in the Pacific Northwest were a good example—strongly believed that their survival depended on invisibility.

We all have our own problems. No one asks about the demons' side of events.

Clary knew conversational bait when it was waved in front of her and was tempted to ignore it. She wasn't sure why the demoness felt the need to explain herself. Still, there was nothing better to do while she slipped back into the stream of traffic that flowed into the city's suburbs.

"Okay," she said, giving in. "Let's hear it."

When the end of the war came, Merlin's final battle spell tasted like ash to the demons, and it smelled as foul as the defeat it was. They all knew the moment presaged living death.

The spell had been stolen from Vivian's own library and crafted into a weapon against them. The thief— Merlin—had slipped from her bed to copy it and then escaped back to his king while Vivian slept. This, after she'd taught him so much and opened his eyes to the truth of his enormous power.

Such betrayal was the last insult in a war that had pitted every species against Vivian's people. The army Arthur of Camelot had cobbled together was an alliance of fleas, but those fleas were legion, and they had won. They strutted and crowed and claimed they were in the right.

True, the demons had fought for conquest and glory. They'd fought for the mastery they believed they deserved. Right and wrong didn't enter into it. Demons didn't bother hiding their lust for power. They were dangerous, but they were—unlike Merlin—honest about it.

Vivian had stood on the ravaged field of battle, among the dead fae and humans and witches. Some of the demons had killed with glee and others, like her, with a grim determination to survive. Her people would succeed, or they would fall. Falling meant banishment to someplace worse than the blood-soaked dirt.

There had been death for demons, too, for immortality didn't mean that they were indestructible. Her kind was made from energy and magic and a rare concentration of power could blast them to nothing. Tenebrius had said noble words about their losses, but they'd been brief. After all, it was the living who were in trouble now.

Vivian had not felt mortality's shadow yet and wasn't afraid of death. Yet she had feared Merlin's spell, because she knew it meant the Abyss.

There were many names for it: Hades, Hell, the Underworld. Wherever demons had come from, they had passed through this desolate place to reach the mortal realms. The operative phrase was *pass through*. No one actually wanted to stay there, given the open pits of flame, rocky deserts and pools of toxic sludge that passed for lakes. Magic could make the odd oasis, but that was a far cry from a truly habitable world. Could anyone really blame them for wanting to stay away?

And yet Merlin was using her own spell to push them off the green earth, with its fresh water and birdsong, into the lifeless pit the petty King of Camelot thought they deserved.

The spell's release was a hot slice across her skin. It was a ring of force radiating from Camelot's highest tower, not quite seen except for a bend in space and time where the ripple passed over the surrounding land and sky. Clouds scudded away like foam in a ship's wake. Trees bowed and broke, the most flexible all but flattening before the force of Merlin's magic. And there was not just one wave of power, but pulse after pulse in concentric rings of crushing force.

The mortal realms would recover, but the demons would not. The spell hit them like a war hammer, the force hurling them across the veil between worlds and sealing their path against return. Vivian flew end over end, losing all sense of her physical being as the magic smashed her to pieces and plunged her into the Abyss, a drop in a torrential waterfall of demonkind.

Down, down into the dark they crashed, into the sunless pit of arid rock. Here no birds sang, no trees stretched tall, no children laughed. Their freedom was gone, as surely as if chains bound their limbs. Here was their punishment on the command of Arthur, King of Mortals—but it was Merlin who had done it.

Vivian raged, yet she might have accepted her fate if it had come another way. But it had come like a knife in the back. She had loved Merlin, and this was the result.

For the first time ever, Vivian had felt the hot kiss of a tear.

Clary pulled her bike to the curb and pulled off her helmet to cool her head a few degrees. Vivian's memory left her solemn, unsure whether to offer her regrets. It wasn't like she sided with the demons, but banishment seemed harsh.

I'm not asking for sympathy, Vivian remarked in her usual dry tone. *Just that you understand we have our own story. There was a rational reason we wanted the mortal realms for ourselves. I, at least, am not a mindless evil who devours infant children on toast.*

"You say that like you're the exception."

Some questions shouldn't be asked. Where are we?

Clary didn't know Seattle well, but could tell this had to be one of the newer suburbs. It still had that semipermanent feel that came from half-finished construction and lawns just sprouting new grass. The afternoon light made all the fresh, colorful paint pop.

Very shiny, Vivian commented without enthusiasm. *There is something here I do not like.*

"In-ground sprinklers?"

Something is watching us.

"I thought you were keeping Merlin off our back."

For now. I am curious to see a little of the modern mortal realm and you have been showing it to me at an alarmingly grounds-eye view. I have been content to ride along.

Clary considered that. Since Merlin had knocked

Vivian senseless in the post-potion aftermath, the demoness hadn't interfered with Clary's physical movements. Nor had she talked quite so much about vengeance. Something had changed.

But now wasn't the time to ponder that. "If it's not Merlin, then who's watching?"

Vivian uttered something Clary assumed was a demon curse word. *Fae, and they are carrying blades hewn from the black rock mined from the roots of the Crystal Mountains. Once blessed by the High Druids of ancient days, such knives can wound a demon. I thought they were all destroyed in the war.*

"Then how did the fae get them?" It seemed a stupid thing to worry about in the moment, but at the same time…

Clary sensed a rush of rage from the demon. It was pure, white-hot and fueled by the instinct to survive. It was also tinged by fear.

Tenebrius has betrayed me. He must have discovered that I lied when I agreed to spy for LaFaye. This is my punishment.

Clary froze. She was still straddling her bike, one foot on the curb and her helmet dangling loose in her hand. Her backpack was strapped with bungee cords to the rack she'd put on the bike for the occasion. The neighborhood had that post-apocalyptic quiet that bedroom communities get when everyone has left for the day. The only noise was a lawn sprinkler making a rhythmic *whoosh-whoosh* from the house to her left.

Her spine prickled in warning. Slowly, casually, she put the helmet back on and buckled the chin strap. "Where are they?" she asked softly.

Behind you. Go now.

Clary crouched over her low handlebars and started

pedaling, rising from her seat a little to pump harder. Pain screamed up her exhausted thigh muscles, but Vivian's fright kept her moving. Now she could hear movement above the hiss of her tires on the pavement. It wasn't so much footfalls—fae were light on their feet—but the jingle of metal. She risked a glance over her shoulder to see two fae, long, white braids streaming as they ran, almost pacing her speeding bike. Despite the heat, they wore battle leathers, weapons belts strapped around their waists. It was the belts making all the noise.

Each fae carried a foot-long blade. They were black and gleaming, curved and tapered like a small saber. *Demon-killers*, Vivian hissed. There was no doubt they'd slice a human just as effectively.

Clary looked back to the road, struggling with the image of neat family homes paired with the deadly fae. Between the houses she could see a main road ahead, although she wasn't sure how to get to it. Like so many new developments, the streets were a maze designed to keep traffic slow and safe.

She'd just decided to forget the road and ride over-land when something bumped the back wheel. Her narrow tire erupted into a sickening *thwap-thwap-thwap*. Clary skidded, just managing to control her fall as the bike went over. Pavement slammed her shoulder as she rolled free. She caught a glimpse of the fallen bike, a throwing star sticking from the mangled back tire. Well, that was one downside of the fashion for no fenders.

A split second later, an ear-splitting crack told her the helmet had saved her skull from the edge of the curb, but pain still flashed white behind her eyes. Hands snatched her upright. The fae was breathing hard, the thrill of the hunt plain in his dark pupils.

"Don't think I'm going to pause to drink your tainted soul, demon child." The fae's voice was low, almost a growl.

Clary was too stunned by her fall to speak. She could only react, and Gawain's fighting drills kicked in. She slammed the heel of her hand into the fae's elegant nose. The crunch of bone and flesh twisted her stomach.

The fae howled in surprise, reflexively clutching his face. Clary snatched at his blade, risking her fingers as she grabbed it free. It all happened so quickly, she barely had time to spin on her heel before his partner reacted.

Run!

Clary sped for the closest yard, but her legs were slow and heavy and the biking shoes that were so good at sticking to the pedals sucked for running. She dodged between houses, nearly tripping over the small, useless hedge separating one empty driveway from the next. The fae was gaining on her with ease.

"If you can do anything," she urged Vivian, "now would be the moment."

As soon as she spoke, she sensed the demon gathering power. It rose like an electric storm, crawling down her arms and raising the fine hairs despite the sweat soaking her skin. Then all at once, Clary was no longer Clary but a being of enormous power. She skidded—no, swaggered—to a halt in a backyard. There were no children there, but a swing set creaked in the silent breeze. She spun to face the fae, who came to a juddering halt and fell back at the look on her face.

Clary fell to one knee, clasped her hands in a double fist around the knife hilt and smote the ground. The world vanished into blackness.

Chapter 16

Vibrating with a mix of anger and worry, Merlin opened his dresser drawer and rummaged inside until his fingers found the amulet. It hung on a chain that had been sliced through by Lancelot as he'd torn it from the throat of Morgan LaFaye's pet assassin. The gem had the power to track magic. It also shielded the wearer from magical attack. Merlin had come by the gem almost honestly—Nimueh, the famed Lady of the Lake, had traded it in return for a favor. Merlin had accepted the deal mostly because he liked Nim and she'd been in trouble. For practical purposes, he was loath to use any tool that might draw the attention of the Queen of Faery. And yet now that his agate scrying stone was broken, he needed the gem's ability to track.

He pulled the amulet out from under a pile of socks. It was silver, star-shaped and set with a large ruby in its center. Merlin picked a piece of fluff from the chain, feeling the power of the stone awaken in his hand. It was a light trickle, but he didn't let the subtlety fool him. After all, he'd charged the stone himself once upon a time, when he was Vivian's student. He knew exactly how it worked.

If only he understood women half as well. Sure, he'd been gone longer than expected. He'd not only had to destroy the infected laptop, but also open a portal for Arthur to conduct negotiations with the goblin king in preparation for the coming war. In that window of time, Clary had fled. Why? He'd trusted her with that one thing—to stay put for a couple of hours. Clary was contrary, but she wasn't foolish. What was more, Clary on the loose meant Vivian on the loose, and that didn't bear thinking about.

But right now the *why* wasn't as important as how to get her back—even if that meant his troubles weren't over. There were enchanters who swore off sex, claiming it damaged the mental faculties, and at the moment he was inclined to agree. If he'd ever needed an argument for abstinence, this insane demon-infested situation was it.

Merlin raised the amulet, letting the star-shaped object spin on the broken chain. The ruby winked with every turn, beautiful and hypnotic. If it tracked magical signatures, surely Vivian would stand out in the crowd.

Vivian, who had suddenly begun to ask awkward questions about their relationship. What would make a demon do that? Then again, she'd always been curious. Experimental. Challenging. He was the one more likely to stick to old ideas. Her unpredictability had been good for him.

With a sigh, he dropped the gem into his palm.

His gaze fell on the stack of tattered paperback books on top of the dresser. Tamsin had put them in Clary's suitcase, but Clary had forgotten to pack them when she left. It didn't surprise him that Tamsin had sent the books, since she knew her sister so well. Clary called them her comfort reads, those favorite stories she read time and again because they were like visiting old friends. Through the course of her training she had apparently needed plenty of comfort because they had appeared again and again during her lunch breaks.

They were tales of adventure and romance, like any minstrel would tell, filled with exotic places and handsome lovers. The one on top—and the one he'd seen most often—featured a tent in a desert oasis, a camel and a harem girl swooning in a studly bandit's arms. That was Clary—smart, modern, independent to the point of madness and willing to embrace whatever she enjoyed, even if it was floridly improbable. She'd pointed out—in response to his acid commentary—that the fact that it *was* fantasy was completely the point.

The memory made his chest ache with an angry sense of loss. He sat on the bed, his senses all too aware that this was where they'd made love. He closed his eyes, unwillingly pulled under by memory for a moment. Her soft skin, the feel of her breath on his cheek, the feeling that once, just once, he was completely welcomed by another person. That was the one thing Vivian had given him that he had never been able to replace. Since Clary had become his student, he'd harbored a secret and unlikely dream that maybe, just maybe... He snapped his eyes open, pushing the emotion away. He couldn't afford to lose himself that way, certainly not now and perhaps not ever. Not with his track record for attracting doom.

The blankets were still tumbled, the light scent of Clary's perfume still lingering in the air. As hard as that was on his concentration, it would help focus the magical connection between them. Merlin straightened the coverlet and set the amulet down, staring into its ruby depths. With a few deep breaths, he slipped into a light trance.

The first impression was of blurred colors and rushing movement, like a film on fast-forward. Then he was seeing the world from—the back of a bicycle? Was there any more inefficient way imaginable to run away? Except, of course, his painstaking and time-consuming search of all the usual transportation routes had turned up nothing. Clary knew what she was doing.

So did Vivian. He sensed her watching for his approach and he faded back before her magical alarms detected his presence. His view adjusted to take in the surroundings. Suburbia. Houses, lawns, newly planted trees that would look good in about a decade. And fae with demon-killing knives. A crushing panic slammed his chest with the force of a train. Merlin jumped to his feet, all too aware that he might be too late.

Clary's gasp echoed in the surrounding blackness. She still clutched the demon-killing knife, but the only way she knew that was by touch. It was utterly dark.

Her memories of the past few minutes were fragmented, as they had been the last time Vivian took charge. She remembered the startled fae, the gathering magic and a thunderclap as she'd skewered the lawn. A portal of some kind had yawned and she'd jumped through. The fae hadn't been able to follow. Apparently, this was a demon-only escape hatch.

So where had the portal gone? Clary prodded the mental space where Vivian should have been, but all was quiet. Had using all that power exhausted her? A lick of panic said that, as little as she liked Vivian, she'd come to rely on her company.

Clary got to her feet, her muscles stiff as cardboard. Her shoulder hurt from falling off her bike and her wrist ached from hitting the fae, and she was trying not to be scared. After a deep breath, she summoned a witch light, the tiny ball of illumination bobbing above her palm until she willed it overhead.

Clary almost wished she hadn't. She was in a tunnel with rounded sides of hard-packed earth. It wasn't much taller than she was but it went on far past the witch light's glow. Behind her, the tunnel ended in a blank wall of dirt. Presumably, that end led back to the yard with the homicidal fae—and her ruined bike, her backpack and the real world. She unstrapped her helmet and set it aside, running her fingers through her flattened hair. After that fall, the helmet would have to be replaced. At least she still had her ID and wallet— although she wasn't sure what good that would do her in the mystical demon sewer.

She wished Merlin were there. Besides his magical skill, few men could appear so calm while cracking an unruly imp over the head—and look so hot while they did it. Not that Clary particularly wanted to remember that incident. She hadn't actually meant to summon a rowdy, seven-foot creature with bright blue skin and a taste for smashing furniture.

Yes, if Merlin was here he would know what to do

and, more important, she could tell him about the fae with demon-killer blades. Cautiously, she stood, picking up the knife. "Any idea what to do next?" she asked, hoping Vivian would answer.

Silence was her only reply. With no other options, she began walking, doing her best to watch in every direction despite the small space. It smelled musty, like a long-neglected basement. There had to be spiders, she thought with a shiver.

She considered what Vivian had said about Tenebrius working with Morgan LaFaye. It raised some interesting points. From what Clary had heard in the past, the demon Tenebrius and LaFaye hated each other. They had openly bickered at a tourney that had been held just before the queen had been imprisoned. Tenebrius had been the judge and awarded Arthur a prize of his choosing—one which Arthur had yet to claim—but the demon had been happy Camelot had beaten the Faery Queen's side. So why would Tenebrius ally himself with the notorious LaFaye now? And hadn't Vivian said she was the demon's friend?

Not in the human sense of the word. Plus, LaFaye is a superior ally. If she regains power, she can offer him freedom.

Clary released a breath, reluctantly pleased to hear Vivian's voice. "Then they deserve each other."

I agree.

Clary took another hesitant step. She'd become aware of a sound she didn't like—a sliding noise barely perceptible over the echoes of her own footfalls. "By the way, are you okay? You went quiet there for a moment."

I am tolerable. The word was curt. *Keep going. This pathway will lead to one of your great cities.*

"Which one?"

Does it matter? I didn't have much time to choose. This path was available, so I took it.

Since Clary couldn't argue with that, she didn't try. The only thing to do was to keep walking through the endless, featureless tunnel.

She had paused to rest for only a moment when the serpent darted forward. It was nearly the same black as the dirt floor and as long as a broomstick, moving with a strange sideways crawl. Clary would have missed it but for the sheen of the witch light on its iridescent skin. She shrieked, leaping backward to avoid the creature.

Kill it!

Without hesitation, Clary slashed with the knife, muscles taking over while her wits froze in panic. The blade bit into sinew, a flare of green light igniting where stone touched flesh. The snake writhed, the head curling back to bite at its pain. It was then Clary saw the fangs unfold like tiny twin scythes. They glistened with a milky yellow poison. She stomped on its neck, holding it still as she lopped off the head. Dark fluid drained from the stump, smoking as it hit the earthen floor and eating a hole inches deep wherever it touched. The blade was unaffected, but Clary backed away before the stuff could touch her shoes. She didn't want to think about what the snake's venom might have done. "What was that?"

A creature that dwells in demon passageways, Vivian said unhelpfully. *They are the realm's response to the wound caused by our magic.*

Like antibodies, Clary thought. Which meant the demons were an infection. Did that make her part of the disease? She stared at the scorched earth and neatly severed head. "Sorry, bud," she said to the thing. "It was you or me."

Vivian's chuckle was faint, but it was there. *You're beginning to sound like me.*

That was disturbing. "Are there more of those around?"

They never come alone.

Clary moved on, picking up her pace to a jog, and then a run when she heard the whisper of skin on stone. She was out of breath by the time she reached a stone wall that abruptly ended the passageway. Vivian opened it with a flash of power, and she stepped through.

Clary stood for a long moment, trying to place the familiar scene. She'd been here before, but without context it took several long glances from left to right to remember the shops and restaurants that placed her on Portland's riverside walk. Clary zipped the long knife inside her jacket, careful not to do herself permanent damage. By then, she was already formulating a plan.

It was late afternoon, the water silvery and the sky filtered through a light haze. Tourists were everywhere, as were the tempting scents of the many restaurants along the route. She hadn't eaten since she'd gulped down a breakfast burrito on the road. She half-walked, half-ran to the nearest coffee shop, stocked up on caffeine and empty calories, and got advice from a pair of teenage boys working on high-end laptops in the corner booth. By the end of the conversation, she was fairly certain they would either own Silicon Valley or end up in prison before they were twenty. Either way, they'd given her the information she needed.

She took a bus, getting off near Powell's Books, and found the store the boys had recommended. An hour and a half later she checked into a modest hotel with a small bag of new clothes and a large bag of tech toys. She'd kept the clerk at the computer store well past closing, but she'd bought enough to make it well worth her while. Besides, when two geek girls started talking, time flew in the nicest way.

The hotel room was old, with a queen bed, a desk and not much else. Still, it made up in space what it lacked in decor. Once she settled in, showered and ordered pizza, it was time to get to work. Neither the boys in the café nor the store clerk had heard of any unusual malware, which meant the demons hadn't surfed the electronic highway beyond Camelot. After all, these were the folks who would definitely notice glowing hands popping out of the screen and immediately try to figure out the code. Arthur's command to go dark had confined the problem, at least for the moment.

Sadly, it was a pretty sure bet that happy state wouldn't last, probably because Perceval would start texting some pretty girl.

And you have a plan beyond soldering Perceval shut in his own armor?

Vivian had gone quiet—and deathly bored—once Clary started talking computers. Clary was unapologetic. "You have your superpowers, kitty cat, and I have mine. Before I came to work at Medievaland, I was a programmer. My job used to involve shutting down computer viruses."

Clary opened another box, dumped the packaging on the floor and plugged in yet another device. She'd paid cash for it all, using up most of the emergency fund she kept in her apartment.

Not that I'm an expert on computer emergencies, but wouldn't a demon infestation be unique?

Clary answered without pausing in her assembly. "Yes and no. With luck they can be isolated and erased. They're just electricity, right?" She opened the laptop and powered it up. It whirred to life with a cheerful beep. Clary's pulse jumped, loving the sound and smell of brand-new equipment.

Erased? Vivian's tone was icy.

Clary's stomach jumped at the sound. There was anger in the word, but also fear. Clary paused to check her thinking. She could understand why the demons wanted to leave the Abyss, but she'd seen a glimpse of the blood-soaked battlefield through Vivian's memory. She'd seen the manifestation that had crawled from Merlin's laptop. Even the snake in the tunnel argued that demons didn't belong in the mortal realms.

They sure didn't belong in her head. Clary's fingers ceased their flight across the laptop's keys. "I'm sorry I have to do this. I wish there was another way, but I can't let this pass. I have to try to stop it."

There was a long pause, and Clary sensed the demoness was considering her options.

I approve, Vivian finally said, her voice subdued but resolute. *Tenebrius does not trust me to guard his interests while he pursues his own, and he has betrayed me. He will not be defeated easily, especially if he is in league with LaFaye. Doubt won't help you survive.*

The demon had barely finished speaking when the door crashed inward, spewing pieces of wood across the floor.

Chapter 17

Clary bounded from her chair, every nerve on alert. The two fae who'd chased her before pushed through the door without a word. She recognized the one she'd hit because of his swollen nose and black eyes. This time, though, he had an automatic rifle slung over his shoulder. Apparently, they thought her worthy of bigger firepower. Clary felt a crazy twinge of satisfaction, but it was short-lived. The moment the fae were in the room, two more crowded in behind them, forming a deadly wall between her and the door. The last fae to enter closed what was left of the door and locked it.

The stone knife sat next to the laptop. She'd been using it to open boxes, but now she snatched it up. It wouldn't stop bullets, but it was all she had.

There was an instant of perfect quiet in the room. She was dimly aware of a chorus of voices in the hallway outside—evidence that the smashed door and parade of fae had attracted attention. The supernatural world was supposed to stay out of the public eye, but clearly that didn't matter to this bunch.

"What do you want?" she demanded.

By way of reply, the bruised fae raised his rifle. Clary's face went numb with panic, the rest of her body prickling as if she'd touched a live wire. She wasn't sure how much was adrenaline and how much was Vivian's rising magic.

He squeezed the trigger. Clary jerked aside, the bullet a hot kiss beside her ear. Her breath deserted her. A witch's reflexes were fast, but Vivian's were faster, and suddenly she was moving too quickly to think. She shrieked in pain as a fireball left her hand. There would surely be blisters if she lived long enough to burn.

The fae scattered as her attack slammed into the wall, leaving a scorch mark on the bland wallpaper. It gave Clary seconds to slash at a fae, but he ducked, sweeping low with one foot and knocking her down. Clary's knife spun out of reach under the queen-size bed. His second blow hit her hard enough that the room reeled.

In a second he was on her, one hand at her throat while he fumbled for the rifle. She was at a bad angle to fight back, her only defense to claw at his face with her already burned left hand. The fae's head jerked back, keeping just out of reach, but Clary grabbed the front of his coat, pulling him down. He pulled away, but not before she grabbed his jaw. The moment her fingers touched his face, Vivian released another blast of power. Clary swore with pain as the fae flew backward. He hit the ground, but didn't move again.

The other fae rushed in as she dived behind the desk. A rush of mad, protective anger flooded her at the thought of all her beautiful new equipment being shot to smithereens. She grabbed the folding luggage rack and hurled it. The gesture forced her to stand, which was a mistake. Three rifles discharged. She dropped to her knees behind the heavy desk, but not fast enough. A bullet clipped her shoulder, the fiery bite giving way to throbbing agony. Nausea swelled as Clary went icy cold, then burning hot with the shock and pain.

Then the wall behind the bed vanished in a blast of icy blue flame. Everyone turned, even the fae who was towering over the desk to shoot Clary like a fish in a barrel.

That's my boy. It's about time these fools learned who they've annoyed. Vivian's voice was nearly a purr.

Not nearly so confident, Clary inched just high enough to see over the edge of the desk. She was sweating, her breathing shallow, but the wound in her shoulder was bearable now, hot pain instead of a howl filling every corner of her mind.

A dark pinprick appeared in the center of the blue light, swirling like a child's top. It grew and grew, flaring outward until the darkness was as tall as a man, then taller, then reaching the high, plastered ceiling. Merlin stepped out, his face set into hard lines of fury. Clary cringed when she saw he held one of the black snakes just behind its head.

He hurled it into the knot of fae. It flew like a knotted rope, unfurling just in time to sink fangs into one of the enemies. A blast of gunfire sprayed the ceiling, shattering the overhead light and raining down plaster dust. Another fae swiped with a demon-killing blade, hacking the snake in two. It was too late. The fae who had been bitten was corroding, pieces of his body collapsing inward as the venom ate everything inside the fragile structure of his skin. A stink like rotten fish sauce choked the room. The only mercy was that he never made a sound.

By that time Merlin had stepped from the portal onto the bed and then jumped lightly to the floor. He had no gun, just a ruby pendant on a broken chain that he stuffed into his jeans pocket. The remaining two fae swiveled to face him, muscles coiled and rifles at the ready. Clary was sure they would have fired, except for the two well-armed fae who emerged from the tunnel and stood to flank Merlin.

With a flash of pleasure, she recognized Laren. The other, named Angmar, she'd met only once before but knew he was a friend of Gawain's and a leader among the rebel fae.

"You!" spit one of Clary's attackers. "Merlin the Devil!"

His rifle twitched, but Angmar shot him dead. In the same instant, Merlin lunged, knocking the weapon out of the remaining fae's hands and throwing him into the dresser. The fae slid to the ground, dragging the lamp and telephone with him. Outside, the howl of sirens split the evening air. Clary rose from behind the desk. Blood ran, hot and sticky, down one arm, but she couldn't stifle a grin.

"Hi," she said. "Thanks for dropping by."

"You're shot," he snapped as if she'd done it on purpose.

"I think I'll be okay," Clary said, answering the question he hadn't asked.

Merlin's expression was slightly wild, as if he didn't know whether to laugh hysterically or burn the scene to the ground. His amber gaze flicked over her, the computer equipment and the wreckage of the room. Finally, it came to rest on the last living bad guy, who was staring defiantly into the barrel of Angmar's gun.

He lightly placed two fingers on the captive fae's forehead. "It's time to tell us what you know."

Merlin was certain his nerves blackened and shriveled to ash when he saw Clary grinning at him, blood soaking her shirt and dead fae all over the floor. She was chaos packaged in a small, perky blond bundle, but he couldn't keep his stomach from dropping in pure relief. Even though the amulet had tracked her to the hotel, he hadn't breathed easy until that moment.

Merlin's interrogation of the remaining fae took less than a minute. When he was done, Laren and Angmar dragged the prisoner through the portal back to the rebel compound. Merlin had saved some of the demon essence from the laptop, and the rebel fae were eager to see if it could be used for a cure. As a one-time special bonus, they had a handy subject to test.

Which left Clary and her makeshift computer lab. Laren had helped her shove it back into its shopping bags and send it through the portal. They'd gathered every last weapon, too, including the demon-killing knife and every cartridge they could find. With the aid of magic, Merlin had scoured the room of evidence. The police had been breaking down the door when he'd hustled Clary through the portal, which he redirected to the safety of his living room.

Once they were there, he rounded on her. "Did you use a credit card anywhere?"

She shifted uneasily. The room was lit only by a floor lamp in the corner. The soft light touched one side of her face, highlighting the gentle curves of brow and cheekbone. It struck him, as it had so often, how she never seemed to notice her own beauty.

"I paid cash as I went," she returned defiantly. "And I registered the room under the name Kitty Salem. It wasn't the kind of place that asked a lot of questions."

Kitty for Vivian, Salem for witches everywhere. Cute, but he wasn't in the mood to be amused. "Good, because the cops are going to be very curious. I'm pretty sure someone got a good look at you and probably the fae. There will be witnesses."

"Or not. People don't go to a no-tell hotel to be good citizens."

She had a point, but Merlin's chest was a knot of anxiety. It wasn't just the fae with demon knives, or the police, or the possibility that LaFaye would know her amulet had been in use and by whom. It was that he might have lost Clary.

"Why, by the blasted Abyss, did you run?" he roared.

Her chin came up. "Can I get a bandage before we dive into the details? I got shot."

"That's not an answer!" he snarled, but he marched her to the bathroom, a hand on her good elbow.

When they got there, he sat her on the edge of the tub and crouched to examine the wound. After rummaging in a drawer for blunt-tipped scissors, he gently began cutting away her sleeve.

"I was afraid, okay?" she finally offered. "On top of everything else, the demons know Vivian's last known whereabouts was inside my head. They sent fae assassins to punish her for sitting out this fight."

The prisoner he'd questioned had said as much, but Clary's frightened words made it personal. Merlin glanced up from his work. Her face was pale, but that was no surprise given the bullet wound, not to mention the day they'd had. What worried him more was the hollow look in her eyes. It went beyond shock and fatigue to a much darker place.

"What do demons do with human babies?" she asked suddenly. "What about Vivian?"

"Vivian?" he asked, trying to figure out where this was coming from. "I think she likes them."

"But she's a demon."

"Humans like baby animals. We don't need to be a cat to like kittens."

"That's weird," she said, then hissed through her teeth as he peeled away the soaked fabric of her jacket and shirt. "We're like pets to them."

"*Weird* is a sliding scale where you and I are concerned." He peered at the wound. "Vivian is as dangerous as a box of vipers, but she's selectively vicious, unlike some of her kin."

"Speaking of vipers," Clary said quietly, "where did you get the snake?"

"The same tunnel you passed through. The amulet was very thorough about tracing your journey. Once I knew where you were, I called for backup." He washed around the wound, relieved to see it looked much better once the excess blood was gone. "Congratulations. The bullet passed through."

"If she is so dangerous and you hate demons so much, why did you study with them for so long?"

The question stripped away centuries, returning him to the hillside where Vivian had first taken his hand. There was bitterness between them now, but it could not erase that golden sun-soaked day when she had come from nowhere and turned him from a disappointed youth into a man who understood his own worth. Her lessons hadn't just been about magic.

"She had something I needed." It was the truth, but it wasn't the whole answer. "There are times I wish I had never met her, especially when I understood the destruction and depravity that come so naturally to her kind."

Clary said nothing. He finished dressing the wound, certain he'd done an adequate job but planning to call Tamsin anyway to be certain Clary had the finest care. He rose, setting his tools aside and offering a hand to help her to her feet.

"Is that all you think of them now?" she asked. "That they're horrible and disgusting?"

Her movement was lithe and filled with energy despite the bandage and ruined clothes. Yes, this was Clary, always full of fire. That was a comfort, even if all her talk about demons was not. "What else is there to think? They did their best to conquer our world. They try to justify it by saying it is their nature to rule. They have no means to return to whatever homeland they came from so they'll rule ours instead. They're cruel and violent and make no apologies for it."

Clary looked down at where his hand held hers. "And yet you were lovers."

Merlin had been about to work the conversation back to the subject of running away, but this stopped him cold. "It's complicated."

Her fingers tightened around his. "Explain it to me. I know it's none of my business but I'm really confused."

He didn't want to have this conversation, but after what had happened with Vivian and her potion, he had to say something. "A relationship like ours was—it's like a puzzle made of a hundred parts. I suppose all are, in a way. One shared experience, then another, then a joke you both laugh at. Before you know it, all those separate impulses become a single bond."

"So it wasn't all bad?"

"No. When I met Vivian, I was lonely and isolated and she was like a breathtaking bonfire."

"But it didn't last?"

"How could it? You know what she is. You saw what she did to me. To you."

And that was completely true. And yet a corner of his heart, one not crushed by regret for his betrayal, had missed her. She wasn't good or kind like Clary, but she had a quick wit and a stunning depth of knowledge.

No, there was no relationship more complex than his feelings for the demon. After an acquaintance of over a thousand years, how could it be otherwise? Awe, lust, admiration, terror, guilt and gratitude were all there. So was resentment. He didn't want to face the fact that he'd pretended to return to her side only to steal that spell. It had been the act of a coward, and it had been the act of a man doing his best to save Camelot from destruction.

And now? It was history, where she should have stayed for both their sakes. He was holding the hand of the woman he wanted now.

A frown pleated Clary's brow. "Do you hate her?"

"I don't trust her, and I hate what she's done to you." He studied Clary's anxious expression. She hadn't moved an inch, still holding his hand as if he might vanish if the contact was broken. "The only reason she isn't working with Tenebrius is because she's here to kill me."

"How can you be absolutely sure of that?"

"She doesn't forgive."

Not like Clary, who had helped bring Laren home to himself even after he'd tried to take her soul. And that was, perhaps, the moment Merlin understood just how much he wanted—needed—Clary in his life. It hadn't hit him all at once, but filled him as gradually as an incoming tide since the moment Clary had taken the fae in her arms. He wanted that kind of redemption. Not that he deserved it.

And he'd talked enough about the past. It was the present-day Vivian he had to worry about now. "Is she awake?" he asked Clary.

She pulled her hand away from his. "No. She hasn't stirred since you knocked her out. As far as I can tell, she's entirely gone."

Chapter 18

The lie all but burned Clary's lips.

Why did you say that? Vivian asked.

The answer was simple and very practical. Vivian was inside her and Clary was beginning to suspect she couldn't leave. Whatever Vivian had said about seeing the sights, there was no reason for her to have gone along on her cycling adventure, or to sit there listening to Merlin call her a box of vipers. No, she was stuck until something or somebody removed her. Therefore, in a sideways fashion, what Merlin thought of Vivian applied to her, as well. Unless, of course, he had reason to think the demon was gone.

That's terrible logic, little witchling. Vivian almost sounded sympathetic.

Maybe, but it was all she had. She didn't want him to think her a demon, or even a demon's walking hotel room.

Merlin's gaze swept over her. "Are you sure Vivian is dormant?"

"Yes," Clary said firmly.

Silence became a tangible thing as if the feeling between them was resonating off the bathroom's tiled walls. Suddenly suffocating, Clary turned and walked out, leading them back to the living room. She clenched her fists to hide the sudden trembling in her limbs. How had this happened? How had she ended up lying to the one man she wanted most to think well of her?

"Ordinarily, I don't think what I did to Vivian should have quieted her for more than a day or two," he said. "Demons are strong. Immortal."

"But not invincible."

"No, and I keep returning to the fact Tenebrius has declared her an enemy. I see LaFaye's hand in that, but I also see Tenebrius's forethought."

Vivian came to attention. *What does he mean?*

"If she has gone quiet, something unexpected occurred. I think that was Tenebrius. It would be easy to sever the energetic bond between realms while she is vulnerable. That would be like pinching an umbilical cord or an intravenous line."

Clary sensed Vivian's startled reaction. *He said that was an accident!*

"What happens then?"

"Loss of strength," he said. "Hibernation."

Clary sat down, trying to digest the information. Was that why Vivian couldn't leave?

It's not untrue, Vivian said in a way that said it wasn't the whole story, either.

"But what about the fae with knives?" Clary asked.

"An instant solution," said Merlin. "Instant death is

better than hibernation if you're shutting down a loose end who knows more than they should."

"That's horrible!"

"That's demon politics," Merlin replied, his expression grim. "I wouldn't wish this on anyone, not even her."

"Especially not her?" Clary asked gently.

"She wants to kill me."

"She didn't."

"I hesitate to take that as a sign of affection."

"I'm just trying to be fair."

"Stopping LaFaye and Tenebrius will help Vivian." He looked away. "Right now things can go back to normal for you."

"Normal?" She gave a faint smile. "I'm not sure what that is anymore."

Merlin knelt at her feet, smiling slightly as he brushed the hair from her eyes. "You'll be fine."

Except Vivian was still there. This would be the moment to confess she'd lied, but then he kissed her, nibbling along the angle of her jaw. "What are you doing?" she asked, a rush of pleasure making her voice husky.

"I'm punishing you for running away." His fingers ran lightly down her arms, carefully avoiding her injury. "It may involve some extended interrogation." Then he kissed her forehead, a soft, lingering gesture that said she was precious to him.

"This is an odd form of punishment." Their discussion had been so serious, she wasn't quite ready for his lightened mood. She hadn't wanted to hear about how much he both admired and loathed his ex-lover, even though it made perfect sense. Take away the supernatural parts—and maybe the killing parts—and it didn't actually sound all that different from anyone talking about their exes.

At bottom, even the most powerful witches and wizards and kings and queens were still people.

"I'm happy you're all right," he said, rising and pulling her to her feet.

"I'm glad you're happy." She should say something, tell him she was far from demon-free, but then he'd get that look on his face. The one that meant he hated demons, and that contempt would be for her.

"We should get you cleaned up and in bed," he said. "You look ready to fall over."

The words were solicitous, but they somehow let her know that if she wanted to fall over in his bed, he'd definitely be there to catch her.

It was everything she'd ever wanted from him, but now it made her breath quicken in apprehension as much as desire. She was playing with fireballs, and she should know by now that she'd get burned.

He kissed her, his hot mouth sending her pulse into triple time. Images from the potion aftermath crowded her head, and her knees grew weak. It was too much.

She pushed away, her stomach in knots. "I need to sleep." She ducked her head, desperate to hide the lie that must be branded on her features.

He stroked her hair, his touch gentle with a sympathy that made her squirm. "Of course. I'll use the guest bedroom. Get all the rest you need."

Clary was certain she wouldn't sleep a wink.

"You realize if this works I've earned my right to fight with the rest of Camelot's forces," Clary said to Merlin the next day. Her voice was bright and cheerful, even if the rest of her was exhausted.

Merlin grunted in typical male fashion—that way of implying volumes they thought other people understood.

They'd both been busy that morning. Clary guessed it was as much to cover the frustrated desire between them as the need to fight their enemies. At least on Clary's side, work was a safe way to avoid the thorny question of Vivian's presence. Maybe in time she'd grow used to the idea of having her lover's ex in her head, but she wasn't there yet.

She'd reassembled her equipment on the dining room table, doing her best to ignore the scorch mark they'd left the last time they'd battled demonic malware. Currently, she was typing code, adjusting a program she'd written before in hopes that it would dissolve a demonic entity. Well, energy was energy, electrons were electrons. She'd give it something that would scramble its zeroes and ones. Meanwhile, she was waiting for Merlin to follow his grunt with something she could respond to.

"Use your words," Clary replied. "Or don't. I just don't want to guess what you're thinking."

He narrowed his amber eyes, reminding her of a disgruntled tomcat. "You used to be an obedient student."

"No, I wasn't." Though she did recall being marginally more respectful. In awe, actually. "Okay, fine, but I had your ex in my brain for a while. It colors things."

Merlin left the room.

Clary sighed but her fingers didn't stop moving. Merlin was avoiding any further conversation about Vivian. Apparently, he'd said all that he meant to on the topic.

Clary wasn't sure what would happen if a choice came along that pitted her interests against Vivian's or if the demon would ever resume her revenge against Merlin. For the moment she had all but vanished from Clary's mind, which seemed to be her way of resting.

The timing was good because Clary needed to concentrate. With this computer emergency, she finally had an opportunity to show what she could do instead of repeatedly screwing things up.

She'd blocked off every one of her workstation's connections to the internet until she had her strategy in place. Now she was typing furiously, all too aware she had no time to waste. In her opinion, the entity would eventually give up on invading Camelot's tech and move on to easier prey, which was pretty much the rest of the world. So far, they'd managed to keep everyone from touching their devices, but it wouldn't last.

And Clary's foe was bound to be unpredictable. Sure, LaFaye hated Arthur because he had Camelot's crown and she believed it should have been hers. Sure, the demons hated Camelot for sending them to the Abyss like bad dogs. It made sense they'd designed an attack specifically to invade the tech toys of Arthur's crew. But Clary understood things that got into the computer ecosystem developed a mind of their own. Infections infected. Trojan horses found things to invade. Someone would slip up and check their social media account. She had to confine the entity and destroy it, stat.

Clary sat back, rereading her last few lines and poking a key when she found an error. Her shoulder hurt, but it was better than before and she could live with the badass scar the bullet would leave behind. Moving on automatic, she drank a mouthful of coffee, not minding that it was cold. A quiver of excitement hovered in her stomach—not random butterflies, but quiet fireworks of pride. She was at the top of her game.

To give credit where it was due, Vivian had made some suggestions about the physics of the demonic collective. Any programmer except a witch would have despaired at translating her supernatural physics lesson into code, but Clary felt good about what she'd done. Very good. This was her personal superpower.

The front door slammed and she recognized Arthur's deep voice. The king, it seemed, had to come to Merlin if he wanted a front-row seat for this particular show.

A shadow fell across the table. She looked up to see the two men blocking the light. As always, Arthur wore his sword, Excalibur. The king's reddish hair looked slightly wild as if he'd been trying to tear it out. Given the circumstances, she supposed it was possible.

"Hello, boys," she said, forgetting for a moment that she was talking to a king and his enchanter. Vivian really was a bad influence.

However, Arthur simply nodded. "How does your work progress?"

"I'm ready." The words left her with confidence. She put one hand on the crystal sphere sitting beside the laptop. It wasn't the precious object Merlin's red stone had been, but a workaday crystal ball. Every witch coven had one. So did the rebel fae. If they couldn't trust digital communications, magic would have to do. "Everyone's on standby."

"Tell me what will happen," said Arthur.

Clary had to hand it to him. For a medieval guy, he made a good attempt at grasping the modern world. All the same, she put it in layman's terms. "If I poke the entity with a big stick, it's going to run. So I've given a bunch of friends their own sticks to keep it from getting away."

She held up a flash drive. "These are the sticks in question. Camelot spent a fortune in overnight courier fees. Mine is the biggest stick and coordinates all the others, which is why I had to write a bunch more code."

Arthur's eyes lit up. "I see. This is like a boar hunt. You will deliver the killing blow, but it will take other spearmen to keep the boar at bay."

"Yeah, okay," she said. "This isn't how one typically eradicates a bit of nasty on the web, but this isn't a usual computer bug."

Arthur gave a small smile. "I understand. Please proceed."

Clary proceeded. She gave the crystal ball a tap and it flashed red, the signal to all her fellow geeks to unleash the code. Then she popped online just long enough to type in a string of characters, hit Return and disconnect again. A heartbeat passed, then another.

"That's all?" Arthur demanded.

"Wait for it," she said. Her screen began to scroll, listing the zillions of places her code was coursing in search of its quarry.

Merlin moved to stand behind her, putting one hand on her shoulder. It was a simple gesture, one a teacher or a friend might make just as easily as a lover. Despite her best efforts, her thoughts chased down what was becoming a well-worn path. They had begun to move toward a relationship, but she was still confused by her—and his—connection to Vivian. In some unconscious way, was he Clary's lover, or Vivian's? Where did they overlap? Would everything end once Vivian was gone, or if he found out the demoness was still around?

She should have been content that, for now, he was behind her and supporting her contribution to Camelot's defense. It wasn't enough. For the first time, Clary wasn't asking why he'd want to be with her. She was certain she deserved Merlin for herself.

Clary's moment of distraction ended with a frantic flutter of orange light from the crystal ball. Laren's face appeared in its center. Lines of tension bracketed his mouth.

"There is something amiss. Our equipment is overheating and there is something wrong with our monitor. The screen is…" He trailed off with a look of disgust, then seemed to gather himself again. "It is not conducting itself as a screen ought to behave."

He'd barely finished before other voices began crowding in. The image in the ball flashed between one face and the next. Clary recognized some of the witches, and others were strangers. All had agreed to help her, but now their panicked exclamations melted into a confused babble.

She smacked the top of the ball, taking control of the conversation. "Hang on, all of you. You're doing great. Help is on the way."

"My CPU's too hot!" someone cried. "The computer is trying to shut down."

Clary tapped the ball again. "You're magical. You fix it."

She began typing like a madwoman. She'd anticipated something like this might happen, and had countermeasures ready to go. She re-established a link and launched one file, then another, before shutting down again.

"What's happening?" asked Merlin.

She jumped at the sound of his voice. She'd been concentrating so hard, she'd nearly forgotten she was in a physical space with real people around her. "Our green gooey friend is looking for a way out of the trap. I've just set bait to draw it back this way."

"What kind of bait?" he asked.

"Something that looks like an escape route." She smiled up at him. "It isn't."

Admiration flashed through Merlin's eyes. He'd watched her struggle so hard with her studies that she knew he'd appreciate her confidence now. She flushed with pleasure, but turned back to the screen, all too aware of Arthur's assessing gaze. Her flustered mood was short-lived. What she saw on the monitor snapped her to attention.

It had turned a putrid shade of lavender that, here and there, shaded to a greenish-blue. That was bad enough, but it was bubbling and lumpy, like carbonated cottage cheese. The smell made Arthur step back.

He waved a hand. "This stinks of a battlefield two days in the sun."

Clary's mouth watered dangerously, but she launched her final assault. The bubbling became more frantic, and Arthur drew Excalibur, holding it in both hands, in case the laptop mounted a savage attack—an image that would have been funny if it hadn't been all too possible. Clary scooted her chair back just in case.

The cottage cheese bubbled into a cauliflower, then began to change pixel by pixel into something else. The change came randomly so that it was impossible to guess what image it might be, but it held its shape, still protruding from the screen. Clary rose from the chair, backing up until she felt Merlin's solid form behind her. One of his hands touched her waist as if to steady her. She heard Merlin's indrawn breath when the picture resolved into a face. Excalibur twitched as if it took all Arthur's willpower not to strike.

The heart-shaped face had large gray eyes and an elegant bone structure that hinted at mixed blood—fae and human or fae and witch, or perhaps some of all three. The hair was black and lustrous, the skin pale as the moon.

LaFaye, Vivian hissed from deep in Clary's mind.

Chapter 19

Clary stared. She'd heard a lot about the Queen of Faery, but she'd never seen the woman before now. "Well, I guess there's no question about a fae-demon alliance now."

The eyes turned Clary's way, and she shrank back just a little. She hadn't expected the image to respond, and there was nothing friendly in the fae queen's glare. "Do not become too confident, witch. This was a scouting party, nothing more."

The voice made them all tense. It came from the laptop's speakers, the tone tinny and crackling with static. If the image noticed the poor audio, it didn't seem to care. The gaze rested on Merlin for a long moment, sparking with hatred, before moving on to Arthur. "I bid you come to the Midsummer Festival in the Forest Sauvage. My emissaries would hold parley with you."

Arthur raised Excalibur until the tip was inches from LaFaye's coldly beautiful face. The apparition's expression twisted with anger. The sword was the one thing she feared, for it cut through every enchantment, even hers.

"I have allowed you the luxury of imprisonment," said the king. "Are you certain you want me to seek you out?"

From what Clary knew, the Lady of the Lake's prison was the best Camelot could manage, and LaFaye's current stunt was proof that the jail was growing weak. Arthur's brave words were equal parts threat and wishful thinking. Even so, there was no mistaking the fear in her eyes as Excalibur's point drew near. She gave a reptilian hiss.

"Come, Arthur," said the Queen of Faery. "Come and face your destiny if you dare."

With that, her image dissolved into a fluttering mass of random black shapes that were immediately pixelated and erased by Clary's code. The laptop's screen flattened back to its normal shape, but Clary's heart continued to pound.

"Is she truly gone?" Arthur asked quietly, lowering the sword but not sheathing it.

"She was never truly here," Merlin replied. "That was a projection, nothing more."

Still, Clary scooted her chair back to the desk and initiated a scan. They were silent as the image of a tiny witch on a broom sailed back and forth across the screen. Eventually, it burst into a shower of stars. "It's clean," Clary announced, voice shaking with relief. "The internet is officially demon-free."

"This is your victory," said Merlin. "You should be proud."

To Clary's utter surprise, the king pulled her from her chair and planted a kiss on her cheek. He gave an infectious laugh. "Praise all the saints. Now Gwen can download her stories and stop threatening to order my knights to the bookstore three times a day."

Clary raised her chin. Morgan might have called the internet invasion a mere scouting party, but Clary knew better. They'd slammed a door in the face of their enemies. That had to be a victory worth cheering about, even if it was just the first of many battles.

Merlin threw open a window, admitting a welcome gust of fresh air. "So who's up for a picnic in the Forest Sauvage?"

Humiliation was a nuanced experience, and Morgan LaFaye had plumbed every depth. She was a skilled enchantress, educated by the finest witch and fae practitioners and possessed of a natural talent unseen in a thousand years. She was a monarch and a warrior in her own right. And yet...

The queen paced her quarters, trying not to notice the threadbare path she'd worn in the carpet. The objects around her blurred with the speed of her steps, but that didn't matter. They were so familiar, she barely saw them anymore.

Fear raged like a storm battering her from the inside out. As good as she was, she had been trapped in this prison. Now she'd suffered the shame of another defeat. Morgan wore that embarrassment like a leaden mantle, not just for herself, but for the whole of her family. They had cleared the path for her to inherit Camelot's throne with cunning and violence, and she had failed to seize that gift and wield it like a queen. Did she even deserve it?

Of course she did. As always, Merlin had interfered. Merlin, who had saved the infant Arthur. Merlin, who had brought him to kinghood. Merlin, whose strumpet Vivian had refused to join with the others and assist LaFaye in her hour of need. Well, Tenebrius would punish that dereliction.

And now Merlin's protégée had shut down Gorm's escape route. There would be no sudden attack on Camelot, no escape for the demons and no freedom for Morgan.

She flung herself into a chair, kicking aside the footstool so hard it flipped over. Why had she trusted her future to a spell she didn't understand? Like most who had spent even a brief time in the modern world of the humans, she was acquainted with smartphones and video streaming, but that was a distant cry from knowing how to write that into a spell. Computers were a crude magic of their own, and one she'd never bothered to learn.

And demon magic? Her power had refused to blend with theirs, unbalancing the incantation. No wonder it had failed. Her magic was too pure to blend with the demon dregs.

LaFaye jumped to her feet. "Gorm!"

The summoning circle flashed, and the tiny demon appeared in a cloud of theatrical smoke. She all but leaped across the room and snatched the creature up by the scruff. It dangled, the expression in its yellow eyes vacillating between being mournful and brimming with reproach.

"You failed me," she said in a low, bitter voice.

"I told you the spell was a prototype," Gorm wheezed. "I learned much. Next time it will work much better."

"Is that an excuse?" she raged.

"It could have worked with some practice. Your magic is a little different than ours, like AC and DC currents."

She didn't want to hear it. "My magic is pure. Yours failed."

The creature waved its hands, begging her to let him go. They were ugly, wrinkled little paws. Rage howled inside Morgan and trembled through her limbs. She hated the monster. She hated that he'd tricked her, exposed her inadequacies. Most of all, she hated that he'd raised her hopes and then failed. As the seconds ticked past, she grew light-headed, the world dimming to grays and blacks around her.

"There won't be a next time," she said, her words quiet now. "I don't permit failure."

She wrapped her hands around his throat, summoning every scrap of her anger and feeding it through her ferocious power. Gorm kicked and squeaked, eyes bulging as she squeezed.

He was just a little demon. When Morgan was finished, there was barely any stain at all.

"The Midsummer Festival is where every species in every realm agrees to a truce and comes out to play." Tamsin grabbed Clary's arm and dragged her forward. Clary followed obediently, still feeling slightly woozy from the portal that had brought them there. The Forest Sauvage was a no-man's land between all the realms. It was wild and dangerous, full of strange monsters and even stranger magic, but it was also home to many wonderful things.

The fair was held in a large meadow, or series of meadows, separated by stands of trees. The vendors' pavilions ringed the main field, each one decorated in a different pattern. There were stripes of green and white, blue with stars and red silk ringed with prancing lions. Each sold something different—wine or gold work or instruments inlaid with mother-of-pearl. At one end of the meadow was a stage and there a band of dwarves played a raucous reel on fiddles and wheezing small pipes. Children of all species romped together on the grass in a bounding, wing-fluttering chaos of delight. The sight made Clary laugh out loud.

"Aren't we supposed to be, y'know, organizing an army or something," Clary wondered out loud. "This feels too much like a vacation paradise after the past few days."

Tamsin's expression turned serious. "Enjoy the peace while it lasts. The crazy is never far off in these parts."

"What are we supposed to be doing?"

"Arthur is meeting with the goblin king, Zorath. Gawain is with him."

Clary nodded. Merlin had been mysterious about his immediate plans, but that was normal for him. "Then I suppose we're free to explore."

The two sisters wandered the booths, and slowly their mood lightened. It was impossible not to be tempted by the bright, fluttering scarves and baskets overflowing with every kind of bead or broach or ring. Clary was a natural magpie, and any fairground could part her from the last dollar in her purse. This was no different; only her wonder was more intense. Each item was exquisite, from the polished statues of tiny dragonets to the huge clay drums that sounded like captive thunder. Best of all were the hideous goblins who had brought their sparkling hoard of gold and gems to market. She'd heard about Gwen's adventures with the goblin king, when she and Arthur had slain a troll and saved the goblins' precious mines. The feat had cemented Arthur's alliance with King Zorath, and the shared peril of the quest had gone a long way to healing the relationship between Camelot's king and queen.

However, as beautiful as the treasures were, it was the happiness of the fair that stole Clary's heart. Everyone greeted her like an old friend, even if they'd never met.

I have not seen this place for many, many years, said Vivian wistfully. *It is as delightful as I remember it.*

"I thought demons still came here once in a while," Clary said in a low voice, not wanting to alert bystanders that she was chatting with her personal hellspawn. While she could talk to Vivian within her own mind, it somehow made it harder to discern which thoughts were her own.

Only Tenebrius comes now. He is strongest and able to leave the Abyss for periods of time. He keeps a castle in these parts.

Clary remembered Tamsin's story about that castle, and fervently hoped to avoid it. "Do you know where LaFaye is imprisoned?"

The Lady of the Lake's white tower. You can see it through the trees.

Clary searched the horizon. "I thought there was a glamour that hid it from view." She finally found a smudge of white against a dark backdrop of green.

The magic is growing thin. Lady Nimueh is a mighty sorceress, but LaFaye is formidable.

To Clary's eyes, the distant tower looked like a broken fang waiting to strike. After the image in the laptop, she never wanted LaFaye's gaze on her again. But then, the evil queen would be hunting larger game than Merlin's student witch.

That is exactly why we shall succeed, said Vivian with bloodthirsty satisfaction. *No one will see us coming, and I will have my vengeance on Tenebrius and his dark queen for what they've done to me.*

"I really don't like the sound of that."

The demon didn't reply, because Merlin appeared at Clary's elbow. "I have set perimeter wards throughout the fair. If Tenebrius or his fae friends arrive, I will know it."

"So, what next?" Clary asked.

"We wait." Merlin gave a careless wave toward an enormous tent that filled a nearby clearing. "Arthur is enjoying the hospitality of King Zorath. Goblins always dine before serious negotiations, and ambassadors from a dozen of the mortal races are there."

"What's there to negotiate? Surely everyone wants LaFaye gone."

He shrugged. "There will be battle plans, plans for dividing up booty and decisions about which champion leads the charge. None of it means much once swords are drawn, but the pride of monarchs is tricky business."

"I bet Arthur misses Gwen for this part." The queen was a masterful negotiator, but she was too close to her time to travel.

"Probably," Merlin agreed. "But he has Gawain, who

can be diplomatic when he chooses. Have you had a chance to look around the fair?"

Tamsin, who had obviously been eavesdropping, looked up from examining a tray of earrings. "You should definitely show Clary around."

She shot Tamsin a scowl, but it was mostly out of old habit. Tamsin had set her up on far too many awful dates during their teenage years. Merlin looked between them, suspicion plain on his face. All the same, he gave Clary a slight nod. "Do you want to see the sights?"

Clary shrugged but she smiled, too. "Okay."

Merlin offered an arm and they set off down the row of pavilions, walking slowly but with purpose. "Don't bother with this part of the grounds. It's just a better version of Medievaland. The really interesting things are outside the main field."

"What do you consider interesting?" she wanted to know.

He gave a slow smile that was actually charming. "Have you ever tasted the desserts that the naiads make?"

"The what?"

"Naiads are water spirits. There are not many left in the human world, but they still live here where the waters are pure." He led her into what was clearly the refreshment area. It smelled of wood smoke and cooking aromas, some redolent of spice and one a savory, mouthwatering blend of mushrooms and sage. She veered that way until Merlin pulled her back. "Don't eat anything made by the spriggans. You can never tell where it's been."

He took her instead to a corner of the meadow where a stream ran close by. After the smoke, the air seemed crisp, an earthy tang replacing the heavier smells of meat and spice. The space was crowded with all manner of folk, some with wings and antennae, others in full chain mail. Clary waved to Beaumains, who was standing in line and chatting with a pretty girl who was green from head to toe. Whatever the naiads sold, it appeared to be a universal favorite.

When they got to the head of the line, Clary saw the naiad serving dishes of what looked like crushed ice. Every time a customer paid—sometimes with gold, but sometimes with a shell or a flower—the naiad knelt and took another dish from the cool stream. Clary was entranced by the creature's grace, and also by the fact she was entirely translucent. It was hard to see where she was until she moved, and the light seemed to bend and curve to show her presence.

Merlin paid in a type of coin Clary didn't recognize. The naiad accepted it—she was definitely corporeal enough to deal with solid objects—and lifted their desserts from the shallow water.

"Thank you," Clary said, shocked a little by the freezing temperature of the dessert. It was only then that she discovered the entire dish—including the bowl and spoon—was made of ice.

"Enjoy," the naiad replied in a lilting voice and then turned to the next customer.

Clary walked away, Merlin at her side. "The trick," he said, "is to eat the whole thing before it melts."

Obediently, she dug the spoon into the ice. The first mouthful made her stop in her tracks. The sun was hot on her shoulders, but her mouth was filled with a refreshing explosion. She couldn't name all the flavors, but she recognized many. There was that earthy tang, but there was something floral, too. There was honey and the rich ripeness of berries, the snow of the mountains and the spice of herbs. It was a mouthful of everything good about the summer forest.

"Oh!" The exclamation was hardly profound, but it came from her heart.

Merlin grinned, and there was something boyish in it. "I have this at least once every summer." And he stuffed a spoonful into his mouth.

Clary couldn't remember him ever sharing an ordinary personal detail. She'd seen his home, even his bedroom, but this was different. Surely someone who had lived for centuries had thousands of likes and dislikes—or maybe the need to define one's tastes changed as time blurred memories together. Or, and this made more sense to her, his heart was here, in this land caught between worlds. Maybe this felt more like home.

She paused between spoonfuls, even though cold water was beginning to drip through her fingers. She was getting an ice-cream headache. "What was it like, being the king's sorcerer in the old Camelot?"

The sadness in the look he gave her broke her heart.

Chapter 20

"What do you think?" Merlin said. "It was the time before everything happened."

Before he had destroyed the world he knew and half the creatures in it. Clary could see him retreating, the relaxed mood they'd shared dissolving like the icy dessert. He looked away as if wishing to be anywhere but next to her. "I mean," she said, stammering a little, "was it like this, with pixies and naiads and goblins? Did the supernatural walk freely, or did they hide from humans like the witches do now?"

He seemed to relent, giving her a sidelong glance. "They were in the open back then."

She took a final spoonful of dessert and set the bowl on a stump to melt in the sun. "It must have been beautiful."

He didn't reply, but walked slowly toward the trees.

Not sure what else to do, Clary followed. She sensed he was deep in thought, maybe lost in memories older than the oaks around them.

When they came to another clearing, he directed her to sit on a fallen log. Clary obeyed and watched as he picked up a fallen branch, breaking off leaves and twigs until he was left with a makeshift wand as long as his forearm. He walked the circumference of the clearing, drawing a line in the grass. A human would not have seen it, but her witch's sight made out the faint yellow glow he inscribed. When the circle was closed, he turned to her.

He'd regained his composure, even offering a faint smile. "It is far easier to show you than to describe it." And then he raised his hands and spoke words of power, showing what Camelot's enchanter could really do.

Clary blinked and gasped as mist rose from the glowing circle like a cylinder that reached the sky. Then it shimmered into focus, turning to pale stone with arched windows overlooking rolling hills and a pristine sky. The view said they were high up, so high that birds flew below and the horsemen on the green seemed tiny as a child's toy. But the enchantment did not stop there. The illusion rolled toward her like an unfurling carpet, showing a stone floor with brightly woven rugs, shelves of scrolls and ornately bound tomes, a worktable with flasks and jars and a crooked inkwell complete with feather pen. Clary discovered she was sitting on a low bed strewn with furs.

"This is where I worked," he said.

The illusion was remarkable. Clary stroked the furs, even lifting one to see what was underneath. The mattress was far thinner than anything on a modern bed, but it seemed perfectly comfortable. "How did you do this?"

I taught him well, Vivian purred from some distant place inside her.

"It is real," he said. "For a brief time, at least. We are invisible to passersby."

Clary rose and walked to the window. The wide embrasure was cool, the stone gritty beneath her hand. Outside, a breeze snapped the rows of multicolored pennons that decorated the rooftops below. There were a dozen smaller buildings inside a crenelated wall. A drawbridge stretched across a moat guarded by pinnacled towers. Everywhere there were people in medieval clothes—ladies on dainty horses, soldiers and many, many workers. A knight rode across the courtyard, his destrier's feathered hooves clopping on the cobblestones. "This was Camelot," she said, her breath barely above a whisper.

"It was," he said. "It was a time that only remains here, in the kingdom of magic and memory."

"But Camelot still exists," she said, turning to look him in the eye. "Arthur and Gwen have built something new. It doesn't look the same, but it's just as real. It serves the same purpose."

"Of course," he said, the words subdued. "It is not in Arthur's nature to give up."

And neither had he. She could see it in the yearning look he gave the scene outside his window. The light limned the clean lines of his nose and jaw, showing off his austere good looks. She imagined him in the costume he'd worn at Medievaland, with the robe of stars and his wizard's staff. He was indeed her rebel prince of magic, filled with storm and daring. He was everything she'd dreamed of in her future mate.

"This was before the spell that destroyed the fae and damaged the witches," he said, "before the demons were banished and Camelot collapsed. Before I sent the knights of the Round Table into the stone sleep. Yes. This is what I crushed beyond recognition with a single act, and if faced with the same circumstances, I'm not certain I could change anything. Camelot had all but lost the war."

In anyone else, the words would have seemed like self-pity. Merlin was stating plain fact. The only thing that softened his statement was the knowledge that he was still trying to fix his mistake. No one could say he hadn't taken responsibility for what had happened.

He leaned on the side of the window, looking out at the hills. His broad shoulders filled the loose T-shirt he wore, the short sleeves baring his tanned and well-muscled arms. One hand rested on the sill, the fingers curled into a loose fist. Clary put hers over it.

"I will take comfort when I've healed the damage I've done," he said.

"That doesn't mean you can't have company." She leaned forward, leaving a light kiss on his cheek.

His hand turned, catching hers, and squeezed it. "My history should frighten you away."

"I know," she said. "You're the greatest enchanter of all time, and the one who fell the furthest from grace. All the little witches are told to eat their peas so they don't end up like Merlin."

His eyebrows arched. "Now you're mocking me."

But she'd made him smile—almost. "We've figured out a cure for the fae. This story of Camelot isn't over yet."

His gaze melted as if her words had far more power than she knew. This time it was he who kissed her, tugging at the tender flesh beyond her lips. He teased her with his tongue, begging permission to explore. She caught his tongue, sucking it deeper into her mouth, sharing the summer-forest taste of their icy dessert.

All the misgivings she'd felt the night before receded in the face of his grief and the need to show him he was not alone. She had to make him believe there was a future without the pain of loss she felt in his desperate kiss. She cradled his face with her hands, holding him as if he was something precious.

He backed her to the bed, pushing her down to the feather mattress. Clary let herself fall, the soft furs tickling the bare skin of her arms and face. She stretched, luxuriating in the unexpected comfort. But then she saw the heat in his amber eyes and suddenly became self-conscious. The hunger was impossible to mistake.

He bent over, resting his hands on either side of her hips, and bent to kiss the bare strip of skin between her top and the waistband of her jeans. The faint prickle of whiskers made her shiver, and then he kissed her again, just above the first spot. His tongue dipped hot and wet into her navel. She curled forward, her fingers in his thick, dark hair, and then he was on the bed with her, straddling her body as he kissed and licked his way upward. She pulled off her top, abandoning it among the furs. She'd wanted this moment, not as Vivian's host, but for herself. She tugged at Merlin's T-shirt until he stripped it off, revealing the sculpted muscles of his chest and stomach. She ran her hands down his torso with gleeful greed.

He stroked her, the pressure of his fingers deft even

through the fabric of her jeans. She squirmed, arching into it, wanting him with a need that went back to the first time she'd heard his name. Then, he'd been a legend, a mystery to unfold. Now she knew him as a real man. She'd found more grief and less fantasy, but she'd turned her dream into something with value. She found his lips again and drank him in, heart pounding as if she would fly to pieces.

With Vivian and the potion, he'd held himself on a short chain, disciplining an almost violent need. This was equally intense, but tempered with a tenderness she had barely suspected. He was offering her the man he kept hidden behind his chill wall of reserve.

They shed the rest of their clothes, one item at a time. Clary was never sure how much of that was Merlin's magic, spurred on by impatience. He slipped his fingers through her intimate folds, drawing a moan of pleasure from her throat. There was something to be said for a man with a thousand years or more of practice.

And then his fingers slid out and he kissed her there, doing everything she had ever imagined, and then a dozen things more. Pressure built and churned, the eye of the storm low in her belly. Desire spiked in short, sharp bursts, each one tearing a piece of her self-control away. She held on as long as she could, refusing to let the moment end, but that was impossible. Eventually, Clary was forced to surrender, pleasure erupting as magic crackled over her skin. The power was neither his nor hers, but a twining web spun of their combined arousal. She cried out, a sound between jubilation and a sob.

And then he was beside her, pulling her close with an urgency that mirrored her own. He slid inside her, the sensation so intense she came a second time. He began to move, a languid rocking that soothed and made her restless at the same time. Until now, he had barely touched her breasts. Perhaps he had been saving that path to fresh sensation because now he set to work with a will, kneading and sucking and rolling the tips with his tongue. Tension corkscrewed inside her again, driving her to push his gentle rocking to deeper strokes. He met her need and doubled it, going deeper and faster. The magic around them became a snapping corona, flaring as he made his final thrust. He roared, a wordless shout of triumph as he came. Clary crested a moment later, shuddering beneath him a final time.

They fell back, exhausted. Clary curled into his side, their limbs tangling. The air was warm and comfortable, the bed soft as a cloud. She should have fallen asleep, lulled by the soft rhythm of Merlin's breath. His hand stroked her hair, twining the strands through his fingers.

Except her mind would not be still. She'd wanted this, no question. It had been a gift between them, the door opened by his unexpected willingness to share his memories of the Camelot he'd lost. Except...

Her thoughts trailed off, hating her conclusion. Merlin didn't know she still held one of the demons he'd sacrificed everything to destroy.

Don't, Vivian said, her voice profoundly sad. *Nothing but unhappiness lies that way.*

Merlin made a sleepy sound and kissed her ear. She rolled toward him and buried her face in his neck.

Then Vivian did something unexpected. At first, it felt like being dissolved in champagne, a million bubbles popping along every nerve. All at once, Clary was wide-awake, filled with unstoppable energy. Vivian wasn't lurking inside her, like a guest sharing the same house. Not anymore. She'd spread herself through Clary like the liquor in a cocktail, an indivisible part of the mix.

Merlin must have sensed something, because he rose on one elbow. Clary glanced down his long, lean form and wanted to purr. It was a strange kind of sharing, and yet it was perfect. They both got the full benefit of the view—and whatever else was on offer. She drew herself up, pushing him down on the bed and imagining a lengthy menu of treats. Merlin's eyes were half-lidded, almost speculative, but his slow smile was that of a very happy man.

Then the ground shook, and not in a good way.

Merlin leaped from the bed, aware the world he'd left beyond the walls of his remembered tower had changed for the worse. How long had they been there? He couldn't be certain, but it could not have been much more than an hour. He began snatching up clothes, tossing some to Clary and pulling on others. It was only when he did not hear her moving that he turned to look at her.

Her green eyes were panic-stricken. "Come on," he said, touching her cheek and forcing her to meet his eyes. "Remember you are the student of Merlin and a powerful enchantress in your own right."

He'd seen her in her element, using her skills to trap and defeat the thing in the computer. He'd seen her fight the fae and struggle to measure up to her own dreams. Courage like hers was uncommon.

She blinked, as if coming awake, and met his gaze. Her eyes had a luminous quality that was hers alone, and they regarded him with a sweetness that almost made him shy away. He was not used to such affection, especially in this place with all its reminders of disaster. He did not deserve it, and yet he would shed his last blood to keep her from changing her mind about him.

There was every chance that might come to pass. For all the terrible things she knew of him, there was more. And yet he couldn't face that now—he wouldn't. Not so soon after the beauty of their lovemaking. He leaned forward, kissing Clary's velvet mouth once more, drawing out their peaceful interlude for another second. She kissed him back, sipping at his lips as if it were the last time they would ever touch.

Then the ground shook again.

"What is that?" she whispered. Then she seemed to snap out of her daze and hastily began pulling on her clothes.

"It sounds as if they started the apocalypse without us."

He waited until her sneakers were tied and then commanded his replica of the tower to vanish. The bed and other furniture went first with a faint explosion of mist that wafted away on the breeze. The carpet receded to the walls, leaving only the grass behind, and then the walls themselves turned to a thick, gray fog, blotting out the view of Old Camelot. With a final wave of his hand, Merlin cleared the air, and they saw the cause of the disturbance. Far in the distance, a huge stone sailed through the air toward the Lady of the Lake's white tower. When it struck, stone sprayed into the air and the ground shook beneath their feet.

"They're using a catapult," he said, answering the question forming on her face. "I believe it's a trebuchet, to be precise, with just enough magic to break through every ward Lady Nimueh has set around her tower."

"Who is *they*?" Clary asked, her voice rising with panic. She grabbed Merlin's hand, and he squeezed hers in reply.

"The fae armies have arrived." He gave her a thin smile. "Shall we go save the world?"

Chapter 21

They did not run. Merlin had seen too many battles, with enemies waiting in ambush and arrows flying where he least expected them. He held Clary's hand and proceeded with healthy caution toward the goblin tent where he hoped Arthur would be. Their path took them first through the clearing where the food vendors had been. It was empty of people, but fires licked at the wounds in the grass where the tents had been. Food, dishes and even articles of clothing were strewn on the lawn. A dead pixie lay facedown, wings torn like a broken kite. He kept Clary moving, hoping she did not see it.

An ax rested beside the path, meant for chopping wood rather than battle, but he took it anyway. Sometimes a weapon was more efficient than any spell, and he guessed he would need all his magical strength before the day was done. As they reached the main clearing he stopped, Clary's soft form bumping into him.

"What's up?" she asked.

The coast was clear, so he pulled her forward without replying. The stage was empty of musicians now. The tents where the merchants had sold their wares were abandoned. A few had collapsed, the colorful silk deflated over the silhouette of the tables beneath. Others had obviously been looted. The goblin's display of treasures was empty, the ground a trampled mess of mud.

He could see figures running in the distance. He was certain by their swaying gait that the figures were dryads, the tree-people who lived deep in the woods of the Forest Sauvage. They were normally peaceful, but like the Charmed Beasts who spoke the human tongue, they had sided with Camelot and its king after Arthur had saved them from enslavement by the fae.

The white peak of King Zorath's pavilion lay ahead. At least it was still standing. Merlin slowed his steps, pulling Clary close to his side. Guards blocked their approach, but he recognized the two knights at once. Owen of the Beasts stood to the left of the pavilion's entrance, and Beaumains stood to the right, one arm still wrapped in a bandage.

"The king was asking for you," Owen said, the soft Welsh lilt of his voice at odds with his stern expression. "There has been trouble."

"What happened?"

"The king will tell you. He said to send you in immediately when you arrived."

Clary released Merlin's hand. "I should find Tamsin."

"She is with the wounded behind the tent," Owen said.

Merlin caught Clary's arm before she could get away. "If there is the slightest whiff of trouble, come find me."

Her eyes widened, the expression pleased and a little rebellious. "What's to say I'm not the cause of it?"

And then she was gone. The remark had been pure Clary, carelessly flippant, but there was enough truth in it to make Merlin wince a little. There were times when the woman could be marketed as a kind of bipedal land mine.

He shook himself and went in search of Arthur. It didn't take long—he was deep in conversation with Zorath, the goblin king.

Goblins were warty, lumpy, peculiar-smelling creatures and the king had all those qualities in spades. They also came in a variety of hues, including green, blue and a scarlet red. Zorath was red, as wide as he was tall, entirely bald and wore a cloak of ermine and a diamond-studded crown. Merlin bowed low to Zorath as well as Arthur, knowing goblins appreciated a show of respect.

"I'm glad to see you," Arthur said to Merlin in a "where were you?" tone.

"I was on the far side of the grounds," Merlin replied. "What's happened?"

"It was a flock of birds," said Zorath, who looked mightily offended.

"I beg your pardon, Majesty," said Gawain, who approached from Arthur's right. "They were not birds as we know them, but like the creatures who attacked on the tourney ground at Medievaland. I have seen such apparitions in the Forest Sauvage. They were the creatures of the demon Tenebrius, whose stronghold lies not five miles away."

"Great," Merlin muttered under his breath.

"The attack is everything we feared," said Arthur. "The fae and demons are working together to free La-Faye from her prison."

"We're outnumbered three to one, and they're better trained and better armed," Zorath complained. "Could it get any worse?"

"Undoubtedly," said Merlin. "And it probably will, but we don't have any other option. We have to fight."

Merlin had said something similar to Uther Pendragon, Arthur's father, just before a battle. There had been war back then, too—the tangled web of royal families were forever squabbling about who got to wear the crown. The witch-born family of Morgan LaFaye wanted it for their darling little sociopath, and Uther wanted it for his unborn human heir. The king had made Merlin promise to look after the interests of his child. Merlin had believed himself more than capable of looking after a single babe.

Then came the day when he visited Uther's castle, expecting a grand victory celebration. The king had defeated the witches in open battle, and his crown was safe. It should have been the start of a new peace.

But suspicion stiffened Merlin's spine as he galloped through the castle gates. The stable yard was deserted. So was the great hall, the bakery and armory. When Merlin flung open the doors of the feast hall, he found the figures of men slumped around the high table. Even from across the room, he could tell they were knights and lords by their dress. Food sat on great platters of gold, but it crawled with flies. Merlin's stomach churned at the sight, but as he drew closer he saw drifts of dead insects littering the table. Warning sounded deep in his gut.

He touched the first man he came to. Stiffness had obviously left the body, because he rolled easily to one side. Merlin sprang back, pulse jumping as he saw the man's face. It was swollen and blue-black, the skin cracked and crusted with fetid fluids. The few drops of liquid left in his cup might have seemed innocent once, but now was black and sluggish and smelled of something foul.

Merlin's mouth turned dry. Poison. A coward's weapon.

He circled the table slowly, looking at each hideous face and trying to put a name to it. When he got to the red-haired man at the head of the table, the one with the jeweled goblet and wolf's-fur cloak, he recognized Uther. Merlin had failed to protect his friend.

He backed away from the horrible scene, barely able to understand what he saw. He knew what poisons a witch could brew and was certain this was the handiwork of Uther's enemies. With a desperate roar, he bolted up the stairs to the chambers of the queen. Bodies lay in his path—servants, page boys and knights. The poison had reached them all, which made Merlin suspect the castle's central well.

The scene in the queen's chamber was a repetition of all he had seen so far. A pitcher and silver cups sat on a tray, though a few of the cups were scattered as if dropped by a suddenly limp hand. Sunlight slanted in through the high windows, shining mercilessly on the fallen ladies of the chamber. Only the queen's visage had been untouched. She was dead and pale as parchment, but her loveliness was unchanged. She had not drunk the poison, but the blood-soaked sheets told another story. She had died giving birth. Merlin spun around, wondering where the child had gone.

And there it was, a boy, in a basket by the hearth. The ashes of the fire were long cold. Merlin bent over the basket, dreading what he would find. The babe's skin was chilled, his breathing uncertain, but the prince alone lived out of all the castle's occupants. A careless oversight on the assassin's part, and one that would be rectified if word of the heir's survival got out.

Merlin gathered the child up, holding him close to share the heat of his body. Anger bit inside his gut, his chest, the back of his throat. Who did this to their fellow beings? To a mere baby? Merlin's own infancy had been filled with everything a child needed—safety, plenty and love. He'd had much while this child had lost everything. Worse yet, the princeling had lost it because Merlin had underestimated their enemies. If he'd been more suspicious, Uther might still be alive.

There was nothing in the place that was safe to eat or drink, so Merlin rode away at once. He knew a knight, Sir Hector, who lived far from this castle and had a family of his own. It would be safe to hide the prince with him until the boy came of age. Then Merlin would help him reclaim Uther's throne.

Perhaps Merlin wasn't meant to save Britain himself, as his druidess mother had believed, but through a great king. He could teach this Pendragon child, show him the way of statesmen and shape his character. This boy would be wiser than Uther, craftier than his enemies and far, far wiser than Merlin.

He decided to name the boy Arthur.

That boy stood before him now, a grown man with ice-blue eyes and his father's reddish hair. Arthur was every inch a king, but he was still Merlin's friend and, in a way neither man often acknowledged, the orphaned child he'd held in his arms.

"What do you need me to do?" Merlin asked, knowing he'd lay down his life to spare that boy's—or his king's.

"We take the battle to the tower," said Arthur.

Horses were brought for the knights, but the goblins went on foot. A contingent remained behind—including Tamsin and Beaumains—to guard the wounded. Merlin wished Clary would stay behind, as well, until he saw Gawain and Tamsin's farewell. Judging by their heartfelt kiss, he wasn't sure if it was worse to leave the woman he cared for behind or to have her with him as they rode into danger. His one comfort was the improved strength and reflexes the connection with Vivian granted her. Still, he insisted Clary wear light leather body armor and strap a long knife to her hip. He did the same, adding his favorite sword in a back sheath.

Their progress eastward through the forest was quick, as if the path itself opened up to speed their way. Merlin rode at Arthur's side, with Gawain in front and Clary in the relatively safe position behind him. Owen of the Beasts rode beside her, ready to be of assistance since she was not a strong rider. No one spoke, leaving only the clop of hooves and the jingle of harnesses. The woods themselves were quiet, as if every living thing was on alert. That made Gawain's shout to halt easy to hear.

Merlin reined in, straining to see what was the matter. It was only when Gawain edged his horse aside that he saw the fox bowing low in the middle of the path. It was a little larger than an ordinary fox, but it looked otherwise the same, with black stockings and a white underbelly. The only extraordinary marking was the splash of green at the tip of its tail, which marked it as one of the Charmed Beasts of the Forest Sauvage.

Owen made a sound of pleasure, for the fox was his particular companion. No one would call it a pet, however. Charmed Beasts were their own masters, though they had allied with Camelot in return for the protection of the Pendragon kings.

"Greetings, Senec," said Arthur to the fox. "What news do you bring?"

"Your Majesty," replied Senec in a melodious tenor. "The Lady of the Lake sends word to hurry. The defenses of the tower will not last."

"How many fae have come to fetch their queen?"

The fox hesitated. The beasts made excellent spies, but their ability to count was limited. "They brought many soldiers. Enough to fly three different banners."

Three different armies of fae translated to thousands. Arthur held a quick consultation with Zorath, and a large contingent of goblins split off, moving at a quick march to approach the tower from the south. Once that order was given, the king spoke to the fox again. "My thanks to you, Master Senec. I have one more task to ask of you."

"What is your command, Your Majesty?"

"There are eagles among the Charmed Beasts. Do you know their location?"

"Of course, Your Majesty."

"Find them and tell them it is time to summon every creature that will fight with me. It is time to make our stand against the Faery Queen and her demon allies, once and for all."

With a final bow, Senec turned and was gone. The company rode on, sunlight flashing through the leaves and dancing on the knights' armor. The ground rose as they went, passing fast-moving streams fed by mountain snows. Eventually, their path opened onto a broad platform of rock that formed one side of a valley. The white tower stood on the other side and some distance to the south. It was a good vantage point—close enough to see the enemy, but well out of bowshot. It was an excellent point from which to mount a charge.

The white tower rose like a delicate spear of crystal, the thick mountain pines forming a dramatic backdrop. At last Merlin spied the gleam of the enchanted lake that stretched near Lady Nimueh's castle. Unfortunately, it was surrounded by what looked like a living carpet of heavily armed fae. They were packed so thickly and in such number the mountainside below the tower could not be seen.

And crouched in the middle of the throng was the trebuchet, a great wooden machine on wheels at least five times as high as a man. Its base was triangular, the long throwing arm balanced on the point. As Merlin watched, the arm swung forward, its enormous slingshot whipping up and over to cast a huge boulder skyward. The stone cracked against the white tower and the ground shook, making the horses sidle.

Merlin had assumed there was a touch of magic that allowed the assault to pierce the enchantments that defended the castle. Now he could see there was far more to it than he'd assumed. There were fae in blood-red robes standing near the machine, scribing symbols into the boulders they hurled. Demonic symbols. It made sense, but now the magnitude of the magic in play became clear. This was the kind of magic that could turn the Forest Sauvage into a desert, or simply erase it altogether.

Cold, prickling fear ran up Merlin's shoulders and perched at the back of his neck. Arthur turned to him, the glittering chill of his eyes confirming that he knew exactly what was at stake.

"Give the signal," said the king. "We engage now."

Chapter 22

Clary heard Arthur's words and the finality in his voice. It was rare that she, who had grown up without kings, truly understood what his crown meant, but she did then. She felt the burden of it in her gut. His order would cost lives, but not giving it would cost more.

With only a slight hesitation, as if he was thinking the exact same thing, Merlin raised his hand and a bolt of bright green light exploded into the air. The signal. There was an instant of quiet, like an indrawn breath. Her insides went tight, holding a gibbering panic at bay. It felt as if every fae head had just turned their way. They'd passed some point of no return.

Then a storm of goblin arrows flew in perfect unison, buzzing as the fletching caught the air. The first volley had barely risen when a second came from the south, showing the fae were trapped in the bowl of the valley.

Fae shields flew up, deflecting many of the arrows, but a respectable number found their mark.

"Loose!" The goblin king's voice echoed off the valley walls, and another flurry of arrows sailed from the goblins' recurved bows. Zorath had shed his regalia in favor of a studded leather cap that had seen much use. This wasn't his first battle.

Gawain, Owen and Perceval gathered protectively around their king, and it struck Clary how few knights there were. She'd heard the original Round Table had numbered one hundred and fifty, but only a fraction had been found and awakened in the modern age. Two were injured, thanks to Vivian's stunt at Medievaland, old Sir Hector had retired from the battlefield and Lancelot was off guarding the white tower with the Lady of the Lake.

And yet, when the goblins finally charged, so did they. It happened suddenly, with a cry and a churn of hooves and a horrible drop in Clary's heart.

"No, wait!" she cried, half rising from her saddle until Merlin caught her arm.

"Be still," he said, squeezing hard until she met his eyes. "The fae aren't going to leave just because we ask nicely."

"But there is only a handful—"

"We cannot ask allies to fight unless we draw our own swords."

But all she could think about was that Arthur was Gwen's husband and Gawain was her sister's husband-to-be. She didn't want to live in a world without Perceval's impudent laughter or knowing that there was no Owen to nurse stray animals back to health. These weren't the shining knights from the movies—these were people she loved. But then, couldn't that be said of all soldiers?

She sank back to her saddle, trembling with fright and anger. None of this should be happening. The urge to smack LaFaye's perfect face rose like a silent scream. "What do we do?" They were the only ones left behind.

Merlin's expression spoke of banked fury. "What we always do, stand on the balcony while the knights battle below. Except this time our magic is aimed at the enemy."

So the shows at Medievaland had been rehearsals. That gave her a point of reference, at least. "How do we destroy their army without hurting our own?"

Merlin dismounted and then helped Clary down before securing the horses. "First, we take care of the trebuchet. The assault on the tower weakens the spell that keeps Morgan imprisoned."

She looked down the valley at the machine, careful not to let her eyes rest on the chaos of men and weapons. If she saw a friend in trouble, she'd lose her focus. As she watched, the fae released the next shot, and the huge beam swung the catapult. A boulder flew into the air, and this time she could see the corona of dark magic sizzling around it. It crashed into the top of the tower, knocking a layer of stone away. The top of the tower crumbled, leaving only a shard like a broken tooth. Clary's chest hurt at the sight, but her curiosity was stirred. "How come the Faery Queen won't be killed when the tower comes down?"

"The spell that jails her will break before the tower falls altogether. I do not doubt that LaFaye already has an escape plan in place."

The knot of tension in Clary's chest made another

twist. "Let's make sure those plans don't do her any good."

Unexpectedly, he kissed her, his mouth hot and urgent. When he pulled away, he rested his forehead against hers for a moment, his eyes squeezed shut. "Thank you for being here."

Where else could she be, when everyone she cared about was in peril? "I'd say no problem, but it probably will be."

He huffed, a kind of half laugh, and turned to the scene below. Clary stood at his shoulder, folding her arms and frowning down at the blasted machine. Then she pointed. "What's going on there, by the wheels?"

Merlin narrowed his eyes. "Dryads."

They seemed to erupt from nowhere, sinking their long fingers into the wood and tearing it to shreds. As they watched, the fae turned as one toward them, dealing swift death to one of the graceful creatures as the others slipped away, only to reappear and attack a different corner of the machine. Their courage shook Clary to the core.

And yet the trebuchet swung again, sending another missile toward the tower. With a jab of his fingers, Merlin shattered the rock to powder. A roar went up from the battlefield, some voices defiant, others enraged. The strike left him panting.

"Don't stand in the open," he said, pulling her behind a screen of trees. "They know we're here now. And watch for anyone attempting to reach us."

Clary nodded. It was her turn next, and she already had a plan. She could feel Vivian stirring, but the demoness remained inconspicuous, merely nudging Clary's spell where it lacked finesse. With her help, Clary launched a very realistic swarm of hornets upon the fae working the trebuchet. All productivity stopped as the otherwise perfect fae launched into a manic dance of slapping and shaking their cloaks and hair. Meanwhile, the dryads finished their destructive work.

"Good one," Merlin shouted, and launched a fireball at a mounted fae general. It struck him squarely on the breastplate and sent him toppling backward from his horse.

Their run of luck didn't last. The next moment fae rained from the trees, trapping Merlin and Clary in a circle. She recalled Merlin's warning that they'd exposed themselves, but she hadn't heard anyone approach. But then again, all fae moved like shadows.

Merlin's sword left its sheath with a hiss, the motion continuing in a downward slash that killed one attacker before the leaping fae touched the ground. Clary shrieked in pure surprise, but had the wits to draw her knife and fall into a crouch. By then, Merlin had run the second fae through, freeing his sword again by kicking the carcass to the ground. Like all the most experienced knights, his sword work was more efficient than pretty.

Clary counted three fae left. One made a grab for her, but she dodged, sensing Vivian's subtle assistance as she weaved and slid a spell onto the blade. When she slashed, it hit its mark, leaving a red stripe down his arm.

"Go away," she snapped, furious that she'd been forced to cut him. He didn't seem to care, because he lunged with his own blade. She twisted away, slamming her heel into the side of his leg. She heard a horrible, wet crack as he slid off the lip of the valley and went tumbling down the path where Arthur had ridden into the fray. She'd probably dislocated his knee.

When she turned back, the other two fae were dead. Merlin leaned on the point of his sword, sucking in deep breaths. His face and arms shone with sweat, and she could see fresh gashes on his armor. The sword ran with blood, but none of it seemed to be his.

"I've never seen you fight," she said, her voice colorless with the shock of what had just happened. "I thought you just trained for the exercise."

His mouth twisted. "I wish."

Clary's chest squeezed at his tone. Knowing there was nothing useful to say, she watched as he wiped down his sword on a rag torn from the tunic of a dead fae. Unwilling to touch the dead, Clary wiped her knife on the grass and put it away. Her hands began to shake as adrenaline left her system. Now that the crisis was over, her mood was sinking fast.

Merlin spun toward the trees, sword raised. Clary jumped in fright, but this time she could hear someone approaching—not fae, then. As the bushes parted, a tall man came into sight, carrying an unconscious female form. Though she'd met them only once, Clary knew they were Sir Lancelot du Lac and Nimueh, the Lady of the Lake. The powerful enchantress was one of the fae who still had a soul, and one moment in her luminous presence had told Clary everything about what the fae people had lost.

The woman was dressed all in white, but the gown was tattered and muddy, her feet bare and covered in cuts. Her tangled hair was unbound, its silvery length almost reaching the ground. Dulac, as he was known among the knights, was in battered armor, and it was plain that he'd been fighting. Clary nearly dropped to her knees. If Dulac and Nimueh were here now, like this, everything had gone pear-shaped.

Merlin sheathed his sword and sprang forward to help the knight lay his burden on the grass. "Nimueh!" he said, urging the woman to wake. When she didn't respond, he looked up at the knight. "How long has she been like this?"

"Not long, but she's exhausted." The knight's face was pale as he knelt beside his lady. "She fought hard as any warrior, but she cannot hold out any longer."

Clary stepped forward. It was on the tip of her tongue to argue that they simply *had* to keep fighting, but she strangled her fear. It was plain the two had done all they could. "Get your lady to Tamsin. Take my horse. There's a hospital set up at the fairgrounds."

Dulac's steady brown gaze met hers. "Thank you."

Merlin nodded. "Let Nim rest now. We'll need her fireworks later."

As Dulac gathered the unconscious woman in his arms again, an enormous crack resounded over the valley. Clary spun to see a diagonal split crawl across the white stone of the tower. The top half slid off, crashing to the earth in a cloud of dust. The lower portion exploded, fountaining rock into the sky. Flames followed in a rush that reached almost as high as the original spire. They died almost at once, but the point was made. The enchantments that guarded the prison were gone and Morgan La-Faye had escaped. Although she was safely on the other side of the valley, Clary began to tremble.

Dulac galloped away with his lady, barely sparing another word. The Queen of Faery would take revenge on her jailers if they were caught. Clary watched them go, so brave and so weary, and wondered if everything was lost. Merlin touched Clary's shoulder, making her jump and then sag against him. Her throat ached with unshed tears.

A long, piercing note rang over the valley. "That's Gawain's horn," said Merlin. "Arthur has sounded a retreat."

And then he threw a spell into the seething mass of warriors. Like a long bullwhip, it seemed to crack and then ripple outward in a blur of violet light. A demon spell, Clary realized as Vivian fed her the knowledge. One that Merlin had learned from her. It seemed to only touch the fae, and not for long, for as they fell to their knees as if struck, they picked themselves up again almost at once, angrier than ever.

That spell takes a great deal of strength, Vivian explained, *and mastery to ensure it does not hurt your friends. No one could perform it twice in one battle.*

But it gave the retreating army a moment, and that was what they needed. Swords swung and spears stabbed, and Clary could see clearly now how badly outnumbered Camelot's allies were. The goblins had borne the brunt of the fight, and far too many lay dead on the valley floor. The remainder took the opportunity to escape.

Arthur and his men reached Clary and Merlin just minutes later, along with the goblin king. A sob of relief escaped Clary. Perceval had an impressive gash over his eye, but they were all alive. The two kings listened grimly as Merlin, leaning with exhaustion against a tree, told them about the Lady of the Lake's flight.

"We must regroup," said Arthur.

"And do what?" Zorath demanded, his voice rough with grief.

Arthur said nothing, his face like stone. Clary bit her tongue, wanting to butt in, but she had nothing useful to say. They couldn't give up, and everybody knew it, but what hope did they have to win?

Merlin broke into the uncomfortable silence. "We have to move before the fae pursue us. There is nothing to be gained if our retreat becomes a rout."

Clary was about to point out that she'd given her horse away when she saw something in the sky. "Look!"

Everyone turned to see the eagles soaring into the late-afternoon sky. She saw a pair, and then two more, and then there seemed to be dozens splitting off in a dozen directions. "Master Senec has delivered my message," said Arthur. "The eagles of the Charmed Beasts are summoning our distant allies."

But seconds later something else was in the air. Scraps of black floated upward from the treeline, seeming to tumble and waver more than fly. They were fast, though, matching the eagles for speed. When a handful caught up to one of the majestic birds, they swarmed it, and moments later the eagle plummeted to earth.

"No!" Clary exclaimed under her breath, not just for the eagle but for the hope it had represented.

"Hellspawn," Gawain snarled. "That is the work of the demon Tenebrius."

Arthur shifted in his saddle, seeming to come to a decision. He turned away from the sky and looked them each in the eyes before turning to his enchanter. "You asked me what I need you to do," he said to Merlin. "I need you to cure the fae, however impossible that may seem. The only way to win this war is to turn them against their own queen."

Chapter 23

The enormity of Arthur's demand left Merlin hollow, but he had promised Uther Pendragon that he would safeguard his child. He had promised his mother to safeguard their people. And there was an inevitability to the task. Merlin's errant spell had damaged the fae, and he had sworn long ago to heal that wound. Perhaps the unlucky stars that cursed his existence had finally aligned. Maybe this was his moment to make things right.

"I agree," he replied. "This is not a war we will win in open battle. This was our only chance for that, and we lost."

"Do you have a plan?" Arthur asked. "Is there anything you need to carry it out?"

"My student—" he nodded to Clary "—and another horse. She rather generously gave hers away to Dulac."

There were no spare mounts, so Perceval offered his. Minutes later Merlin was cantering to the west, Clary just managing to keep up. When they finally reined in, she was breathing hard. "Where are we going?" she asked. "What is this plan of yours?"

The sky had turned to the dusky blue of early evening, that rich color that came the hour before sunset. The sunlight had turned Clary's skin to a pale honey shade. He watched as she self-consciously combed her fingers through her wild mop of hair. Somewhere in her past there must have been people who told her that if she only dressed like a lady or tamed that spiky tangle of locks, she might have been beautiful. That would be like telling a wood violet to climb into a window box, or a robin to sit quietly in a cage. It made no sense. She was flawed and unruly, and that was part of her perfection.

He realized she was waiting for an answer. Reluctantly, he turned his thoughts back to the coming disaster. "It's more of a guess than a plan."

Her look was dubious.

"It's a good guess," he said, just a little defensively. "Do you remember the fae Laren and Angmar dragged away?"

"Yes. I doubt I'll forget them trashing my hotel room anytime soon."

He supposed not. "Angmar called me just before we left for the Forest Sauvage. I'd given them a sample of the demonic essence that corrupted my laptop. It restored the soul of the fae who attacked you, just as a taste of your soul cured Laren."

Clary's eyes widened, showing off their green depths. "Really? I guess it kind of makes sense. The demon essence, or whatever they call it, must have demon DNA. Do demons have DNA? And why does demon DNA restore fae souls?"

Merlin shrugged. "Because it was a demon spell that stole them." He really hoped it was that simple. There was a lot of guessing going on in the conversation, but that was the problem when it came to demons. Nothing about them played by ordinary rules.

"However," he continued, "an enormous number of soulless fae requires an enormous amount of demon essence for a cure. Happily, the material Tenebrius used to infect the computer was extremely dense. A modest amount will go a very long way."

A silence fell as she digested that. An evening breeze was rising, bringing the smell of earth that had baked in the sun.

"And so you think if we got our hands on more of that goop, we could use it to dose the fae?" she asked.

"Yup. And on a battlefield a whole lot of fae will be in one convenient place."

"I couldn't figure out a good disbursement model," she said. "I couldn't figure out the math."

"Container." Merlin made a shape with his hands. "Spell." He mimicked an explosion, with particles raining on the earth below.

"Oh." She nodded her understanding, but didn't look enormously happy about it. The light was fading, blurring and softening her features. A distant bird trilled its evening song. "And so where are we going to get the goop?"

"Tenebrius had it, or at least I assume he was the one who did, to carry out the attack on Camelot's tech. Only a top-level demon ever has access to their essence. I'm hoping he has more stored there." He pointed at a distant roofline that appeared past a broad apple orchard. "That's his castle."

"Are you crazy?" Her words were quick and low. "When Gawain and Tamsin went there, they barely got out alive."

"Do you have any other ideas where to get what we need?" He nudged his horse forward, picking up the broad trail that led through the abandoned orchard. "I don't think demon goop is available online, though I've never checked the dark web."

Clary made an exasperated noise, but followed. "What do you want me to do?"

"I can send you back home, if you prefer."

"And sit around biting my nails? No, thanks."

"Good, because someone has to tell Arthur if my plan doesn't work."

It was almost too bad that Vivian had gone dormant. He could have used her firepower. But if it was only magical talent he needed, he would rather have taken Nim. Gawain would be a far better guard, or Master Senec a better spy. But Clary alone understood the whole problem, from Laren to the laptop to Tenebrius's betrayal of Vivian. She'd proven herself a fighter and could think on the fly. All things considered, Merlin couldn't wish for a better partner.

They rode in silence through the rows of trees, the horses' hooves muffled on the soft ground. Green apples were just forming on the trees, filling the air with a hint of their tartness. The beauty of the place was broken once, when they found the corpse of an eagle. It was one of the Charmed Beasts they'd seen attacked, and its feathers were all but torn away.

"This means Tenebrius left LaFaye and came this way," he said. "Another reason to remain alert."

Clary nodded, tears standing in her eyes as she gazed at the fallen bird. They stopped just long enough to bury it in the loamy soil and then resumed their ride.

The moated grandeur of the demon's castle loomed ahead. Twin towers guarded an archway that framed a portcullis and drawbridge. No guardsmen were visible, but that didn't fool Merlin for a moment. The place would be watched.

When they reached the edge of the orchard, they stopped again. The first stars were showing against an indigo sky as he dismounted. "I could tell you to stay here with the horses, but I doubt anywhere in this area is safe."

She dismounted stiffly. He was sore, so she had to be in minor agony. "If it's all the same to you, I'd rather stay close."

He nodded, scanning the drawbridge and towers. Using magic would act like a beacon. If he was going to get in quietly, he would need to use old-fashioned burglary skills. "Can you swim?" he asked, eyeing the moat. At least there was nothing nasty about the water itself or the stream that fed it.

"Sure. I was a lifeguard in college."

"Good. If anything touches you in the water, kill it. It might just be a fish, but I wouldn't take any chances."

They removed their armor, shoes and weapons, keeping only their knives. Barefoot, they crept to the water's edge. Merlin slid into the moat without making a noise and dove, the chill darkness swallowing him whole. He kicked forward, sensing the movement of water that meant Clary was behind him. The distance to the castle's outer wall wasn't far for a strong swimmer. He came up for breath when he touched stone, but still barely raised his head above the waterline. He knew from Gawain's adventures in this place that there was a watergate that led to the castle yard. Clary bobbed up beside him, spitting out water. Merlin pointed to his left, and they began their search for the gate.

It didn't take long, but they were wet and cold once they were back on land. Lights shone inside the main keep and guided them across the yard.

"How do we get inside?" Clary whispered.

Merlin craned his neck to see a window above. It was just an opening in the stone, without glass or shutters, but it was large enough to climb through if they could reach it.

Clary followed his gaze. "Give me a boost."

He did, feeling the distracting blend of muscle and softness as he hoisted her upward. Then, like a shadow, she was through the window. Merlin dug his fingers into the stone and, using main strength and bruising his toes, followed her upward. When he pulled his chin over the broad sill, he saw the window opened into an empty passageway. With another heave, he swung himself up and in.

Clary was crouched against the wall, all but invisible in the shadows. Her tense posture told him she felt the heavy atmosphere of the keep the same way he did. Dark magic filled the place, thick and cloying, as if the air was filled with heavy smoke. There was no smell, and yet a sense of alarm filled him, primal as a fear of flames. It was the scent of a predator, and they were the prey.

He crouched beside Clary, putting an arm around

her to stop her shivering. "Gawain said there was a library in this tower," he said, keeping the words barely audible. "We should start our search there."

They rose as one, thinking they were safe for that moment. They had been quiet, so quiet, and yet not silent enough. Merlin looked toward the staircase, but the shadows thickened into a solid shape that turned and tilted its head to fix them with a black, glittering eye. It wore a hooded robe that hid most of its face, but he knew what was beneath the folds of cloth. It had no name, but he'd seen it long ago. It was Tenebrius's watchman and a kind of horrific pet. It had the face of a crow, the body of a man and the appetite of a ghoul.

He gave Clary a shove in the opposite direction, and she ran. The crow sprang forward, the hood falling back to show its razor beak. Merlin had no weapon but his knife, which seemed tiny against the slashing talons of the creature's hands and feet. He snapped a kick to its chest, grabbed the beak and twisted, smashing it headfirst into the wall. Then he ran for all he was worth. Clary was far down the hall, and he had to sprint to catch up. He could hear the birdman stirring and knew the smart thing would be to get out of sight.

There was a door ahead, with a round arch and a plain iron knob. Clary looked over her shoulder, a question in her eyes. Merlin nodded, and they ducked through the entrance. Merlin fished his key chain from his pocket, and lit the tiny flashlight he kept there. It was cheap and the beam was small, but it worked well enough when magic wasn't a good option. The light revealed an earthen tunnel that existed, for no apparent reason, twenty feet above the ground.

"Demon tunnel," Clary said softly. "How come we

got in?" She was pressed against him, shivering slightly in her wet clothes. He pulled her closer.

"This might not lead anywhere," he said, choosing not to answer. "Sometimes they were built for storing things the demons wished to conceal."

"Like the goop we're looking for?"

"Exactly."

They walked on a few steps. The space was honeycombed with chambers, though most appeared empty. Merlin swept the beam around, then up, and then in the corners just in case of snakes.

"You know about these places," Clary said, keeping no more than two steps away. "Vivian must have taught you about them."

It was a statement, but he knew there was a question inside it. "Yes, as her student I lived in her household for some time before the demons were exiled to the Abyss."

She was watching him closely, and he wondered how much Vivian had told her about those days before she'd gone dormant. Some things were best left alone. Vivian, of all people, would know that. It was with some relief that he found a chamber with shelves to the ceiling, each one overloaded with objects. "Here," he said, leading her forward.

The room had a moldy smell as if some of the contents were ancient. On the first shelf alone there were earthenware jars that looked vaguely Egyptian, wooden apple boxes filled with old uniforms and an ice-cream maker still in its original box. Demons were natural pack rats. The next held magical paraphernalia, most of it old and rickety. The third shelf held only one object, and Merlin knew it was what he was looking for. It was oblong and papery, like a giant egg or cocoon, and about the size of a football. But it wasn't the appearance that told him that this object alone held demonic essence. It was the aura that radiated from it, the same suffocating dread he'd sensed in the hallway above.

Yes, he'd lived with demons. At first, he'd thought them all-powerful, and then he had seen them as simply *other*—a species that didn't quite belong. Like a foreign plant that escapes the garden into the wild, they overran the other species around them. What they wanted, they took—livestock, houses, children, wives. It was easy to believe they'd come from some other world where there might be natural predators to keep them in check.

Merlin had understood it all the day Tenebrius had found a tiny Hebridean village that sat on an island the demon desired for himself. He'd drawn a claw across the throat of every inhabitant and tossed their corpses into the sea. Then he had done the same to the neighboring islands and burned any house that spoiled his view.

After that, Merlin fled from the demons, ashamed of his association with them. Ashamed that he had studied at their feet. Revolted by what they were, and what his time with them said about him. It was only when Arthur had begged him to rid the mortal world of the demon scourge that he had returned to Vivian one last time. He'd gone back to betray her by stealing her battle spell, and then that had horribly backfired. He should have known that nothing good ever came from a demon.

The thought made him wonder what terrible blunder he was making now. Yet now, as before, he couldn't see another way forward. The object on the shelf before him was the fae's best hope, Camelot's hope, and maybe even redemption for himself.

"What are you thinking?" Clary asked, worry puckering her brow.

"Nothing good."

He reached out, grasping the container, and lifted it from the shelf. It was solid, but not terribly heavy. Still, it took all his willpower not to drop it and back away in disgust. It hummed with energy, the thousand upon thousand potential individuals swimming in an unformed state. This was the primordial ooze of demons, and Tenebrius had tried to weaponize it. Merlin tucked the egg under his arm, hating the papery feel of the cover. It felt like dead skin.

He glanced at Clary, using the sight of her as an antidote to his mood. They'd found what they needed and they could leave this place. The egg might give them a cure. There was still a chance to turn everything into a win.

Clary gasped, her face turning to a mask of horror. "Snakes!"

Chapter 24

The strip of winding shadow struck, arching into the air. Speed blurred all detail, but Merlin saw the flash of deadly fangs aiming for his leg. His power flared, but he throttled it at the last moment, remembering the danger of using magic here in Tenebrius's private domain. Saving himself would expose Clary.

But she moved fast, driving her knife through its skull. Merlin jumped back to see her blade quivering in the stone floor, the serpent pinned like a specimen in a display case. Its tail twitched once, and was still. She backed away slowly, disgust twisting her features.

"How did I do that?" she asked hoarsely.

Merlin let out a shaking breath. Lucky for him that even if Vivian was dormant, she'd left some of her reflexes behind. But there was no time to talk about that now. Another rope of darkness skittered across the floor in a strange, sidewinding motion. Clary squeaked as it twisted toward her.

Without thinking, Merlin scorched it with a handful of flame. For an instant, the serpent glowed bright white edged in orange, its body stretching and drooping like molten glass, and then it collapsed to ash. Clary grabbed his arm, fear and gratitude plain in her tight grip. As the light faded from the ash, the room grew dark, and that was even worse. Merlin knew there would be more snakes hiding in the inky shadows. There always were.

"We need to leave," he said softly. "I've used magic, and now Tenebrius will know we're here." He'd managed to stifle his power when it came to himself, but he hadn't been able to hold back when she was at risk.

Clary swore under her breath, then freed her knife from the stone floor. "How do we get away without running into more wildlife?"

Merlin considered. Even if they survived the snakes on their way back to the main castle, the creature with the crow's head was outside the door to these hidden rooms. Plus, they'd already tripped whatever magical alarm system the demon employed. A speedy getaway would be more valuable than a stealthy one.

With one hand, he drew an archway in the air. A thin line of luminous white followed his fingers as if he was sketching with light. The white thickened and seemed to crack apart, like the seal around a door. Brilliant blue rays escaped the gap like windblown banners, flaring wide. With a swipe of his hand, Merlin cleared the doorway, settling it back to black. Soon the dark orchard shimmered into view. The branches of the trees swayed in a silent wind he could not feel. It was just an image, the reality far away—and yet close enough to reach in two strides. With the egg of demonic essence under his arm and Clary's hand in his, he stepped through the portal.

The horses whickered as they stepped out of nowhere, but stood obediently as Merlin stashed his prize in the saddlebags. Merlin and Clary donned the clothing and equipment they'd shed to enter the moat and within a minute, they'd mounted and set off at a brisk pace.

They rode in silence as if holding their breath. It was possible that Tenebrius wouldn't notice the egg was missing for some time, the same way no one noticed a missing golf club until it was time to use it. All the same, Merlin expected spies, or magical trip wires or a perimeter alarm to sound as they left the orchard for the road. Nothing came.

"That was too easy," Clary finally muttered.

He wanted to tell her not to jinx their good fortune. Instead, he tried for a reasonable explanation. "Perhaps the demon goop masks our presence."

"What, like disguising our scent?"

"Perhaps."

But he might have spoken too soon. He reined in, hearing a sound like the wind in a ship's sails. It was moving across the sky toward them like low, rhythmic thunder. His chest tightened so hard it felt as if his heart had been forced to beat sideways. Without hesitation, he nudged his horse into the cover of the trees, grateful when Clary's mount automatically followed. They hid just in time. The creature in the sky flew low, the skirts of its tail rustling against the tips of the trees. A smell like rotting carrion swamped them, making the horses stamp and quiver. Merlin's own stomach did an uneasy roll.

"Tenebrius, in his hunting form," Merlin whispered.
They said nothing more, watching the dark shape
pass over them. He reached forward, patting his horse's
neck and whispering comfort into its flattened ears. The
spell was small and simple, yet it was enough to keep
their mounts from panic until the demon was gone. Even
in the dark, they could see the great carrion bird had
savage claws and a beak hooked like a scythe. But it
moved on without pausing or so much as looking their
way. It was searching for something or someone else.

He waited a few minutes, then a quarter hour, listening to the wingbeats pounding the air. They seemed to
go north, then east. Once they faded, Merlin continued
to listen, his ears almost physically straining to catch a
last clue to the demon's destination. If he hadn't been on
another mission, curiosity would have made him follow.

They waited a long time to ensure the coast was
clear before they moved. Then Merlin turned his horse's
head toward the fairgrounds and set off at a gallop with
Clary at his heels.

As with most trips, the road back seemed shorter.
Even so, the sky was turning from the black of midnight to the indigo of earliest dawn when they crested
the ridge that marked the halfway point of their journey. From there, the path they followed descended to
a wider road that ran the length of the forest. Merlin
almost relaxed, but then he saw a flash as steel caught
the silvery gleam of starlight. Alarmed, he reined in,
signaling Clary to do the same.

"What is it?" she asked in a barely audible voice.

"Fae." Now that he knew they were there, he could
see past the glamour that hid the army. Thousands of
soldiers marched along the road below, their column

stretching as far as he could see in either direction. Their armor did not match, but nonetheless it gleamed with careful polishing. White hair hung in long braids, and slender hands held bows that curved like wicked smiles. They moved silently, as only the fae could. Merlin sat straighter in his saddle, the awareness of danger awakening his own urge to fight. LaFaye must have ordered the hills of Faery emptied to gather this army.

Clary reached out to touch Merlin's arm, and then she silently pointed. Merlin followed her gaze to a small figure on a gray mare. Merlin's stomach burned with sudden hate. He knew that dark-haired woman from a hundred nightmares. It was Morgan LaFaye herself, freed from Nimueh's prison. Beside her horse's head was Tenebrius, striding in step with the others. He was dressed as usual in beautiful silken robes and seemed utterly relaxed as if he hadn't just flown there in haste to greet them.

The queen turned to say something to the demon, and Merlin caught a glimpse of her face. The pale oval was indistinct at that distance, and yet he knew it was the same as they'd seen in the laptop, exotic and beautiful as a poisonous bloom. Merlin clenched his fists on his horse's reins, making the beast toss its head.

"Where are they going?" Clary asked.

"I don't know," Merlin replied, wishing again he had the leisure to spy on Tenebrius and the queen. "But if I don't get to safety with this egg, it won't matter."

It would have been so easy to draw another portal, or send a message through a spell, but Merlin knew La-Faye would sense another enchanter's magic this close. He'd take that risk for himself, but Clary was no match for the Queen of Faery or for Tenebrius. He would have to rely on other skills. Merlin turned his horse's head and retraced his steps, leading them away from the marching fae at a brisk pace. As if there weren't enough reasons to hurry, soon dawn would deprive them of the cover of darkness.

He glanced at Clary's worried face. "Change of plan," he said. "We can't get back to Arthur. This army blocks our path."

"I guessed that much," she said, and he saw how tired she looked. "Where can we go?"

There was only one place he knew of in the forest with strong walls, decent beds and no monsters. "The castle at Camelot."

Her look was pure confusion. "Camelot?"

"You were expecting a five-star hotel?"

"Wasn't Camelot in England?"

"The castle is here, too." It was not the same place where the Knights of the Round Table had lived so long ago, but an almost-identical twin created by the magical realm for reasons deeper than anyone knew. It was solid enough, every detail preserved without decay down to the raisins in the larder and the oats in the barn. The main difference was that none of people who had lived and worked in the real place dwelled in this twin. To Merlin, the joyless silence made going there like visiting a grave. Tonight, however, that grave was their refuge.

The path he took led them through the deepest part of the forest, where the track disappeared in places and in others led them to bogs, or bramble patches or streams too treacherous to ford. Merlin, however, knew the land and found a route despite its tricks. All the same, dawn was breaking by the time the castle came into view. It stood on a rise overlooking the surrounding land, the round, pointed towers and crenelated walls gleaming in the rosy light. He heard Clary's indrawn breath and saw delight wash the fatigue from her face.

"It looks like something from a storybook. Which tower is yours?"

Her words struck dagger-sharp. "It's not here anymore. It hasn't been since Arthur banished me after the war." Arthur's wrath had been worse than any punishment, but Merlin had deserved it after what he had done to the fae.

She stared in disbelief. "But you're not banished anymore."

"It is true that I am welcome at Arthur's court again," Merlin agreed. "It seems the forest still has reservations." He spurred his horse forward, putting an end to the discussion.

They passed over the drawbridge and between the towers that guarded the entrance, the hooves of their mounts ringing off the walls. The sound crawled over Merlin's skin as if an invisible pen were writing out his sins in a tattoo. It was too quiet here, just like in Uther's castle of death.

They found the stables and tended the horses before anything else. Caring for one's mount was the first lesson any warrior learned, and they'd ridden the poor beasts hard. Besides, if magic failed they were the only means of escape. He had to be sure they were there for Clary.

She got as far as removing her animal's saddle before she sank onto an old three-legged stool and leaned against the side of the stall, her face white with fatigue. She watched Merlin work, her eyes slightly glazed. "I should be helping you," she said, voice thick with guilt.

Merlin had been watching her fade, and smiled at her words. "Rest and don't worry about it. I'll look after both horses."

She lifted her head, blinking owlishly. "You need to be doing stuff. Magical stuff. I should be doing this."

Clary was tired to the point of being useless, but she wouldn't thank him for pointing that out. "Physical work is good for thinking."

That much was true, and he liked the warmth and smell and gentle sounds the horses made. Merlin was reluctant to end the peaceful interlude, knowing it would be the last. Finally, though, he retrieved the egg from the saddlebags. "Let's go inside." He put an arm around Clary and led her toward the keep.

"To a nice, soft bed?"

He nodded. That was where she was going—to Guinevere's old chamber. It was hung with green silk and the bed was piled high with down pillows. Plus, Arthur had built his queen a bathing chamber lined with a mosaic of tiny marble tiles. Clary could sleep there safely and in as much luxury as the forest could provide. They entered the door of the keep, and Clary halted for a moment to stare openmouthed. The grand entrance was hung with colorful banners. Weapons and shields hung on the walls, evoking all the pomp and grandeur of Arthur's court. To one side was a sweeping stone staircase, the banister carved in the likeness of a sinuous dragon with its head as the newel post. He observed her wonderment with a twinge of pride. The old place hadn't lost its sparkle.

He helped her up the stairs to the chamber he sought. "Rest," he said, giving her a gentle kiss as he sat her down on the bed.

Clary looked up at him, cracking an enormous yawn. "I can't just sleep. What's happening with Arthur? What's that army doing? Don't you have a big spell to prepare?"

All that was true, but she'd pushed herself to the point of exhaustion. He kissed her again, this time on the forehead. "A warrior sleeps while she can, because she doesn't know when the next opportunity will be."

"And what are you going to do?" she asked, stifling another yawn she obviously resented.

"Nothing much. I'll be back in a few minutes."

It was a lie, but she was already settling back onto the bed, too exhausted to notice. He left the room before she could argue, carrying the egg back to the main floor, and then down another staircase into the bowels of the earth. Few people knew that Camelot had a dungeon, much less how to reach it, but Merlin did. He'd put it there, after all.

This was where the battle would be won or lost, and he had a great deal of work to do before everything came to an end.

Chapter 25

Clary woke with a start, unaware that she had even fallen asleep. She pushed off a thick blanket that had been spread over her. She didn't remember it from when she'd first entered the room, so she guessed Merlin had checked on her at some point. The thought brought heat to her cheeks. For months all he'd done was scold or challenge her, or teach her in that strangely terse but patient way he had. Tenderness still wasn't something she was used to from him. As she sat up, she realized he'd also pulled off her shoes. The sight of them lined up neatly beside the bed made her stomach do an odd flip. They'd stripped when they'd made love, but caring for her as she slept seemed twice as intimate.

Light streamed through the open shutters of the window, telling her that the day was far advanced. There was a bathing room adjacent to the bedchamber with a round wooden tub that was filled with water scented with rose petals. A minor spell heated it enough that Clary was able to wash thoroughly and dry herself with the soft linen towels folded beside the tub. A change of clothes was laid out on a nearby trunk. Merlin again? Clary guessed the hip-length tunic and loose pants were made for a page or squire. They were far from flattering, but they sort of fit and they were clean.

She pulled on her shoes and went back downstairs, looking for Merlin and breakfast. She would have called his name, but the formality of Camelot's castle, with its intricate sconces and miles of embroidered tapestries, awed her. For all that she loved Medievaland, she was a hamburger and binge-TV kind of girl. Besides, she had no guarantee what might show up if she began shouting at the top of her lungs.

She wandered outside the huge front doors, vaguely remembering from history class that castle kitchens were in a separate building so that they couldn't burn everything down. She began a circuit of the yard, pausing to say hello to the horses and finding a smithy and a carpenter's workspace before finally locating the kitchen.

It was there she found Merlin sitting at a large trestle table and frowning into a cup of smelly herbal tea. The familiarity of the image struck her. The wood, brick and sparse furnishings were a lot like his apartment. His decorating choices, not to mention his fondness for weird beverages, weren't fashion forward, as she'd assumed. They were what he was used to.

When she sat on the bench across from him, he pushed a platter of cheese, fruit and nuts her way. "Sorry it's a bit primitive, but this is what was in the kitchen stores," he said. "Breakfast cereal hasn't been invented yet."

She fell on the food while Merlin poured her a cup of the tea, which turned out to taste better than she expected. In fact, everything did. It might have been a function of her hunger, but she didn't think so. This was food as it was meant to be, pure, raw and grown as nature intended. She had to force herself to chew slowly before she inhaled it and gave herself a stomachache.

Merlin watched her with something like amusement in his amber eyes. "I trust you slept well?"

"Like a rock," she said around a bite of the soft, creamy, white cheese. "What about you?"

He looked into his tea. "I caught a nap. I had things to do."

It must have been a short nap, judging by the circles under his eyes. Grim lines framed his mouth. She reached out and put a hand to his cheek, feeling the brush of his stubble. "Talk to me." It was a demand, not a plea.

His glance was sharp, but she saw his defensiveness wane and she caught his gaze and held it. "I sent a message to Arthur, telling him where we were and what we'd seen," he said. "I expect he'll join us here. This castle is defensible."

"Won't we be sitting ducks? LaFaye will know exactly where we are."

Merlin's smile was sharp. "There are some advantages to that."

Like gathering all the fae in one place so that they could cure them. That led to another question. "Where's the egg?"

"I put it in a safe place and, to borrow your slang, warded the hell out of it."

"Do you know how we're going to use it when the time comes?"

"I have some ideas." He'd put a hand over hers where it touched his face. He pressed his lips into her palm, sending tingles up her arm and into her core. When he looked up, his eyes were hot with an emotion she couldn't quite read. "I don't know what will happen in the next twenty-four hours, but parts of it will be ugly."

Her breath stopped for a moment, but she deliberately calmed herself. "I know."

She felt Vivian stir. The demoness had been unusually quiet that morning, but now her presence reminded Clary of just how much she was hiding from Merlin. She had no illusions that they'd make it through an entire battle without Vivian showing up.

If you are going to destroy LaFaye and her demon allies, Vivian said in something close to a growl, *you will indeed need my help. I have knowledge only a demon can provide. Together we shall crush them to ash.*

Which was great for Camelot, but would probably kill her. Even if it didn't, there was the whole demon-ex-girlfriend-in-my-brain issue. Clary's relationship with Merlin would be toast.

Merlin was studying her expression. Whatever he saw there did nothing to lighten his mood.

"Come." He held out a hand. "There's something I want to show you while we have a little time."

"How much time?"

"Enough. The fae are still hours away, and I have prepared everything that I can."

She rose from the table and grasped his fingers. His skin was warm from the earthenware cup he'd been holding, and the sun caressed her shoulders as they stepped back into the courtyard.

All the same, his words sent a chill through her. Whatever was going to happen was not far off now. The happiness they had in that moment, in the sun and quiet of Camelot, was measured in scant hours.

She moved close to him, wanting to lean into him like an affectionate cat. On a primitive level, she recognized his physical strength and skill as a warrior. He was also the greatest enchanter in the mortal realms. It was natural that she would turn to him for protection, but there was more to her need than that. He understood her. He saw Clary Greene for herself.

The whole time she'd been his student, from the first lesson to their adventures in the demon's castle, he'd watched over her but never stifled her. He'd let her take her share of danger and learn from her mistakes. No one had ever shown that much confidence in her. No one had cared enough to give her that much space while still catching her every time she fell. For that reason, she was as prepared as she could be for whatever job she'd be asked to do in this war.

He was ever thus, Vivian said, startling Clary. *Some lovers try to grant one's every wish. He will teach you to grant your own wishes. Sadly, fools mistake that for lack of passion. They don't see the genuine care in his actions.*

For a demon, thought Clary, that was deep insight.

I've learned much from you, said Vivian. *One cannot be a teacher without having the curiosity of a student.*

Clary couldn't help wondering what on earth her demon visitor was finding in the chaos of her brain.

That mortal relationships are as complicated as a painting. So many colors. So many layers, one atop the other until it is the combined effect that we see. A de-

*mon's existence is far simpler in that regard, but I am
grateful to understand another point of view.*

With that, Clary sensed Vivian fading into the background once more, no doubt to dig up some new and
juicy contradictions from her subconscious. Or plot
some suicidal revenge fantasy against her demon buddies. Yup, there was nothing but good times ahead.

Merlin led her to a garden behind the keep, set out
in neat squares like a checkerboard. Clary recognized
many of the herbs from her studies. Some were for
cooking, some for dyeing cloth and others for medicine. The combination of scents made an intoxicating
aroma in the warm sun. Bees swarmed the plants, the
low buzzing an instant invitation to a nap. Merlin drew
her to an arbor festooned in a red and white climbing
rose. Clary paused to sniff the striped petals.

"This variety of rose has disappeared from modern
gardens," said Merlin, touching a cluster of blossoms
with something like affection. "But that's not what I
brought you here to see. Go through the archway."

Clary did, and stepped from day to night. She spun
around, looking up into a sky crowded with stars. Beneath her feet was an endless stretch of pale sand.
"What is this?"

"It's from your book," he said with a lopsided smile. "An
oasis in the wide desert, alone with the midnight stars."

She spun around to see the same unlikely purple tent
as on the cover of her favorite romance. Gold fringe
festooned the sides, and lamps of pierced metalwork
hung from poles staked in the sand. The lamps threw
elaborate patterns of light on the sides of the purple
silk, tiny cousins to the stars above. A slight distance
away, she saw the lumpy silhouette of a sleeping camel.

Beyond the tent was a dark pool surrounded by palms that waved languidly in the breeze.

"Awesome," she whispered, unable to find her voice.

He came up behind her and his hands slid around her waist. "It is a fantasy, nothing more."

But it was *her* fantasy, her favorite one, and he'd remembered it. She closed her eyes and leaned back against his chest where the steady beat of his heart reassured her. "I always came here in my mind when I needed to escape. You made it real."

She understood why he'd done it. With demons and fae and war, anything could happen. They might never have another chance to be together. This might be farewell.

"Come inside the tent," he said, distracting Clary from her dark thoughts.

The tent flaps were already drawn up, showing a spacious interior. A scatter of Oriental carpets covered the floor, creating a thick, springy surface. An ornate couch—or bed, she couldn't tell which—occupied one end of the space. The other held a table covered in golden dishes. Clary looked closer, lifting a cover to release a cloud of spiced steam. Clary identified saffron rice, almonds and a medley of pears, squash and roast lamb in a peppery sauce.

"There are figs in honey," Merlin pointed out, "spiced wine, and shaved ice with quince and lemon."

Clary knew without asking that these were his weaknesses. A pang of uncertainty assailed her until she saw yogurt pretzels, pumpkin pie and a golden platter laden with neat rows of seafood tacos. Her weaknesses.

"You know what I like." She shouldn't have felt so astonished, but she was. "You know what we both like."

"There is fantasy enough for us all," he said softly and

turned her in his arms. She slid against him, her body fitting perfectly in his embrace. "There is enough to please every part of you, which is what I want to do right now."

Merlin was seducing her. He'd built an entire world to do it. Clary tried to swallow, but her tongue was thick and unruly. "You don't need fantasy," she said. "You had me the moment you remembered the oasis. That was the real you, not any daydream."

He gave a slight shrug. "If you've got the magic…"

She kissed him then, taking his mouth with all the frank hunger that rose in her like a drug. He tasted of tea and of himself. She gripped his shoulders, rising on her toes to balance as she drank him in. When the kiss finally broke, she drew a deep breath. "You built this place for my dreams. Where are yours? What do you want?"

Merlin hesitated. "I want you to be happy." Every last, delicious inch of her.

The scene he'd created was born of the same skills the demons used to create their pockets of comfort in the wastelands of the Abyss. Once in a rare while, he appreciated the beauty their power could weave. Was it possible that their legacy was capable of good or ill, and the outcome dependent on the one who wielded it? Some people said that of guns. Others said guns were a temptation to do wrong.

Merlin wanted to believe he could make things come out right. He knew better than to think one woman's love could change him—he had to do the work himself—but she could make the journey so much better.

He slid his hands beneath the neckline of her tunic, finding the wing of her collarbone. He bent and kissed it, smooth skin scented by the rose petals in her bath.

He groaned, kissing his way to the cool flesh of her shoulder. Clary was a delicacy more delicious than any food and more intoxicating than the rarest wine. "You're everything I need."

She pouted, and it was adorable. "Still, you must have more vices than naiad ice cream and spicy rice."

"My favorite flavor is Clary." He cupped her face in his hands. "We fight well side by side. Do you know how long it's been since I could say that?"

Her brow furrowed. "I don't think that's in any magazine quiz about finding the ideal life partner."

"I'm not ideal. I'm not even particularly good. If you knew me, I doubt you'd remain in the same room."

"That's not true," Clary said in a low voice.

But it was.

He finally found out the truth after living with Vivian for years. They had shared a long day of labor, conjuring a spell that strengthened the borders of demon territory against encroachment by trolls. Demons regarded the monstrous creatures the way gardeners viewed slugs—a nuisance, but one possible to contain.

That night Merlin lay on the furs at Vivian's feet, drowsing as she read to him from a tome of history. Books were how they spent their hours, reading or being read to, for not even Vivian ever stopped studying magic. As subjects went, it had a learning curve that stretched to infinity.

"This passage was written by Agoricus the Great," she said.

Merlin knew the name of that demon. It had taken all the druids of his island homeland to destroy him. "Do I want to hear what he has to say?"

Drunk with relaxation, Merlin rolled to his back, staring up at Vivian's beautiful, feline figure. The firelight played with her form, kissing the curves and shadows of her face. Her violet eyes were intent, regarding him with speculation.

"You should. He was the mightiest of the demon princes of his time, and it is significant that he was slain by your mother and her friends."

"He was an arrogant fool?"

Vivian's smile had teeth. "Didn't you ever wonder why I took an interest in you?"

Something in her tone was different, and cold foreboding made Merlin sit up. "Tell me."

"Didn't you ever wonder why demon magic came to you far more easily than any other kind?"

But now Merlin was mute with apprehension. By this time, he had seen what Tenebrius had done in the Hebrides, and a thousand other cruelties. The only thing that kept him with the demons was the gratitude he felt for Vivian.

"Agoricus the Great was your father," Vivian said almost smugly.

"What?" He was on his feet.

"Your mother conjured the strongest warrior to sire her babe. She neglected to specify what species." Vivian shrugged. "When I learned that you existed, I wanted you for myself. Half-demon, half-druid witch. What a fascinating specimen you would be."

She leaned forward, caressing him with her gaze. "What a weapon to hide among the mortals."

Revulsion hit him, and not just because Vivian had withheld that truth. He was half a demon. His mother had slain his father in order to protect her tribes from the demon's devastation. Worse, Merlin had sworn to protect his people and yet here he was, fawning at the feet of his demon mistress. He disgusted himself.

He grabbed the book from Vivian and flung it into the fire, letting his father's words burn to ash. "How did you know?" he roared.

Vivian raised a single brow. "Agoricus bragged of bedding the great druidess, Brida, and of siring a son. He knew you would be a power in the world. When he fell at your mother's hands, I searched for you and coaxed your steps my way. When you arrived in that olive grove, you all but knocked on my front door."

Merlin sank to the floor, his head in his hands. Where did he belong? He was too much a mortal for the demons, seeing their cruelties for what they were. But if the humans discovered his father's name, they would do their best to kill him on sight.

He hated Vivian for plucking him from his penniless ignorance.

He hated himself for being her tool.

He hated himself for being stuck between worlds.

He had returned to the human kingdoms that night, and did not return again until he came back to steal her accursed spell. If Vivian had done her best to turn Merlin into a weapon to use against mortals, he would thwart her and be a weapon *for* the mortals. He'd banished her kind to the Abyss, freeing the world from demon evil.

And he'd broken Camelot, and the fae, the witches and, yes, the demons doing it. If he'd needed proof of his father's blood in his veins, it went far beyond his unusual amber eyes. He'd inherited a demonic talent for destruction.

Merlin deserved whatever doom befell him.

Chapter 26

Clary ran a hand over Merlin's forehead. Her touch was warm and firm as it smoothed his brow. "A penny for your thoughts. You disappeared somewhere inside your head for a moment."

"I wouldn't waste the money," he said, turning his face into her palm as she stroked his cheek. "They weren't good thoughts."

Clary smiled, but it was tinged with determination as if she flatly refused to be anything but delighted. In many ways she was an innocent who deserved all his protection. In others, she was every bit a fighter as the rest of Arthur's court. The contrast fascinated him.

"If they're bad thoughts," she said softly, "I'd like to hear them so I can chase them away."

He cupped her face with his hands. "If I asked you to return to Medievaland, would you go?"

"No," she said simply. "I came to fight. I have magic, too, you know."

"I know. I taught you."

"And you're a good teacher."

"I can take everything but watching you get hurt."

"Right back at you. But you're not leaving, so I'm not, either."

And they kissed, mouths teasing in tentative nips. He bit the tender flesh inside her lips, bidding her to open to him. Once their tongues tangled, he lost himself in the taste of her. It was the sweetest, most sensual reprieve from the darkness eating at his heart. Clary was the antidote to everything he was.

In one swift move, she pulled off her tunic, dropping it at their feet. He traced the edge of her bra with his tongue, exploring the rough lace and smooth skin beneath it. Tension built between them, rising until they could take no more.

It was impossible to say who moved first, but suddenly they were fumbling with their clothes, trying to undress without ending their embraces. He lifted her in his arms, her bare legs wrapping around his hips. The skin-to-skin contact, hot and frantic, almost broke his control. He carried her to the bed, but she stayed where she was, clinging to him, her lips locked with his.

Her bra was gone. Merlin's tongue found her nipple and began a teasing assault. A shiver rocked through her and she tilted her head back, inviting him to take more of her. He did, laving her in long, teasing strokes and rolling the tips of her breasts until they were flushed and erect. She writhed beneath him as he suckled one breast and then the other, blowing on her wet nipples until she shuddered with need.

Finally, she released her grip, sliding down his body with her own. The promise of her lithe, soft flesh ripped a moan from his throat. Her fingers were clumsy with haste as she unbuttoned his jeans and when she sank to her knees, his pulse pounded like war drums. She touched him, first with her palms, stroking his fullness until it throbbed with need. He buried his hands in the wild mop of her hair, the silk of it between his fingers a sensual delight.

His breath hitched as she stroked him and took a long, slow lick. If he knew her preferences, she knew his. In the spirit of wickedness, she nibbled at all the points that would unravel his self-control. He shifted uneasily as her teeth grazed him.

"Please," he moaned.

"Please stop?" she teased, giving another lick. "Or please keep on with what I'm doing?"

"More."

She gave him more, until he hovered on the edge of explosion.

"Enough." He pulled her up, all but tossing her to the silken covers of the bed. "Now I please you."

The thundering of his pulse countered the ragged syncopation of their breath as they tried to kiss and move and bite all at once. He kneaded her breasts, drawing a sigh from her lips as she arched into him like a cat begging for attention. He drew a nipple into his mouth, letting his teeth graze the point as he sucked it to a stiff peak. She writhed beneath him as he attended to the other, bucking against him in her quest for relief. He slid his fingers between her thighs, testing her readiness. She was hot and slick with need.

And yet, he went slowly, drawing it out with kisses

that began at the clean angle of her jaw and worked slowly between her breasts. The scent of their desire made his head swim with lust. He wasn't just loving her, but claiming her for that moment in time, and he did it thoroughly. He devoured the sweet and salt of her skin, the softness of her thighs and the delicate architecture of her bones. He found the hidden points of pleasure and brought her gasping with surprise. He wasn't a wizard for nothing.

When he finally entered her, they were both ready for the intimacy, making it a slow communion of body and soul. They had made love before, but this time he gave more of himself to it, pleasuring her but also sharing everything that pleased him. Clary took the lesson to heart. Soon it was impossible to hold back, and his body took over. Clary gave a lusty, hiccuping cry and dissolved with pleasure, digging her nails deep into Merlin's flesh as he drove hard to the finish and filled her with heat and warmth.

She spasmed her release around him, squeezing tight in wave after wave. Then his mind broke apart, and there was nothing but delicious female flesh and the need to possess it. He dissolved in the ecstasy of her and cried out, a sobbing, triumphant shout.

He relaxed into the mattress, letting the silken softness cradle him as he held Clary in his arms. She buried her face against his chest, her breath like a featherlight kiss. She seemed so small, the fire in her quiescent with satisfaction. He ran a hand down her back, tracing the slope of waist and hip. She was perfection.

Merlin's thoughts rested there, refusing to acknowledge the darkness gathering around them. He'd created this moment for them both, one taste of bliss before the storm began. He refused to look ahead into the gale. It would do no good to break their hearts now, when they needed all the courage they could get.

She propped herself on one elbow, her gaze soft with their lovemaking. "Thank you. I never suspected you had such a romantic side."

Merlin wasn't sure he'd call that lost corner of his heart romantic, but it was intensely private. At least, it had been until now, when he'd shared it with her. He stroked Clary's cheekbone with his thumb. "I wanted to show you a side of me no one else ever sees. I want you to know how much you matter."

He said nothing more, because there was nothing more to say. Tears stood in her eyes, though a faint smile hovered on her lips.

Remember me this way, he thought. When he kissed her again, there was pain in his heart, for they would not get through this war without baring all their truths. He wasn't ready to face what she would see in him.

The Queen of Faery felt regal once more. She was bathed, her hair dressed by expert maids, her midnight blue riding habit was trimmed with sapphires and her mount was a black mare of the finest bloodlines. Best of all, she was freed of that blasted tower—literally blasted free—and able to roam where she willed. And best of all, she had flunkies to do her bidding. She had let it be known that her royal will was to expunge Merlin and his puppet prince, King Arthur of Camelot, from existence once and for all. Merlin first, then Arthur and then all the rest.

Her spirit would feel infinitely lighter with their corpses lined up for her inspection. She would walk from one to the other, admiring each in turn and knowing she had established the ultimate power over each one. Hers to hold, and hers to destroy. It would be like Christmas or an especially satisfying day of shopping. They would never threaten her happiness again.

It would not be without risk. Arthur possessed the sword Excalibur. She feared that enchanted weapon, for it was the one blade that could cut through her enchantments and end her life. For years, that had stalled her plans out of pure cowardice, but no more. If she'd learned nothing else from captivity, it was that being careful had gained her nothing. No more caution.

The endgame was well in motion now. She rode through the Forest Sauvage at the head of an army, the tall, silent trees standing sentry on either side of the road. They'd had archers poised to kill any of Arthur's spies, whether on foot or in flight, but she'd called them off now. It didn't matter what Arthur knew, because nothing could help him anymore. She spoke little, too agitated for ordinary conversation. Besides, the only words that mattered had been the order to march on Camelot, for that was where Arthur was sure to flee. By the time the sun set, his crown, his sword and his life would be hers.

And better yet, she'd have Merlin and his witchling. Why he had taken on a student after so many centuries, she'd never know. She supposed it didn't matter, because what could a beginner do in the face of the Queen of Faery's superior power? Morgan mentally pictured them roasting on a spit. After today, neither would have the chance to interfere again.

Tenebrius appeared at her left stirrup. The demon had joined them some miles back, but went on foot. It was doubtful any sane horse would carry such a creature. Morgan looked down, enjoying the sensation of rising above him.

"Do you have a plan for battle?" he asked.

"Of course." She flicked a fallen leaf from the skirts of her new riding habit. "I have discussed it at length with my generals."

There, that put him in his place. This was need to know, and he wasn't in the inner circle. Why would a demon expect more?

He bowed with a humility that had to be fake. "How would you like me to contribute my magic, my queen?"

She recalled the disastrous outcome of the computer attack. Filthy demon magic that had crippled her own. Resentment colored her tone. "Keep your spells to yourself until I give the order."

He laughed. The sound brought heat to her cheeks. "What is so amusing?"

"Nothing. Your advice is wise. It is difficult for any but the most accomplished practitioners to use demon power if they are not born to it. Some never do."

She raised her chin. "Few wish to. It is unclean. Besides, I am not using it, you are. We will each stick to our own spells."

He snorted, his yellow eyes narrowing to slits. "Have you seen Gorm, by the way?"

Alarm skated through her, though she did her best to hide it. "He is not my employee or my pet. I do not concern myself with his whereabouts unless he is summoned."

She spurred her mare forward, leaving the demon behind. In a dozen yards the forest road ended and a view of Camelot's castle opened up. Morgan reined in to stop and stare. The pale towers seem to float above rolling green hills, a prize that until this moment had been untouchable. "No more." The words were barely a breath, but they carried all her intention like a spell.

The moment was spoiled as Tenebrius came up to her once more. Morgan inwardly cursed at the demon for breaking into her daydream, but said nothing.

He fixed her with his strange yellow gaze. "You know that even I, who am stronger than any other of my kind, can only remain outside the Abyss for a limited period of time."

"You are confessing this weakness for what purpose?" she asked tartly.

"Now that you are free, what of my freedom? That was our bargain. We both get out of jail."

"I will attend to that when Camelot is mine." She was asking more than their original bargain, but what was he going to do?

He stood motionless, as if holding in a string of curses. "Would you like me to watch the skies as I did when your prison fell?"

She nodded. "Be on guard for a dragon of Merlin's acquaintance."

"A dragon. That's all?" His sarcasm was plain. "And what will you be doing while I tackle that detail?"

"There is but one thing left to do before the fall of Merlin Ambrosius and Arthur Pendragon begins." She turned to her sea of exquisite, heartless fae. A greedy glee assailed her at the sight. They were hers. *Hers.* She commanded them, and they would smash Camelot's court to pulp and hand her the glittering crown.

"I need a volunteer," she said to her shining host. "Who here would like to fetch my secret weapon against the king?"

Chapter 27

"It's time."

Clary heard Merlin's words. For a long moment she pretended to be deaf, but the inevitability of the moment dragged her to her feet and made her dress. They did not speak as he did the same. She dawdled, stretching out even these few minutes, and was still holding her shoes when they turned to face each other. He touched her cheek with the back of his fingers.

"Listen to me carefully," he said. "I'm going to need your help. Arthur is going to bring his men to Camelot and will need to get in the front gate. I don't know if he'll reach here before the fae. You need to help him get through the gate safely. Find a good vantage point and offer covering fire like we did at the tower."

It sounded simple enough, but she was paralyzed

as she understood what he was actually saying. "You won't be with me?"

He shook his head. "I have to launch the spell that will cure the fae."

Her pulse kicked into a gallop. "Without me?"

"I have to work alone."

That meant they wouldn't be there for each other—but then, this was war. Things were getting real, and she couldn't rely on him for everything. "I'm afraid. I'll be all right, but I'm scared."

He kissed her brow. "You can do this, Clary. You're ready. This is everything you've trained for."

It is, said Vivian, surfacing from wherever she had gone. *This is the moment we fight.*

Tears burned the backs of her eyes as the razor's edge of panic cut through her. This was goodbye. "Be careful."

"I will," he said.

Even if they both survived, Vivian was inside her, itching to fight. Even if everything went perfectly, nothing was going to be the same. If she let Vivian fight—and why wouldn't she unleash a weapon like the demoness to save Camelot?—she would be obviously possessed, a hated demon. The alternative was to hide the truth, and that only served herself.

You do not hide from a just fight. Neither of us do. It is not in our nature.

That was the truth. Clary squeezed her eyes shut as Merlin kissed her lips one last time. Tears leaked from her lashes and she swiped them away before he could.

"Save the world, okay?" she said in a choked voice.

Clary ran, bursting from the tent and across the starlit sand. The camel gave a surprised snort, but the only other sound was the wind in the palm trees of the oasis. She stopped to pull on her shoes, not caring that she had sand on her feet. She looked back over her shoulder, but Merlin hadn't followed. She was glad and heartbroken at once.

The warm wind touched her cheek. She knew deserts were cold at night, but she'd always dreamed this one would be warm, suitable for gauzy harem wear and dancing naked under the moon. A pleasant, harmless untruth, like the rest of this desert scene. Merlin had made it just so that they could enjoy a moment of perfect joy.

She'd never be able to read that book again without thinking of this oasis. She couldn't help resenting that a little. Before today her daydreams had been easy, demanding nothing from her. Now Merlin had tangled her heart in them. But if he'd complicated Clary's hopes, he'd also given her tools. She wasn't the incompetent witch she'd been when she'd arrived at his doorstep.

"And I have a demon," she muttered. "I will not be afraid to use it."

Vivian sprang to life. *I thought you'd never ask.*

Clary finished knotting her shoelace and rose, trepidation seeping in. "Tell me."

The Queen of Faery ordered my death. I want her head on a spike. I have a plan.

Clary's brain froze at the audacity of the words. "Excalibur is the only thing that can cut through her magic. Not even the Lady of the Lake could beat her."

But I'm something she's never faced before.

The delighted anticipation in Vivian's voice sent chills down Clary's spine, but then her mind snagged on an important point. "What do you mean LaFaye ordered your death?"

I have been examining my state. Tenebrius told the truth when he said that I would die in your realm. Merlin assumed my trapped condition meant hibernation, but all connections to the source of my energy have been completely severed. I have limited time left.

There was fear in Vivian's voice, but also bloodthirsty exhilaration as if she was betting her last chips in a high-stakes game. Clary understood. Vivian had been mortally wounded, but she would go out in her own way and hold nothing back in one last, glorious fight.

Help me, Vivian said. *Help me with my revenge and you will be free of me and a clean, pure witch once more.*

"But you're dying!"

I will fight for the new life the queen carries, and for you and Merlin and your dreams. I will paint one of the many layers of your love before I am no more. I will be a chapter in your romance of camels and desert stars.

Clary's mind reeled. What would it be like to be mortally ill and alone, cut off from everything familiar, even your own body?

I will die fighting, as I must. Besides, I'm stuck with you. I couldn't be alone if I tried.

Clary swallowed back her tears, knowing Vivian wouldn't want them. "We'll fight together, then."

Clary would fight for a new Camelot, and Gwen and her baby, and the wedding Tamsin and Gawain would have if they ever stopped dithering about cake and decorations. Everyone Clary loved was on the line, and hadn't she trained with Merlin just so that she could fight when the time came? They always knew the fae would come. As Merlin said, it was time.

"Merlin should know what you face."

He will know when I choose to tell him. Now go back to Camelot.

Clary's hands were shaking, but she obediently crossed the sand and used her own magic to shove the portal door open, leaving her fantasy behind. She blinked as reality swam into view. It was still bright in the garden, though the sky had hazed over with a thin layer of cloud. As the portal closed behind her and vanished, Clary had the sense that only an hour or so had passed. And yet something had changed. The garden continued to release its heady aura of lavender and thyme, but the bees were gone. The birdsong, including the incessant cooing from the dovecote, had stopped. It was as if everything that could hide had fled to a safe retreat. "This isn't good."

LaFaye has moved the first piece on the board. Find out what that is.

Clary sprinted to the keep, mounting the winding stairs as fast as her feet would carry her until she reached the highest chamber. She was breathing hard as she took stock of her new surroundings. The room was empty except for some trunks, but it had windows on all four sides. She ran to each one in turn, seeing mostly sweeps of wood and meadow, but the west-facing view told her what she needed to know. There were fae as far as the eye could see and nothing between them and the castle.

They'd arrived much sooner than expected. Merlin had underestimated LaFaye's battle plans.

Merlin finished dressing himself, his movements so brisk they were jerky. It had taken all his resolve not to imprison Clary in some far distant realm where he knew she'd be protected from battle—but that was a coward's way to ease his heart. Trust was the greatest tool he could give her, and Clary had earned the right to do her part. He believed in her too much to put her in a cage, even to spare himself pain.

He left the desert, releasing the magic that had formed it the moment he had safely returned to the castle garden. He would have kept the oasis for Clary's future use, but he needed all his strength for the coming fight. She was nowhere in sight, which was a relief. The aching lump in his chest was a warning that his resolve wouldn't have survived another parting.

It was the same reason he hadn't told her that he loved her. If anything went wrong, an admission like that would have been a millstone around both their necks. He'd loved before, certainly. He had a heart and the world was filled with lovable people. But he hadn't loved like *this*, with a woman he wanted to be with forever. Ironic, given what they would face that day. Or perhaps it was fate's gift to him, a glimpse of who he might have been. There might have been a Merlin who was a good and loving man, content to at last find safe harbor and home.

His vision blurred, but he blinked his eyes clear. Nothing good came of being with him. His parents had created a monster capable of ripping the souls from an entire race. His only possible redemption was to become the man who healed the world, regardless of the cost. He would use the cursed power he'd been born with for good. Then, only then, would he deserve mercy.

Merlin started for the dungeon, his long strides carrying him across the courtyard as they'd done so often before in better times. Back then he had the love of a king and every opportunity to indulge his curiosity. A word would send servants scurrying to bring him rare ingredients. There would always be an audience to gasp and clap at whatever magical wonder he desired to show off. He'd been an insufferable idiot who never realized how blessed he was until it all fell away.

He entered the keep and unlocked the secret door, passing through the layers of wards he had set last night. The stairs were narrow and dark even with the aid of the light he summoned. The dungeon was not a large space, but it had a table and a brazier and a tall pedestal that held the egg inside a cage of deadly magic. That was all he needed for now.

Merlin had broken the world, and now it was time to fix it. There was a very good chance the spell would kill him. The downside of giving Clary her fantasy of perfect happiness was that now it meant something to him, too.

He clenched his jaw against the agony of loss that splintered his heart.

Clary had found her way to the tower roof so she could see even better. More fae had arrived, circling the castle in a noose of steel. There had been losses at the white tower, but the troops she'd seen on the road last night had doubled the size of LaFaye's forces. More were coming from the forest and falling into place behind the others, rank after rank arriving as she watched. She had no idea how many fae there actually were in their homeland, but she had a sense every good fighter available was present.

And she could see another one of those freaking catapults in the distance. The wheels of the trebuchet turned slowly, bumping over the rolling grass while two long lines of soldiers pulled on ropes as thick as their arms.

Common sense said that Clary would have to leave the tower once it began its work, but she had some time yet. The army was still gathering.

"Where is Arthur's army?" she wondered.

He is not far, but he hides himself.

Clary wondered how Vivian knew, but this wasn't the time for idle questions. Instead, she continued to search the enemies' lines and finally spotted LaFaye herself. Instinctively, Clary ducked behind one of the huge merlons, the square teeth of stone that made up the crenelations along the tower's edge. A wild terror surged through her as if she were a rabbit and the queen a hungry hawk.

Fear is smart, said Vivian in a voice that came close to a purr. *Every good predator is careful and crafty.*

Clary's stomach rolled over, panic threatening her breakfast. But she peered around the slab of stone, taking a second look. She used a farseeing spell that Merlin had taught her to bring the queen's face into focus. She looked the same as when she had bulged out of the laptop—beautiful except for her contemptuous expression. She rode a black mare and her dark blue gown was spangled with gems. She carried no weapons that Clary could see, but who needed a sword when you were Morgan LaFaye?

Clary shivered when the first goblin arrows flew, their song filling the sky with a deadly hum. As Vivian had said, Arthur's forces were hidden and the fae wheeled around in confusion, bringing their shields up a moment too late. Dozens fell to the deadly shafts, even in the small slice of the army Clary could see.

Yes! Vivian exclaimed.

Clary scanned the woods, finding no sign of the bowmen. Down below, LaFaye was doing the same, twisting in her saddle. She flung out a hand, and Clary sensed her power rippling outward. It peeled back the concealing magic that hid Camelot's troops.

Clary just had time to glimpse the goblins shooting from the trees when the knights charged. They came up the rise to her right like a silver spear of armor and horse, driving deep into the flank of the fae. It was all Arthur could do, she realized. The fae army was between the king and his castle. It belatedly occurred to her that she might have wanted to pull up the drawbridge, but that would cut off both friend and foe.

Leave it, said Vivian. *There are better ways to help.*

Clary leaned out to get a clear view of the knights, and understood what Vivian meant. They were driving toward the front gate, which would give them some cover, but their momentum had run out. With so many fae, they were mobbed. And yet, she couldn't help but wonder at the skill of Arthur's men. Lancelot lay about him with his battle-ax, hewing down fae with bloody efficiency. Excalibur flashed, and enemies fell as if a scythe had passed through them. It was lovely and terrible and everything she'd dreamed of when she'd read their stories as a girl.

Then a fae's spear struck Arthur's side, and he slumped forward. Clary's fireball struck before she'd so much as formed a thought. The fae went up in flames. And then she became a kind of witchy sniper, giving cover as the other knights circled around their king.

"By all the pointed hats in the coven, I'm doing this," she muttered. She was fighting like a pro.

Fae arrows skittered like claws against the stone of the tower as the enemy returned fire. She ducked, as safe as one could be in a battle, but aware that it would only take one shaft to end her warrior career. Perspiration ran into her eyes.

The goblin army clogged the area before the drawbridge, preventing the fae from storming in, but there was still a sea of swords between the knights and safety. Progress forward was one step at a time, the battle so thick that Clary could sometimes barely find her friends inside the thickets of steel.

It seemed hopeless, the ranks of goblins thinning as LaFaye ordered attack after attack. The fae queen had not yet unleashed her magic, but Clary guessed she was holding back, saving her strength for a final, fatal blow. Numbers were enough for now.

Likewise, Clary kept Vivian in reserve and used her own smaller power to ease Arthur's way to the gate. Soon he wasn't the only one wounded. Perceval's shield arm drooped, leaving his side dangerously exposed. She covered him as best she could, but there was too much to watch at the same time.

And then a frenzied yell came from the left. A portal blazed to life in an explosion of light, and another army streamed through, some on horseback and others on foot. They were fae, but completely unlike the fae surrounding the queen. These were alight with passion, swords raised and eyes blazing, their long, white hair streaming with the speed of their attack. Clary recognized Angmar and Laren among them. These were the rebel fae, the ones with souls who had escaped from LaFaye.

The cavalry had come, but as the queen turned to face them, even Clary could see at once that the desperate rescue wouldn't last.

Chapter 28

Merlin knew the battle raged outside, but he could not afford distraction. The work he did was too delicate to let his mind wander. He'd cast the ritual circle first, building it strong enough to hold the magic he needed. Within it he scribed shapes, first in chalk and then in his own blood. That would direct the energy out of the dungeon and into the sky above the fae army he knew brawled outside the gates. Energy would be the first step of his ritual. The second and more dangerous stage would be igniting that energy with enough force to disperse it over the fae.

He removed the wards from the egg and placed it in the circle. It seemed so common—like something from an animal's burrow—and yet the power that surged from it crawled over his skin. Now that he'd taken away the wards, he was certain LaFaye could feel it, too, even at a distance. For an instant he remembered her as a skinny girl with serious gray eyes—smart, adventurous and stubborn. She might have been an ally if she'd grown up with a different family around her. But she hadn't, and something essential in her personality had been irreparably broken. After the harm she'd done, there was no turning back for her now. Pity stabbed him when he thought of that girl, but she was no more real now than the Merlin who might have been. They hadn't reached this point by accident. They'd both made choices. Now they would do their best to destroy one another.

He sat cross-legged on the floor and held the egg between his palms. The energy crawled over his hands like tiny claws, streaming between his fingers and over his wrists. It was thrumming as if aware, a slow, inhuman heartbeat that sent surges of power deep into his core. Merlin let his mind go blank, falling into the sensation. Images flickered by, but he didn't attempt to catch them. Riding a pony as a boy, his mother with her hair braided for war, the Mediterranean Sea, and Clary, her laughing eyes green as the first buds of spring.

He had promised himself to let her go. She had trained hard to take her place in this battle, and she had succeeded. Her triumph was his, as well. But he loved her, and that made everything hard. There were a thousand reasons he was here alone—for the fae, for Arthur, for all of Camelot and even for himself—but she was the most important. He had to win and if that demanded the sacrifice of his own life, so be it. It was the only way he could truly protect her.

There was a moment of regret, and the awareness of his own vulnerability. But Merlin Ambrosius didn't matter anymore.

He crushed the egg and let the demonic energy consume him.

* * *

The battle shifted as the queen's forces turned to rebuff the attack of the rebel fae. As much as LaFaye hated Merlin, the fae despised their rebel kin more, for they represented all that the fae had lost.

As the fae's attention swung away, Arthur's advance toward the gate picked up speed. Clary's fire knocked off the fae that remained behind to block his path.

In the distance more unexpected aid came as a stream changed course, flooding the path from the woods and turning it into a bog. The trebuchet was quickly mired, and all the fae heaving on the ropes couldn't prevent it from sinking deeper and deeper into the mud. Clary guessed the naiads were responsible, but caught no glimpse of the transparent beings. Then ropes of ivy snaked up the beams of the great machine, pulling it down into the muck. When the fae pulling the trebuchet drew their swords to hack the vines away, they were pulled down, too. It was a small victory, but it raised Clary's hopes.

She returned her attention to the knights. LaFaye had put her troops back in order, and Clary was hard-pressed to clear a path for Arthur's last rush to the gate. LaFaye hurled a spell at the towers guarding the draw-bridge, shearing off the top three rows of stone blocks as neatly as if she held a hedge trimmer. The only thing that stopped her was the number of fae struck by falling stone. Clary didn't breathe until the last knight was safely inside and the remaining goblins manned the castle walls, raining arrows down on their attackers. The drawbridge creaked upward, leaving LaFaye's armies on the outside of the moat.

From where she stood, Clary couldn't see the knights

once they were inside the castle walls, but she could hear orders shouted for water and bandages and for weapons from the armory. Instinct urged her to go help, but she had another job to do.

LaFaye was clearly up to something. The queen moved forward, a phalanx of guards around her. There was someone with her on a white horse, but Clary couldn't see who it was. The fighting around the queen stopped and the army parted. Those allies who weren't inside the castle had withdrawn for the moment, leaving their dead on the bloody banks of the moat.

"Arthur," called Morgan LaFaye. "Show yourself."

Silence followed, leaden and intense. Clary could hear the wind hum through the chinks in the castle's rock, as if the stone sang softly to itself. At last, a door opened below. Clary peered down to see four goblin archers emerge onto a stone balcony. Then Lancelot and Gawain followed, their shields held high. Finally, Arthur stepped out, moving carefully. His tunic was bloody, but he held his spine straight and his head high, and one hand rested on Excalibur's hilt. With his other hand, he moved Gawain's shield aside. It was clear that Arthur would allow his men to guard him, but he refused to hide.

"There is no victory for you here, Morgan," said Arthur, his voice carrying easily over the field. "It takes more than swords to rule the mortal realms."

"My army is insatiable for human souls. I command with an authority that you can only dream of."

Which was why, Clary knew, LaFaye had used her own sorcery to keep the fae from healing naturally. Merlin's spell had only begun the damage to her subjects. Time had healed the witches, but LaFaye had ensured her people never recovered. It was a hideous abuse of her power.

Arthur was clearly thinking along the same lines. "You command through treachery against your own. Gloating ill becomes you."

Clary's scalp prickled, distracting her from the exchange. She looked over her shoulder, but no one was there. The sensation was power cycling from below. The dungeon. Merlin. The spell that would return souls to the fae.

She had little idea how the spell would work, or how far along it was, but anything involving that much power was highly dangerous. A knot gathered in her gut and twisted hard when she thought of the risk to Merlin. She had intellectually understood that battle could bring death, but this was too real. This was something she couldn't face. She loved him. She loved him!

"How can I help him?" she said to Vivian. "I have to do something!"

Be patient. Everything depends on choosing the right moment.

Clary was about to make a scathing comeback when one of the queen's guards dragged the white horse forward. All thoughts flew from Clary's head as an outraged cry rose from Camelot's men. Guinevere sat on the white horse, her face rigid with fright. Clary's heart dropped like a stone.

"I know your sorcerer is at work, Arthur," said LaFaye. "I can feel his spell like an itch along my skin."

Clary saw Arthur and his men stiffen. This was news to them. "Let my queen go, Morgan!" the king bellowed.

"And return your precious heir? I think not." Her

reply was clipped and businesslike. "Not unless you hand Merlin over at once."

Arthur's fists clenched as he seemed to weave on his feet. Blood dripped from the hem of his tunic, showing his wound was still open.

"What do we do?" Clary demanded. "And don't tell me to be patient!"

Vivian didn't reply. She didn't need to.

A roar of amazement sounded from both armies as energy whooshed into the sky like Roman candles on the Fourth of July. The force of it hurled Clary backward, her nerves tingling as if she'd touched a live wire. She crawled to her hands and knees, teeth chattering. "M-Merlin," she breathed, gazing up in wonder.

Energy sparkled against the cloudy sky, white and gold and pink and blue, each fleck swooping up to crest and flutter down again like the spray of a fountain. It was beautiful, but the magic needed to command such power would tear anyone apart. Not even Merlin could survive it.

Agony yawned open inside her. "I should have told him that I loved him."

Vivian's sympathy was a light and unexpected touch. *He knew.*

A gasp escaped Clary as if she'd taken a wound. The thought of Merlin, of that time in the garden, was more than she could bear. Hot tears washed down her face.

It is time, said Vivian, but Clary was turned to stone. *Now!*

Clary's attention snapped back to the field, blocking the wall of pain that threatened to unravel her. Gwen sat forgotten, the speed of events saving her from the spotlight, at least for the moment. LaFaye rose in her saddle, pointing toward the multicolored rush of energy. Her lips moved feverishly and a moment later a bolt of green lightning hurtled toward Merlin's spell.

Vivian sprang into action, her power ripping through Clary so fast it felt as if she would turn inside out. Perception scrambled, all sense of size and space dropping away as she fused with the coruscating light. The flow was powerful, but lacked the will and intelligence to defend itself. The green lightning struck, but Vivian batted it away, absorbing the impact with her own strength. The impact sent her spinning around, and she suddenly understood what she needed to do. Tenebrius had done his best to rip her power up by the roots, but she had conserved her magic for just such a moment. She had lain quiet, watching and waiting to pounce.

Merlin held a pillar of light, the stream of energy coursing between his hands and the sky. He jolted as Vivian's consciousness joined the stream. Relief and trepidation arrowed through him, making him drag in a noisy breath. He'd thought her gone, but she was definitely present now, the bright, lush hue of her personality adding its mark to the stream.

"Hello!" he said softly. Maybe he had betrayed her, and maybe she had struck back with her potion. Now, with the future balanced in his hands, those things seemed less important than her brilliant mind and incandescent spirit.

Hello, she replied. *You can't do this alone.*

He felt the juddering impact of the faery queen's attack and the force of Vivian's counterstrike. The gyrating twist the blow caused nearly knocked him from his feet. By the time he caught his balance, he knew what Vivian meant to do. He nearly staggered again.

"No," he said softly. "Let me. I owe you recompense for what I did."

Don't be a fool.

There was kindness in the voice that traveled through the steam of sparkling light, and that was worrying all on its own. Vivian had never been kind. Not in the way humans were.

You arrogant mouse. Did you think I was incapable of learning? Of choosing who I am?

"Why?"

Your Clary is quite a teacher herself. This time there was deep affection in her voice. For him. For Clary.

It humbled him. "I'm sorry. For everything."

I know. That's why you always frustrated me. You could never see how I cared for you.

He was too shocked to find the words to answer.

The plume of energy exploded into a fine mist, hurling Merlin into the stone of the dungeon wall.

Clary screamed and fell, the agony of the explosion seeming to tear holes in her mind. She curled into a ball, cradling her skull as the pain made her retch and twist. Only when the white-hot threads receded from behind her eyes did thought creep back to her. Something very, very bad had happened to Vivian. It felt as if the demoness had been torn away, with only a gaping hole left behind.

Shocked, Clary rolled to look upward at the shower of sparks in the air. *Dispersion*, she thought as the wind caught the colorful energy and floated it across the fae army. It was the second part of Merlin's spell, the dangerous process of showering the energy over the fae. Vivian had taken Clary's math problem and spreadsheets and solved the issue with the subtlety of a sledgehammer. And damaged herself irreparably in the process.

Clary closed her eyes, weeping. She'd wanted the demoness gone with all her soul, but still she felt her loss. What remained had been so drained by the explosion that it felt little more than a memory or a shadow. Vivian had been dying and she'd given everything to strike one decisive blow—one that would turn the fae on their evil queen.

Clary swallowed, praying this meant Merlin was safe, but knowing he'd been holding the energy stream when it had exploded. Sobbing, Clary scrambled to the edge of the tower. The demon essence fell everywhere like a fine snow. The fae stood transfixed, their eyes wide and faces upturned. The Queen of Faery waved her arms and screeched, but whether she was summoning a wind or ordering her troops to flee, Clary couldn't tell. The sparkling magic seemed to float by unaffected as if her power had little effect on what Vivian had done.

As the demoness had said, LaFaye hadn't seen her coming.

All at once, the sky went dark as dusk. She spun to see a dark mass covering the sun. Shading her eyes, she craned her neck to make out a dozen kite-like shapes. She instantly dropped to the stone in terror. Demons, probably something Tenebrius had cooked up. She'd seen the ragged scraps of darkness from a distance during the last battle, but here they were close enough to make out the wicked claws and inky feathers—or perhaps it was tiny paws and bristling fur. The creatures seemed to shift before her eyes, though the jet-black eyes remained fixed on her. They were coming to wreak punishment on someone for that spell, and Clary was visible. They swooped, a stink of dead flesh staggering her senses.

Clary ran for the stairs, but she hadn't gone a dozen steps when they got her. She screamed as five of the things snatched her up, clawing fingers grabbing handfuls of her clothes. She flew upward, hoisted from the rooftop like a bale of hay. Clary squirmed as a toenail stabbed into her back, but went still as the edge of the tower disappeared and the distance to solid ground grew suddenly far. Vertigo swam as wind scoured her face and roared in her ears. She fought the instinct to fight free, trying hard to go limp until the grass swung upward and the creatures let go. She fell to her hands and knees, teeth clacking with sudden impact. With a thundering flap, the creatures were gone, circling around with sudden urgency.

Clary scrambled to her feet. A handful of fae ran toward her, weapons in hand. Demon sparkles still drifted through the air, but with a sinking heart she realized they weren't having any effect. Merlin's spell wasn't working. Why not? Fear hit her like an icy wall.

As the cold-eyed fae crowded around her, a spear tip touched her throat. Then Morgan LaFaye shouldered her mare between the guards. The queen's gray gaze was as furious as her henchmen's were blank. "Oh, look," LaFaye said through gritted teeth. "Tenebrius brought me a present. Merlin's little witchling."

Chapter 29

"Bring her," said the queen. "Put her with the other hostage, but beware. She has a little magic."

A huge fae grabbed Clary's arm and pulled her forward while LaFaye returned her attention to the castle. "Call off your enchanter, Arthur," she cried. "Call him off or I will destroy your queen!"

Did she not realize that the spell was done, and that Merlin would have spent all his magic and possibly his life? Clary clenched her teeth, fighting back a scream of frustration and sorrow as the fae tossed her to the grass. Gwen was there already, her back to a tree, while the white mare she'd been riding cropped grass nearby.

"Are you all right?" Clary asked in a low voice. Her friend looked flushed, a faint sheen of sweat on her brow.

"Why are you here?" Gwen asked. "You should have stayed on the tower."

"The demons brought me."

"Where's Merlin?"

"In the dungeon, I think. It wasn't supposed to happen this way," Clary protested, that old, horrible feeling of incompetence washing over her. Anxiety sped her heart, making her light-headed. "The spell should have worked."

"What spell?" Gwen asked and then gripped her distended belly with a groan.

"Are you in labor?" Clary asked in horror. It was possible, she supposed. Gwen had been dragged through a portal and forced to ride. That couldn't be good this late in her pregnancy.

"Not yet," Gwen said firmly. "I refuse."

"Sure," Clary said doubtfully as Gwen moaned in pain again.

"Silence!" one of the fae guards commanded, prodding Gwen's shoulder with the butt of his spear. It was the same big fae that had dragged Clary to his spot, and the queen hissed in a breath and clutched her collarbone.

Clary's self-control snapped. She sprang to her feet, pushing the guard away. "Don't touch her!"

It had been a stupid move. He was armed, while she was not. The guard casually flipped his spear around and presented the blade-sharp tip. "The queen has value. You do not. Be careful how you try my patience."

Still shaking with anger, Clary didn't back down. Instead, she planted her feet and folded her arms, taking up a position in front of her friend. "Right back at ya, bud."

It wasn't the best line, but it made the point. The fae's brows bunched together. "Do you think to challenge me?" He sounded more bewildered than anything else. Evidently, disobedience didn't happen often in his world.

Their argument had attracted LaFaye's attention. "Deal with her," she said coldly.

The fae struck. Gwen screamed, but the sound was drowned by the noise of the spear splintering against the wall of Clary's magic. Toothpick-size bits of ash wood flew into the air. The fae ducked to guard his face, just avoiding the blunted spearhead that ricocheted past his shoulder. Clary's heart pounded, but she grinned. The spell was hers, but the reflexes and power were Vivian's.

Surely you didn't think I'd miss this fight? Vivian's voice was very faint, but it was there.

"Welcome back," Clary said softly, knowing she'd just had a narrow escape. "I've never been so glad to have a demon for a friend."

That doesn't say much for your social life.

The faery queen was off her horse and coming their way. The light flashed off the sapphires decorating her dark gown, giving her the look of a serpent in motion. She flicked a hand and a massive force struck Clary from the side, sending her tumbling across the field and away from Gwen. It felt like a dragon's tail had thumped her, knocking the breath from her lungs. She dragged it back in with a whooping gasp as she scrambled to her knees. She lifted her head to see LaFaye regarding her with open contempt while the surrounding warriors laughed. The mocking sound held a dangerous edge that reminded Clary of hyenas.

"Is this how Merlin trains his apprentices?" the faery queen scoffed. "You're hardly fit to mend his robes."

Clary crawled to her feet, aching in every joint, but

Vivian's power was rising, winding round and round in the strange, humming dynamo she'd felt on top of the tower. This time it seemed different, though. Harder. Darker. Sharper. She wasn't holding anything back because LaFaye had ordered her death and this was the moment of her vengeance.

When LaFaye flicked her hand again, Clary struck back, Vivian's power driving the blow. The queen doubled over with a scream of surprised agony. Clary danced back, energized by the small win. The demon's magic was filling her with a whirling sensation so vast it made her ears ring. She felt ten feet tall and crackling with potential. Fae warriors rushed to stop her, but she swept them aside like flies.

When she struck again, the queen deflected some of the power, but not all. Blood ran from LaFaye's nose in a thin, scarlet trickle. Clary was panting, exhausted and exhilarated at once. She feinted, struck, and feinted again, her blows lighter now but coming so much faster. She was moving as one with Vivian, relaxing into the flow of the battle.

But the demon had given too much of her strength already that day, and LaFaye wasn't so easily beaten. The faery queen made a two-handed gesture and a column of white fire sprang from the ground, trapping Clary in its midst. It squeezed inward to cut off her air, blinding her vision and numbing every other sense. She began to gag, her ribs unable to move.

Vivian's magic wobbled dangerously, and Clary grew unbearably hot as the fire began to consume her. Slowly, inexorably, her feet left the ground as LaFaye's geyser of flame forced her upward. Death seeped in like a stain.

* * *

Merlin staggered into the courtyard and squinted against the daylight. Between the backlash of magic and the blow to his skull, his head throbbed as if he'd been on a three-day bender. His memory of the last hour was a senseless montage of light, color and ear-splitting explosion. He had one clear thought and he clung to it stubbornly—where was Clary and why hadn't she told him that Vivian was anything but dormant? She'd lied, and it had been a dangerous lie. An irrational urge to strangle her pounded inside him.

He couldn't explain what had happened at the end of the spell, except that Vivian had saved his life. He fell against the courtyard wall, propping himself up because his legs would no longer hold him. Grief and confusion wrenched his core.

She'd sacrificed herself. A demon. Out of love.

Merlin's world had changed in that single moment, but it would take much longer to make sense of it. He'd used his bruised magic to call out to her, but received no answer. Had her sacrifice been worthwhile? He didn't know. The spell would work and save the fae, or Arthur's forces were doomed.

Merlin had to know what had happened. He had to know if Clary was safe.

He looked around. Goblin soldiers milled about the courtyard, distributing weapons from the castle's armory. Sir Owen was tending to a horse's shoe while somewhere in the distance Lancelot argued with the king. Merlin recognized the French knight's voice and Arthur's terse reply. He followed the voices to the balcony, hoping for a clue to Clary's location.

"She has my wife!" Arthur bellowed, but it obviously hurt, because he gripped the side of his blood-stained tunic.

Dulac steadied the king with one hand, his brow furrowed with concern. "You are in no condition to ride or fight, and Gwen is in the middle of the enemy's forces. Let me go."

Merlin went suddenly cold. The blood, the look on Arthur's face, sent him forward. "You're hurt." He touched a hand to the king's side, murmuring a spell to stop the flow of blood. His demon ancestry meant that he'd never be a good healer, and the repair was crude, but it would do for the moment.

"Where were you?" Arthur demanded.

"Working," he replied, deliberately vague. It would take too much time to explain. "Have you seen Clary?"

"There." Dulac pointed to the battlefield. "LaFaye has her, along with Gwen."

Merlin froze, then raised his eyes to Arthur's and saw what he felt himself. Rage, terror and the overwhelming need to shield the woman he loved from a monster. The instinct to protect was an almost mindless drive.

He turned to see where Dulac pointed. At first he saw thousands of heavily armed fae attacking the castle's defenses. The goblins were holding them off, but that wouldn't last forever. Then he saw the gentle snow of his spell—which was doing exactly nothing. Merlin staggered, the enormity of a second failure ripping the strength from his spine. He sagged against the wall, only a last shred of pride keeping him upright. His mind balked, refusing to admit that he'd risked so much only to lose again. It didn't seem possible—and yet the evidence was plain.

And despite monumental failure, his work wasn't

done. His gaze found the knot of guards surrounding
LaFaye, who was facing off with Clary, Gwen huddled
on the ground behind her.

"By the Abyss," Merlin muttered.

Broad shadows slithered over the field. He glanced
skyward, receiving a fresh shock when he saw flying
black demon-creatures above the castle's towers. An
aerial attack was a whole other problem—but he saw
something else, as well, first as specks on the horizon,
and then like tiny, distant kites. Dragons! Some of the
eagles had made it to the Crystal Mountains, and Rukon
had brought his kin.

He'd never seen so many at once. There were red and
green and blue dragons, some slender and some small,
but most were huge males, their wingspans as wide as
any house. They circled above the battlefield, coast-
ing between lazy flaps as a ragged cheer went up from
the castle's battlements. When one of the dragons shot
a lick of blue-white flame and seared a handful of the
black demon creatures from the sky, the demon's flapping attack receded like the tide.

"Rukon!" Merlin cried as the green dragon sailed
past. "Rukon Shadow Wing!"

The whiskered head swung his way and he banked.
"Enchanter?"

"LaFaye has my mate!" he shouted, gratified when
the dragon's head snapped around in surprise. "Take
me there!"

Merlin jumped to the edge of the battlement and
leaped as the dragon sailed past. He grabbed on to the
long, sinuous neck and straddled the bony spine. It was
a madman's move, but it took him straight toward Morgan LaFaye.

Rukon sailed low, daring spears and arrows to bring Merlin close to his destination. LaFaye shot a fireball, but it flew slowly through the sparkling snow, its magic confounded by the demonic energy. The dragon dodged it with lazy grace. When Merlin slid off Rukon's back, he landed in a knot of fae who rushed toward him with swords drawn. Merlin belatedly realized he was unarmed, but that was soon remedied. His magic wasn't hampered by the haze and soon he had a sword, and his closest attacker did not.

A fae sprang at him and he slashed, the sheer force of the blow sending his opponent reeling. It was then he saw the column of light trapping Clary, and he lost his mind.

Magic slammed through Merlin's body, lashing out from his palm to smash through Morgan's spell. It was pure instinct, firing along each nerve with complete clarity of purpose. He was there to protect.

The column flared a brilliant scarlet before flying to shards of light and energy. For an instant, he was blind. Then he bolted forward, for Clary was falling and needed his arms. He caught her, cradling her warm weight as he lowered her to the grass. With a relief that left him hollow, he saw the rise and fall of her chest.

Then he rounded on LaFaye, his anger turning to something distant and deadly. The fae around them must have sensed the threat, for there was a sudden silence in their corner of the battlefield. Morgan's broken spell had washed outward, absorbing into the sparkling haze and turning it scarlet. It looked as if the sky was snowing flakes of blood. The fae stared upward, seemingly befuddled by the sight.

The Queen of Faery stumbled, clearly weakened by

the blows she'd taken and the unfamiliar magic clogging her powers. Fear paled her cheeks, but she was far from surrender. Merlin put himself between LaFaye and the women. He held the sword casually, every sense attuned to her slightest move.

"This is it, then," she said, making it a fact more than a question. "I will make you beg."

"Believe that if it gives you comfort," he replied.

She lashed out with her power, and this time she put all her force behind it, cutting through the haze. Merlin raised the sword, making a mirror of the bright steel and deflecting her power away. His counter tossed her to the ground. She rolled quickly to her feet and threw a spell that locked her power with his, grappling like a wrestler trying to pin her opponent.

This was it, as LaFaye had said. Merlin fell to one knee, shaken by her strength. The impact jolted him, focusing the truth in his mind. He was fighting for his life, and if he fell everyone he loved was vulnerable—Arthur, Gwen and all of Camelot. Most of all, Clary would be unprotected.

LaFaye's power dug deep, and he howled with pain as she sought pieces of his soul to rip free—hopes, dreams, memories. Some things he might have gladly surrendered, but others he could not part with. Clary's sleepy face over breakfast. Her laughter as they fell into the silken bed at the oasis.

LaFaye's gray gaze locked with his, and there was no mercy in it. Merlin struck with everything he had, and she fell, her mouth open in a silent scream.

He grabbed her throat, ready to throttle her, but she found her voice. "Help me, my warriors. I am your queen!"

But there was no answer. One by one, the fae were falling as Laren had fallen, shuddering and foaming at the mouth. It had taken Vivian's magic, and Merlin's power, and the catalyst of LaFaye's spell, but together they had turned the demon essence into a cure for the fae. After so many centuries, their nightmare was over.

LaFaye wailed in grief, but no one cared. Merlin continued to hold her down, his hands still around her slender neck because he dared not let go. Not yet.

There were many ways to bind power, most of them unpleasant. Merlin had no potions or syringes to use, as he had with Vivian, but he had the advantage of the demon essence still lingering like a mist of blood in the air. LaFaye had never bothered to learn its ways, and now it hobbled her like a crude anesthetic. Merlin reached inside the Queen of Faery's magic, twisting her own power tight around her so that the more she struggled, the more energy she fed to her own bonds. It was a painful kind of noose, but she had done nothing to earn his sympathy.

When he finally let go and backed away, she thrashed, howling with pain and rage. Merlin spared a quick glance at Clary, who was sitting up now, her arm around Guinevere. The two women looked back at him with faces blanched by shock, but they seemed unhurt. He yearned to go to Clary's side, but he could not risk it yet. Giving in to his need might jeopardize everything.

As if he'd foreseen it, LaFaye chose that moment to lunge. Even deprived of her powers, she was dangerous. He grabbed her wrists before she scratched out his eyes. Using his greater weight, he forced her down to her knees. She glared like a madwoman, hatred bright in her eyes.

"What do you want, wizard?" she snarled.

He thought of so many things: Uther, the fae, the war, and all the wars before this one. He recalled Lancelot holding Nimueh's exhausted body in the woods. If that was not enough, Morgan had endangered Gwen and Clary and ordered Vivian's death.

"I want justice," Merlin said, his voice cracking with anger.

LaFaye laughed, a harsh, contemptuous sound. "Oh, be careful of your prayers, wizard. You just might get your wish."

Chapter 30

"Wait!"

Merlin turned his head to see Angmar, Laren and those of the rebel fae who had survived the battle approaching the scene.

"She is our queen," said Laren. "We must have a voice in deciding a fit punishment."

Merlin nodded, but he did not take his hand from LaFaye's wrists. "She used your people. She kept the fae from healing and turned their hunger into a weapon. What would you have me do?"

"Return her to us."

Merlin stiffened. "What?"

"You were my lover," LaFaye whispered to Laren. "Surely you recall the pleasure we shared?"

Laren's face cleared of emotion, and it took a moment for Merlin to identify the expression as blackest shame. "I remember," he said, his voice as strained as the look in his eyes. "The fae do not forget."

"Then do not be foolish. Not all of our people are here," said the faery queen. "There are others who are still mine to command."

Laren came closer, but not so close that his feet touched LaFaye's skirts. The dark blue velvet pooled on the trampled ground, the hem richly embroidered, but he recoiled as if she were rotting with the plague. "We will help the others. Your power over us is broken and time will heal the afflicted."

LaFaye said nothing, but Merlin felt the tension cording her every muscle. His shoulders tightened in response, wondering what she might do.

Laren looked up into the sky, his lips forming a bittersweet smile. "What a difference there is when I look around me now. Without my soul, I saw the world, but I could not see the beauty in it. I knew I was blind, but I could not perceive what I missed. It was as if the universe had drained of all color."

LaFaye and Merlin both went utterly still. They shared the guilt for the fae's pain, and though neither said it, that guilt was the thing that bound their fates together.

"The nightmare we've lived will never leave altogether," Laren added, "but it is dawn at last."

As if on cue, the haunting note of Gawain's horn sounded over the trampled fields. The king was coming. Laren drew his sword, lowering the point to the Queen of Faery's throat. Angmar did the same, and then another fae joined in. Cautiously, Merlin released his grip and stood. LaFaye was trembling, the agony of her binding no doubt profound, but he doubted it cut her as deeply as her failure. All around, her army lay senseless in the mud, though here and there one of the fallen warriors was stirring. Above, the dragons circled with majestic grace, having cleared every last demon from the skies. Then the castle gates opened and the knights rode out, Arthur mounted on his charger and Dulac at his side. The king was upright, but even at a distance Merlin could see he was in pain.

But though Arthur would always be his king and his friend, Merlin's heart belonged to Clary. Now that La-Faye was no longer a threat, he turned to gather her in his arms. She was soft and warm, and he understood Laren's smile when he looked into the blue and lovely sky. In many ways Clary had restored his soul the way she'd healed Laren. She was everything.

"Are you well?" he asked.

"Yes," she whispered.

"I have many questions about what happened on the battlefield. Vivian—"

"Don't ask," she said, tears glittering in her lashes. "Please don't ask."

He wanted to, and in many ways had to, but he bowed to the plea in her eyes. Besides, she was free of the demon taint now, wasn't she? How could Vivian have survived such a spell? "Yes, it's over. Nothing else matters but that we are both safe."

Merlin pulled Clary close, content to breathe in the scent of her hair. Somewhere behind them, Gwen and Arthur were playing out a parallel scene, happy to be alive and embracing the one they loved. They had come through their personal version of the Abyss and were safe on the other side. What more could anyone ask?

Then LaFaye burst free, giving a mindless shriek of

fury. She launched forward, heedless of the fae's swords even though they slashed her flesh without mercy. Like a dark arrow, she flew toward Guinevere, her hands outstretched like claws. LaFaye had one last way to hurt Arthur and Camelot, and she meant to take it.

"Stay here!" Merlin ordered Clary, and bolted after the faery queen. He had bound her power, but that didn't mean she was harmless. With a wordless shout of warning, he saw LaFaye launch herself through the air. Gwen tried to dodge, but she was weary and heavy with child and only managed to fall.

Excalibur flashed as Arthur drew it. There was a sudden silence as if the whole of the Forest Sauvage froze in shock—except for the graceful arc of the blade. It whistled through the air, somehow anticipating where LaFaye would be when she spun, black hair flying, to face the king. Her expression had hardened to lines of malice, only her eyes widening as she realized what was about to happen. The blade found its mark, beheading her as she lunged.

The impact was not merely physical, for Excalibur was an enchanted sword. The Queen of Faery's magic ignited as the blade sliced through it, sending a rush of flame into the air. Heedless of his injuries, Arthur swept his wife to safety. Merlin stopped his forward rush, the fire's hot draft against his face so intense it nearly burned him. The smell reminded him of acid and ash.

This was how Morgan LaFaye met her end. She had been the greatest threat Camelot had known—cruel, ambitious and half-mad with jealousy, and yet Merlin couldn't stop a twist of regret. She could have lived a life that was brighter than this fire. Instead, she had chosen a path that left no conclusion but this.

"She knew the fae would do far worse to her than a clean death," Laren said. He'd suddenly appeared at Merlin's elbow, his face painted by the hues of the dying fire. His eyes held more anger than pity for his queen, but there was still compassion in his words. "She chose her end on her own terms."

"By attacking a woman heavy with child," Merlin said drily.

"She was never kind or wise, only certain of what she wanted."

They both fell silent. As if LaFaye's death had broken the last chains that held the fae, more and more of the fallen warriors were coming to their senses. Some seemed transfixed by joy, others overwhelmed with sorrow. Many sobbed. Laren excused himself and joined the other rebel fae who walked among them, comforting where they could.

The scene, already chaotic, was unraveling as the armies realized the war was over. The goblins were calling for beer. Still reeling from the sudden change of fortunes, Merlin turned from the smoldering patch of earth that had been one of the greatest enchantresses of all time. There could be peace now, rebuilding and time enough to plan a future. Merlin could afford to be happy now, couldn't he?

Then Clary gave a yelp of terror. Merlin snapped to attention to see Tenebrius stepping through a ragged portal to seize her by both arms. The demon towered over her by a full head and more. He pulled her back to his chest, bracing one thick arm under her chin.

"You!" Merlin roared, summoning his power. "How dare you show your face here?"

"I am here for justice!" Tenebrius bellowed, making

Clary wince. "I demand retribution for what you did to us, Merlin Ambrosius—to the witches and fae and demons. None of what happened here today would have come to pass if it had not been for your deceptions."

Merlin's hands fisted at his sides. His eyes locked with Clary's, doing his best to exude confidence while he scrambled for a way to snatch her from the demon's arms. "You don't care for anyone but yourself, Tenebrius. You were counting on LaFaye's promises to free you from exile. Now that she can't keep them, you're playing your last card."

"And if that card is a long-overdue reckoning?" Tenebrius shrugged, making Clary clutch at the arm pressed against her windpipe. "You didn't think you could walk away a free man, did you, wizard?"

"Why should Camelot bow to your threats?"

"I have the hostage. Besides, Camelot claims justice should be for all. Why not for the demons, too? What about the wrongs done to our kind?"

Arthur approached, Dulac at his side. The king walked slowly and stiffly, his surcoat streaked with fresh blood as if the fight with LaFaye had reopened his wound.

"Tenebrius," said Arthur. "I wish I could say it was a pleasure to see you once more. We last parted on much better terms than this." There had been a tourney in the Forest Sauvage, Arthur's knights on one side and LaFaye's on the other.

"It seems you've won against the Faery Queen once more," said the demon.

"Release Clary," said Arthur in frigid tones that signaled all pleasantries were over.

"No. While I have her I also have your attention," said the demon.

"You always have my attention, though not in the best way," Arthur replied. "The demons were banished because they tried to conquer and enslave everybody else. I have to protect my people from your kind."

Clary closed her eyes, her face strained with fear. Merlin strategized five different rescues, but each plan ended with her neck broken or all of them blown to bits. Force was not the answer.

"We need to conquer, that is true," the demon answered. "We have lost the path to our homeland and have no place of our own to rule. What would you have us do?" He looked directly at Merlin as he asked the question.

"That is not my decision to make," Merlin replied, nodding to Arthur. "It is the king's. However, I will trade my life for Clary's. Take me hostage, not her, and we will give you an answer."

Tenebrius gave a mocking smile. "Are you certain that is a trade you wish to make? I know how you regard demonkind."

Clary made a strangled noise and tried to twist from his grasp. Tenebrius gave a soft, bitter laugh. "The violent combination of magics in the field today fused what was left of Vivian into Clary's being. One soul, one body, one mind, one consciousness. Your snow-white witchling is tainted by the wild essence of my kin."

Clary shrieked. It was not shrill and filled with rage, but plaintive with fright and confusion. If she'd known something was different inside her, she hadn't understood.

Merlin surged forward, just as bewildered but knowing she needed him. Tenebrius held out a hand. "Wait, enchanter, do not approach. Let me consider your offer."

A beat passed, and a thousand thoughts crashed through his mind. Clary must have kept the truth about Vivian from him all the way along—or at least since the last time he'd knocked Vivian out. Clary had hated that, and no doubt sheltered the demoness from any more of his efforts to get rid of her. In return, he suspected Vivian had protected Clary.

And just as well. In the end, Vivian had saved them all because Clary had taught her what kindness meant. Vertigo swept through him as the truth became plain, and he took a long, steadying breath. There would be almost nothing left of Vivian now, but the effect on Clary would still be profound. She would be much more than a witch—she would be immortal, powerful, an enchantress in her own right.

But at the moment, she was staring at him with round, terror-stricken eyes. A complicated pain inside Merlin rose to all but strangle him as he held her gaze. He knew what it was like to be told he carried demon blood. But was it the same for her? Did she have Vivian's memories? Did she recoil as he had and believe herself corrupted?

But then, Clary had joined with a demon who had grown and changed and sacrificed herself for love. Perhaps Clary would make her own choices about who she would become, just like she always had.

Merlin took a deep breath and released it, making up his mind.

He loved her. Nothing else mattered. "What is there to consider, Tenebrius? My life for hers."

Clary's eyes went wide with shock. She hadn't expected that. He tried not to look as the surprise faded to a confusion of grief and hope. This moment could still go wrong.

Tenebrius gave a fang-tipped grin. "You are a poor bargain, wizard. She is a tasty treat."

Merlin reached into the pocket of his jeans and withdrew the ruby amulet he had used to locate Clary. "Then I will add this to your compensation. It belonged to LaFaye."

He held it up, letting it spin on the long, gold chain. The ruby flashed in the sunlight, dazzling with the promise of power. The demon's goat eyes glowed with greed.

"I recognize the amulet and know its worth," said Tenebrius. "I will accept it as part of the bargain, but there is one thing more I want, and it is not gold nor is it an object of power."

"Name it," said Merlin.

"Truth." The word hung like doom over the battlefield, with its confusion of bodies and sobbing fae and the wounded king leaning on Excalibur.

"Tell your friends the truth about yourself." Tenebrius swept a hand across the scene. "Tell the truth of who you are and how you came by the spell that cast us into the Abyss. The fae deserve to know why they suffered, and your king should know the real nature of the man he calls his friend and protector."

Arthur's look was puzzled and angry. "What is this monster implying?"

"That I am equally a monster," Merlin said softly. He felt as if he was falling down, down a well and would not stop until he drowned. "Vivian cursed the spell I stole from her—that is why it caused such great damage."

"Who is this Vivian?" Arthur asked, looking from Merlin to Clary to the demon.

"A teacher of mine. And more."

So much more. Merlin closed his eyes, wishing one of the dragons circling far above would snatch him up and carry him far away. This was too private, too great a flaw to expose. Shame ate through him as if it would turn his bones to powder. From the day he'd discovered who his father was, he'd tried to scour away every hint of association with the hellspawn.

"Merlin?" Arthur asked in a voice that edged toward command.

He met Clary's eyes again, but quickly looked away. He'd told her she would not want to know him if she found out his true nature. After what she'd seen in the past few days, she would understand why. He hated demons because he was as much one of them as he was a part of the mortal world. As Tenebrius had pointed out, he had caused monumental devastation. Agoricus the Great would be proud.

The only thing good he could do was save Clary. No doubt it would be the last gift she would ever accept from him.

"I have my father's eyes," he said. Then he told them the rest.

Merlin talked, and he talked. After LaFaye's brutal end, Guinevere had been taken to the castle to rest, but Arthur and the knights remained, as did many of the fae. He was aware of them, but his gaze strayed most often to Clary, who listened with a fixed expression he could not read. He tried with all his might to guess what she was thinking, but she kept her thoughts completely guarded. The only movement she made was to swat the demon's claw away when he tried to stroke her cheek.

When Merlin had finished, he expected Excalibur's edge against his throat, or a fae blade or even the kiss of dragon breath. Instead, there was a soft murmur that died almost as soon as it began. The afternoon was fading, the shadows deepening to a dusky purple.

"I have no more to say," Merlin concluded. "I have upheld my side of the deal."

Tenebrius held out a clawed hand. "The amulet?"

Merlin tossed it to him and walked slowly forward. Tenebrius kept his word and pushed Clary away.

To Merlin's intense relief, she paused slightly as their paths crossed. Now her eyes were wide and thoughtful as if seeing him for the first time. For an instant he fell into their green depths. He expected to see elements of both Clary and Vivian there, but it was not so simple. She was neither and both, and yet someone new and stronger than before. He silently took Clary's hand and raised it to his lips, savoring the scent of her skin before letting her pass.

"Hello," he said.

The corners of her mouth turned up, the expression both fond and challenging. "Hello."

He desperately needed more, but urged her away to the safety of Camelot's knights. Then he turned to the demon. "I am your prisoner."

"And now," said Tenebrius, digging his claws into Merlin's shoulder, "you shall pay for your crimes, Merlin Ambrosius."

Chapter 31

"Not so fast," said King Arthur. "We have been patient and bargained generously, but you push too far, demon. At that tourney you judged, I won the prize. You promised me anything of my choosing that was in your power to grant."

Arthur had never claimed his prize. Merlin's breath caught and he turned to Arthur with a sudden, almost bewildered realization that his friend hadn't abandoned him after all, even if he was half a demon.

Tenebrius's face fell. "I don't remember," he said, although it was plain he did.

"I choose Merlin," said Arthur.

"Under one condition." Angmar stepped forward. "As the fae suffered in consequence of the stolen spell, we put a condition on Merlin's freedom."

"Oh?" Arthur said tightly. He had just ended a war

with the fae and could not afford to offend them, especially not the rebels who had come to his aid. "What condition would that be?"

"That Vivian agrees," said Angmar. "She was deceived by her lover. It is up to her to decide if he has truly been redeemed."

Tenebrius burst into a belly laugh that made Merlin long to punch him. "You are asking a demoness to forgive?"

Merlin's heart plummeted. He could see Arthur drawing breath to argue, and held up a hand. "The decision is hers to make," he said softly. "I wronged her."

Tenebrius made a doubtful snort. "How would you rather serve me, wizard? As a scullery boy or the slave who scrubs my dungeon's floors?"

Clary took a step forward, opened her mouth as if to speak and then hesitated. Licking her lips, she tried again. "A long time has passed. He deceived me, that is true."

She looked confused as if processing memories that were only half her own. Merlin tensed, wondering what memories Vivian had kept, and how much had slipped away before she'd fused with Clary. Some of those early times had been joyous.

Merlin took a step forward, and Tenebrius did not stop him. Merlin knelt at her feet, thinking how everything had come full circle. Vivian had taught him, and he had taught Clary and now Clary had taught them all about matters of the heart.

"My love," he said, feeling the words true but strange on his tongue. "Forgive me. Forgive what I did, and that I compounded that crime by distrusting you now.

You saved me from a certain death, and you saved us all from defeat at the hands of LaFaye."

"Who are you speaking to?" she asked.

Merlin took her hands, feeling the slight bones of her fingers curl around his. Blood pounded in his ears at the thought of her walking away, dismissing him because he had betrayed her. "I thank both Clary and Vivian for our salvation, because you both saved us. It was not just Vivian's power and Clary's heart, but Clary's courage and Vivian's willingness to learn. If you are one, then you are the most wondrous creature to walk this enchanted forest."

"Even if I am a demon?"

Merlin bowed until his forehead touched her hands where he held them. "You are unique."

"So are you. We all are. That's the point."

He looked up, but she was scanning the crowd, her gaze going from the fae, to the king, and finally to Tenebrius.

"Merlin betrayed me, but he's also stitched my wounds and taught me the right way to build a portal and helped me clean up when I accidentally summoned all the chocolate custard in the Pacific Northwest. He's been a mentor when I chose to start my life over, and he's never held me back when I wanted to see what I can do." Clary paused, finally looking down to meet his eyes. Hers were warm, but with an edge of laughter. "I think I'll keep him. And in the end, he did cure the fae, so I suppose we all should forgive him. He has done much good in the world, although he cannot see it for himself."

Arthur cheered, and the men of Camelot cheered with him. After an initial hesitation, the fae applauded, too. They were too overjoyed to be cured to hold a grudge. As for the goblins, they had found the castle's cellars and were delighted with pretty much everything.

Merlin didn't need any more encouragement to rise and grab Clary so he could kiss her soundly. Nothing mattered but that she believed in him, and that he wanted her, and that there would be a future.

"And what of me?" Tenebrius asked Arthur. "Are the demons to remain locked away until we dwindle to nothing?"

The demon was fading around the edges, a sure sign that the pull of the Abyss was taking effect. He could not stay in the Forest Sauvage many more minutes, and it would be some time before he could visit again.

"What is Camelot," said Arthur, "unless there is justice for all?"

"Surely we owe the demons nothing?" complained Gawain.

Arthur put a hand on his friend's shoulder. "We don't. But justice is not solely the payment of a debt. It is meant to put things right, and sometimes that means growth and better choices. Last time I chose war against the hellspawn. This time I will ask the finest minds in all the realms to study the path the demons traveled to reach this place. If they have a homeland, there must be a road to send them back. With a little effort and common sense, maybe everybody can be happy."

After the battle came the sad business of mourning those who were lost. Then came feasts of celebration, and then came farewells. Arthur's allies returned to their homes. So did his former enemies, although the fae, with Angmar as their new king, left with promises of friendship. The war with the fae was over at last.

Eventually, the court of Camelot returned to their new homes in Carlyle, Washington. For Merlin and Clary, that meant his condominium. Except it didn't feel like his place anymore and he wasn't sure why. He wandered from room to room like a restless cat while Clary sat at the dining room table scowling at the scorch marks left by the possessed laptop.

"Are you going to come sit down?" she asked him. "We should order in. After all that roast beast and spiced wine, I'm dying for a good pad thai."

He came out of the bedroom and leaned against the wall. "Then order enough for two."

"Have you got some menus?"

Merlin went to the kitchen and began opening and closing drawers. "I thought I did, but I can't remember where I put them."

She laughed, and it was a wholesome, merry sound he'd come to count on. "Two of the most powerful beings on Earth, and we can't manage to order dinner."

Merlin closed the last drawer and turned to face her with a grin. His heart lurched at the sight of her at his table, wearing one of his old shirts because they hadn't moved her things in yet—but they would. They were together now in all the ways he'd never dreamed would happen.

At first, he'd worried it would be strange to be with a woman who was his first love and his current love in one. It wasn't. In the end it had felt like his heart coming home to him, healed and renewed. And those that knew Clary best, like Tamsin, had said that the biggest difference they could see was that she had much more magic and a whole lot more confidence, especially when it came to her wardrobe. They adored her just the same.

"I love you." He'd never actually said it like that before, all three words together.

"I love you back." Her smile was slow and a little wistful.

He finally spotted the stack of menus on top of the microwave, but he ignored them. The moment was too important.

"You don't think it's too weird, what happened to me?" Clary asked softly—and for the zillionth time. "It doesn't freak you out?"

"There are things that freak me out," he said, sliding onto the chair beside her. "Ghouls, animated slime, those purse dogs with bulgy eyes."

"Purse dogs?"

He kissed her forehead. "You don't freak me out, okay?"

On the contrary, she intrigued him. She had Vivian's passion and Clary's compassion, as well as Vivian's temper and Clary's stubborn streak. All of the Clary he loved was there, but with an added spice he truly appreciated—and if he had his way, they'd be together forever.

"I'm part demon," she said.

"So am I."

"You hate demons. You don't get over that in a couple of days."

They were simple words, but they held so many layers of feeling for both of them. He realized this was what was making him restless, this thing he needed to face. "I do not like what the demons did. I will never see the world the same way most of them do. But I've learned from what happened. I've had choices all along. Like you said, we're individuals and all of us get to pick who we become."

The statement made him think of Morgan LaFaye, the graceful girl she had been and the evil queen she'd grown into. An unutterable sadness twisted inside him.

"We do choose, and we do change," she said.

"I know that now," he said, holding her hand. "It's like I've been wearing dark glasses all my life and finally took them off. Everything is lighter."

And now, with a little help from his friends, the fae were cured. He'd only understood the complete weight of that guilt after it had lifted, and now he wanted to live.

"New beginnings," she said, sliding onto his lap and pressing her lips to his.

The kiss pushed the last thoughts of pad thai from his head. Things were just getting interesting when Clary's phone buzzed. To his profound annoyance, she answered it. "Hello?"

He watched her face light up. "Really? A second one?"

Merlin heard the babble of Tamsin's voice and guessed she was referring to yet another knight showing up at Arthur's door. Long ago Merlin had put one hundred and fifty knights into the stone sleep, but only a few had ever awakened. It had been another case where one of his spells had gone wrong, but now—perhaps with LaFaye's demise or Vivian's forgiveness—it had fixed itself. First Sir Bors had turned up at Arthur's door, then Sir Geraint, then Sir Kay, and on and on. Getting so many medieval warriors acclimated to the modern world was going to be a heroic task all on its own. Still, Merlin was glad to see each and every one. They were old friends, and with this many willing and brave hearts, there was a lot of good Camelot could do.

Clary thumbed the phone back to sleep. "Gwen's gone into labor."

Merlin's heart leaped. "How is she?"

"Just fine. She's had her boy. Now she's working on her daughter."

"Twins?" Merlin frowned. "No one said anything about twins."

Clary shrugged. "Arthur's delighted."

"Did he know?"

She grinned. "No. But Gwen and Tamsin did. Women have to have some secrets, after all."

"How did she get away with keeping two babies a secret? What about ultrasounds?"

"Arthur's old-fashioned." Then Clary cocked her head, peering into a future Merlin couldn't see. "But I'll bet he gets with the whole prenatal program next time around. I think this surprise package is Gwen's way of making him pay attention."

"I promise I'll pay attention when the time comes."

"I know you will," she said in a way that left no options.

They both laughed, although he wondered what Clary would try to get away with down the road. She'd already hid a demon from him, after all.

"I want to get married in Camelot. In your tower."

That was right—the tower was back. "Why not at the oasis?" he asked.

"That's just for you and me."

"Ah."

She chuckled. "Do you think we could tie tin cans to Rukon's tail and get him to fly us to our honeymoon?"

"I'm guessing no." Then it occurred to him he was missing a step. "Aren't I supposed to go down on bended knee?"

She looked up from under her lashes. "You've done that already in front of the king, a bunch of hysterical fae and an entire army of drunken goblins. Show me what else you've got."

He kissed her again, nibbling and nipping and making it count until, with a sigh, she tossed the phone onto the table. She straddled him, winding her arms around his neck and paying his affection back in kind. She was definitely the best kisser he'd met in his long, long life. This new amazing creature was going to take centuries to learn.

He couldn't wait.

Dinner was gleefully, gratefully forgotten for a good many hours.

* * * * *

SPECIAL EXCERPT FROM

Ⓗ HARLEQUIN®

ROMANTIC suspense

*Detective Belle Granger knows she must stop the
serial killer on the loose in Midnight Pass. But as she
gets closer to the killer—and her ex, Tate Reynolds—all
of Tate's fears from ten years ago surge to the surface
and threaten their love once again.*

Read on for a sneak preview of
The Cowboy's Deadly Mission
*by Addison Fox, the first in her brand-new
Midnight Pass, Texas miniseries.*

"Tate. Someone's out there."

Her words finally caught up with the shift in mood and Tate focused
on her. "What?"

"Someone's out there. Watching." With her free hand she kept a
firm grip on the back of his head, holding him still before he could shift
to look around. "Kiss my neck so I can get a look behind you."

Tate complied, the light taste of salt from her skin coating his lips.
The joy he'd have taken from that move only a few moments before
had vanished, replaced by the overwhelming urge to cover her with his
body while he wrestled her into the safety of the car.

"Do you see anything?"

"No. The lot's clear and I don't see anybody walking around." She
arched her neck, the move appearing to anyone watching that she was
in the moment, enjoying the pleasures of the man she was with. The
bulleted description he received, matched in the rumble of her vocal
chords beneath his lips, told another story.

She was back on the job and his presence had become unnecessary.

Tate pulled away, that reality as effective as a cold shower. He
wasn't going to apologize for the past few minutes but he was damned
if he was going to stand there and play undercover stud, either.

"Where are you going?"

"You seem to have a handle on things. I don't think my lips are necessary any longer."

"You're picking a fight with me?"

"Geez, Belle, I don't know. One moment we're kissing each other's brains out and the next you're ready to race off into the night. I'm not gonna lie, it messes with a man's head."

"I'm not going to apologize for thinking we were in danger. You of all people should understand that. We found a dead man practically on your property this morning."

"I'm well aware of that."

"Then why the sudden pout?"

She always knew the right turn of phrase to reduce their exchange to a heated debate and had succeeded once again. Tate turned in a wide arc, his arms held high and his voice rising several decibels. "Anyone out there? Anyone watching?"

"Tate!"

She tugged at him but he stepped out of range, his gaze roaming over the parking lot as he kept up the steady shouting. "Who's out there? Getting your rocks off on a couple making out in the bar parking lot? Where are you hiding, you bastard?"

"That's enough!"

Belle got a better grip on him this time, dragging on his arm and pulling him toward her. The move was enough to catch him off balance and his other arm windmilled as he stumbled a few feet over the gravel parking lot. He caught himself and added his own personal layer of armor, pushing every ounce of smart-ass he had into his tone. "If this is how you get a man on his back, I'd say you're not very good at this game, Belly."

"I'm trying to keep you from being a target."

"Of what? Some perv's attention?"

"Or a killer."

Don't miss
The Cowboy's Deadly Mission *by Addison Fox,*
available August 2018 wherever
Harlequin® Romantic Suspense books
and ebooks are sold.

www.Harlequin.com

Copyright © 2018 by Frances Karkosak

HRSEXP2088

Need an adrenaline rush from nail-biting tales
(and irresistible males)?

Check out **Harlequin Intrigue**®
and **Harlequin**® Romantic Suspense books!

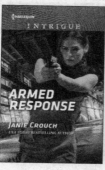 

New books available every month!

CONNECT WITH US AT:

Facebook.com/groups/HarlequinConnection

Facebook.com/HarlequinBooks

Twitter.com/HarlequinBooks

Instagram.com/HarlequinBooks

Pinterest.com/HarlequinBooks

ReaderService.com

**ROMANCE WHEN
YOU NEED IT**

SGENRE2018

Reward the book lover in you!

Earn points on your purchase of new Harlequin books from participating retailers.

Turn your points into **FREE BOOKS** of your choice!

Join for FREE today at **www.HarlequinMyRewards.com.**

Harlequin My Rewards is a free program (no fees) without any commitments or obligations.

MYR1